MICKEY
TAKE

STEVEN HAYWARD

ACKNOWLEDGEMENTS

My sincere thanks go to Leila Dewji for her editorial wisdom; to my fellow authors: Jacqueline Andrews, Michael Tappenden – for the many delightful days of Critters critiques and Kaf1 lunches – Josie Aston, Dominic Canty – for the tireless support and encouragement through my frequent and, at times, torturous plot diversions – and Fred Nath for the unique insights of a novel-writing brain-surgeon; to Angela Docherty, whose strength and tenacity are an inspiration, and the many generous supporters of New Ways (newways.org.uk); to the Beagle Club who listened graciously to my musings every Saturday morning; to all the many other friends who gave invaluable feedback on the early drafts; and, finally, to my wonderful family who have been so supportive of this ex-banker who unexpectedly decided one day to resign the job and follow a dream to write stories.

For Helen, the love of my life

– x –

And for my dad, Peter,
the rock on which my family is built.

PROLOGUE

December 1983

Monday, 5th

Fog hangs in garlands from the sparse trees along an unlit road. The night is frozen, bone-deep. It's no longer silent. Neither is it holy. Branches weep from the shudder of impact. Screams of agony splinter the air. And hot metal pings. Two cars have recoiled, face off, astride white lines. Festooned with shards of silver and gold, the tarmac glistens like Christmas.

Minutes later, beyond the next bend, another motor stops abruptly. Seeing the blue flickering trees ahead, the driver's brain immediately spikes. He kills the engine and snuffs the headlights and, once out of the car, checks all the locks before disappearing into the shadows.

At the turn in the road, his first glimpse of the scene is the rear of a white hatchback. Viewed from behind, it appears unscathed, its street cred emblazoned in black letters across the tail. The other car facing him is crushed beyond recognition. Its red bonnet curls upwards like a tin lid. Ahead, at the foot of a tree, a heap of limbs and clothing lay deathly still. On seeing the traffic cop, the watcher instinctively drops to the ground. He breathes deeply as his knees soak up the muddy verge, until the piercing screech of metal clears his head.

Failing noisily to prise open its door, the cop speaks softly to the driver of the red car. With no more than a sideways glance at the woman on the ground, whose living eyes wouldn't stare that way, he hurries on, past the steaming bonnet of the hatchback, ignoring the gaping hole in its windscreen. The exchange with this

1

driver is more animated; two deep voices with an edge of familiarity talk at length. Eventually, the cop crosses the road to check on the body.

The watcher remains concealed, aroused by the carnage.

It's a futile gesture when the plod holds his fingers to the woman's neck. Even the awkward rearranging of her coat to cover her exposed flesh is made to look dignified. But when he deliberately pulls on his gloves, lifts the limp calf and roughly removes her shoe, the unseen witness sneers.

He's seen it all before. Where were the bizzies when a fleeting uncle broke his arm in a drug-fuelled rage? Or when his ma smacked his head against the wall to back up the story of how the clumsy five year old had fallen downstairs? Where were they a few years later, when he was forced to beg for her on East End streets, so she could score her next fix? They just moved him along. And the one time he went to them and opened up, they ignored his cry for help.

Nothing surprises him now. Not when the pig walks back to the white car, opens the nearside door and drags the screaming driver across to the passenger seat. Nor when he goes back to the driver's door and hurls the woman's shoe into the foot well. Not even when he returns to the body, removes her blood-soaked scarf, wraps it around his baton and slams it through the shattered windscreen, widening the hole. When the silk snags on the broken glass, he leaves it hanging there like ribbon.

Only then does the scum return to his patrol car and call for paramedics. Only then, with all the justification he will ever need, does the watcher return to his car to await the blare of sirens that will cover his retreat. And only then does his mind return to the task of dumping the body parts bagged up in his boot.

1.

September 2009

Wednesday, 16th

No taller than five-four, she shoulders her way through the pack with the wiry strength of a fly-half. As a gap opens she falls forward, unsteady in three-inch heels, leaning against my arm with one hand, whilst deftly cradling two glasses in the other. I move awkwardly to make way, but rather than try to pass she smiles and says, 'I've been watching you.'

She asks my name; hers doesn't register. After the evening I've had, you wouldn't blame me. But I must look a complete imbecile when all I can say is, 'Uh?'

'Grace,' she repeats, and this time the adolescent in my head whispers, *Amazing.*

She really is. An innocent, heart-shaped beauty with big, docile eyes set deep into sculpted cheekbones, reminding me of those sultry caricatures, popular in the 60s. The only outward signs of the gregarious nerve that allows her to approach a complete stranger in a crowded bar are the upturned corners of her smile. The way they exaggerate the mischievous dimples at either side of her mouth only competes for my attention with the sparkle in her eyes.

'Macallan, isn't it?' she says, offering me one of the drinks. 'I prefer something a bit peatier, like a Lagavulin or Laphroaig, but this'll do for now.'

She downs the whisky with only a slight grimace, and continues to press the second glass into my hand, before looking at me with a fixed grin, probably wondering if there's anyone in.

Hello? I pull my eyes away from hers, zooming out for a wider view. She's obviously not long out of the weather because her shoulder-length blonde hair hangs down in shaggy, damp twists like she just stepped out of the shower.

Okay, I'm going to hold that thought...

Hot Shot

My name is Michael Field. If you thought I was going to say: *My name is Michael Caine*, you'd be wrong. The only thing we've got in common, some say, is he talks like me. I suppose you'll be the judge of that. Anyway, call me Mickey.

I'm here in my local. About nine miles east of a place I've affectionately dubbed Bleak House. I've just covered twice that distance getting back. You've seen the movie with the guy, freaked out and running, flushed into the underground labyrinth. That was me. Going north on the Central line... over the loop to Hainault... above ground, through busy streets... another tube, heading south... first bus, going anywhere... District Line, eastbound... one beyond my usual stop... off at Hornchurch... walk a random circuit back... before slipping unnoticed into the sanctuary of a familiar watering hole...

After that, the first single malt wasn't likely to touch the sides. Was I followed by a thug wielding a torch? I don't think so. Did I see any psychos along the way? Well, it *was* London. But no, none of them were in hot pursuit, so I thought I was in the clear.

Unusually for a Wednesday, The Feathers was heaving when I squeezed my way to the bar, avoiding any eye contact. The barmaid was another new face out of the usual mould – chirpy, young Antipodean with a mercenary smile, razor-sharp wit and a mood that could turn on a sixpence. She was being chatted up by some lads along the bar and didn't given me a second glance as I twitched down the first glass and immediately called for another.

The second scotch had been sitting on the bar for a couple of minutes. My heart had stopped pounding, and I was feeling confident I could pick up the glass without spilling any this time. As I did, a hand rested on my shoulder and I lurched forward with a jolt in horror at the thought of a guy with a Maglite grabbing my arm and hauling me from the pub. It was just some reveller getting carried away and tripping towards the bar. I called him an arsehole under my breath while licking whisky off my hand. I could tell he was too drunk to notice me and too arrogant to give a shit. He was wearing a dark suit and fancy cuffs, just like I used to. The Feathers is always full of drunken City tossers on an England match night. They slowly regress into unlikely hooligans – voices become more raucous, language more colourful – as they direct all that suppressed male aggression at the big screen.

Having shifted position to let him in, I feigned nonchalance and cast my eyes around the pub. The bar in The Feathers is like a big horseshoe, with an island in the middle that the staff can circle around. Evenly spaced around it are elaborately-carved pillars, supporting glass shelves above, framing my view through to the other side. That's when I saw her, an absolute babe, leaning against the bar directly opposite and staring straight back at me.

Without a TV screen, that side of the pub didn't seem so busy, and I thought she might have been on her own. On one side of her was a space that was soon taken by an old guy, waving a fiver vigorously towards the landlord who was covering that part of the bar preferred by his football-indifferent regulars. On the other side was a middle-aged couple in conversation, their backs to my apparent admirer. She was being served. The landlord put down two tumblers. I was relieved, though slightly disappointed, because that surely meant her boyfriend was at one of the far tables. I looked away, mildly bemused by the intensity of the moment.

I tried to keep my cool but I could still feel her eyes on the back of my head. I had to look back. By then the barmaid was standing right in front of me, setting down two pints of lager for City Boy. When she moved back to the Guinness pump to fill the final third of a glass, my view across the pub returned and I was looking at a gap at the bar next to the old guy talking to the landlord. Game over. I downed the second scotch without a further spillage and contemplated taking the back roads home.

While the last couple of hours had felt like a nightmare, I knew I wasn't dreaming. But what occurred next surely only happened to guys like me in a fantasy world of our own making, in the depths of a beer-induced coma. I turned to make my exit and thought about nudging The Suit's drinking arm as I pushed my way to the door, when the gap I was trying to open up was suddenly blocked by the girl from across the bar, squeezing her way towards me.

Alarm bells started ringing in my head and this evening's main event flashed through my mind...

Bleak House

When you fall on hard times, there's no knowing how low you'll stoop. But believe me, I wasn't doing it for fun. And although I knew what I was looking for, I didn't really understand why it was so important to Herb, nor why it was worth the four figures he was paying me for this little bit of breaking and entering.

The thought crossed my mind: if the place looked like it had been deserted for years, was it still technically a crime to break in? Either way, it wasn't like it was the first I'd ever committed. It might have been fair to say that everyone had done the odd ton down the motorway or had a few too many sherbets and didn't want to leave the car at the station overnight. But that's not what I was thinking. My previous experience was somewhat more serious than antisocial behaviour behind the wheel. That was a long time ago, and then I had some help when it came to tidying up the loose ends. Suffice to say, nothing ever came of it and I was able to get on with my life.

I'd always fancied myself as a lucky boy, a charmer, what

they used to call a Likely Lad. Even so, I couldn't help feeling there was something very iffy about this job. I was about to commit only my second attempt at burglary and, much like twenty years ago, I didn't really know what I was letting myself in for.

Undeterred, I slid effortlessly through an open sash window onto a squalid, threadbare carpet. At one time it might have had a swirling pattern, but more of its mesh backing was showing than any of the abstract scrolls of its former glory. It wasn't quite as dark in this room as it had been out the back. While a single streetlight shone in from the front, my eyes still found it hard to adjust. Outside, its intrusive glare had been subdued by the irregular shadow of a large oak that conveniently obscured the side path from the road, allowing me a discreet way around from the garden.

If I said the light was casting an amber wash around the room, glowing and fading rhythmically like a mood lamp as the tree swayed gently in the breeze, I'd be having you on because I was completely unmoved by the ambience of the place. If I went on to say the sepia hue made the room seem welcoming and benign, you'd know I'd lost the plot. But I did sense a strange contradiction in the apparent tranquillity. That feeling I'd had – that something wasn't right about this, not just morally and legally – it hadn't gone away. This was too easy. The window on the side of the house hadn't even been latched for Christ's sake; not exactly breaking and entering when all I had to do was lift the bloody window and step in. I couldn't believe my luck. Although once I was in and looking around that dingy little room, any optimism I had began to dampen.

I couldn't make out the colour of the floor or the fringed, partly-shredded bedspread, thrown untidily across the single bed that ran the entire length of the wall. The bed was basic, reminding me of a prison bunk: metal-framed, no headboard, a thin striped mattress, visible where the cover didn't obscure it, no pillow, or any other sign of comfort. Apart from that, a frayed wicker chair in the corner by the window and an ancient wardrobe opposite, the room was empty. It was the wardrobe that held my attention, one of its doors gaped and the remains of an inner mirror were strewn in flickering shards across the floor.

Tiny slivers of glass crackled underfoot and the carpet clung to my shoes like Velcro as I stepped out into the hallway. To my right, I could only just see the bottom step of a staircase that ascended off to the side. I shuddered, barely suppressing the memory of a stranger looking down at me from the landing. That was another staircase, in another house, long ago. Beyond this one was the front door, its rippled glass glimmering orange from the neon outside. Across the hall were two more rooms. The door to the front room was shut. The other was open, and I could see a linoleum floor, streaked with what looked like oil.

The floorboards creaked in protest as I took a step towards the open door. The edge of a rolled-top bath, the kind that would cost a fortune to buy, came into view. Above, I could only discern the outline of a small frosted window, presumably facing out onto the wall of the neighbouring house, because it added no illumination to the room. Without opening the door wider, I could only see one side of the bath; its once pristine white enamel looked grey and dull, seemingly smeared with the same greasy muck as the floor.

I tried to ignore the flashback in my head, reminding me what pools of blood looked like in the dark. Too late. What little I could see was already combining with vivid memories. My confidence was ebbing away on a wave of revulsion at the disgusting state of this place. Nausea was creeping up on me as the smell registered with my senses. A dank, suffocating odour of decay permeated the walls and rose from the floor in an acrid vapour; a stomach-churning cocktail of stagnant piss, sour milk and vomit.

And there was something else: a sweet, pungent edge with the tang of rotting meat and the bitterness of cold metal.

Moments before, easing through the window, my mood was bright. This was easy. No problem. Grab it and go. Now I felt sick. What the hell had I walked into? I was frozen, in the middle of the hallway, unable to move.

What possessed you to get involved in something Herb's tied up with? The voice of Michael the Banker echoed in my head.

— *Stick with it. Into the kitchen, two more paces and you're there. You know where it is. Get in there, pick it up and leg it back out through that window.*

Mickey the Resurgent Rebel won the debate and I was moving again.

Old instincts took over and I strode headlong towards the door at the end of the hall. Like the bathroom, the door was ajar and beyond it there was only darkness. I knew, once in the kitchen, I'd be able to get my bearings and locate what I came for. I slowly pushed the door, letting in light from the hall, and stepped over the threshold. I stopped abruptly, confused and disoriented. What I was looking at wasn't the kitchen.

It was a connecting room, wider than the hall, no more than ten feet long. I had to assume it led in turn to the kitchen. I tried to make sense of the unexpected layout, comparing it in my mind to the outer perimeter I'd had to skirt around. That's when I realised there were two other rooms, one on either side of me, and I was merely standing in another rectangular hallway, this one with a door on each of its four walls. The one ahead had to be the kitchen and it was partially open, whereas the solid doors on either side were both closed.

As I looked from one to the other it was apparent that although the rest of the house hadn't been maintained for donkey's years, these internal walls had been added in more recent times. Left un-plastered in bare cinder block, their dull grey doors were set into unfinished metal frames, each with robust bolts top and bottom – the ones on the door to my right were secured by heavy duty combination locks. The concrete floor, also not an original feature, was levelled only to a rough screed.

In any other circumstance I'd have been intrigued by the industrial nature of the renovation, in what was otherwise an uninhabitable dump, but my head was spinning with the reek that intensified as I got deeper into the building. It was like I'd entered a huge corpse and was being drawn towards its putrefying guts. The smell assaulted my senses, adding to a surging feeling of dread at what surrounded me. I tried to stay focused as I pulled up my collar to cover my nose and mouth and walked straight ahead, into the kitchen.

Scanning the mountain of rubbish on the table, it didn't take me long to see it. There, wrapped in an oversized brown envelope, a package no bigger than a paperback. I could tell before I even looked inside, it was the object I'd come for, and I put it in my pocket. It was so light I knew I'd need to keep checking it was still there. A feeling of satisfaction lifted me and I headed back with renewed confidence, reaching the doorway into the original hall, ready to get the hell out of there. That's when I took leave of my senses.

— *Hey, what's the rush? It's cool. I've got what I came for, no problem. This is easy. I got in quick. I can get out quicker. No one's seen me, there's no one around. Let's take a quick look at this added room – the one with the bolts drawn back. Maybe there's something else in there that would be useful to Herb.*

Ever the opportunist, the Resurgent Rebel took control and, with a newfound enthusiasm, I was heading back to investigate the chamber.

The handle turned readily, and I pushed. The door yielded quietly, smooth yet heavy on sturdy hinges, inward into total blackness. Although there were no windows, it wasn't the darkness that I noticed first. Released from its confined space, the stench hit me like a train and made me gag. Reeling at the thought of grisly scenes that might have played out in this hellish cell, I retched and almost added to the assumed matter on the floor.

Somehow I mustered the mental and physical gristle to step into the room, and my eyes began to adjust to what tentative light had dared follow me in. All I could see was a metal bench, scattered with an assortment of tools: lump hammer, pliers and a hacksaw. Don't be fooled, this was no DIY workshop.

10

The meat cleaver and various butchers' knives and skewers removed any lingering doubt, as clinically as they would any other surplus appendage. I'd seen enough and was ready to leave when I spotted something else on the bench. It was another brown envelope, at first sight, much like the one nestling in my pocket. That was just another trick of the light. No, this one was like a brick, a solid wad, constricted by rubber bands, stretched taut around its length and width into a thick, twisted cross.

I was drawn to it. Maybe I was thinking it would make a good counterweight in my jacket, like ballast for the voyage home. *Yeah right.* Maybe I wasn't thinking at all because even before I put it in the other pocket, I knew it would tip the scales *so* far the other way.

Pulling the door behind me was surprisingly easy and it picked up its own momentum and slammed with a reverberating clang. While it gave me some reassurance the door would keep whatever evil had occurred there contained, it also shattered the stillness of the house and echoed noisily as I retreated to the main hallway.

No sooner had I turned to enter the bedroom on the right, I heard another sound – a hideous, muffled scream – a human cry so desperate and pathetic that it reached through my chest and tore at my lungs. I froze again, not knowing what to do. I was convinced the voice had come from the locked room. The last thing I wanted to do was go back in there.

I didn't get far before a loud rattling sound shrink-wrapped my testicles. It was the front door, ten feet behind me. Someone else was trying to get into the house. Okay, call me a coward, but if I said something like this had happened before, you'd forgive me the perverse sense of relief as I abandoned all thoughts of chivalry. Besides, this was way too much aggro for the sake of a thousand quid, and my instinct to flee was stronger than any human urge to stay and help whoever might be suffering in that room. I was through the bedroom and out of the window quicker than I came in, moving silently and swiftly back down the garden, towards the high fence along the back.

I glanced over my shoulder, expecting some knucklehead to be pursuing me, the open window of my escape surely obvious to anyone coming into the hall. I was relieved to see no one chasing. It was only when I'd clambered up, and was about to drop down the other side of the fence, that I got a good look back at the house and saw the torch illuminating the kitchen like a strobe, while a ghostly silhouette ransacked the room.

Before I lowered myself to safety, the shadow of a giant appeared at the window and the searchlight's beam swept across my face.

Bunny Girl

Since escaping down the gravel pathway that runs along the backs of the gardens of Bleak Neighbourhood, I'd been replaying the scene in my mind. Between anxiously looking about to see if I was being followed, and frantically scouring the tube map I'd pulled from one of the station racks en route, I wasn't able to get the thought from my head that someone had been suffering in that place and I'd just run away.

Now here I am, being chatted up by the most beautiful, young woman I've ever seen.

Maybe she's the girlfriend of the guy with the torch. It's The Banker again, trying to cramp my style. *Maybe she's going to soften you up and lure you into a dark alley where he'll be waiting with his toolkit.*

— *No. That's just being paranoid.*

Maybe she's a prostitute?

— *She doesn't look like one.*

Like you'd know what they look like.

— *Yeah, I'm pretty sure they don't go around buying their prospective clients drinks as if they're selling time-shares. Even tarts have standards.*

Fair point.

I'm confused. Amidst the conversation in my head, my brain can't find the right connections to work out what to do. It's trying to recall the last time a gorgeous girl with a taste for single malt introduced herself with a sexy smile and a free drink.

When I was a young guy – ready, willing and able – this never happened to me. In twelve years of marriage, this never happened to me. Yet here I am, well past my prime, down on my luck, in an old Barbour coat that hangs down on one side, and looking like I've spent the evening with Freddy Krueger. And completely out of the blue, I'm supposed to know what to say.

'Thanks' is the best I can manage. God, I'm so pathetic. I need to get a grip soon before she comes to the conclusion that I have some kind of mental impairment and a nightly visit to the pub is part of my care in the community programme. All I can do is raise the drink and sip it like a girl.

Fortunately, the kick of the spirit jolts my brain from its inertia and I look around for somewhere we can sit or at least have some space to move. There's a small table in the corner and I nod in its direction.

'Sorry,' I say as she sits down with her back to the window. 'You must think I'm a complete moron. It's just that... you caught me a bit cold. Hello, I'm Mickey.'

'I did start to worry I'd made my biggest chat-up mistake ever,' she teases, 'but I'm always ready for rejection.'

I smile at the Betty Boop tilt of her head that confirms my belief she's never had to worry about that.

'So, Mickey... were you heading off already?'

Her eyes seem to shine into mine, like she's driving towards me around a sharp bend, intentionally leaving them on full beam. I'm blinded, mesmerised, imminent road-kill, unable to avoid staring back into them. I try to retain some composure and take control, but I'm hopelessly outwitted at every turn.

'Oh, I only popped in for a quick one,' I reply, instantly aware of the clumsy innuendo. My obvious discomfort is met with a naughty smile that lights up her face.

'I'm sure I counted two,' she says, lowering her gaze from my eyes. 'You're obviously a guy who doesn't hang around.'

Unlike mine, her double-entendre is both subtle and

intentional, and I feel my face flush and my pulse quicken. I grin like a schoolboy and shift awkwardly in the chair.

For God's sake get a grip; you're probably old enough to be her father.

I try to assume some semblance of seniority by finishing the rest of the scotch and asking her if she'd like another drink.

'This time, I'll get them to add some peat,' I joke embarrassingly as I turn to go to the bar.

'Okay,' she calls after me. 'But if Pete's not around, I'll settle for Mickey.'

Now, as I walk to the bar, everything is different. City Boy moves aside to let me through and I'm served without waiting by the Aussie barmaid who smiles sweetly and even says 'Thanks, mate,' when I hand her a tenner. It's turning into one very interesting night, and already I've completely forgotten about the odd packages in my coat pockets and the anguished cry for help that turned my legs to jelly less than two hours ago.

Grace brings me back to reality with a bang when she asks what I've been up to this evening. She admits she's been watching me from the other side of the bar and thought I looked seriously worried about something. Where do I start? Those big eyes are hard to deceive, and I have to keep looking away as I come up with some cock and bull story about Mum being ill. She seems to fall for it and gives me lots of sympathy. She says she spent the evening helping her brother with his homework. I think I got away with my little white lie about poor mother's gout, but they say it takes a bull-shitter to know one, and I'm having serious doubts that Grace is being completely straight with me.

For some reason I can't fathom, the conversation seems to be getting tense. I suspect I'm reacting subconsciously to her apparent change of mood. She's trying too hard to make meaningless conversation and I'm wondering if things aren't moving a bit too quickly for someone I've only just met. The grown-up in me takes back control and I start looking for a way to bring this interesting and very flattering fantasy to a close, at least for the time being. Apart from anything else, I'm getting really anxious to call Herb.

The rabbit in the headlights analogy begins to take on a more sinister meaning as I sense Grace realising the evening's conquest is coming to a premature end. The bunny's in serious danger of being boiled and the cheeky banter is turning into sarcasm and resentment.

'Well you'd better head off home if you've got a better offer waiting there,' she says after I start making noises about needing to get an early night with a busy day ahead.

I want to see her again, I really do, but all I can come up with when I get up to leave is, 'I'm sure I'll see you in here again sometime.'

'Probably not the best offer I'm going to get tonight,' she replies brutally.

Harsh... but fair. The Banker gets the last word as I squeeze my way to the door.

* * *

Another Mother

The soothing sound of violins drifts along the hall to the room he's checking first. The music adds to his relief at finding the door untouched. He's been caught off-guard – came back to clean up too late. It's much earlier in the evening than he'd expected, though it's not for him to reason why. Ask no questions; tell no lies. Do as he's told... most of the time. As for the rest... he's only trying to help. That's what's concerning him now. The fact it's all still here. That wasn't in The Plan. Opening the door, he exhales loudly. Everything's as he left it. But that other room... that's another matter.

Lighting it up, his first concern is addressed; still there, in a bucket, behind the door. He'll get rid of it later. That's two off his

15

list – the worst half. The other two, they're not bad things. Not really. But they are of more value... at least to him. He looks around and his jaw tightens at the sight of an empty space where he'd left the first. Ought to be more careful...

'How many times do I have to tell you not to leave your shit lying around?' He hears her voice and freezes. 'How... many... times...?' Each word accompanied by the sting of her hand.

How many times? How many times had he gone to his bed hungry... to grip with little fingers the red imprint swelling his thin, freckled arm... to feel the comforting warmth soak through his scants... to spend the night praying to be dry by morning...

Seeing the other thing still there brings him back. His face softens and he relaxes his fist. Crossing the room, he smiles and, lifting it gently, wipes the glass with his sleeve. She smiles back and he takes it with him, his steps lighter as he cradles it in time with the music.

2.

Double Income...

So much for Mickey Field, the lucky boy. I don't know, some would probably call me a barrow boy. There was certainly a time when I was proud to be considered a YUPPIE. Back in Thatcher's glorious eighties, so the theory went, if you worked hard, played hard and kept your nose clean, then you either ended up a Well-Off Older Person, otherwise known in the vernacular of the time as a WOOPIE, or Burnt-Out But Opulent, aka: a BOBO. Trouble was, many got rich too quick and ended up a complete LOMBARD – Loads Of Money But A Right Dickhead.

I was late to join the party, but I was doing alright. Don't get me wrong, I was never in the big league. When asked for my occupation – on those forms with a hundred different tick-boxes – I would reluctantly select "Banker". I never really felt much like a banker though. To me, bankers were the bigwigs who flew around the globe doing mega-deals to finance construction projects or corporate mergers and acquisitions. Then again, I suppose that was a view from the inside. On the outside of City life, most people haven't got a clue what goes on. All they see are the bonuses, the arrogance of the few who gamble other people's money away with impunity, and the rewards for failure when the ones who screw up are given big payoffs to leave quietly. I have more sympathy for this viewpoint now I'm on the outside, banker-bashing with the rest of them, but with the hypocritical fervour of a reformed smoker. And if I'm honest, in the end, I think I even surprised myself by sticking at it as long as I did.

Okay, I have to accept, to those on the outside I was a banker and, they may have assumed, a successful one at that. But

I'm not going to bore you with the details of what I spent twenty-odd years doing in the world of high finance. First, because it's pretty mundane a lot of the time, and second, well the chances are, you're one of the "most people", and wouldn't have a clue what I was talking about anyway – or more likely, wouldn't care. Let's just say, things were looking sweet. Looks can be deceiving.

What about Mickey the Charmer? Well... maybe not. My happy marriage of twelve years came to a sudden end when I realised Sam was playing the field; trouble was it wasn't this particular Field. She had her own City career, and together we made the perfect couple, or so you might have thought. When it all came crashing down I was left alone, empty and bitter, and worst of all, feeling very stupid. That's the problem when your wife spends so much time in the company of her colleagues, longer than she ever spends with you, the one she's supposed to love. For Sam, frequent evenings working late soon became a quick drink with Dean and the rest of the nightshift to de-stress for the journey home.

While some people in the City do early mornings or late evenings, depending on whether they're trading in Eastern or Western markets, nightshift in this context is simply gallows humour for workaholics. If you want the big bucks, you have to be prepared to do the early start *and* the late finish. Oh, the joys of working in London at the centre of the global business day. It's enough to make you cry into your Bollinger!

Before long, Sam's quick drinks with the team became drinks just with Dean; an hour became three or four. Occasionally, the last train was missed and one of the cheap hotels that sprang up in the Square Mile ten years ago, presumably for this purpose, was a last-resort bed for the night.

'Sorry Mickey. I'll be able to make a flying start in the morning,' she'd say on the phone, supposedly from a post-modern, eighty quid a night B&B within walking distance to the office. 'I'll get home early tomorrow and we'll go out for dinner.'

And I would fall for it, time after time.

'No worries, sweetie,' I'd say. 'Get your head down and I'll see you tomorrow.'

Get your head down! What a mug. What a stupid, trusting, loyal, never-been-with-another-woman-since-our-first-date, bloody fool.

When I found out, she had to go. She didn't want to, but once a cheat always a cheat in my book, and there was no way back for her. She left with a suitcase and I gather Dean took her in. His wife left him years ago, the first time he strayed. Sounds like she shares my principles – maybe I should meet her. Well, that was the end of the marital bed of roses. But were that the only problem in my life. I quit my job the day after she left.

Enter Mickey the Likely Lad. Picture the scene. I'm in an interview room with some kid from the bank's compliance department, young enough to be my daughter, the day after I'd watched Sam get in the back of a minicab and disappear from my life. She's asking me what I know about some missing cheques.

Sure, the book was in my charge, kept locked in a cabinet to which I had the key. All cheques issued were logged in the register, which was also under my supervision. I even signed most of them before they went out. There were two signature lists: I was on the A list with my boss, and all the senior staff in my department were on the B list. One signature from each list was needed on every cheque issued. In reality, I countersigned them all, unless I was out of the office when my boss, the anally-retentive Rick, would grudgingly lower himself from his ivory tower to sign one or two.

More often than not, my guys would avoid running the gauntlet with Rick and wait until I got back. They seemed to prefer my approach. If the transaction had been verified and the cheque already signed by someone on the B list, it was good enough for me. As I saw it, my signature was there to add authority. It was a demonstration of confidence in the integrity of my team. Clearly not a view shared by Rick, who always wanted to know the inside leg measurements of a flea before he would sign anything.

So, you could say I had almost total control over the

chequebook, which was pretty much what Little Miss Smarty Pants was making clear during our interview. I could see the glint in her eye; confident she was about to take her first employee scalp, all the better for it that I was a ten-year veteran at the firm, with leadership responsibilities. That same sense of superiority was pretty much what I was trying to convey to her by the total contempt with which I was responding to her questions.

On any other day, I would have easily taken the sting out of this "misunderstanding", smiled reassuringly, nodded agreement with the seriousness of the issue, calmly voiced my concern this could possibly have happened in my department, set out clearly what I intended to do to investigate the lapse and, inevitably, disarm her with that old school charm. She would have made some notes, offered a few pointless suggestions for improving my management controls and agreed to meet again in a week to review progress with my enquiries. We would have smiled and left amicably, probably both still thinking the other was an arrogant piece of shit, but it would have ended well enough.

As it happens, it didn't end well.

Instead, I said what I really thought. By the time I'd finished, she was promising to report me under every code of conduct and harassment policy she could find. At least I left the interview smiling. It was about as charming a smile as Jack Nicholson's, leering through the shattered door with an axe. I really didn't give a toss.

I went straight to my desk, grabbed the half dozen personal effects, excluding the photograph of Sam that lay face down in the drawer, hoping for a reprieve that would never come, put on my jacket and walked out. I caught a fleeting glimpse of Rick's startled face as I marched away from his office and down the corridor.

And you know what, it felt bloody marvellous. In that moment, I finally allowed myself to accept something that had been eating away at me for years. I had spent my entire adulthood acting out someone else's idea of a decent life. And

God, had I hated it.

And then there's Herb. The guy who put me up to this. I suppose you could think of him as an old family friend. Everyone knew he wasn't entirely kosher, yet nobody ever seemed to be able to put a finger on why. He was always good to us kids when we were growing up – my brother John and me. He lost his wife in a car accident in the early eighties, a couple of years after we moved into the same road where he lived. Local gossip at the time said they had been expecting their first child, which also perished in the crash, but he never talked about it.

We hadn't really noticed him until John and I started walking home from secondary school together. Then we'd see him leaning against his gatepost most afternoons. Occasionally we'd stop to talk and be late home. Mum would remind us of what she always said about talking to strangers, but Herb was alright. We never went inside his house; he never invited us in. He would want to know if my team had won on Saturday and whether I'd scored. I always replied I was only a fullback, and yet that didn't stop him asking every week.

As I got older he usually had some good advice for dealing with girls. When I was fifteen, he'd occasionally slip me that month's *Playboy* and say with a wicked grin that he was always happy to help educate a fellow gentleman in the ways of the world.

A couple of years later, something terrible happened and Mum and I moved to another street. That was a tough time for us both; before my eighteenth birthday I became "the man of the house". I tried to support her the best I could, but she'll never know how hard it was for me. And at a time when I might have gone completely off the rails, Herb became the father figure I never really had before. He dusted me off and gave me another chance. Ultimately, he gave me the confidence that allowed me to move to the City in '89 in the hope of positioning myself for the next boom. Of course, back then I wasn't sure whether I could really settle into that City routine. I was never one of those who had it in their blood. Still, there was money to be made and I wanted to give it a shot for a few years.

After that, Herb and I stayed in touch for awhile, and I would drop in on him if I had time when visiting Mum. But once Sam came along, even our occasional phone calls fizzled out. Although they never met, she didn't like the sound of him, and wouldn't even let me put him on the guest list for our wedding. After that, our paths diverged completely, even though he continued to live alone in the same house. So, until quite recently, I hadn't seen him for years.

Maybe I should have kept it that way.

Calling In

Now, back home from The Feathers, I punch the number into my mobile and wait to hear Herb's voice.

I'd written his number on the back of one of my old business cards. An unopened box of them was one of the few things I grabbed from my desk when I'd made my recent exit from a stable life and a steady income. I'm not sure why. It's not like I can ever use them again. I don't know; maybe it's something to cling to – a memento of that tiny speck of authority I so readily abandoned.

The phone keeps ringing and I let it continue in case he's otherwise engaged. It must be five minutes and there's still no answer, so I let it go on for another ten rings before hanging up and deciding to try again in the morning. Maybe he pulls the plug on the phone when he goes to bed. That seems unlikely. Surely he'd have waited up for my call tonight.

I seriously doubt Herb is the kind of guy to be out on the razzle of a Wednesday evening. He has to be knocking sixty-five if he's a day, and when I saw him recently he made it sound like he wasn't in the best of health. But what sticks in my mind the most is that his house was immaculate. Some old widowers' houses can be pretty grim. Unidentified stains on the carpets, net curtains that hold themselves up, dried egg yolk on the tablecloth. And I don't even want to think about the assortment of smells.

Well, that's what I was expecting. But no, for an old boy he keeps the place modern, clean and tidy. It wasn't always like that. I suppose when his missus was killed all those years ago, you could have forgiven him the state of the place back then. And yet, somewhere along the line, since I was last there, it looks like he decided to make her proud. All that time living along the street and everyone assuming it would still be a junkyard in there. Just goes to show, you never know what goes on behind closed doors.

It was last Tuesday that he caught me completely off-guard when he phoned out of the blue...

I'd not long got a new mobile number and was still getting to grips with the free handset. Apart from anything else, the bloody thing doesn't give much warning before running out of juice. So, not for the first time, I'd been carrying it around all day without realising it was completely useless.

Of course, I got home and plugged it in without switching it back on, and didn't realise until an hour later that I'd missed a call. Not recognising the number, I instinctively deleted it and forgot all about it. Well, here's another thing that was pissing me off about my new mobile phone. With no conceivable reason for the delay, it rang at two o'clock in the morning, and when I answered it with an unintelligible grunt, an ambivalent pre-recorded voice informed me I had one new message. I didn't even get the chance to swear and throw it across the room before I had Herb's dulcet tones in my ear.

'Bugger! Sodding answer machines,' was his opening line. 'Mickey? Michael Field, is that you? Sorry to trouble you son, it's your old friend, Herb. Herbert Long. From your old stomping ground – I helped you out a few years back. I'm sure you remember. Look Mickey, the thing is I wonder if you can help me with a spot of bother I've come up against. I hope you don't mind me calling on your portable number. I hope to hear from you.'

23

It may have been the voice of an old man, but I could tell the words were carefully chosen, and that their meaning was intentionally underplayed. Though my eyelids refused to open, my brain was wide awake and playing drums on the inside of my skull.

As I replayed the message, I realised he hadn't left his number for me to ring back. No problem, it'll be on the missed call log. The Banker started grinning long before I remembered deleting it earlier. The phone skidded to a halt across the floor where it laid, defiantly illuminating the room until plunging me back into darkness just as my eyes were starting to adjust.

Last Week

Wednesday, 9th

I felt guilty being so close to Mum's house without going in to see her; I suppose I only ever went south of the river for that reason, and I was sure there'd be hell to pay if she knew I'd been in Gravesend and not even popped in to say hello. The day after Herb's message I had another reason for being there, and I just hoped he would make the trip worth my while.

Mum doesn't miss much that goes on in the neighbourhood and she has spies everywhere, so I decided to park in one of the side roads. It seemed very strange opening the gate and walking up the path to Herb's front door. Given the years that had passed since I'd been beyond this particular gate, maybe I shouldn't have been surprised at the apprehension I felt as I rang the doorbell.

Herb answered almost instantly and, apart from a momentary pause for recognition, followed by a failure to disguise a furtive glance up and down the street, he welcomed me into the house as if I was still a regular visitor.

'Mickey, it's good to see you,' he said, shaking my hand. 'You've just caught me on the phone, but come on in lad.'

He released his firm grip on my hand and led me into the

24

long, narrow hall, through the first door on the right, to his front sitting room. He seemed strong and upright, and moved confidently, but the thinning wisps of grey hair, cropped closely over his angular head, and the lines chiselled in the granite of his face hinted at the years that had passed since I'd seen him last. The only frailty I noticed was that his left hand trembled uncontrollably; an impairment he seemed oblivious to and did nothing to conceal.

He gestured for me to sit down on a leather sofa that not only dominated the room but also filled the air with its heady musk of opulence. In front of me, on a stylish glass coffee table, was a cordless phone facing upwards and a black Moleskine notebook, open alongside it. He smiled awkwardly and picked up the phone, covering the mouthpiece with his large hand before he spoke.

'If I'd thought for a moment,' he said in a subdued voice, 'you'd have come straight down here, I would have got some provisions in.'

With that he took the notebook and the phone and stepped out into the hall where he continued his call in a voice low enough that I couldn't hear.

I noticed the distinctly modern, masculine styling of the decor and furniture as I sank into the soft tan cushions. And as I looked around the room, I tried to reconcile the quality and affluence in front of me with my expectations. It was like I'd stepped through a time warp – outside you approach the front door of an austere detached house, cloned between the wars; inside you're greeted by a contemporary show home, uncluttered and minimalist. Everything looked new and without a speck of dust. I knew a lot of young guys in the City who would have worked fourteen hours a day just to rent a place like it. Apart from the dramatic change from how it looked the last time I was in here, I couldn't help wondering how the hell an old guy like Herb managed to maintain it so spotlessly, let alone afford such luxury.

'Just get it done!' he said bluntly, as if for me to hear, and his eyes flashed like blue steel as he walked back into the room.

He replaced the phone in its cradle behind the door, while I struggled to sit forward in the seat to show my concern. But when he turned back to me his expression had changed, like everything was tickety-boo.

'Sorry Herb,' I said. 'I didn't get your message until it was too late last night and I couldn't find your number this morning, so here I am.'

'No need to apologise, lad. It's very good of you to come, especially after all these years. What is it, ten?'

'Longer than that,' I said. 'Nearer fifteen.'

'Well, you certainly don't look a day older, lad. I was almost expecting to see young John standing behind you on the doorstep.'

I smiled uneasily.

'If only,' I said.

'Yes, quite,' he said, his voice dropping again. 'We've all got things... back then, that we'd change, given the chance.'

I nodded solemnly before he lifted the mood with a big smile. 'And your mother, lad; she seems to have held up well. Always cheerful when I see her. And always telling me about you – so proud she is.'

'Yeah, she's keeping well, on the whole. Has a bit of trouble with her legs now and again. She's quite resilient, all things considered. You know what it's like; none of us are getting any younger.'

'You're not wrong there, lad. Can I get you a drink? I've only got tea and coffee, unless you fancy a drop of scotch.' He winked on the last word but must have seen the alarm on my face because he looked over at the solitary gilded clock standing dead centre on the mantelpiece. 'I thought it was later than that. Look at me plying you with whisky when the sun isn't even over the yardarm. Have some coffee.'

'Thanks Herb, that'll be good – milk, two sugars. Can I give you a hand?' I followed him out of the sitting room and down the hall to a large modern kitchen. An expensive Italian coffee maker and a matching chrome microwave were the only objects adorning the black granite worktops that contrasted tastefully with solid cherry wood cabinets. I felt horribly outclassed in the ideal home stakes.

'Nice place,' I said, the words totally inadequate.

'I like to keep it tidy,' he said, and as if to prove the point, hurriedly gathered an array of paperwork that was scattered across the sleek top of a button-less hob into a pile and lowered an opaque glass lid over it.

Despite the spasms in his left hand, he deftly produced four shots of espresso from fresh coffee beans that were automatically ground, dispensed and filtered into two cups he'd placed under the machine's twin spouts.

'Do you want your milk frothy?' he looked at me doubtfully and I read the signs and declined in favour of cold milk – the steamer on the machine looked unused, but then again everything in this house looked brand new. He placed the cups onto saucers he'd put on a tray, along with a plate of chocolate digestives, and then added milk to one of the cups whilst looking to me to signal when was enough. Without another word, he walked out of the kitchen and back to the front room. I instinctively followed him with the tray.

'It's great to see you doing so well, Herb… after all this time,' I said. 'It was quite a surprise to hear from you. I'm just not really sure… I mean, why now?' I tried to maintain some decorum by perching on the front edge of the sofa, cup and saucer in hand, declining the offer of a biscuit, in spite of the growl of protest in my stomach. I had always looked up to Herb, but knowing so little about his particular line of business, beyond all the idle gossip, made me very nervous about what he was going to ask me.

'I gather you've come up against some bad luck,' he said without looking up.

'It's fair to say I've had better months,' I replied, wary of what Herb knew of these recent events and, more to the point, *how* he knew. I still hadn't fathomed where he'd got my new mobile number from, but I wanted to give him the benefit of the doubt and see where this was going. 'You never met Samantha, did you?'

'No, lad. Your mother showed me a wedding photo a few years back. She looked like a real beauty. What went wrong?' He looked genuinely concerned.

'She was... is a real beauty,' I agreed. 'I suppose I just wasn't enough for her in the end.'

'Did you know the other guy?' He was looking at me intently.

'I'd met him once or twice. He was her boss – a complete arsehole as far as I'm concerned. I suspect Sam will be just another of his casualties and one day she'll realise what she's lost.' I was becoming melancholy and I didn't like it. I knew I needed to stay strong and focused. Sipping the coffee helped. 'What keeps me going is reminding myself she made a choice the first time she played away. Even though I threw her out, it was her decision at the outset. I'm sure I'll be better off without her.'

'You're right Mickey. There's never room for three in a marriage.' His voice dropped slightly as he added, 'I'm sure one day you'll get your chance to take him out.' My cup clattered noisily in the saucer as he continued talking. 'And I'm sure all that high-powered City life wasn't good for you in the end.'

'Yeah,' I said nervously. It was starting to feel like Herb already knew everything about me, even though I hadn't spoken to him for years. 'I was ready for a change. I didn't need hassle at work and at home, so I've dumped them both. I haven't felt this liberated since I was a teenager back down here.'

'That's what I wanted to hear, Mickey.' The devilish smile had returned to his face. 'I imagine all those years of pinstriped conformity got a bit restricting for a man of your potential.' This time, when he held out the plate of biscuits, I couldn't resist.

'When I heard you'd made these changes and were heading out in a new direction...' He had suddenly become animated. 'I thought to myself, perhaps you might be keen to get back to a... less conventional lifestyle? And I thought you might be in a position to help me with a problem I have.'

'Sure... if I can,' I said cautiously, wondering what I could possibly do to make his life more comfortable.

'The thing is Mickey, I doubt I have a lot of time left. And I'm buggered if I'm going to let them destroy me and take everything I've fought for while I've still got the strength to defend myself.' He was looking straight at me, his face had set like cement, and he spat his words like bullets. 'They say they've got evidence that would put me away for life, and they want me to pay a heavy price for it. For a guy like me, prison might as well be a death sentence. The alternative they're offering would put me on the streets with nothing. And that would amount to the same thing. I know I've done some things in my time. But I've tried to keep a low profile these last few years and stay out of the deep end, so I don't know what they think they've got on me. I'm pretty sure it's all a con. My problem is there's plenty of Old Bill still waiting to take me down, and so it's a risk I can't afford to take for any of the past to be stirred up by some fabricated evidence that even suggests I'm still a player.'

I was sitting there, chocolate melting on my fingers, trying not to drop crumbs on the upholstery, and listening to his confessional on a life of crime. Mum always said Herb was trouble, and I knew he was no angel, but I had no real idea what he was involved in, and hearing all this from the horse's mouth was raising more questions than it answered. But the one burning a hole through my skull was: what the hell was he going to ask me to do to help him? Before anything came together in my head, he got to the point.

'They say they've got photographs and they've given me a fortnight to come up with the first instalment. I have no intention of giving the bastards a penny, so I need to get those pictures and I've got just over a week left. They've got a shit hole of a place they use as a hideout not far from where you are. Do you know South Woodford? Of course you do, lad. Well, it's not really my domain. I've been up there a few times but I don't have the stomach to go back. I've still got a few contacts who owe me

29

favours, and I'm told the photographs they're talking about haven't even been printed. Seems they're not in a hurry to put them on paper. Apparently, they're on one of those disposable cameras, you know the sort. Well, as long as that camera stays intact, I figure I've got a chance to call their bluff. That's where you come in.'

He finally paused and I sat there in stunned silence. I'd managed only the occasional nod, trying to convey the impression this was no more than a normal conversation with an old friend. Herb might have been convinced; The Banker certainly wasn't buying it. He was crapping himself.

More questions came thick and fast into my head: did he really say disposable camera? Could you even get them anymore? In the iPhone age, why the hell would your average blackmailer have relied on last century technology? I remembered my old instamatic on which half of the photos I took missed the most important part of the main subject altogether – usually their head – and occasionally all but the right arm of the person standing next to them. And yet these guys were sure they had material worth exploiting without even developing the film? Before I got a chance to voice any of these concerns, Herb continued.

'The place is empty most of the time, unless they've got a job underway,' he said, staring straight into my eyes, despite what must have been a look of bewilderment across my face. 'I'm told there's something big going on tonight and the place will be deserted again next week. They tend to stay well away until things cool off. All I'm asking you to do is go along and take a look inside. See if you can find the camera. It'll help me sleep better at night knowing the film hasn't been developed. It'll make me very grateful… generously so, you understand… if they no longer had it. So here's the deal. I'm sure you used to be able to claim expenses at the bank and expect… what do they call them these days?'

'Variable benefits?' I heard myself say.

'Bankers' bonuses!' he said and his eyes lit up like a cash

register. 'Well, if you can take a trip up there a week from tonight, let's say your travel expenses would be a hundred. Does that sound reasonable?'

He seemed to be getting carried away and was clearly enjoying this, despite my obvious discomfort. Before I could even start to contemplate what he was asking me to do, let alone work out how many times I could make the return trip on the tube with £100 credit on my Oyster card, he continued.

'And if you can establish whether the camera is still in one piece and the film undeveloped, let's add a subsistence allowance of two-fifty. I suppose that might just cover a nice meal and a bottle of wine in one of those fancy bistros up there.'

I nodded involuntarily.

'Okay, here's the real performance incentive,' he continued, parodying my previous remuneration arrangements. 'If it's still there and you can acquire it for me without leaving a trail, we'll round it up to a grand and call it a golden handshake. What do you say?'

The room was silent for several agonising seconds as he stared straight into my eyes. I was unable to look away, but I didn't know what to say either. Where to even begin?

'Look, I really don't need the money,' was all I could come out with, and he nodded like he already knew that. 'Things aren't great,' I continued, 'but I've still got the house and some savings that'll keep me going until I get back on my feet.'

That's probably what he was expecting me to say. Still, he wasn't getting the message. He kept looking at me, his wry smile increasingly out of place as I tried another tack.

'Herb, what I'm saying... This really isn't my scene. Not anymore. I'd love to help you, really I would. It's just the last thing I need is to be getting involved in something I don't understand. I'm sorry... you're asking the wrong guy.'

He nodded slowly back at me, the fun no longer in his eyes, replaced by a distant look that made me believe I had been his only hope. I felt like a complete loser and a heartless bastard and it was pathetic, I know, but I needed a way to break the tension.

'Sorry Herb...' I said. 'I need to use your loo.' He huffed and shook his head, and at least there was some humour back in his smile.

I exhaled deeply as I got up to leave the room. It seemed like for twenty years we'd been heading in opposite directions, but to Herb nothing had really changed. I felt bad that I'd probably blown any credibility I had in his eyes, because I suppose I did want to show him that I had a backbone, and I really didn't want our reunion after all these years to end so badly. But I was relieved to be momentarily off the hook as he eased back in his chair and directed me to the door along the hall.

Ahead of the kitchen door were two others, either side of the hall, and I was drawn to the one on the left. An easy mistake you might say, but if I'm honest I had noticed the twin Chubb locks in the centre and the deadbolts at the top and bottom. No one's *that* security conscious when they're taking a dump. Back in the lounge, Herb's phone had started ringing, and hearing the low hum of his voice gave me the push I needed. I didn't think for a second it would open and if it hadn't, I'd have gone through the other door, stood in the cloakroom for a minute or so, flushed the toilet, washed my hands and gone back in to give Herb my final answer – no 50/50, no phone a friend – I definitely wouldn't be helping him out. That's if it hadn't opened. But it did. And I found myself looking into an integral garage, organised like something I'd seen only once before.

In the centre, with barely walking space around them, were cardboard boxes of every shape and size, stacked neatly, floor to ceiling. Around the outside, shelves were filled with cellophane sealed packages that protruded in irregular bulges, reminding me of the kind of serious luggage you sometimes see wrapped in heavy duty cling film on airport carousels. Standing at the threshold, with the only light coming in from behind me, I wasn't able to see any labels on the boxes. I glanced furtively back along the hall, anxious not to move abruptly for fear of rousing a treacherous floorboard. My heart was pounding, but there was no sign of Herb having finished his call, so I slowly shifted my weight and took a step inside. The first package on the shelf at eye level lit up, its symmetrical two-tone pattern clearly visible beneath the plastic covering. At first I only saw the shiny glint of metal in the shape of the letter G. As I stretched the plastic with my fingers, a second G, a mirror image of the first, intersecting it like links in a chain, completed the unmistakeable logo of Gucci. Looking along the rows of shelving that filled the rear wall, there must have been fifty pieces, and I had to assume the sidewalls were similarly stacked.

I closed the door quietly, tiptoed across the hall into the toilet and coughed loudly as I flushed. With hot water draining away wastefully, I looked at myself in the mirror above the basin. The eyes that stared back told me this little respite wasn't helping in the slightest. I was struggling with what I'd just seen and trying to reconcile it with what I knew about Herb. In particular, I was trying not to think about a particular night some years ago when I'd last seen a similar array of high-end merchandise. The night I'd got in over my head. The night Herb had come to my rescue.

I returned to the front room and sat down opposite Herb without saying a word. He was still on the phone and this time he continued without regard for my presence.

'Yes, Ying-Son. Exactly as you said it would... More? Perhaps... Let's see how this goes. Same terms... yes? Good. I like the sound of that. I'll be in touch.' He put the phone down and wrote something into his book and I waited for him to finish.

'Why don't I make us some lunch?' he said and got up to leave the room, taking the Moleskine with him.

'Herb. No, really. Don't go to any trouble. I was going to pop in to see Mum so I'll have a bite to eat with her.' I hated using her as an excuse to leave but he had already disappeared, I assumed into the kitchen.

'Herb?' I called after him, 'Don't make me anything, I'm going to walk round to Mum's.' I sat there for a while and could hear him moving around. I started to think he hadn't heard me and was out there making sandwiches, but when I walked out into the hall he was standing at the door to the garage with keys in his hand. We both seemed to freeze for a second until he casually dropped them into his pocket and came towards me.

'You're a good lad, Mickey,' he said, 'visiting your mother whenever you get a chance. Watching you grow up all those years ago and seeing you now, I'd be proud to have a son like you. I really thought we could have helped each other out.'

He looked down at his quivering hand and I could only shake my head and hope that he would just thank me for visiting and let me go. Instead, he looked straight back into my eyes.

'I've got no one else to look out for when they put me in the ground, and that could be anytime soon. Life's all about lending a hand where you can. I scratch your back, you scratch mine and we all get along.' Though I might have imagined it when he tilted his head back in the direction of the garage door, there was no mistake when he added: 'You know what I mean... don't you Mickey?'

There was something sinister in the way he said those final words, and I understood the unspoken reference to the favour he did for me all those years ago, the one he'd made a point of alluding to in his telephone message. I could no longer meet his stare and had to look away, stung by the realisation this was far from an optional proposition. It wasn't his style to spell it out for me; nevertheless this was payback time.

'Look Herb,' I said, reaching for the door handle. 'I'll call back in to see you again before heading home.' A light seemed to come back on in his face as I added: 'Let me think about it, okay, and we'll talk some more this afternoon.'

As I opened the door, I already knew I would be helping Herb with his little problem. It was madness, but what real choice did I have?

Walking down the path, the white-collar conformist within me began his usual descent into the realms of self-pity and victimisation, like he always did under pressure. Then something happened as I reached the gate. It was like all those years had slipped away; the veneer of respectability shed like an old skin. The Rebel was re-emerging inside, keen to reclaim the excitement of his youth.

It might have only been a remnant of The Banker's paranoia, but as I walked away from Herb's house, I felt I was being watched. It was bound to be someone Mum would know so it was probably for the best that I was going to see her anyway. She doesn't generally like surprises. I can't say I blame her; she has good reason not to. But she was thrilled I'd driven down just for her.

* * *

That Night

Dry, hardened eyes dart around a cold, bare chamber, mouldering in the bowels of an abandoned house that stands detached and unseen by the night-blind neighbours of a suburban street.

The sound of breaking glass makes her shudder, but fear is no stranger. It's usually temporary, replaced by the pain of punishment. And followed by relief and frequently disgust at her abusive husband's pitiful remorse. But this man is different. Dispassionate. Clinical. She tried talking to him, at first. He wouldn't look at her eyes or acknowledge her voice, even when it changed from a reasoned appeal to a desperate scream. He ignored her protest, remained distant. Unmoved.

Rarely has fear escalated to panic. Yet these last few hours, maybe days, terror has been her constant state of mind. Even the physical trauma and the resulting throb, gnawing at the side of her head, can't disguise that.

Like a dilating pupil, the door opens slowly and an arc of light invades the room, at once eclipsed by his looming shadow. Soft heels, bound at the ankles, dig vainly into the rough concrete floor, pressing her back into the comforting darkness of the corner.

But the walls won't yield. And the movement only tightens the cord that binds her hands and ends in a spiteful loop around her neck.

Onto the sturdy bench he drops a small plastic box, its wrapper criss-crossed with rubber bands. His note, scrawled in red, matches its grisly contents:

> *KNOW WHAT YOU DID RIGGS, NOT*
> *FORGOTTEN. WHAT ABOUT THIS ONE -*
> *WHAT'S HER LIFE WORTH?*

In a different hand, large black words cut across it like a stamp:

> *TAKE IT OR LEAVE IT*
> *EITHER WAY, GO TO HELL*

Lifting a large metal tray from the bench, he carries it towards her, and only the refocusing of her eyes conveys any change of expression. The ceramic ball held with gaffer-tape in her mouth denies her face its instinctive response. Blood pulses in her disfigured ear, reopening the wound. He stares at the black scab that begins to glisten red again. A slow trickle paints a fresh track along the contour of the vein swelling in her neck as globs of snot pulse like molten pistons from her nostrils.

'Aye... she's... already... there.' The only words she'll hear him say are punctuated by the sounds of tools being placed on the floor. They mean nothing to her, but the sound of his voice at last is strangely soothing. Mercifully, she can't look down. She doesn't see the Stanley knife, the cleaver or the bolt-cutters. Only when he removes the small heavy hammer and begins to grind it into his palm, does urine seep through denim into a warm pool around her feet. And when he raises it above his head her eyes finally close. He holds it there for eternity.

3.

Thursday, 17th

A week later and here I am driving south over the QE2 Bridge again; heading back to Herb's. I'm dosed up on coffee, three shots already this morning and it isn't even seven o'clock. Sleep came at a high price. After failing to reach Herb on the phone, I laid awake for hours, being tormented by the thought of a torch-lit shadow peering at me through the darkness. When my conscious mind succumbed at last to a fitful sleep, it was punctuated by a claustrophobic sense of dread and nausea, accompanied by a cry for help, initially distant and weak, but which seemed to grow into a resonating scream of Hammer House proportions.

I gave up on any chance of a lie-in, having woken at five-thirty in a sweaty contortion of pillows and sheets. Through the mist of a single malt headache came a vague and disturbing recollection of Torchy's menacing shadow breaking into my subconscious and, with the bony hands of the Grim Reaper himself, throttling me whilst demanding his money back.

Oh yeah, the money. That other package languishing mysteriously in that torture chamber; The Banker wanted me to leave it there. I managed to persuade him the two brown envelopes looked very similar in the gloomy light and it wasn't easy to be sure which was which.

Yeah right. He reminds me how that's bollocks. *Even an idiot like you could have told them apart.* But he's no longer calling the shots. He's going to have to start trusting me a bit more.

Maybe, he says. *Remember what happened the last time The Rebel called the shots.*

The Banker may have only been a pretentious, junior management pen-pusher who liked people to think he was a big shot, but he knows how to bring me down. I manage to shut him up, only after he repeats something he said before: that I still don't really know what I'm dealing with. It's a fair point. But at the end of the day, I took the other package. It was an opportunity too good to miss.

Tossing coins into the automatic booth at the end of the toll bridge, I'm reminded how last night, as soon as I reached into my jacket for the heavier of the two envelopes, it was pretty bloody obvious I was holding a serious stack of bank notes. You'd think The Banker would have known this instinctively. But no. The closest I came to seeing, let alone handling a bundle of cash in my whole career was as a senior clerk, when I took my turn on the rota to seal the vault. Even then there was always another locked grille between me and the goodies.

No, he's right again. Any fool would have known the feel of a meaningful pile of hard currency. Apart from the obvious size and shape of it, you'd recognise the way it curled around your hand, the tentative handshake of an old friend, bending and wedging like the pages of the phone book.

Well, that's the first thing that came into my mind anyway – the phone book. They've become a lot thinner these days, whereas the business directory seems to keep getting fatter. That's the reason I have a brown envelope locked in my glove compartment containing a neatly stacked two and a half inch block of yellow paper the size of £50 notes. Ignore the colour of its contents and I bet by holding that envelope you'd easily believe you just became twenty-five grand the richer. Anyway, I figure it might be a good idea to keep a decoy now the real stuff is safely hidden.

The lighter of the two packages is in my pocket, still with its original content. Mind you, it's a different pocket in a different jacket to the one I wore last night. Call me paranoid, but each article of clothing has gone into a different plastic carrier bag, along with an anonymous sample of the contents of my dustbin, and each bag has been dumped into different street bins all the way to Lakeside. The last bag contained the gloves I wore last night; the ones I put back on this morning to examine the camera. I'm not sure what I was expecting to find. It's a disposable, the sort you used to get in Woolworths for a couple of quid. Kids would buy them to leave lying around at parties so anyone could take a photo, and when they got them developed everyone would have a good laugh. There'd be the usual assortment of gurning faces, sneaky peeks up girls' skirts and drunken lads' lily-white arses. Until it's been opened and the film processed it's just another innocuous glitter-wrapped box with a lens. And that's exactly what was in the envelope – nothing more, nothing less.

Right now, in the warming sunshine of a pleasant Kentish morning, the trauma of my recent criminal act, with its associated mysteries and consequent nightmares, has already started to fade, and I'm thinking about the money Herb promised me. I know I told him I didn't need it, but with the job done, as far as I'm concerned, I'm eligible for the full remuneration package and keen to get my hands on another bundle of cash. Whilst a thousand quid is a poor relation to the stack I've hidden away, at least Herb's money will be earned and I feel like I deserve it. I'll decide what to do with the other windfall another time. All I'm focused on is handing the camera to Herb and walking away with the reward – no more questions asked. Debt repaid. Honour upheld.

For the second time in eight days, I'm also hoping to avoid detection by Mum's neighbourhood watch, as I park in another side street and walk the last few hundred yards.

Unexpected Withdrawal

It's still early as I walk up the front path. The curtains are already drawn back, not that I'm concerned about waking him. I've already grappled with that dilemma earlier this morning, only to then get no reply again when I rang his number. That's what prompted my decision to just turn up. I'm not so sure of the rationale ten minutes later, when I'm still here ringing the doorbell and peering gingerly through the front window. No answer. No movement. Silence. By seven-thirty the street is coming to life; people are leaving their houses for work and I'm feeling increasingly conspicuous standing at the front door for so long. All I can do is walk back out of the gate and down the street back towards the car. Driving slowly past the house again, I think I see a silhouette move across the front window. I can't be sure. I'm starting to doubt myself. Just lately, I've been seeing shadows everywhere.

I continue in the direction of Mum's and try to come up with a credible reason for visiting again, unannounced and this early in the morning. At the same time I know she'll never tire of being pleased to see me, and in no time I'm sitting in her kitchen, waiting for bacon and eggs.

'There was a chance of some work down here,' I say to her as she pours my fourth coffee of the morning. I hate deceiving her, but at least there's some truth in it.

'Oh, that would be good,' she replies. 'It would be nice to see more of you. I knew you'd find something soon.'

'I wish I was so optimistic,' I say, gesturing to the TV where the breakfast news programme is announcing more redundancies. 'Things are looking pretty grim in the City. My old firm just let a dozen middle managers go.'

'Isn't that awful,' she says with genuine concern. 'All those poor bankers losing their jobs. Makes me think you got out in time.'

'Maybe,' I say without conviction. I can't share her sympathy for guys my age walking away with six-figure packages. If only I could have kept my cool, I might have been considered an operational liability and been one of the lucky ones. I try to imagine how it would have felt, the short walk of shame from the MD's office, followed by the long skip of joy out of the building.

'It's unlikely I'll end up back down here though,' I add,

hastily backtracking so as to manage any expectations my recently regular visits are set to continue. 'I might take on some temporary work closer to home.'

As I say it, I can't ignore the irony of my recent foray into local casual labour, and get a flashback of myself legging it over a fence and down some back alley. Not exactly a placement through Office Angels.

'Have you seen Herb Long lately, Mum?' I ask, barely changing the subject.

'Well, it's funny you should ask,' she says, her expression sharpening. 'I saw him only yesterday coming out of the bank on Perry Street. It was really quite peculiar.'

'What was?' I say, steering a corner of buttered bread from yolk to ketchup to mouth in a single movement.

'The way he completely ignored me. I know some say he's a rogue, but he's also a gentleman, holding doors open and raising his hat, smiling and saying "Good Morning". Well you know me, I'll always stop and say hello when people are civil, and no matter what they say, he's always been very courteous to me.' She pauses long enough to flip the last crispy rasher onto my plate and return the frying pan to the hob. 'Then yesterday, it was as if he'd looked straight through me. He must have seen me because I walked right in front of him. He didn't acknowledge me – no smile, not a word – just kept walking. I was so surprised, I was left standing there like a lemon. And rather than heading back towards Pelham Road to get the bus home, he got into a car that was waiting by the side of the road and it drove off in the opposite direction.'

I sit there trying to get my head around what she's saying. It doesn't seem so strange that Herb would get into a car after a visit to the bank, but I have to agree, it seems odd for him to blank her like that.

'I just hope he's alright,' she goes on. 'Whether he was a scoundrel in his day, I don't know. Now he's an old man. I'd pop along and knock on his door to check on him if I had the nerve. He's always been such a private person. I don't know anyone who's ever been over the threshold into that house of his. Some say it's a pigsty.'

'Mum, you shouldn't listen to all that gossip.' I look up from wiping my plate with the last piece of crust. 'He looked clean and tidy the last time I saw him,' I add, unintentionally defending a man I supposedly haven't seen for years, probably sounding a little too knowledgeable in the process.

'Poor old soul,' she says, seemingly without hearing me. 'He always asks after you though. A couple of weeks ago he was very interested in how you were doing, especially when I told him you'd had some bad luck of late.'

'Really?'

'Yes. And besides, when *was* the last time *you* saw him, Michael?'

'Oh... um... it's been a while.' I shrug and start clearing the table. As if that isn't uncharacteristic enough, I grab the tea towel when she begins washing up.

If you'd done that more often, maybe Sam wouldn't have given up on you. While she doesn't say it, and I doubt she's even thinking it, the words echo in my head regardless.

'When you saw Herb a couple of weeks ago,' I ask, keen to continue a real conversation, 'did he say he wanted to speak to me?'

'No, why would he have wanted to do that?'

'Oh, it's nothing really,' I say, polishing an old fork like it's sterling silver. 'I got a garbled message on my mobile and couldn't work out who it was. I thought it sounded like him, only I don't know how he would have got my number.'

There's no way Mum would have given it out and not asked me first. And given the opportunity to say if she did, she just shrugs.

After we've put everything away, I offer to take her into the town centre to get some shopping she says she needs. Nothing much, only a few bits I'm sure could have waited, but she never passes up the chance of the company and the possibility of seeing one of her friends and showing off her big-shot son.

Ironically, when her chance comes to tell Iris or Rita or Joan how successful I am in the City, we're surrounded by bog rolls. Mum doesn't mention my recent change of fortune. I play along for the sake of her pride and try hard not to think too much about my latest career direction.

On the way back, she wants to call into one of the elderly ladies in the neighbourhood she keeps a charitable eye on. She takes the jumbo value pack of toilet tissues in with her and I stay in the car by mutual consent. It seems this is one old-timer not in the best state of domestic or personal hygiene.

The diversion means we pass Herb's on the way home and I glance again at the front of the house. There's still no sign of life. I help Mum unpack the shopping and decline her offer of lunch. Instead, she sends me off with a box full of emergency rations, in case I should starve before she sees me again.

Feeding Disorder

I'm back in the car, parked around the corner from Herb's house, trying to decide what to do next. I unlock the glove compartment and take out the envelope with the camera. Maybe I should drop it through the letterbox. All my instincts tell me that would be a bad idea. First, if there *is* something dodgy on the film, I'd rather put the camera in his hands and not leave it lying around. Second, if what Mum saw the previous day is in any way connected, his house is probably the last place I should leave it. The thought strikes me like a hammer blow: the house may even be being watched. And there I was hanging around the front door for ages earlier. I might as well have had a big cardboard arrow pointing at my head. The third reason sits slightly uncomfortably on my conscience, but I don't like the idea of giving up the goods without getting paid.

I decide to write a cryptic note I hope won't incriminate me in the wrong hands. It reads: "Good match away from home last night. Apart from the changing rooms and a spectator too close to the Field! Caught offside but managed to evade the home defender. Thankfully no injury time or penalties. Guess who got the goal and lifted the trophy? Not bad for a fullback! Waiting for transfer news – MF".

Approaching the front gate, I scan the street. It's deserted, and I'm satisfied the little two-seater parked within sight of the house is empty. Walking up the path, everything is exactly as it was earlier. This time I only ring the bell once, wait a few seconds and without dwelling to look through any windows, put the note through the letter box and walk away.

Driving home, I can't get the sense of anxiety to subside. I'm concerned there might only be two explanations for Herb's absence. The first is that he's been taken by whoever was trying to blackmail him with the photos. I imagine him, having handed over the cash he was forced to withdraw from the bank yesterday, suffering physical abuse at the hands of violent, ruthless thugs, as a direct consequence of me having taken the camera and *their* money last night.

This is the malignant hypothesis that makes me feel sick to my stomach, not only at the thought of what Herb might then be going through. There's also the realisation I'll be their next target. At least I can console myself that there is nothing I could have done differently to help him. That's where the problem arises with the benign alternative, which at first seems more reassuring.

Having accepted it's perhaps less fanciful to assume that Herb is sitting still and cold in his favourite chair, in a rear room of his house, with a book open on his chest, having expired peacefully from natural causes, I wrestle with the fact I've done absolutely nothing to raise the alarm, and here I am just driving away.

I consider calling the local police anonymously and telling them I've just witnessed a disturbance at Herb's address, and that maybe they should go and check on the owner. Problem is, of course, if for whatever reason they had to break in, the first thing they'll find is my note, which will soon start to look more that a bit odd if there *are* signs of foul-play. Even if everything's fine and he seems to have just nipped into town for the day, they might have a rummage around anyway and find all that interesting stuff in the garage. Either way, I'll have been responsible for tipping them off to my old friend's lucrative trade in illegal merchandise.

Reluctantly, I decide there's nothing more I can do right now. If I haven't heard from Herb by mid-afternoon tomorrow, I'll drive back down again after dark and have a snoop around. For the second time in as many days, I find myself calmly and rationally contemplating breaking into someone's house.

The further I drive beyond the river, the worse I feel, and once I'm off the motorway, I have to pull in and try phoning Herb again. There's still no reply and I sit here, staring out of the windscreen for ages. That's when I decide, enough is enough. I need to talk to someone about this predicament I'm in. I'll ring Greg. I've known him for years. He lives near me, is a man of the world and, as a bookmaker, a good guy to have on-side in a crisis. I'm just hoping he's free tonight.

'GB Ra-cing,' the receptionist sings at me down the line.

'Hi, can I speak to Greg Bell, please? Tell him it's Mickey Field.'

'Put-ting you through,' is followed by a few seconds of silence.

'Field-o! How you doing mate?'

'Yeah good, thanks Dinger. How's business?'

'Ticking over, mate, ticking over. You? Still enjoying your time off?'

'Yeah, not bad. You know, just taking it easy for awhile.'

'Nice one. Look, I'm up against it a bit mate, so what can I do for you?'

'Sorry mate, I won't keep you. I was just wondering if you fancy a beer tonight that was all.'

'Great idea Mickey-boy. Definitely. Look, I'll ring round the lads later and see who's up for it, yeah?'

'Yeah... that would be... I was just hoping we could...'

'Yeah, brilliant idea... Hold on mate...' his voice goes muffled and I realise he's keeping two conversations going. 'Yeah, no worries, Mickey. I'll get the boys onboard and we can give it the full treatment. Can't remember the last time we all got together.'

'Yeah... sure. But what I...'

'And God knows you could probably do with a serious blow-out, me old mate.'

'Yeah... but...'

'And you don't even have to get up for work tomorrow. Lucky bastard... Anyway, sorry mate. The three-thirty at Lingfield Park's not looking good. Red-hot favourite's gonna walk it. You heard it here first – go and put your house on it. Not good for us though. Need to lay off some of our risk. Gotta dash... King's Head, right? Eight o'clock. Can't wait. Laters.'

At that the phone goes dead and I sit back and shake my head. Rather than a quiet chat with a trusted mate, tonight's now going to be a riot.

Assuming they are all up for it, along with Greg there's Tom, who I've also known for years from when the three of us worked together at another firm. And then there are the two guys from my last place, Harvey and Jake, who were always more like friends than colleagues. The four of them know each other pretty well since I introduced them all, and we tend to get together a couple of times a year. It always ends up being a major piss-up and so I like to prepare well for the alcoholic binge.

Before getting home, I think about my usual lads' night out speciality and wonder if I've got all the essential ingredients to make it when I get in. Four slices of bread, overhanging the plate, each with its own slice of ham, are covered in baked beans, topped with a generous layer of grated cheese and the whole thing is finished off for a minute under the grill. All chased down with a large glass of semi-skimmed. Manna! The plan is to load up to the point where I can absorb ten pints of beer; we usually get two rounds in each, and no one ever wants to shirk their turn as the evening wears on. Truth be told, most of us have usually had enough after six. The real art comes from leaving room in the tank for a quarter-pounder with cheese, salad and chilli sauce as we stagger home afterwards.

4.

Fixed Odds

We meet up in The King's Head as arranged and the evening is swinging along nicely. By nine o'clock, I've completely forgotten about Herb. When I was still sober, I made a point of getting The Banker to agree, regardless of how drunk I got – even in the unlikely event of getting five minutes with Greg on his own – not to allow me to make any mention of scary houses, cries for help, shadows at the window, disposable cameras, large bundles of cash and enigmatic, old men who set little tasks and then mysteriously disappear.

After three pints I'm entertaining the guys with an embellished version of the meeting I had with the girl from Compliance about those missing cheques some weeks ago. The way I tell it now, my accuser was only nineteen, blonde and gorgeous...

She kept crossing and uncrossing her legs and dropped her pen very close to my foot and reached across seductively to pick it up. Her ample bosom jiggled playfully between the open buttons of her crisp white blouse as it brushed against my knee.

'You're probably wondering what I've asked you here for', she said with a husky voice and a seductive grin.

The guys are laughing sarcastically, I suspect only partly in contempt of my pathetic daydream. Also to disguise what's going on in their own underpants.

'Have you seen my Sexual Harassment Policy?' She said as she loosened her blouse.

'Why, is it compulsory?' I said.

More sniggers from the boys.

'Oh yes!' she exclaimed, removing her glasses and unpinning her hair, letting it cascade like a golden tide over her slender frame. 'And when you've done it once, you have to keep doing it.'

'Really?' I asked. 'How many times?'

'Again and again... and again.'

'I don't know if I can.'

'Oh, you have to.' She looked into my eyes. 'I need you to.'

'But it's been such a long time...'

'Come on, don't be shy,' she said. 'I'll help you. It's just like riding a bike.'

The beer-fuelled laughter increases.

'I don't think I can remember how.' I looked away, ashamed.

'Really?' She seemed to be losing patience.

'No,' I said, fiddling with my tie. 'You seem surprised.'

'Yes.' She scowled. 'I can't believe you haven't been doing it regularly.'

'Why do you say that?'

By now the guys are completely lost in their own worlds and I hold onto the moment long enough for mouths to start opening.

'Because, according to your signature on the Compliance Record, you've read the bloody thing every year since you've been here!' she hissed, throwing the Staff Handbook across the table at me.

Amid the groans and laughter, I can hear slow clapping coming from behind me, and I look around to find the girl from last night in The Feathers, standing with her back to the bar watching us. She's sneering and applauding sarcastically, and I can feel myself blushing. Not least because several strangers are also staring at me. That and the fact she's with some guy who's looking at her in spiteful bemusement. To make it worse, my mates are rubbernecking from her to me, with mixed expressions of confusion and admiration.

'Thank you. Thank you very much,' I say in a terrible Elvis

voice and turn back to our huddle.

'You're in there!' Jake murmurs, to which there's conspiratorial muttering from the others. 'She's really hot. Do you know her?'

'No,' I lie. 'And it looks like she's with someone.' I'm dying to turn around to see if they are still looking, but I don't dare. I'm also dreading that she's going to walk over at any moment and make some acerbic comment. Thankfully, I can't sense anyone approaching from behind.

'Are you sure she's not the Compliance girl, checking up on you?' Harvey chips in, and they all laugh.

'Yeah, that's the only trouble with figments of your imagination.' Tom takes up the baton. 'When they *do* come true, you usually end up screwing them up.'

I smirk back at them, unimpressed, suddenly feeling very sober. In the hope of dismissing her unexpected intrusion as an everyday occurrence, I attempt to make a serious point in a hushed voice.

'She's obviously one of those feminist types who's overheard something out of context and thinks I'm a sexist bastard, and can't resist making a scene to embarrass me.' I'm wasting my breath. The boys have the bit between their teeth.

'Why don't you go and have a chat with her? See if you can convert her from the feminist path,' says Greg. The guys are getting louder and I can almost feel eyes drilling holes into my back, but I still can't bring myself to turn around.

'Yeah, she probably needs a good seeing to, that's all,' Tom chimes in.

'Sure, just like you should have done with the girlie from Compliance. I bet you'd still have a job then,' says Harvey.

'I reckon you would have probably been promoted.' Jake completes the circle, and they all howl at my expense.

The volume of their banter has returned to its earlier boisterous level, and I cringe at the thought of her enjoying all of this. I almost feel sorry for the guy she's with. I give up trying to contain the situation and turn around to apologise. To my surprise and relief they've gone. I'm the only mug in the group with my back to the rest of the pub, and when I look back the guys are all smirking.

'Don't worry, she went and sat down on the other side of the pub after you ignored her,' Greg explains. 'Her bloke seems *well* hacked off.'

'Look at him though, little squirt,' Harvey adds, straightening his frame to its full five feet, five and three-quarters to see over my shoulder.

'Must have something going for him though,' Tom says, leaning forward to rest his bristly chin on Harvey's head. 'How's it feel, Harv, looking down on a bloke like that?'

'Piss off!'

'Uh-oh!' Jake looks past me with raised eyebrows and a hand over his mouth, blatantly failing in any attempt to look inconspicuous. 'Don't look now. He's just got up and walked out with a face like thunder.'

'What'd I say?' Harvey says, finding another three inches to get a good look. 'I knew Mr Bean wouldn't be able to keep a girl like that for long.'

This time I can't resist looking around in the direction their bulging eyes are indicating. I'm expecting another wind-up, but the warning not to look is genuine, because as I stare across the pub, sure enough she's sitting alone, looking straight back at us with a hurt look meant just for me.

'Now you've got to go for it, surely,' Jake says, and they all mutter in agreement, breaking out into more schoolboy sniggers, prompting me to make a rash decision to even things up a bit.

'Okay, fellas, put your money where your mouths are. I bet I can pull her with a single line.' I stun them into silence with misplaced bravado and forge on while I still have their attention. 'The odds must be against me if the boyfriend's just stormed out. Chances are she'll go after him before I even get across the pub. I reckon it's got to be worth twenty quid from each of you. Who's in?'

'So what's the wager then Mickey?' Harvey asks, without

giving me the chance to respond. 'How about, we each stump up twenty quid if you succeed in sitting down at her table, spend at least thirty minutes talking to her, and then get back here with her number? I'll be the official time-keeper.'

'I'm in,' Greg says, reaching for his wallet a bit too eagerly. 'I need to make up some of my losses after the day I've had.'

'Hang on, what's my down-side risk, Dinger?' I ask, considering that he's the expert since swapping investment banking for bookmaking a few years ago. Not such a big career change as you might think.

'If you fail, we'll just take you for a tenner each.' Harvey cuts in, looking around at the rest of the group. 'Agreed?'

Everyone's nodding. I'm sure they think at those odds they're robbing me blind.

'Okay guys, I think what I'm hearing is: two to one, yeah?' I tilt my head and hold up my palms in a show of confidence.

'Two to one,' Greg says, signalling in tic-tac with a right-hand touch of his nose, before pointing back at me and adding, 'Bar the *field!*' They all laugh again at my expense.

'Deal,' I say, cutting them dead. And without a second thought, I head over to where she's sitting.

Cheeky Boy

Surprisingly inhibited laughter fades behind me as I stride confidently around the corner of the bar and see Grace looking down in contemplation of the tall glass on the table.

'Not drinking scotch tonight?' I say, approaching her quiet corner with a nervous grin.

She looks up, slightly startled, and a brief look of surprise is followed by a sombre smile that suggests her playfulness from earlier has gone, possibly with her companion, who's left an unfinished pint of lager on the table.

'Is your friend coming back?' I persist. I'm already feeling uneasy about my mission, and sense she is in no mood to be chatted up for a bet, if ever a woman was. I can feel the guys watching, so I at least try to gesticulate like I'm delivering a masterful opening line.

'I doubt it. He's always been a spoilt little brat who gets his own way.' Her words ricochet in the confines of the alcove, leaving me feeling very exposed. 'No, I won't be seeing him again tonight. Thank God.'

'Can I sit down?' I gesture towards the vacated chair. 'Or would you rather I left you alone?' I'm still trying to gauge her vibe, when she unexpectedly smiles up at me and pulls the chair out. At that, a completely unconstrained cheer erupts from the other side of the pub.

'What's the bet?' she says, her perceptiveness like a blow to my stomach. She's looking from them to me and I sit here feeling like a kid caught with his trousers down.

'I'm sorry. Maybe I should go.' As I say it I feel pathetic, but she just laughs.

'Don't go,' she says. 'This could be fun. What's the deal?'

'I'm two to one against to sit here for at least half an hour and take back your phone number.' I'm cringing until I notice the sparkle in her eyes has returned and she seems to be flattered to find herself at the centre of my mates' attention. She looks back at them, almost relishing the audience.

'That doesn't sound like much of a challenge, does it Mickey?' She shifts seductively in her chair. Once again, this girl has me exactly where she wants me and I'm struggling to keep my cool. At the same time, I find myself becoming intrigued about her, the coincidence of seeing her again, the guy she was with, and how her mood has quickly changed. I also feel a sense of anxious excitement that I haven't felt for years. Her blatant flirting and innuendo is as unsettling as it is arousing. She's very sexy, if slightly scary with it; the kind of girl I would have steered clear of when I was younger. Too much to handle. Now I'm older and wiser, perhaps I'm ready for the ride. Okay, maybe just older.

'I thought we might need to start from the beginning again.' I look up at her, alluding to how badly things ended last night.

I'm being sincere. She still wants to play.

'So did you get a better offer?' At least this time she's smiling, maybe not sweetly, but without any of the venom from before.

'No, I didn't.' I feign disappointment. 'Truthfully, I didn't sleep well either. And I really did have an early start today. Sorry, I was a bit strung out last night. There's been a lot going on.'

'It felt like you were in a hurry to get away from me.' She seems genuinely hurt. 'And after your performance over there and the way you just dismissed me in front of your mates, I'm surprised you'd want to try again – even if it *is* for a bet.'

'I know. Look, last night was...' I sigh, not sure how to finish that particular sentence. 'As for just now... I'm sorry. I thought you were with someone. And the bet... God, that must look pathetic. I wouldn't blame you for thinking I'm a complete prat. What if I said I'm not here for the bet?' I look back across the bar where the guys have re-grouped in a huddle, like a football team at half time, three-nil down and a man sent off, in resignation that the match is already lost. They shouldn't be so worried; if I gave a damn about the game, I'd be feeling far from confident of making it to full time, let alone getting her name and number in the book.

'So why *are* you here?' She continues to tease, like a cat pawing at a dead mouse.

'I haven't met anyone like you before.' I'm trying to be serious without sounding like a loser. 'I was flattered last night, I really was. It's just that I'm a bit out of practice with all this and I must have got cold feet.'

'That's sweet,' she says and seems to mean it. 'I realise I can be a bit full-on at times,' she continues, 'if you'll excuse the understatement.'

'Not a word I'd associate with you.' I dig back gently.

'Touché!' she raises her glass and I reciprocate. She finishes her drink and accepts my offer of another. At the bar I order her a Tia Maria and Coke; a far cry from single malt, The Whisky

Snob in my head observes. I settle for another pint of Guinness.

As I'm waiting, I feel a sharp dig in my lower back and one of the guys hisses into my ear, 'Get in there my son.' I look over my shoulder and the whole group is giving me the thumbs-up. I make sure Grace can't see me and wink back at them, extending a suggestively curled tongue. They explode into rowdy laughter she can't have failed to notice.

Warm Front

'They must be licking their wounds and emptying their wallets by now,' Grace says as I put the drinks down. She's looking at her watch and I realise she's counting down the minutes when she adds, 'Of course, I might just get up and walk out on you. So you know how it feels.'

'Fair comment,' I say. 'Then again, your bloke might have left his drink, but I don't think you're the kind to waste good alcohol.'

'You're only half right,' she says with a wink. 'As for him, he's actually my brother.'

'Oh, right,' I chirp, failing miserably to hide my relief.

'Yes, he's a student. He only ever hangs out with me when he wants something. The rest of the time I hardly see him. And when he *is* home he's either playing computer games with his geeky mates or locked in his room. We used to be quite close in the early days...' her thoughts tail off as she chases ice around her glass with the tip of a manicured French nail, just like Sam's. The recollection distracts me from challenging her strange turn of phrase and anyway, I sense a knot of tension beginning to form in the brow of her downcast eyes. Then, in an instant, the strain evaporates and she's back with me and asking about my family.

Before we realise, another twenty-five minutes have passed and I've told her about my previous job and my soon-to-be-equally previous wife. She laughs when she realises the skit she overheard earlier was a parody of the last moments of my banking career. When I get to the end, it occurs to me this is the first time I've been able to talk about recent events so openly and objectively. I'm unburdened and realise I feel completely at ease talking to her.

'I'm sorry,' she says. 'I feel really bad I've been giving you such a hard time. No wonder you were a bit edgy when I came along and stuck my big ego into your life yesterday.'

'No, really, I'm glad you did. You gave me the reality check I needed. I've been going round with my head up my arse, blaming everyone else. I'm starting to see I need to take some responsibility for myself and move on,' I blurt out. She doesn't respond and I realise the conversation has become a bit too heavy too soon. So I'm grateful when she lifts the mood by looking at her watch again.

'How much have we won?' she asks with a triumphant smile.

'Ah, well, I haven't got your number yet.'

'There's plenty of time for that,' she says.

'If you say so.' I can't help looking pleased with myself. 'Why don't I get you another drink, just to keep them guessing?' She smiles her agreement and I head back to the bar with our empty glasses.

I look across to the guys who appear resigned to defeat. Harvey nods back with eyebrows raised, and stretches his thumb and little finger from ear to mouth. I shake my head. No phone number yet, but I'm well into extra time.

Back at the table, Grace has made herself more comfortable, removing the chunky knitted coat she's kept herself wrapped up in all evening. I'm greeted by a candy-striped Ralph Lauren polo shirt that fits her like a second skin. The narrow bands of alternating pink and cream map the shape of her perfect breasts like the contours of a benevolent weather front. It's certainly getting warmer in our cosy snug and, following her lead, I take off my jacket and hang it on the back of the chair, without shifting my gaze.

I close my mouth, careful not to drool, and casually raise

my eyes back up to her face. I'm sure my lustful appreciation hasn't gone unnoticed. I'm equally sure that's exactly the reaction she was hoping for.

'So tell me something about yourself,' I ask, trying to keep my concentration, 'apart from the geeky brother I've already met.'

'What's there to know?' She pauses briefly, just for effect. 'Grace de Manton, age twenty-five, flunked out of school at sixteen with one GCSE, trained as a hairdresser for two years before realising there's more money in fake tans, so now I spray white people brown for a living. That's about it really.'

'Interesting,' I say, still getting my head around that surname. 'We'll come back to some of that later. First, I'm intrigued to know what the real Grace is like.'

'Fire away,' she says with a slightly perplexed look in her eyes.

'Alright.' I pause briefly, though not for effect. I haven't really thought this through. Not that it matters; I'm enjoying myself now the pressure is off. 'Here we go... what's the nicest thing, the meanest thing and the most outrageous thing you've ever done?'

'In that order?'

'However it comes.'

'Okay. I think the nicest thing I've done recently is to take pity on a poor, lonely old guy in a pub and buy him a drink!'

'Hey! Enough of the old if you don't mind.'

She smiles, very sweetly this time, and goes on, 'Then of course, I was very mean to him the next time I saw him and showed him up in front of his friends.'

'Yeah, yeah, yeah. Very funny. Not exactly telling me anything I don't already know.'

'Hmm, let me see, something outrageous.' She pauses and looks up at the ceiling. Each time she seems to have thought of something, her brow knits together in an expression of pained recollection, and then she shakes her head as if to say there must be something else more outrageous than that. Slowly, a very girlie grin starts to stretch her lips and widen her eyes until it spreads and lights up her whole face.

'No,' she says. 'I can't tell you that.'

'What?' I'm now desperate to hear the story.

The beaming smile has turned into a naughty giggle, which she's trying to control. That only succeeds in making it worse, until she's laughing hysterically into her hands. Her laughter is infectious and I'm joining in without even knowing what's so funny; other than watching her completely losing it.

'You're going to have to tell me,' I plead, 'and it had better be good.' At that she bursts into another uncontrollable fit, until tears start rolling down her cheeks.

'Sorry,' she manages to say, wiping her face with a tissue. 'I won't be long.' She walks towards the ladies' room, when another wave of hysteria grips her and I'm left alone and confused.

Two middle-aged women are sitting at the closest table and I'm sure they've been drawn into the contagion. They are still smiling across at me as if I've just told the funniest gag ever and they've missed the punchline, but laughed along anyway. And now it's like they want me to repeat the joke. All I can do is shrug and shake my head as they turn away disappointed.

Model Student

Grace is back sitting next to me. After a big swig of her drink she seems to have it all under control.

'If I tell you this,' she says, and I can tell she's being serious, 'you have to promise not to tell anyone else. Especially that lot over there.' She looks across the pub to where my mates have abandoned all hope of me re-joining them.

'Scout's honour,' I say, and cross my heart with my finger. I'm not trying to be funny but her face cracks ever so slightly, and she only just manages to hold back another fit of the giggles.

'Well, I wasn't quite sixteen at the time,' she says, finally starting to open up. 'It was an all girls' school and I was a bit of a rebel.'

'Now *that* I find hard to believe,' I quip.

She goes on undeterred. 'My art teacher was probably your age – what's that, about forty-five?' She smirks with instant revenge and I almost choke on the Guinness.

'Excuse me,' I blurt out. 'Thirty-eight if you don't mind.'

'Well, like I said, he was about your age and *soo* handsome. The other thing he had in common with you was we all fancied him rotten.' She tilts her head to one side and sighs dramatically. I grin back bashfully as she continues. 'Art was one of my favourite subjects, and not just because of Mr Johnson. It was the only thing I was any good at.'

'Hence the GCSE.'

'That's right. Don't tell me, you've got ten.'

'No,' I said, feeling slightly uneasy.

'I don't suppose they had GCSEs when you were at school.'

'What, back in Tom Brown's schooldays? Are you kidding? We were lucky to have books back then.'

'Tom Brown? Who was he, your BFF?'

'My what?'

'Never mind,' she says.

'If you must know, I only got one O-level too. Can we get back to the story?'

'Okay. Well you can imagine, there were a lot of hormonal teenagers in the art class who would have liked a piece of Mr Johnson. In almost every lesson he had to contend with one girl or another asking him a completely irrelevant question about the Old Masters in her most seductive voice – about Rubens and his buxom maidens, Raphael's flighty nymphs, Michelangelo's cherubs. You get the idea – it was always about nudes. One girl asked him if he thought she would make a good model to recreate a scene, and another looked at the statue of David and asked him if he would be an authentic stand-in. Hardly a lesson went by without him blushing profusely and having to rapidly change the subject. It got so bad...'

She takes a sip of her drink as if she needs a moment to

compose herself, before continuing, 'between classes, girls started daring each other to come up with the worst things to embarrass him with. There was a girl called Paula Harvey, who always sat at the back of the class with Julie Dixon, and whenever Mr Johnson asked either of them a question, they would hold hands suggestively and look into each other's eyes before answering him. I don't think they were that way inclined; it just seemed like a funny thing to do. Well, things got out of hand when I foolishly challenged them to take it a step further. I never thought they would do it, but sure enough at the next lesson, as if drawn to them like a bee to a honey pot, Mr Johnson asked Paula what she thought might have been Da Vinci's motivation for the smile on the face of La Gioconda.'

'The Mona Lisa,' I chip in, as if to show I'm not completely stupid.

'Correct. Well, the girls even surprised themselves when they turned to each other and locked in a passionate embrace before French kissing for five seconds to complete the dare.'

'Wow!' My lips form the word but no sound comes out. 'I thought my challenge tonight was a tough one. What did Mr Johnson say?'

'That was the best bit. When they finished, all he could say was, *"Okay, you might be onto something there. Anyone got any other ideas?"* And we all collapsed into a riot of laughter and applause.'

'Fantastic! So where did that leave you?'

'What did you say your mates are on the hook for if you win the bet?'

'Twenty quid each.'

'I should've been so lucky,' she says. 'I was petrified when I caught up with them in the corridor after class. Rather than put me out of my misery, they said they'd come back to me in a couple of days once they'd thought of something appropriate. Well, when they told me later that week what I had to do, I was stunned. I suppose I could've refused and told them to come up with something else... but once I got used to the idea I decided to go for it.'

I'm on tenterhooks, willing her on to say what it was she had to do. She knows she's got me captivated and takes another long gulp of her drink before continuing in a single breath.

'At least I had until the end of term to achieve it. The bad news was I had to put a portrait of myself onto Mr Johnson's classroom wall and it had to stay there for at least twenty-four hours and in it I had to be naked.' She pauses again to enjoy my reaction. I'm sitting here mesmerised, staring back at her, eyes agog like an adolescent in awe.

'I'm starting to feel very pervy,' I admit, laughing uncomfortably. 'I'm wondering if you were allowed to keep any of your uniform on.'

'Dirty old man!'

'Guilty as charged,' I say and really feel it. 'How on earth did you get out of that?'

'I didn't,' she says with a wicked glint in her eyes. 'Mr Johnson made no secret that he was a member of a private artists' club; he was always bringing stuff in he'd done there. So I knew they met fortnightly, and every now and again it seemed they'd sketch or paint a model. One evening, while they were meeting, I wangled my way in to see the club secretary, and with a dark wig, coloured contact lenses and high heels, I was able to convince her I was nineteen and interested in being a model for their next life study.'

'How old did you say you really were?'

'It was about a month before my sixteenth birthday. But I had all the equipment by then if that's what you're thinking about.'

'I'm trying not to. It doesn't seem right, but go on anyway.'

'She said they didn't get many younger volunteers and felt sure the club would be delighted to sketch me and booked me there and then for two weeks' time. As I was about to leave, I noticed Mr Johnson talking with a lot of much older men, and I started to have some doubts about what I was doing. To my horror, the secretary called him over to meet me. I felt sure he would recognise me beneath the wig and heavy make-up, but I suppose the brown eyes must have also helped. He just smiled warmly and shook my hand and thanked me for volunteering.'

'You must have been terrified.'

'I was shaking all the way home. But, it was weird, at the same time I felt really excited to think I might get away with it. Two weeks later, without a word to anyone, least of all Paula and Julie, I donned my disguise again and went back to the village hall. I had to pee when I got there and nearly freaked out in front of the secretary when I saw myself as a stranger in the mirror. I managed to hold it all together and took up my position behind a screen. I could hear them all coming into the room and taking their places; it sounded all very professional. The secretary asked if I was ready and before I could answer she pulled the screen away and I was left sprawling across an old sofa wearing nothing but a wig and a nervous smile.'

My jaw drops. I don't think she's noticed. She's lost in the moment. I can imagine her there in one respect, totally vulnerable, and at the same time, even back then, relishing the spotlight.

'I have to say, it was the most tedious hour I've ever spent with my clothes off,' she says, snapping the moment like a twig. 'Before long I was freezing. It was December and I'm sure they left the heating off on purpose. Not only that but everything started to ache and I got pins and needles in my arms and legs. In the end my bum went completely numb and I was glad when it was over.'

'Well they do say you have to suffer for your art.'

'Yeah,' she smirks. 'Anyway, just as I was leaving I noticed most of the other artists gathering around Mr J's easel and I started worrying he'd twigged and drawn me with imaginary clothes on.'

'In your school uniform, like I said.'

'Right. But instead, they seemed to be genuinely impressed with his portrait.'

'So he didn't recognise you?'

'No, he must have sat there for an hour, studying every inch of me, without ever thinking I looked familiar.'

'I don't suppose he would have spent much time looking at your face.'

'That's what I thought, but when I eventually got to see it, the likeness was really good. Not that I hung around to see any of the sketches on the night. I got out of there as quickly as I could. I remember walking up the road with a huge grin on my face. I actually enjoyed it. It was really quite liberating.' She pauses again, reflecting on this early realisation of something I'm beginning to get a good sense of: this girl will do just about anything for attention.

'So, there were loads of artists' impressions of your underage skin on canvas,' I say. 'Surely you were still a long way from completing the challenge.'

'Well that's the bit I couldn't have anticipated,' she says with a grin and a shake of her head. 'My biggest concern was that he wouldn't even bring his portrait of me in.'

'I'm guessing you got lucky,' I say.

'Well... yes and no,' she says and drains her glass. 'Back at school I didn't dare breathe a word. All I had was a flimsy plan to find it and put it on the classroom wall one evening after school. As far as Paula and Julie were concerned, I still had two weeks of term left to complete the mission. Thankfully, I didn't see Mr Johnson before the next art class came around and it must have been nerves, because that morning I felt really ill with a terrible stomach upset and had to go home so I missed it.'

'I'm not surprised,' I say. 'Having to face him in the classroom again.'

'Well I was going to have to eventually. Anyway, the next day I went in and who's the first person I see running towards me? It's Paula and she's shouting across the crowded assembly hall. "Oi! You devil. You did it! Eat your heart out, Mona Lisa!" Everyone else looked at us totally confused. Yeah... just like that.'

'So how did she know?' I say, smiling to un-crease my brow.

'It turned out Mr Johnson was so proud of his new portrait, he'd only gone and put it on the wall himself. He labelled it: "Example of a true-life likeness. Model in repose." Not only that, he also used it in the previous day's lesson to illustrate the perfect model who, according to Paula, he'd said...' Grace tilted her head and sharpened her voice in fake condescension, '"*had exhibited an elegance and professionalism every girl in this class who has previously mocked the great works of art could only ever dream to aspire to.*"'

'Priceless!'

'That picture stayed on the wall for the rest of my time at school. And only Paula, Julie and I ever knew it was me. As far as I know, they never told a soul. It might even still be there. To think, after all those years, poor old Mr Johnson still has no idea.'

'Bloody hell,' I say. 'One false move and he could have ended up on the sex offenders' register!'

'God, I've never thought of that!' she says and we both collapse into fits of laughter.

This time I'm the one who needs to head to the loo. I wink at the two women who, stone-faced, watch me with eyes that now roll more in disapproval than disappointment.

Kitten Heels

On my way back I'm aware it's getting late, and I can tell the guys are getting a bit agitated. I've missed several rounds, including at least one I should have paid for, and their usual banter seems to have run out of steam without me. Grace senses my concern as I look back across the pub.

'It's okay. I need to head off soon,' she says, 'and, before you ask, no I don't have a better offer. I've already taken you away from your friends for too long and you didn't come out tonight to spend it with me.'

'Surely that's their fault for taunting me,' I protest, whining like a brat when the biscuit tin's about to be taken away. 'Seriously, you don't have to go because of them. I thought we were just getting to know each other. If I'm honest I could do with a different kind of friend right now.'

'I know Mickey,' she says, touching my arm. 'It must have been tough for you losing your wife and your job like that.'

'Yeah, but that's not the half of it,' I blurt out, unable to stop myself, despite my earlier conviction not to discuss recent sinister activities this evening. She's been very open with me and I feel a sense of shared empathy with her that I haven't felt with anyone else for a long time. Forgive me for excluding Sam from that comparison, having discounted all the emotional ties we once shared, and that I once foolishly believed were unbreakable. As I feared earlier, The Rebel is oblivious to my impaired inhibitions, and wants to tell her everything.

'There's some other weird stuff going on I wish I hadn't got myself mixed up in. I'll spare you the gruesome details... I'm just feeling a bit out of my depth.' Fortunately, The Banker is still in there somewhere and stops me going any further except to say, 'And talking to you has made me feel like it's all gone away, at least for a while.'

I'm rambling, and, I realise, in danger of scaring her off. Who's the bunny boiler now? I needn't worry because she seems totally unfazed.

'Look Mickey.' Her piercing blue eyes lock onto mine. 'You're a really nice guy and I'd like to see you again – ideally without a side bet next time.' I flush with embarrassment. 'So let's just say goodnight nicely for the benefit of the boys and you can go and put them out of their misery and enjoy the rest of your evening as planned.'

'Okay. You're probably right.'

'And whenever you need to talk again, give me a call.' She hands me a small page torn from a diary with her mobile number written on it. 'Maybe you can tell me one of your secrets next time.'

With that she gathers up her coat and bag and walks away from the alcove. I grab my jacket and follow her until she stops and turns. We're facing each other in full view of the guys and, despite her fancy heels, she has to reach up to give me a respectable peck on the cheek. At the same time she reaches behind me out of view and firmly squeezes my arse before cat-walking confidently past my mates and out of the pub.

* * *

Eye Shine

Dying leaves rattle like ribbons in the early autumn breeze. And the moon casts their shape-shifting shadows onto a dirt track, imprinted with hooves, crescent and cloven.

The car rolls unlit and silent to a halt behind a barbed screen of holly. From the open boot, he hauls its black-shrouded cargo and, cursing the brightness of the clearing, lurches off into the dark heart of Epping Forest.

He's been here many times. Knows the man-made pathways laid out in daylight by hordes of strollers, and avoids them in favour of the night-time trails. He prefers the lines and furrows that plants instinctively avoid, where animals navigate their nocturnal terrain. In the moon's full glare, inquisitive eyes flash, luminous. He discards the contents of the polythene sack. Without seeing the waiting foxes drool, he knows their instinct to flee will be abandoned under the intoxicating scent.

Leaving another country road onto a gravel path, he lets the engine run. The headlights sweep rose-scented borders until the tyres crunch to a halt. Entering the house through a side door, he empties the holdall he's carried from the car and places it in a vacant slot on a shelf amongst identical others. After fiddling with surveillance controls in a room full of monitors, he opens an inner door. With the contents of the bag still in his hands, he descends stone steps into a pitch-dark vault.

Loosely winding a length of nylon cord around his hand and

66

elbow, he ties it off with a knot. Then he removes a cleaver from a plastic bag and wraps them together in an old towel. Feeling his way in the dark he counts the rows of metal frames and slides the bundle into a recess. The plastic bag he'll dispose of after removing the white ball that he'll clean and return to its rightful place, hopeful its absence has gone unnoticed.

Back upstairs, stepping out into a hallway, he opens a heavy door slowly and glances across the room. The older man slumped in the chair remains still as the grave.

5.

Friday, 18th

Eight o'clock, the morning after the night before and I don't want to open my eyes. I've made it to the bathroom where I'm leaning against the wall, vigorously massaging my temples. I'm painfully aware that the last few hours back with the lads got pretty ugly. Talking of which, there's a gruesome stranger peering back at me when I eventually squint at the mirror. He bears a passing resemblance to me, only ten years older.

I hate seeing my own reflection; it never seems to look quite like the person in my head. My version of me still has thick black hair that grows strong and defiantly untamed, and a thin, confident mouth that kinks very slightly into a raffish grin, framed by a perfectly honed jaw. This morning I can forgive the red eyes and even the dark circles below, but the face looking back at me also appears to have an excess of plucked goose-skin under its jowl, which The Banker accentuates by dropping his head forward and pushing his shoulders back, before pulling at the resulting goitre with his fingers. I wish he wouldn't do that. Not only does it make his dimpled chin look like the parson's nose, I can also see he's starting to go thin on top. The only thick hairs sprouting rebelliously now are growing out of his eyebrows, nose and ears. I manage to stop myself looking any lower, because I know he's not as athletic as me. I don't want to see his gut – it keeps getting bigger. As for his wedding tackle, just lately that seems to be going the other way – definitely a case of use it or lose it.

For some reason, Grace jumps into my head and the old boy in the mirror covers himself with a towel. Seems he's still bashful this morning. Not me, I'd want her to see the effect she's having. I look down, but all that's bulging under the towel is my own beer belly, and I'm reminded of the unsettling conclusion to the events of last night...

Still Buzzing

I had a lot of catching up to do once I rejoined the guys. They'd included me in every round I'd missed, and I had to drink the three pints that were lined up waiting for me, in quick succession, while they quizzed me about what they'd just witnessed. I don't think they could quite believe it. And if I was honest, neither could I.

'Not bad for an old git, horribly out of shape and out of practice.' It was Tom who said it but they were all thinking it.

Of course they wanted to know all about her and so I told them the basics and embellished the rest, to hide the fact we'd met before. Even I was surprised that after just two encounters we had clicked so well without really knowing much about each other, and in spite of such a bumpy start. They seemed totally gobsmacked that I could bag such a young beauty, Jake almost said as much.

'Yeah, don't forget, I do have a good track record,' I reminded him. 'Sam was also a real looker.'

'Sure,' he agreed before taking great delight in adding, 'That was then, this is now. You're no spring chicken, mate.'

'No, but she sure as hell is,' Harvey chipped in. That was the part they were struggling with and, to tell the truth, so was I.

I didn't want to take their money. It didn't seem right in the circumstances. But they insisted. And they wouldn't let me buy another drink either. They said I'd had to invest into the game and so the least they could do was cover my costs in beer. My only contribution was to buy everyone supper on the way home.

When I stumbled into the solitude of my big, empty house, feeling very drunk and a bit queasy, the burger and chips drowning noisily in a stomach full of gas and ale, the reality of the day nagged away at my stupor, forcing me to confront the fact I still had a dodgy camera and a large wad of someone else's cash hidden away. I also realised I had no idea what had happened to Herb and, come to think of it, what the hell I had got myself mixed up in.

I sat on the floor where I'd landed, with one sock in my hand, trying to force myself to focus on the big issues. All I wanted to do though was think about Grace. I must have thought about her for quite a while – in particular the relief map her bosoms made in that stripy top, the slight touch of her tongue on my lips when we kissed and her hand cupping my bum with a little too much firmness in her middle finger... Disappointingly, thinking about her was all I could manage.

Perhaps not surprisingly, but with hideous consequences, The Banker had retired for the night. He might have even stopped me from making the phone call in the first place. But somehow I must have found Herb's number and hit the connect button. I heard his phone ring twice and then a click as it was answered. Euphoric in my drunkenness, I waited to hear his voice. Instead there was only the sound of breathing.

'Herb? You're there.' I said in a rasping whisper.

'Huh?'

I heard a grunt that persuaded me he'd just woken up. 'Herb, it's Mickey. You okay?'

The breathing got louder and he mumbled again.

'Hmm?' he said, the gruffness of his voice not unreasonable in the circumstances.

'Sorry I woke you, Herb,' I sang out, like it was completely normal to be calling him at one in the morning. 'It's so good to talk to you. Thought you were in trouble.'

'Na,' he said, sounding like he was finally emerging from unconsciousness. And for a fleeting second, in my brain-addled stupor, I was ready to believe that he had just been asleep earlier in the day, and my concerns since had all been groundless paranoia.

'Been calling since last night,' I said, feeling the need to justify all that pathetic anxiety I was glad to finally disown. 'Even drove down today but you weren't there. Where you been? I was getting worried about you.'

'Don't.'

He still sounded strangely guttural, like he'd woken with a sore throat, but his breathing had quietened noticeably and I figured he was beginning to get over the rude awakening.

'I got it Herb.'

'Wha?'

'The camera... I got the camera. What shall I do with it?'

Then the sound of breathing stopped and there was nothing. Even in my state, I was worried. Surely he should have recovered his senses enough to be able to say something intelligible by now. Even if he was comatose thirty seconds ago.

'Herb?'

'I'm very sorry...' Suddenly the words were crystal clear, but they were spoken in the deep voice of a stranger, stinging me like a cold flannel to the face. 'He can't come to the phone right now.'

'Who's that?'

'Oh, it's not important who I am, Mickey. What matters is who you are. And what was all that about a camera?'

'Piss off!' I disconnected and dropped the phone, my fingers twitching from subliminal burns.

Shit...! Shit. Shit. Shit.

I picked it up again and hit redial. It rang twice and then went silent.

'What have you done with him?' I screamed and waited for the voice. That time I couldn't hear any breathing. There were no background sounds at all. Until the silence was replaced by a continuous buzz. I redialled and it buzzed again. After three more attempts getting the same response, I gave up and slumped back onto the bed. I wanted to do something, I just didn't know what. I was too inebriated to think straight. My conscience wanted to fight, but it was a token effort, and I settled for wrestling the corner of the duvet over my shoulder. Once it had me in a headlock, I gratefully submitted to the count.

Neighbourhood Watch

I leave my own personal portrait of Dorian Gray shut in the bathroom, and Mickey the Younger staggers into the kitchen in search of coffee and aspirin. My next priority is to prove the brain cells reminding me of the call I'd made to Herb's last night have not been terminally impaired. I call his number and hear the hum of the dead line in the cold light of day. Slowly unpicking a woolly tangle of memories, I'm forced to accept the deeply disturbing voice that answered last night wasn't just a bad dream. I stop rubbing my head, reopen my eyes and decide there's only one thing to do.

That's why I'm now sitting in my car in a queue of traffic eighty yards from Herb's house. Bear with me. It's almost nine-thirty and this isn't a busy road. Seventy yards from Herb's house... even in the rush hour you never have to queue along here. Sixty yards from Herb's house... it's not a through road or a short-cut to anywhere. Fifty yards from Herb's house... the only people that use this road are either just arriving or just leaving.

Did I say Herb's *house*? I was using the term loosely. My head's still throbbing as bloodshot eyes struggle to take in the scene. All they can see is the roof. I'm using that term loosely too. What was once a grey slate pyramid, much like every other roof in the road, is now a cat's cradle of charred timber.

The car in front edges forward again and I almost bump it as I pull away, unable to take my eyes from the point of mutual interest, and the reason for our slow progress. I should be able to see the sidewall above the attached garage. I can't because it's not there anymore. It's now a heap of rubble on the flat roof below. Moving forward again, the front of the building comes into view. The wall looks structurally sound, although the rendering is blistered and smoke-stained, and the two big upstairs windows are shattered. Their distorted frames have arching brows of soot, giving them an expression of shock, and making them look like the school runt stunned by the punch that broke his glasses, crying white tears of molten plastic.

Getting closer I catch a glimpse into the front garden. What was once a small lawn with tidy borders is now a mosaic of shattered roof tiles. The front door is still intact and, off to the side, the garage also appears to be untouched. In fact, the whole of the downstairs looks to be largely unscathed, but a thin mist of vapour continues to rise out of the gutted hulk that was once the upper floor.

A fire engine stands in the road immediately outside the house and two police cars either side serve as the outer corners of a perimeter, marked out in blue and white tape: *Police Line / Do Not Cross*. Traffic is being directed in a contraflow through the narrowing in the road, and as I finally drive past I can see a small group of scene of crime officers, dressed conspicuously in their white hooded overalls and masks, entering the front gate and studying the surrounding pathway. I look at the front door, seemingly undamaged by heat or smoke, and imagine the SOCOs examining it for traces of evidence before eventually opening it. In my mind, the first thing they see is my scrap of paper sitting folded on the mat, undisturbed but for a light dusting of soot.

The traffic moves quickly once we're through the restriction, and I have to force myself to stop looking over my shoulder and concentrate on driving. It's been a full five minutes since I first joined the queue of traffic halfway down the road, before seeing the reason for the hold-up. As I've approached and then passed the house, the thing playing on my mind is the assumption it's already being considered a crime scene. Is that just a precaution with any domestic fire where some accidental reason isn't immediately obvious? Or do they already know something?

I take the car into one of my usual decoy roads and find a gap to park. Back into Herb's road on foot, I cross over so I'm approaching the house from the opposite pavement. When I drove past, I noticed a small group of onlookers being marshalled by a single copper, who kept them back from further disrupting the flow of traffic through the bottleneck. They are still there and I mingle in to listen to what's being said.

It seems the alarm was raised around two o'clock when a passer-by saw flames coming from the roof. He was much the worse for drink and woke up half the street shouting *'Fire! Fire!'* The woman doing most of the talking, to anyone who'll listen, is standing in the front garden of the house opposite Herb's; the rest of us are gathered outside her gate. She hones in on my arrival and proceeds to tell me she was the person who called the fire brigade and that she has spent most of the rest of the morning making cups of tea.

'The first fire engine was here in fifteen minutes,' she says. 'Then two more came. It was over an hour until they got it under control.'

She refocuses on her wider audience who are beginning to lose interest in information they've already heard, and announces there's one small area at the back where the remaining fire crew is still working to make it completely safe for the police to start their investigation.

'They said it's probably where the fire started. In the kitchen,' she says before telling me what I really wanted to hear. 'I didn't *think* there was anyone home last night, but I was so relieved when they said they hadn't found anyone inside.'

I soon realise this woman probably knows as much about Herb's recent movements as anyone else I know, so I drop in a few seemingly innocuous questions.

'Was it a family living there?'

'No dear, it was a widower. Lived alone in that big house; been in there for years.'

'What, has he gone to stay with family then?'

'No, he hasn't got any family. Wife died long ago. Twenty years I've lived opposite him and all he's ever said to me is "hello". Never once invited me in. And yet, there's always people in and out. I would have thought it was a tip in there, but one of the firemen said it was empty.'

The word minimalist flashes into my mind, but I stop myself correcting her. This is getting me nowhere. Maybe I know more about him than she does after all. As she continues rambling I start to lose interest in her commentary and look back towards the wreckage where the front door is now wide open without any sign of my note on the mat.

'...no furniture, no mod cons,' she says and I turn back to face her with a frown.

'What? Nothing?' I say, realising she really did mean empty.

'Not in the house,' she says. 'Unless everything was in that garage. That's where there was always a lot of coming and going.'

'What do you mean?'

'Well, that was the strange thing about him. The way he was always having things delivered. You'd have thought the place would be heaving with stuff. Big vans backed up there all hours of the day and night. It's motorised you know,' she says pointing across the street to the only part of the house that isn't a charred wreck. 'That garage door... he doesn't even have a car. And it would always roll back down before the van pulled away, so you never got to see what was going on inside. Not that I'm one to pry.'

'So what made you think the old boy wasn't there overnight?'

'Oh, that's easy,' she says looking me right in the eye. 'A big silver car turned up yesterday morning. It stayed there at the kerb for fifteen minutes and then the front door opened and the old fella walked down the path, bold as brass. Very smartly dressed, as he always is, suit and tie, cashmere overcoat, all topped off with a smart brimmed hat. And carrying a small suitcase.'

'He went willingly.' The words slip out before I can engage my brain.

'It certainly looked like it. And that driver,' she says, reaching up on her toes while puffing out her chest, 'huge bloke he was. He got out of the car like he was a chauffeur, opened the back door for the old chap to get in and they drove away.'

'So he wasn't forced to leave.' Again, it's not a question, merely the noise the cogs are making in my head. She starts to respond anyway.

'Well... I never thought about that. Why? Do you think...'

'Oh, no. No, ignore me. Just thinking out loud. I don't even know the guy.'

'No... it seemed more like he was going off on holiday. No, I remember now, he talked to the driver like he knew him. As if they were old friends.'

I'm trying to think of a subtle way to ask if she noticed what make the car was or whether she by any chance had written down the registration number. God knows what I'd do with the information even if she had it.

'I haven't seen him since,' she continues. 'Although, as I told the fire chief, we didn't get home until eleven last night so I really couldn't be sure.'

She tails off and I think about slipping away when she stops me dead in my thoughts.

'You're very interested... for someone who doesn't even know him.' She's raised her voice and is suddenly staring at me intently. 'Oi!' she hisses, and one or two of the bystanders who've been largely oblivious to our conversation turn to look. 'Haven't I seen you around here before?'

'Have you?' is all I can say.

'Hey, you're not that bloke who was snooping around over there yesterday are you? Knocking on his door he was and looking through them windows when most decent people were still in their beds.' Her voice is getting louder and I'm starting to worry the copper standing by the roadside will hear her. 'Looked just like you he did. There's not much goes on round here I don't notice, like I told that detective earlier.'

Fortunately, my wits haven't abandoned me completely and, before I've even formed the words in my head I'm saying in my calmest banker voice: 'I'm Anne Field's son. I grew up at number 44 until she and I moved to Hamilton Road East. I went north of the river a few years back. I visit her quite often, so I'm sure you *would* have seen me around.'

'Annie's boy? Annie Field's boy? What, young John...'

'No, I'm Michael.'

'Michael. Yes, silly me... wouldn't be John... no, of course not.' She loses herself for a second in flustered embarrassment and I stand there cringing. Then she starts up again as if someone pushed her reset button. 'Well, why didn't you say? I'd have made you a cup of tea if I'd known you were Annie's boy. Leaving you standing on the pavement all this time. How is she? I haven't seen her for weeks.'

The tension dissipates and the people nearby turn back to resume watching the last of the fire fighters position a hydraulic jack beneath the garage door. For the next few minutes, I have to exchange small talk with this woman and refuse countless offers to come in and have a cup of tea, whilst constantly turning my head to watch as the metal door starts to flex under the strain of the lifting gear. The woman gasps when the mechanism inside gives up its resistance with a loud bang and the fire fighter steps in to take the weight of the door by its bottom edge. A silent hush of expectation descends on the small crowd as he begins to slide it upwards...

...and a collective sigh rings out when a completely empty space is revealed inside. I'm probably more relieved than any of them, and not just because it gives me the opportunity to pull myself away and head back to the car.

It's becoming a familiar dilemma. My intention was to have a quick look around during daylight and then go to the cinema, maybe get some sleep, grab a pizza or something, and sneak back tonight to break into Herb's house. Of course Plan A's now gone up in smoke – literally. Even if I'd had a Plan B, it wouldn't have involved visiting Mum again. It's going to be impossible to explain my presence a second day running, and the third time in just over a week. But I can't risk Herb's neighbour turning out to be one of her most enthusiastic informants, and letting it slip she'd had a nice chat with me on the morning of the fire.

77

Foxtrot Uniform

Sticking to the back streets, I turn left into Mum's road. Her house is fifty yards up on the right and the first thing I see is a police car parked outside. My head starts to pound so that I can feel every heartbeat in my temples. Although my first concern is whether Mum's been taken ill – she seemed fine yesterday – the underlying anxiety is a long-forgotten but re-emerging unease with the boys in blue. As I've said, I'm no angel; I'm no villain either. If you'll forgive me the notion, I can exclude recent lapses on the basis I was acting in good faith and trying to help a friend, though I realise there's not a judge and jury in the land that would agree with that. As it is, I already felt a bit edgy chatting idly with Nosy Neighbour, standing so close to the copper outside Herb's house. Now I'm going to have to confront one of them face to face.

I consider driving straight past and heading home but, if nothing else, I need to know Mum is okay, so I pull over and park behind the cop car. As I approach the gate, the front door opens and a thickset WPC steps out with my mum, holding the door behind her. I'm relieved to see that Mum looks fine. When she sees me she half smiles in my direction and I look back with a questioning frown. She reads my concern and remains inside the house, stifling her customary welcome as I open the gate. I watch as the constable thanks her for the information and the tea, puts her hat on, and turns and walks towards me, her black tights converting friction to static with every step.

'Good morning,' she says. Her gesture is empty and goes unreturned. Instead I reciprocate the sideways scowl she fires at me when my grip accidentally loosens on the heavy-sprung gate just as she reaches it. I'm dismissed with the shake of a head as she reaches to lift the latch. Closing the gate behind her with a ceremonial flourish, she gets in the car and drives away.

'Hello my son,' Mum says. Hers is a different frown, greeting me at the doorstep. 'You can't stay away from your dear old Mum, can you?' I ignore the sarcasm and try to divert the conversation, because I haven't thought of a good reason to tell her why I'm here again.

'What did *she* want?' I say, stepping into the hallway and following her into the kitchen.

'Oh, I called them,' she says with total indifference and turns to put the kettle on, thankfully missing the recoil of my eyes. 'I'd been worried about Herb Long after the other day, and then I heard the terrible news this morning.'

I fail to say 'What news?' quickly enough and she turns in time to see the expression on my face that says I already know.

'His house went up in flames last night.' She says it anyway and pauses, waiting for my reaction. I just nod for her to continue. 'Well, I thought I should tell them I'd seen him...'

'Mum!' I cut in as she gets two cups and saucers from the cupboard. 'Just because you saw him come out of the bank and get into a car, doesn't mean a thing.' I probably sound a bit too animated and realise I need to tone it down. 'I've just been talking to one of your friends, the lady who lives across the road from him, and she saw him get into a car yesterday, right outside of his house, all dressed up and carrying a suitcase. Sounds like a chauffeur-driven limo service. I mean, it's not like he's short of a bob or two. And more than anything else, if there was something dodgy going on, I don't think you should be getting involved by volunteering information to the Old Bill.'

'When you've quite finished, Michael,' she says in the tone she used to adopt when I was a sulky teenager. 'I'll tell you what I told that policewoman.'

'Sorry, Mum. It's just I don't think you should be inviting them in here. I thought we moved here to get away from all that.'

She glares at me for daring to allude to the unmentionable, before looking away momentarily to compose herself.

'All I told them about was last night,' she says.

'What about last night? They already know the guy's house burned down – I've just driven past and there's fuzz everywhere. What could you tell them they don't already know?'

'Tea or coffee?' she asks, blatantly changing the subject as the kettle billows out steam and switches itself off.

'I need the caffeine,' I say, pointing to the jar on the table. 'It turned into a heavy one last night.'

'Another reason why I'm surprised to see you again today,' she says, without looking up from spooning coffee granules into one of the cups.

'Mum? What did you tell her?'

'That I saw Herbert Long,' she says, nonchalantly.

'Last night?'

'*Yes Michael!* And if you'll just let me finish.' She proceeds to tell me how she'd been in to settle Gladys down for the night after the daughter of the old lady we dropped in on yesterday lunchtime had rung to ask her...

Night Flight

Mum walked home the same way I'd driven her earlier in the day. It was already dark, almost eight o'clock by the time she got to Herb's house. As she turned the corner, she saw a silver car parked outside with its lights on. When she got closer she realised it was the same one Herb had got in outside the bank the day before, a big fancy saloon.

All the glass was tinted, so she couldn't see inside, but there was a man in the driving seat with the window down. A huge hand reached out to polish the wing-mirror, but she couldn't tell if it was the same driver. She thought he seemed very shifty though; the way he quickly raised the window when he saw her approaching.

That's when she realised there was a van backed up to the opened garage, and that she could hear voices and noise, like things being moved around inside. She couldn't stop to look because by then she was right in front of the man in the car and she sensed he was watching her. All she could do was slow down a bit and try not to be too obvious.

When she was right in front of the house, she caught a glimpse through the gap as the platform at the back of the van was raised, and she could see a big, fancy brown sofa being rolled in.

She couldn't see who was loading it, but did hear someone pulling down the door at the back. It made a big bang and then the van pulled forward onto the pavement, straight towards her. She almost had to jump back to get out of the way. The van driver must have been in the front all along and, without even looking at her, he drove off up the road.

The garage door was still open and there was a light on. The walls were lined with empty shelves, otherwise the space was completely bare; not so much as a toolbox or a paint pot to be seen. For a moment she thought she'd witnessed a burglary and they'd just taken everything. She could see that the garage was empty and at first that's all she noticed. Until she saw Herb, standing inside, looking straight back at her.

'Hello Mr Long, are you alright?' she called. He looked right through her as if she wasn't there, just like he had outside the bank. She gave him the benefit of the doubt, thinking maybe he couldn't see her, looking out into the dark from under the bright light. But it did seem strange the way he stepped back slowly and, she assumed, must have pressed a button, because the garage door started to lower.

All she could do after that was keep walking. By the time she got to the end of the road where she could glance back over her shoulder, the car was gone. It must have turned around and headed off the same way as the van. Whether Herb got in it or not, she didn't know.

Teenage Kicks

'Did he look like he was okay?' I ask. 'Did you get the feeling he was doing it against his will? Maybe that's why he didn't acknowledge you.'

'No, I don't think so. I can't be sure, but something about it all made me feel like he was in control. Once I realised it was him in the garage, I knew it must have been his voice I'd heard.'

'Who was he talking to?'

'I suppose there must have been someone else with him. Whether he got in the back of the van or walked down the other side and got in the passenger door, I don't know. He might have even gone back into the house. Before the van pulled away, what must have been Herb's voice said something to the driver. Something like: *"Okay, that's it. See you later."* And it sounded like the driver said: *"Okay guv."* I'm not sure. It was the tone of their voices that made it sound like Herb was the boss.'

'So if Herb was in charge,' I say, feeling uncomfortably like I'm interrogating my own mother, 'what made you suspect there was something dodgy going on worth telling the filth?' A slight wince of disapproval crosses her face on the last word, but I know deep down she shares my antipathy.

'No, I wasn't suspicious. I was just concerned for the poor old man, that he might have been trapped in the fire, that's all,' she says, finishing her tea. 'That's why I told them... *the police...* that I saw him there last night with some other people and I didn't know if he'd left the house with them or not. I was really just trying to make sure they hadn't found him in there. I wouldn't be able to live with myself if I thought I was the last one to see him alive and I hadn't done anything to help him, especially after being worried he was acting so strange. Like I told her, maybe he's getting a bit forgetful.'

'And what did she say?'

'She thanked me for being a good neighbour and said there weren't many about these days. Then she reassured me Herb hadn't been found in the house.' She sits back and folds her arms as if to say the cross-examination is over. 'Now drink your coffee before it goes cold.'

I drain the cup and put it back on the table, but I'm not finished with the questions. 'Did she say if they're treating it as a crime scene?' I ask, without looking up.

'Not in so many words. She did ask me how well I know him... or his business arrangements. I told her not very well and that he always seems to be a very private person.' Now it's

Mum's turn to look down and she starts picking at crumbs on the tablecloth.

'Was that it?'

'There was one other thing. Two things I suppose.' She looks back up at me. 'She asked if I'd ever seen any young people going into his house.'

'Huh? What was that supposed to mean?'

'I said no, I've never seen *anyone* go into his house and don't even know anyone who has.'

'And the second thing?'

'Before she left she asked me if he'd ever offered anyone I know any photographs.' It's just as well I've finished my coffee as an involuntary jerk of my hand sends the cup clattering off its saucer across the table. I pick it up quickly as if she won't have noticed.

'Photographs? What sort of photographs?' I ask, trying to keep some semblance of composure.

'That's what I said. And then she started to backtrack as if she'd said too much. All of a sudden she was in a hurry to leave. And that was when you arrived.' She's clearly seen the look of horror cross my face and isn't in the mood to take prisoners because she's looking at me with a curious frown. 'So, Michael, are you going to tell me why you're so interested in all this?'

I can't lie to my mother. I can try to mislead her slightly, divert her from the scent with some half-truths and leave out the odd key fact along the way, but I can't lie to her. Equally, I need to keep her out of this. The less she knows the better. Especially as she's already volunteered information to the police. I can imagine Thunder Thighs returning to ask some more questions and pulling out a piece of paper found at the scene with my writing and initials on it.

'He called me a while ago looking for a favour and I told him I couldn't help,' I say. Mum listens to every word, forcing me to choose them carefully. 'He offered me money and I said I didn't need it.' Okay, all of that's true. But I miss out the part about subsequently agreeing to break into a house and steal something for him. And you wouldn't blame me, in the circumstances, for especially avoiding any references to dodgy cameras and mysterious photographs.

'And you've just been popping down to make sure *I'm* okay?' she says, testing my honesty to the limit.

'Well, yesterday I was following up on that job opportunity I told you about last week.' Okay, I realise that's a stretch. I'm ashamed to say I then completely manipulate her anxieties about Herb. 'All that stuff you said about Herb got *me* worrying about him last night and I tried calling. His phone was dead so I decided to drive back down this morning to make sure he was okay.'

'Hmmm,' she says, with that accepting look only a mother could give her son. 'So what was the nature of this favour? Nothing to do with photographs I hope.'

The word is like a knife in my throat. I'm already reeling from the inference to Herb's social network potentially revolving around young people and photographs and I need more time to think this through.

'Oh, that. No, that was nothing really,' I splutter. 'No, he just wanted me to go and check something out for him near Woodford. No big deal.'

'Michael?' she persists and I shift awkwardly in my chair and find it hard to look at her. Before I completely give myself away I pull off a masterstroke of diversion. Although I'm not sure it's a road I'm ready to go down yet, least of all with my mother, it's the only thing I can come up with that will take the conversation in another direction.

'Oh yeah, I meant to tell you... I won't be taking up that job offer down here,' I say, before looking up with a broad grin and adding, 'not now I've met someone new back home.'

'Oh, Michael, that's wonderful news. What's her name and when will I get to meet her?'

6.

Saturday, 19th

It must be something to do with having a sense of purpose, because this morning I wake up refreshed and free of any ill effects from last night's liquid supper. I vaguely remember sitting alone in my lounge, cradling a three-finger tumbler and staring out at the empty street below...

It had been almost an hour and I hadn't moved; hadn't even tasted the scotch. Its mellow aroma was giving some meagre comfort, but I hadn't felt the need or desire to drink it. The early evening gloom had already stolen the daylight and the ochre glow of the street lamp permeated the room. Even though the light might have danced seductively with the whisky through the cut crystal glass, frankly it was doing sod-all to lift my mood.

Nothing made sense; all I had were questions. Why did Herb act so strangely with Mum? Twice? What was he doing at the bank and who was he with? If it was the same car each time, who was driving? And was Herb a willing passenger or merely doing what he was told under some threat of violence? On the other hand, why pack a suitcase and appear to be chauffeur-driven away from the house in broad daylight, only to come back later and start moving things out of the garage? And if he was in charge, as Mum had thought, why was he orchestrating his own house clearance under the cover of darkness? And who the hell was it, a few hours later, that had answered his phone when I made my drunken late-night call? Then there was the big one: why had his house just gone up in flames?

Being totally selfish about it, the killer questions all of these boiled down to were: why hadn't he been able to take my calls that he must surely have been waiting for and, more to the point, if he still had his free will, why hadn't he tried to contact me?

These final thoughts circled my head like vultures. So much for an evening of quiet contemplation; they weren't helping to ease my anxiety. I could feel the stress boiling up in my chest and I tried to douse it with a single mouthful that emptied the entire glass. That only added to the burning.

What was hitting me hardest was the thought that whatever was going on and whoever was involved, I'd put myself bang in the middle of it without any understanding of what and whom I was dealing with. Herb seemed to be the only person I could talk to, yet I had no way of contacting him. Something else was disturbing me far more than all my self-pity. I kept coming back to the same haunting question. Perhaps I was making too much of the policewoman's inference of Herb as a photography enthusiast with a specialty in adolescents, but what if I wasn't? And what did that mean for the undeveloped contents of the single use camera, wrapped ominously in brown paper on my coffee table? Sitting silently in my empty house, for only the second time in my life, I felt completely out of my depth.

After two more glasses and a large packet of salted peanuts, I took the precaution of ensuring my mobile phone was fully charged. For no discernible reason I also checked the landline was connected. It was barely nine o'clock as I crawled into bed, more in hope than expectation that an early night would give me a better chance of a deep and dreamless sleep. I wasn't only mentally drained, I was slightly the worse for wear, and at least hoped the booze might help to keep the demons away. Before I drifted off into a comatose state, I was forced to contemplate the two things I was convinced I'd have to do next. One was perhaps obvious if far from straightforward, whilst the other fed my paranoia and filled me with dread.

First, I was going to have to get the film developed in order to have any idea of what I was up against. Second, if I still hadn't heard from Herb, I would have to confront the possibility, no matter how remote, that he was locked in one of those terrible chambers and make a return trip to Bleak House.

Close Up

Well, if I dreamt at all, my would-be tormentors must have smelled the scotch and decided I was too inebriated to take any notice of them and buggered off to screw up someone else's night. I slept like a corpse – in fact I'm feeling so focused today I don't even find that analogy the slightest bit disturbing. I'm also famished and make myself a fried breakfast Mum would be proud of.

By eight-thirty, I'm outside a photographic shop on The Broadway, holding the brown envelope in my pocket that contains the disposable camera. It all seemed so obvious last night, but here's the bit that was never going to be straightforward. How do you walk into your local Jessops and hand over a camera with a film for developing when you don't have a clue what kind of photos are going to come sliding out of the printer? Especially when, at best, they could be bad enough to blackmail someone? But it's the thought they might also be connected in some unspeakable way to "young people" that's making me shudder.

I'm weighing up the worst that can happen. Maybe some dubious if not downright appalling images get mixed up with someone's baby photos. Even in the best-case scenario, where the pictures are your average run-of-the-mill blackmail shots, the machine operator is bound to have a good look through the prints before putting them into a nice anonymous packet ready for me to collect.

I try not to dwell on it, and decide the only way to approach this is to ask for the film to be developed while I wait. Of course that might just highlight the fact I've got something to hide, in which case they are even more likely to want to have a gander before handing them over, or worse still, calling the police. I'm guessing they have some duty to report certain kinds of images. I really don't fancy having to explain: *Oh no, it's not my camera... Um, I don't know whose it is... How did I come by it?*

I'm hoping that going in early on a Saturday morning will give me an advantage. I've got here in time to be first through the door when the shop opens, but there's a young lad waiting and he's clearly anxious to get ahead of me. He's looking in the window with his back to me and gradually edging towards the door. I was here before him and I hold my ground. When another spotty youth unlocks the door, I manage to get in first, but he ignores me completely because he obviously knows the other boy and they start chatting across me. I don't believe it. What am I? Some sad bastard who likes to come in at the crack of dawn just to browse? On any other day I would have blown my top. Of course, today I have to hold it all in. I stand here, at least outwardly relaxed, and casually remove the camera from the envelope.

They're talking about some piece of kit the other customer's produced from his bag and they move to the counter where they huddle over the lens that's being removed from its box. I look around the shop in frustration, but no one else appears from out the back to serve me. Maybe it's unusual for them to have a queue at the door first thing on a Saturday.

Bollocks! I can't believe I'm making excuses for them. I'm standing here like a pug with Rottweiler delusions, all suppressed aggression and nervous energy. I'm also feeling very intimidated by these two techno-geeks because, before I know it, they've got several other lenses out on the counter and are comparing technical specifications, as if the customer's from NASA and he's looking to buy a new telephoto for his next mission to Mars. Bugger this. After ten minutes, I've had enough. Then, as I open the door to leave, the shop guy calls across to me.

'If you give it another minute there'll be someone else out to serve you. Is it developing you wanted?' I glance back over my shoulder and he's looking at me as if I'm being unreasonable for not waiting.

'Yeah, okay. There's no hurry.' I look down at the camera in my hand. It's too late to conceal it. And I'd prefer to avoid a public discussion across the shop about developing my dodgy film.

At that point the other customer looks up for the first time from studying one of the lenses and I instantly recognise him. With a face at least five years older than his diminutive stature would suggest, it's the guy who'd arrived at the King's Head with Grace on Thursday night. I remember she said he was her brother. I'm about to nod to him in recognition but he looks away without any acknowledgement and I turn and walk out of the shop.

I get no more than ten yards up the road when I hear my name being called and someone running up behind me. I turn to see Grace tottering towards me, immaculate in straight-legged blue jeans and tanned high-heeled ankle boots that match her caramel suede jacket. My spirits are lifted, along with my eyes, as they complete their journey and rest on her beaming smile.

'Hey you. How're things?' I say as she reaches me. I step forward to embrace her and she seems to hesitate slightly, and initially offers a gentle hug, before kissing me full on the mouth.

'This is a nice surprise,' she says, looking down at the envelope I'm carrying. 'I didn't know you were into photography.'

'Oh, that. No, it's not a big part of my life. Not like your brother, it would appear.' I glance back towards the shop, hoping to divert her as I return the package to my coat pocket.

'Oh yeah, Simon,' she says rolling her eyes. 'He cadged a lift from me because he wanted to get a new lens or something. He said he wanted to get in there early ahead of all the morons with their holiday snaps.'

'Aah, how sweet,' I say in fake admiration of this unlikely display of sibling affection, remembering how she first described him to me.

'Yeah, lovely!' she sneers, before adding: 'I really don't know why I do it. He never does anything for me. And in case you're starting to think we're joined at the hip, don't worry, I don't need to wait for him.'

'Glad to hear it. Looks like he's going to be in there a while.'

'Probably.'

'So what brings you into this bustling thoroughfare?'

'*Me?* God, no. I just parked near the station,' she says with a playful glare. 'I'm taking the tube out west for some serious retail therapy. Then I saw you waiting outside the shop when I dropped him off. And since you haven't called me...'

'But, I...'

'... I decided to walk back and see if you were still in there. I'm in no hurry. Do you have plans? Apart from hanging around outside a photo shop with a brown package in your pocket.'

'I'm going to start thinking you're stalking me,' I say. Her smile drops momentarily until I add, 'Don't get me wrong; I've got nothing against stalkers, especially the really attractive ones.'

'That's nice,' she says and the sparkle returns to her eyes. 'Look, if you don't have anywhere else you need to be, why don't you tell me your other favourite characteristics of a stalker over breakfast?'

I haven't the heart to tell her I've already eaten so instead gesture across the road to a local bakery where a couple of aluminium table and chair sets have been put out on the pavement. We order coffee and croissants at the counter and sit outside. While we wait, I compile a list of my top ten stalker qualities. The first five are easy – petite, shaggy blonde hair, seductive blue eyes, sexy smile and perfect size-eight figure. Beyond that it gets very silly – occasional single malt connoisseur, full-on character (of course, in an understated way), charitable to unworthy family members, helpful to the aged and, at number one, a propensity to share lewd secrets with strangers. After we've finished laughing, Grace leans across to me and we kiss as if the earlier embrace was just a rehearsal. The waitress, who can't be older than thirteen, interrupts us. She blushes and puts the coffee and plates down and hurries back into the shop.

The coffee tastes good, but I can only manage a few flakes

of pastry. Meanwhile, Grace pulls apart the croissant mercilessly and dips torn pieces into the raspberry lagoon on her plate. The Broadway is starting to get busy, although the outside world fades into the background as if someone's turned the volume off.

'I wouldn't call you a stranger, but I do believe you owe me a secret in return,' she says and I flinch uncomfortably. 'So, tell me, Mickey Field, what's the most outrageous thing *you've* ever done?'

'If I told you that right now, you wouldn't believe me,' I reply without hesitating.

'Oh, I think you'll find me very open-minded,' she says. 'And besides, I thought you said you've been a man on a leash for most of your adult life. What can you possibly have done that could shock me?'

Until a few days ago, she'd have had a point, and I would have bored her to death trying to impress her with my lifetime's most shocking revelations, excluding of course the one small incident about which I've never told a living soul and won't dwell on here. That was in a different life.

She already knows about my recent and uncharacteristic acts of impulse, throwing Sam out and then walking away from the only other stable thing in my world, a well-paid job. In this lifetime, these would have rated pretty highly on my list of outrageous deeds, but how do I even begin to tell her how the camera in my pocket came to be there? And do I even want to?

Although I desperately need to share all this crap with someone, right now, in Herb's mysterious absence, I'm not convinced telling Grace is going to help. I not only risk scaring her off, but also compromising Herb's safety, the more people I tell. I've already said too much in my drunken stupor to a complete stranger on the end of a phone, for which The Banker is still not speaking to me. For once I agree with him; the fewer people that know about this, the better.

Grace is looking at me with a fixed smile on her face and, as much as I try, I can't think of anything else to tell her.

'Oh, come on Mickey, it can't be that difficult,' she says.

'No. I can't think of anything,' I say. 'Like you said, I've lived a very sheltered life.'

'Okay,' she says, letting me off the hook. 'But I won't let you get away with it that easily. And I'll want to know all the juicy details... just like I've shared with you.'

'I'll think of something. I promise.'

As I ease back in my seat, the camera shifts in my pocket and bounces against the chair leg. It catches Grace's eye and her face lights up.

'While you're thinking, why don't you just tell me what's in that brown envelope,' she says and I flinch.

Reluctantly, I take it from my pocket.

'What, this?' I say, removing the camera and setting it down on the table.

'Ah,' she says. 'Long time since I've seen one of those.'

'Me too. It belongs to a mate. I said I'd... you know, get it developed.'

'What's on it?' she says, clearly intrigued.

'Ah... I, er. Well that's kind of the problem. I don't really know.'

She looks at me with concern, acknowledging my obvious discomfort, but clearly intent on maintaining the playful mood. She then snorts loudly. 'And... without knowing what's on it,' she says, covering her mouth with her hand to stifle the laughter. 'You seriously took *that* into Jessops to get it developed?'

'It's a long story.' I join in the laughing, but only nervously.

'So why can't this mate of yours do it himself?'

'It's silly really. It's like a... dare.'

'A dare? At your age?' she says. I just smirk and shift awkwardly in the chair. 'I suppose I shouldn't be surprised,' she adds, 'having met your mates.'

'It's not one of...'

'So what's the consequence,' she says and I frown back at her. 'There has to be a consequence... when you fail a dare.'

'But I haven't failed yet.'

'Looks like you've decided against Jessops. What's your

next move... Boots the Chemist?'

By now I'm cringing inwardly and trying to laugh along with her at the same time.

'No, I'll think of something,' I say. For the second time in as many minutes the same words lack any conviction.

'Maybe I can help,' she says suddenly serious.

'Really?'

'Maybe,' she repeats. 'But first, you'll have to come up with something about you that's a bit more outrageous than that.'

I nod in resigned agreement and she puts a gentle hand on top of mine. For a second I think she means I still have to come up with something here until she raises her index finger.

'But... not right now.' She yanks me back into the noisy world of early morning shoppers and slow-moving traffic before finishing her coffee and waving into the shop for the bill. 'I'm losing valuable shopping time. You're welcome to join me and help choose a new outfit if you like. Later on we could grab some food and I'll make you dinner, but if you've got things to do, we could just meet up tonight.'

'No, I've definitely got nothing better to do. I feel I should warn you though,' I say, grinning like a happy fool. 'I'm a lousy fashion consultant. Unless we're choosing lingerie.'

'Maybe,' she shrugs enticingly, and hands a tenner to the waitress before I've even taken out my wallet.

Retail Rewards

I have to admit, I've never enjoyed shopping so much. At one point she even manages to smuggle me into the changing room, where I sit mesmerised as she tries on a rail full of dresses, jeans and tops. I can't keep my eyes off her, and struggle to keep my hands to myself as she parades around in her powder blue underwear, her body every bit as awesome as I've already started to imagine.

By early afternoon, we're both carrying three bags each. Most of what she's bought is at the quality end of West End couture, with prices to match, and her credit card has taken a serious hammering. I suggest lunch at a little French cafe I know off the beaten track and soon we're slumped into comfy chairs and sharing bread and olives, Caesar salad and a half bottle of Petit Chablis.

When we finish eating, I tell Grace how the guys reacted when I returned triumphantly with her number the other night.

'I suppose we'll have to keep up the pretence when you introduce me to them properly,' she says.

'Yeah, definitely. Remember they coughed up eighty quid for our little performance so we can't let them down.'

'I can't believe you took their money. I thought you were their friend!'

'What? I bought the burgers,' I protest.

'You wait until I meet them. That'll make you squirm,' she says, stabbing the last olive with her fork. 'Besides, I reckon forty pounds of that is mine.'

'Talking of making me squirm,' I say. 'What if I told you there's someone else who wants to meet you?'

'Really? Who?'

'Don't laugh, okay? It's just that I told my mum about you.'

'Oh my God!' she says with a hand over her mouth. 'You *really* don't hang around.'

'I know I shouldn't have. It was stupid. I just couldn't help myself.' I feel like twice the pillock: once for telling Mum and now for telling her.

'I'm only joking,' she says. 'Really, I'm flattered. It's very sweet and I'd love to meet your mum. I bet she's really lovely. So, when are we going?'

'Uh... well,' I say, backtracking sharply. 'There's no real hurry.'

'Okay. I'll be ready when you are,' she says with a *whatever* kind of shrug. 'Talking of which, we've got more shopping to do. And what do you fancy for dinner?'

I make sure I've got my wallet ready, but this time she seems happy for me to get to the waiter first.

Back at my house, I open a bottle of Sancerre that's been chilling alone in the fridge for weeks. It's been replaced with scallops, steak and mascarpone cheesecake, and the kitchen counter is stacked with fruit and vegetables. The house hasn't seen fresh produce like this for over a month. In fact, the house hasn't been cleaned for over a month; something I'm acutely aware of as Grace returns from the bathroom.

'Sorry, you've caught me a bit lax on the domestic front,' I say.

'Don't worry. Compared to living with my brother, I'd have to describe you as house-proud. Nice place, have you been here long?'

'Yeah, a good few years...' I stop short of adding that Sam and I moved in the day we returned from our honeymoon.

I pour two glasses and hand her one before carrying the other along with the bottle through to the lounge where the sound of Alicia Keys' rippling piano intro builds to a crescendo. The street lamp is already glowing through the window, even though there's another hour of grey daylight ahead, and I decide to leave the curtains open and the light off. That's where the similarity with last night's vibe ends. We sit down together on the sofa and clink glasses. The wine tastes surprisingly good, given how long it's been in the fridge.

'Do you want to see the last outfit I bought?' Grace says, getting up and heading to the mountain of shopping bags covering the dining table.

'I'd love to,' I reply, remembering the La Perla bag she'd mysteriously acquired after leaving me in Harrods' Food Hall, with the challenge of finding something reasonably-priced for dinner. 'Do you want me to draw the curtains?' I call after her as she leaves the room.

'Not on my account,' she shouts back, laughing.

'No, I didn't think you would,' I say to myself and get up and draw them anyway. After a few minutes, she calls to me from the bedroom.

'Mickey?'

95

'Yes Grace, what is it?' My pulse is starting to quicken.

'Could you do something for me?' she calls in a girly voice of fake innocence.

'Sure, what do you want me to do?'

'Why don't you come in here and I'll show you?'

Opening the bedroom door, I find her lying across my bed – a vision in black and violet silk and lace. My last coherent thought as I enter the room and close the door behind me is one of relief that at least I've changed the sheets.

Developing Solution

Over an hour later we're back in the kitchen preparing dinner, and not long after that the scallops, sautéed with bacon and garlic, have barely touched the plate and now, still ravenous, we're tucking into fillet steak with Roquefort, and washing it down with Châteauneuf-du-Pape. Grace has showered and is wearing the new black dress she bought in Karen Millen. She looks so stunning I feel obliged to make an effort. It's a bit odd sitting at my own dining table in a Ted Baker suit and purple Armani shirt, but she seems to appreciate the transformation.

If I wasn't certain before, then our intimacy has convinced me I can probably trust her with some of my baggage, but I get the feeling she's completely forgotten that I owe her a secret. Hopefully, she's feeling relaxed enough with me now to let it go. She also hasn't mentioned anything about the camera. But if I'm going to find out how she thinks she can help me, it looks like I'll have to make the first move, which feels a bit unusual in our short and intense relationship. I decide to wait until we've finished eating the main course. I don't want to ruin the meal and, more to the point, I need to clear the table on account of Grace wanting her steak rare. There's just too much blood left on her plate for me to even think about where I got that camera.

'Grace?' As I say it, she stops swirling her wine around in the oversized glass and looks up at me. 'You know this morning; you said you would help with my little challenge?'

'Aha! The dare. I wondered when you would get around to that,' she answers with a grin. 'I said I *may* be able to help, remember.'

'Yeah, you're right. Well, what did you mean exactly?'

'I suppose that all depends on what you need. I thought you said there was a long story. I'm in no hurry.'

'Er... yeah. Okay. I mean... I would tell you the story...' I look up and her beautiful blue eyes are now burning a hole in my forehead. Already I'm floundering. 'I just... don't want to drag you into something I'm not even sure I understand.'

'Now I *am* intrigued,' she says. 'Why don't you start at the beginning and we'll see where that takes us?'

'Okay. Well, my mate... he's actually an old guy living on his own. His name's Herb,' I say, and Grace leans forward slightly, her brow creasing momentarily. 'I knew him years ago but we lost touch. I thought his call came out of the blue, and then he already seemed to know I'd be available to help him. He said he was... worried about some photographs. I just had to help him.'

'Worried?'

'He doesn't know what's on the film...' I say, choosing each word carefully, 'but he thinks it could embarrass him.'

'Is he being blackmailed?' she says. The look on her face is probably reflecting my own anxiety. While hers seems to be genuine concern for some random mate of mine, the horror that's no doubt crossing my features is in realisation that I'm losing control of the conversation. It seems too late to retreat and I find myself nodding back to her. 'And he wants you to get the film developed?'

'Er... yeah, in a manner of speaking.'

'Who's he being blackmailed by?'

'Grace,' I say and hold my hands up. 'I really don't think this is a good idea.'

'Why's that?'

'Well... it's just... I hardly know you.'

'Oh!' she says slumping back in the chair.

'What?'

'Well it's okay for me to tell you all my dirty secrets. And smuggle you into the changing rooms. And I didn't get the impression earlier that anyone else has ever been quite so... giving, in your bedroom before. But when it comes to you sharing, suddenly you *hardly* know me.'

'Grace... please... don't be like...'

'No Mickey. I thought we were getting on well.' She suddenly stands up. 'But if you're not prepared to give and take, then maybe I've made a big mistake.'

'Grace, no... please... sit down. Please.' She does as I ask and I reach across to take her hand, which she passively allows me to hold. 'Okay. Well it's a good question: who's the blackmailer? It's one I probably should have asked... before agreeing to... get it for him.'

'So...' she says, instantly brightening again, 'first you had to find it?'

'Uh... he knew where it would be. It was just a rundown old place... a few miles from here.'

'And then you had to steal it?'

'It wasn't... really like stealing, though...'

'But you managed to get it, okay?'

'Yeah. It was left out in the open and I saw it through the window before I went in.'

'Even so, it must have been difficult for you.'

'That was the easy part.' I pause, remembering how strange it felt. 'The side window was unlocked.'

'No, I meant it must have been an awful thing for you to do. It doesn't sound like your kind of thing; career banker one minute, cat burglar the next.'

'No,' I say and inwardly suppress an ironic flinch.

'So, how long have you been holding onto the camera?'

'That night... in The Feathers, I'd just got back with it.'

'My God, no wonder you were so strung out.'

'What was it you said? Bunny in the headlights!'

'Yeah!' She nods her head and grins. 'I do seem to have a habit of catching you in awkward situations.'

'Yeah!' I say, like an echo.

'Why don't you just give it back to this Herb character, rather than try to get the film developed yourself?'

'That's the hard part,' I say, not intentionally pausing for effect. 'I don't know where he is.'

'What do you mean?' she says, her anxiety level having suddenly ratcheted up again.

'He didn't answer my calls and wasn't at home when I went back to see him the next day. I went down there again yesterday and the house was... deserted. I'm starting to worry that he's either in hiding because someone's putting him under more pressure after one of them saw me take the camera...'

'Someone saw you? How do you know?'

'Well, as I was about to leave I heard someone unlocking the front door. I managed to get out in time and, from the bottom of the garden, I saw a torchlight being pointed out of the kitchen window straight at me. They're bound to have realised what I'd taken.'

'Oh!' she says and there's genuine shock on her face. 'You said you were worried... that Herb was either in hiding... or what?'

'I just hope they haven't already caught up with him.'

Grace is looking back at me open-mouthed. I'm feeling momentarily uplifted; my burden halved. She seems to be stunned. I can't tell if she's more shocked that I actually broke into the house or with the prospect that someone might have seen me. Then of course, she might be just as concerned as I am that Herb has seemingly disappeared off the face of the planet.

I wish she would say something, but she stays uncharacteristically silent. Now I'm feeling bad I've dumped all this on her when I was trying so hard not to. Maybe she doesn't give a shit about me. Or Herb. Maybe she's feeling like she's just got to know Buddy Love, and then over a pleasant post-coital dinner, Mr Hyde has put in an appearance. Either way, I shouldn't have blurted all this out.

'Wow!' she finally mouths silently.

'Yeah, wow!' I repeat back to her with a sigh. 'And that's why I'm carrying around a throwaway camera. I wish that's what it was. Literally. And I could just throw it away. I've also thought about breaking it open and destroying the film, but I don't know whether I'll be helping or making things worse for Herb.' I'm hoping if I keep talking she might give me a clue as to what she's thinking. It seems to be working because the colour is returning to her face.

'Well, well. Mickey Field. I would never have thought you had it in you. I'm really impressed. You actually managed to shock me!' She's shaking her head and smiling at the same time. 'And I think I *can* help you. But you're going to have to trust me.'

'What have you got in mind?' I ask the question that's been bugging me – on and off – since she first said it this morning.

'Simon has access to a darkroom at uni. He holds the keys because he runs some photographic society. He spends all night there sometimes, even at the weekends. And...' she says, raising her eyebrows, 'I know he's printed dodgy stuff for his mates before.' She looks up, as if to gauge my reaction.

With both elbows on the table and hands together against my lips as if in prayer, I breathe out deeply through my fingers and close my eyes.

'What would you tell him about it?' I say.

'Oh, I'll come up with something,' she says far from convincingly. 'I'll tell him it's mine. Chances are he won't take a lot of notice, whatever comes out. He's so wrapped up in his own little world and so disinterested in anything I do.'

'I don't know, Grace. It's a big risk.'

'It's got to be a better bet than taking it into Jessops,' she says with a wry grin.

'Well that's probably true,' I say, and continue mulling the implications of something hideous on the photos being seen firstly by a complete stranger in a university darkroom and then by Grace, potentially exposing them both to whatever the hell Herb is mixed up in.

'I could probably catch him tonight,' she says, looking at

her watch. 'He's bound to be going there at some point over the weekend.'

'Oh, right.' I struggle to suppress my disappointment that the evening would have to end here, but without any other plan, I reluctantly accept it's probably the best opportunity I have. 'So, you think he'll be able to do it tomorrow?' My head's spinning and I've gone from reluctant to impatient in three seconds flat.

'Well, I suppose I might be able to convince him it's urgent. That all depends if I see him tonight though.'

I glance at the clock. It's only just gone ten.

'Okay,' I say with a deep sigh. 'I don't suppose I'm likely to come up with a better idea.'

'It'll be okay. Don't worry,' she says with a glint in her eye. 'The dessert will keep for another time.'

'But do you really have to go now?'

'If I go soon, I'll probably catch him before he goes out. Otherwise, he won't be back until the early hours.'

'Right,' I say reluctantly. 'Should I call you a cab?'

'No, I'll be okay. I've only had a couple of glasses. I'll take the car,' she says, and I shift uncomfortably in the chair.

'Are you sure? I'd feel much better if you took a cab. Your car will be okay outside.'

'No really, I'll be fine,' she insists and stands there looking at me expectantly. 'The camera?'

'Oh yeah... of course.' It's still in the pocket of my coat that's hanging on the rack by the front door. I help her to gather up all her bags and she follows me downstairs. I descend slowly, wracking my brain for a better option than handing the camera over to someone I've only known for three days. It seems like madness, but once I reach the bottom step, there's no going back.

I retrieve the brown package and as she reaches out, there's a second or two when we're both holding it before I let it go. She strokes the back of my hand and puts it in her bag.

'Mickey, I realise how important this is to you,' she says. 'And how serious it is we keep this close. I know I've not exactly painted Simon as a little angel, but don't worry; I'll deal with him. Trust me.'

'Okay,' I say, looking into her eyes. 'I trust you.'

'I'll call you later to let you know if he can do it tomorrow. If he can't, I swear I'll bring the camera straight back to you in the morning. If he agrees, then as soon as I have the prints I'll ring and we can decide where to meet later in the evening. Either way, I promise you'll be seeing more of me again tomorrow.' She gathers up her bags and we hug before she kisses me gently and leaves.

'Thank you Grace,' I say as she walks to her car. She turns and smiles. I watch her drive away, still wishing I could have persuaded her to take a cab.

Back indoors, my disappointment at the abrupt end to the evening and the separation anxiety I'm already feeling towards the camera gives way to a new energy. The night is still young and so part B of my plan is back in play.

In the bedroom I can smell a delicate hint of Grace's perfume and, as I instinctively pull the bed together, I see her new lingerie under my pillow. The tooth fairy was never so good to me.

Bus Pass

Almost midnight and the street is deserted. Somehow, in the half-light, Bleak House isn't quite so bleak. Don't get me wrong, Happy House it ain't, but from the front it could certainly pass for Ordinary-if-slightly-neglected House. If it wasn't the only detached property in a street of semis, and if an unruly Virginia creeper hadn't spread like flames to engulf the side fence and half the front wall, it would almost blend into its lacklustre neighbourhood. I walk straight past with only a casual sideways glance. I already know there aren't any lights on from the fleeting view I had from the top deck of the bus.

Having decided last night to come back if I still hadn't heard from Herb today, I'm no longer entirely sure what I was expecting to find. There's no sign of any activity. Maybe this wasn't such a great idea. Still, I'm here now; I may as well see it through. I remember the access lane that leads to the gravel track, running along the backs of the gardens, and keep walking to where it joins the street. Soon I'm through the gap between the two houses and feeling my way along the dark side of one of the garden fences. The last time I came through here I was hurtling the other way in a blind panic, convinced I was being followed. My heart flinches with adrenalin and my neck goes clammy. I notice for the first time a chill in the night air.

As I follow the path round to the left, I stay close to the hotchpotch of walls, hedges and gates defining the ends of the gardens. This time it's not so difficult to work out which house I'm looking for. Opposite is a row of assorted wooden garage doors in varying states of decay. Even in the darkness, the yellow one stands out fifty feet ahead. When I reach it I find the two breeze blocks I'd used before as a step up to the fence.

I take a quick look around. Everything is still and very quiet, the garage doors are all closed and there are no lights on in the upstairs windows of the neighbouring houses as far as I can see. I step up onto the blocks and peer over the fence. The garden below is a jungle, a conservationist's dream, untouched by human hand for at least a decade. Beneath a tangled lattice of nettles and bindweed, a vague central pathway, defined intermittently by crumbling concrete, is the only discernible evidence of man-made order.

I look at the rear of the house and, but for the absence of a torch-lit shadow at the window, my déjà vu is complete. A shiver courses through my body. The protruding wall at the side of the house draws my eye and I think about the two added chambers and wonder if anyone is locked inside. In particular I'm thinking about Herb.

With that in mind, I'm struggling with the non-negotiable condition The Banker insisted on including in the plan: under no circumstances go back inside the house. I'm bracing myself for an argument because just walking past for *a quick look* is telling me bugger all, and if I've summoned up the nerve to come back here, what the hell is the point if I don't establish with any certainty whether Herb is inside? The Banker decides not to rise to the debate and, with his deafening silence ringing in my ears, I lift a leg over the fence and lower myself into the wilderness.

The scene through the kitchen window is the same as before, except for one notable difference. With its previous load now littering the floor, the table's bare surface contrasts starkly with the rest of the room.

Around the side of the house, the sash window I was able to open last time is not only locked at the catch, it won't even rattle in the frame when I push a gloved hand against it. On the inside I can see nail heads protruding haphazardly from the lower ledge as if from some medieval instrument of torture.

I continue around the perimeter. There's no sign of any activity and, apart from the side window, everything looks exactly as I left it; it seems no one's been here since Torchy made some quick repairs and left. The enthusiasm is draining like sap from my veins as I accept that the chance of Herb languishing in one of the cells is remote. And any sense of heroism to attempt a rescue of whatever damsel might have previously been in distress here is also fading fast. The place is deserted.

Keeping to the shadows, I pace back towards the rear of the house and estimate the distance to where the new interior is likely to be. On the outside, the wall remains original London brick, with no visible signs of alteration. A row of decorative airbricks runs just above ground level and I kneel down for a closer look. I must be so edgy that when I brush my hand along the line of ornate ventilation, I think I feel a cold breeze. Even when I convince myself that the chambers' concrete floors wouldn't have any airflow, the skin on the back of my neck won't stop prickling. That's when I hear a muffled humming and feel a vibration against my leg.

'*Shit!*' I jump away from the wall as if it's red hot. I doubt that anyone would have heard my squeal; it was probably audible only to dogs. I wish I could say the same of my pounding heart, which can doubtless be heard in the next street. Oblivious to being totally exposed in the neon glare, my instinctive reaction is to try to rationalise what just made the wall reverberate. From deep in my subconscious I hear power tools and hammer drills, and circular saws start to whir around in my head. I grit my teeth into a hideous smile to suppress the nausea and scramble back into the shadows. That's when I notice the buzzing coming from inside my pocket. Jesus!

A moment later I've regained my composure and I'm reaching for the phone. If I was worried before that someone might have heard me, now I've got a different reason to be glad no one's seen me. *What a prat!* By the time I get it out, it's stopped vibrating and the backlight has gone off. I don't want to wake the thing up again. It was probably Grace and hopefully she'll have left a message.

I'm feeling done in and decide there's nothing new to learn here so I climb the fence and head back along the gravel track and out onto the pavement. I want to call my mailbox to see what Grace had to say. First I need to walk past the front of the house again to get to the end of the road and catch the night bus back towards home. This time I cross the road before passing the house that remains dark and still; my final sideways glance only confirming the trip has been a strangely reassuring waste of time.

At the bus stop I get my phone out and look at the missed call. I know it's pathetic, but I've already added Grace to my contact list and so I'm surprised when the phone displays a mobile number and not her name. Maybe she was using her brother's phone. I dial my mailbox and listen to the greeting that announces I have no new messages. I'm confused but too exhausted to be disappointed.

Before long the bus arrives and I'm sitting on the top deck with the rear seat to myself. The route takes me back towards Bleak House for one final pass and with the road completely empty of traffic, the bus is able to pick up some speed. When we go by everything is a blur of trees and streetlights. But as I focus on the front garden I get a quick glimpse of the entrance and what I see almost sucks the eyes out of my head. The door is open and someone's coming out.

I catch a fleeting glimpse of a tall dark figure in an overcoat before another tree obscures my view. I turn and look through the rear window. The big white Bedford that's parked outside definitely wasn't there ten minutes ago. Before it disappears from view, as the bus takes the curve in the road, the man reaches the van, opens the passenger door and gets in.

At the end of the road the bus is held at traffic lights and I can see headlights rounding the bend towards us. The box van draws to a halt directly below my line of vision. I look down on it and all that's visible through the windscreen are the driver's huge hands, like the paws of a panther clawing at the wheel. The lights change and the bus pulls away, slowly turning left. The van is indicating right and I slide across the seat for a better view as it eases forward past the back of the bus. The glass reflects back the bus's bright lights, but the passenger's window is halfway down and I get a fleeting look at the side of a stern face with sharp features that stare straight ahead. Before I have any chance of identifying him, the man raises a hand in front of his face and the angle of light shifts with the change in direction, leaving the passenger in darkness as the van picks up speed and pulls away in the opposite direction.

The missed call on my phone is from a number I don't recognise. Without hesitating I thumb the call button and hear a phone ring twice before it's disconnected. I swing my feet up onto the seat and stare back at the empty road.

Distress Call

'That was easy,' I say. 'Maybe he's not so bad after all.' I'm back home and on the phone to Grace. She's told me she managed to catch Simon before he went out and he agreed to take the camera to the darkroom tomorrow.

'Oh, I wouldn't go that far. It is weird how he's being so nice to me lately. I don't know what he's been up to. He does seem very keen to stay on my good side all of a sudden.'

'Sounds like you've got him where you want him.'

'Maybe, we'll find out soon enough. He said he'll get the prints back to me in the afternoon, so I'll ring you and we can meet up. Talking of which, I rang your landline earlier but you were out. I didn't have you down as the clubbing type, what've you been up to?' She asks the question I'd been hoping she wouldn't, at least not tonight.

'I went back to that house, where I got the camera,' I say. 'I was worried about Herb; I thought it was worth another look.'

'Why would he be there? I thought you said he asked you to get the camera because he couldn't bring himself to go in person.'

'I thought he might have been... held there against his will.'

'You think he's been taken by the people who were blackmailing him?'

'I know it sounds crazy and paranoid,' I say, trying not to sound crazy and paranoid. 'Since he went missing I've been imagining all sorts of gruesome scenarios. I thought he might have been in serious trouble, especially in that house of horrors.'

'What do you *mean*, house of horrors?' Grace's voice has gone up several octaves.

'Yeah, sorry, I didn't want to tell you before. When I was in there the other night I noticed there were two rooms that seemed to have been added recently, with metal doors and heavy locks.' I pause hoping to gauge her reaction. The line remains silent so I continue. 'Anyway, one of them was unlocked and I looked inside. I couldn't see much but I just knew something nasty had been going on in there. It felt like a prison cell or... something.'

I spare her the graphic details of how bad it smelled and decide she definitely doesn't need to know about the cash I found. 'Grace? Are you still there?'

'Yeah, still here.' She's almost whispering.

'Are you okay?'

'Yeah, sorry, that's a lot to take in. It sounds awful. What did you find when you got there tonight?'

'Nothing. Well at least nothing I could see from the outside. I couldn't get in because the window I used before has been nailed shut. Otherwise everything looked like it did last time.'

'So you don't think he *was* there?' She sounds very apprehensive and I find her concern for my old friend endearing.

'I can't really be sure,' I say, hoping to reassure her and lift the mood a little. 'There was definitely *someone* there.' Instead of any obvious signs of relief I hear a sharp intake of breath at the other end of the line.

'So it could have been him.'

'No,' I say, still trying to get my own thoughts straight. 'I mean I don't know. At first I didn't think anyone was there. But it's possible someone was inside the whole time I was snooping around.'

'You said you didn't go inside. You said everything looked the same. Do you think he's okay?'

'Grace, calm down,' I say, trying to hide my surprise at her unexpected interest in Herb's wellbeing. 'I didn't get a good look at his face but whoever it was, he was a picture of health when he left the house and got in a big white van.'

'Oh, thank God!' she says and I think I hear a slight crack in her voice.

'Grace?' I'm feeling slightly embarrassed at her emotional reaction, particularly as it's in stark contrast to my own feelings of confusion, but at the same time I want to comfort her. I really wish I could hold her.

'I'm okay,' she says, with more composure. 'Mickey, it's getting late. I'll call you tomorrow.'

Before heading to bed, in the hope her lingering perfume on my pillow will incite sweet dreams, I pull the scrap of paper from my pocket and read the registration number aloud. It occurs to me that apart from any clues that might be revealed tomorrow in the photographs, it may be the only other link I have back to Herb.

7.

Sunday, 20th

Today doesn't start for me until the early afternoon; sleep has been so graceful, I don't want to wake up. When my mobile rings at ten past twelve, I almost don't get to it in time. After I've dragged myself clear of the duvet and staggered around the room searching, only to find it cupped in silk and lace at the bottom of the bed, it's displaying a number I don't even recognise. I stand there looking at it for a while. Either I'm getting a ton of wrong numbers or I'm becoming totally paranoid about people calling me who aren't on my contacts list.

'Yes?' is all I say, half expecting the rude bastard to hang up on me without so much as a sorry.

'Is that Michael Field?' It's a voice that sounds strangely familiar.

'What if it is?' I try to sound aloof without being aggressive.

'It's about this camera.' The voice comes straight to the point and I almost drop the phone.

'Who is this?' I bark back.

'You don't know me but I've got some prints I'm told you're very interested in. Before you can have them I want to know what you're up to.'

I finally recognise the voice of the camera geek in Jessops yesterday and say: 'Hold on, you're Grace's brother, right?'

'Is that what she said?'

'It's Simon, yeah? She said you were her...'

'Look, whatever... we're not doing this over the phone.'

'What do you have in mind?'

'Somewhere discreet... I mean, what the fuck do you think?'

'Okay,' I say, trying to stay calm and buy some time. 'Do I need to... bring anything?'

'Well, as you've mentioned it first, I have gone to a lot of trouble and risk to develop your bizarre set of photos. I wouldn't object if you wanted to make it worth my while.'

'Look, mate, this was just supposed to be a favour.' I try to keep it friendly. 'Maybe you should be having this conversation with Grace.'

'Believe me, matey,' he says, 'I *am* doing you a favour. You wouldn't want her to see these first and, yeah, I think you would put some value on me delivering them directly to you.'

I have no idea what I'm dealing with here. It's already obvious that Grace and Simon aren't the fondest of siblings, but she at least told me I could trust her to deal with him. Instead, she seems to have told him everything, including my phone number. Although I weighed up the risk of handing her the camera, I certainly wasn't expecting this. And without any knowledge of what Simon has already seen, I've lost any control I thought I had.

'Okay, how much?' I say with resignation.

'Two hundred.' The reply is instant and it's obvious a counter-offer is pointless. This isn't a negotiation; I've been totally shafted. He says a time and place and the line goes dead.

Sister Act

A few hours later I'm sitting alone at the back of a greasy cafe about a mile from home. I've been waiting twenty minutes and this is starting to feel like yet another wind-up. I wouldn't be surprised to see Grace come breezing in with a cheeky smile and a pack of photos in her hand. But it's Simon who eventually walks in, empty-handed, and straight over to my table.

'It's you,' he says, a sardonic smile forming momentarily on his lips. The grin morphs into a suspicious scowl when he adds: 'What are you up to with Grace?'

'Look Simon, I'm not taking advantage if that's what you're

worried about. I'm sure she can take care of herself. Besides, I didn't think there was much brother-sister love lost between you two.'

'She's no sister of mine and, believe me, I couldn't give a monkey's about her feelings. I just want to know what she finds so fascinating about you.' He leans forward, his chicken-wristed hands grip the back of the chair, forfeiting any attempt at intimidation and height advantage he had standing up straight. Undiminished, he leers at me, eye to eye, before adding, 'Given what you're into, you sick fucker!'

I squirm in disgust and frustration at an accusation I can't even contemplate, let alone defend.

'Look, we've only known each other a few days,' I say, sticking to the only facts I have. 'We seem to be hitting it off and she offered to help with that film. It's really not that compli...' Irony sucks the word back into my mouth. Truth be told, this is getting very complicated. I'm starting to wish I'd waited five more minutes in Jessops.

'So if you've only just met her, what were you doing with *that* camera?'

'It's a long story. I can tell you what I know if you're really interested.' Of course, I have no intention of telling him anything and it feels like a pointless offer anyway, given that he's seen the photos and therefore already knows more than I do. 'But for the moment, Simon, you've got *me* by the balls because I really don't have a clue what was on that film. Whatever it is you've seen, I can't explain without looking at those prints.'

'You're telling me you didn't know?'

'I honestly don't.' He glares back at me unconvinced and I continue anyway. 'Ask yourself, on the basis of what you've seen; do you seriously think I would have taken it into Jessops to be developed if I did?'

'And Grace didn't know either?'

'How could she?' I yell before dropping my voice back to a spitting whisper. 'Look, if you've just developed the prints and no one else has seen them, then you're the only person I know

111

who has a clue what's on them.'

He's still standing in front of me, but no longer leaning across the top of the chair. He steps back and rubs his spotty chin, whilst keeping his eyes locked on mine. Momentarily, he looks away and starts raking his lower lip with his front teeth. I follow his gaze around at the empty tables.

At least no one's been listening; even the woman behind the counter is still flicking through the same magazine she barely managed to pull herself away from to serve me. Finally he sits down opposite me.

'Okay man. I don't need this shit,' he says. 'Here's the deal. Give me the cash now and they're yours. Not a word to Grace. As far as I'm concerned we didn't meet. The film was ruined. That's what I've told her and you'd better act like you believe her when she tells you.'

After the exchange, one thin brown envelope for another, from one inside pocket to another, he stays for coffee but, call me unsociable, I don't feel like getting to know him better. For one thing, I've just handed over 200 quid of someone else's money to a guy I don't know. I was assured he could be trusted by someone who said he was her brother. He's disowned and double-crossed her. What's bugging me most is the fact she lied to me.

I only hope the package in my pocket does actually contain a set of negatives and matching photographs originating from that camera. I couldn't bring myself to look at them in front of him and now I just want to get home. So, naturally, my greatest anxiety as I step onto the bus is the possibility I've been duped again. I'm starting to lose count.

It's a short ride back and I try to stay positive; Simon just wanted some money for his trouble. Job done. Hopefully I never have to see him again. Lurking mischievously behind that thought is a spark of excitement. I'll soon be able to see what was on the camera. And finally begin to understand what all this is about.

Long Shot

If only life was so simple.

Just five prints slide out of the envelope when I empty it onto the coffee table, along with the negatives cut into strips. I'm not sure what I've been expecting, but five photos? And it's even worse than that. I flick through, purely to count them, with a cursory glance, and quickly turn to the negatives to check they tally. Sure enough, there are only five frames exposed. The rest are all completely blank.

Okay, now I'm wondering why I didn't look closely at the camera, because I would have seen a number somewhere to indicate how many exposures had been taken. But it's only a fleeting thought because looking back through the photographs only confirms my next biggest fear. I can't see a single thing in them that seems to relate back to Herb, and certainly nothing for him to get blackmailed over. And to make matters worse, I can't see any reason why Simon had to make me feel like such a slime-ball.

Set in a pub against the backdrop of a Happy New Millennium banner are five shots of a group of young friends in various combinations and poses; all very salubrious and innocent I should add. I can't say I'm really studying each of the pictures with any great scrutiny at this point, apart from noticing there are five or six kids, boys and girls, probably in their mid-teens. They're totally unremarkable. They look like any other kids mucking about in a pub on New Year's Eve. I sit on the sofa and stare out of the window in disbelief. *This* is what Herb sent me into Bleak House to get?

I grab the scotch and empty the first glass without ceremony and start to pour another. Looking down at the table where I've left the prints lined up like solitaire, I notice something vaguely different about one of them. It's the only shot that isn't staged and the only one with a single subject. The other thing that strikes me is that the angle and distance are different to the others. It's as if it was taken from some way across the pub, while all the others are much closer and more candid. Instead of looking directly at the camera, the girl in the centre of the photo is facing off to the side as if she's talking to another member of the group. So I can only see her profile. She's holding something in her hand at the bottom of the shot, but it's blurred as if it's overexposed, so I can't make out what it is.

I've not really taken much notice of any of the faces in the group shots; they're just anonymous kids having a laugh. This picture stands out though and I pick it up for a closer look. Compared to the others I get the distinct impression this one was taken discreetly, probably without the girl's knowledge. I suppose it could have been taken by one of the others when they went to the bar or were coming back from the toilet.

I don't know, maybe I'm looking too deeply, trying to find something significant. Close up, the blurred area looks like a lighter or a match, although that doesn't make a lot of sense. The pub doesn't look very full and the people in the background don't seem overly animated, so it's unlikely it was approaching the big countdown when they might well have lit sparklers or started waving glow-sticks around. I give up. At the end of the day it's still just another party photo. No big deal. I put it back on the table.

Holding up the length of negatives with the exposures on it, I can barely make out the images in the dull light. I turn the light on for a better look and find the picture of the girl on the end of the strip, confirming it was the last picture taken. That's when I notice the numbers on the film's edge.

I'm momentarily confused when I see this one is frame six. Looking back along the edge of the strip I realise the numbers start at two. A quick look at the other blanks confirms I only have negatives for twenty-six of the twenty-seven frames. Number one and its corresponding print are missing. I can only draw one conclusion. Simon kept it back. The realisation sends me into a rage and without a further thought I grab the phone.

'What do you want?'

'You know what I want, you snivelling little shit.' I'm livid and failing hopelessly to keep my cool.

'Oh yeah, I forgot to say. There was a problem with the first frame. It must have got stuck in the mechanism. I had to cut the film to get it out. You're lucky all the others came out in one piece. How old was that thing anyway?'

I have to think quickly. He sounds very calm and believable and he certainly has a point about the age of the camera. No, I'm not buying it. It's too much of a coincidence. I have to believe there's more to the fishing trip Herb sent me on than a bunch of kids celebrating Y2K. There must be something else on the missing photo and Simon has to have seen it to think that *I'm* the sicko. I'm guessing he decided to keep it to exploit some further financial opportunity.

'Simon, listen very carefully,' I say as menacingly as I can. 'If that negative and print are in my hands within twenty-four hours, firstly you get to keep the money. More importantly, you get to keep the use of all of your fingers. I'm sure you're going to need them if you're serious about a career in photography. So, before you give me any more bullshit, take your time and think it through. Whatever Grace has told you about this little assignment of ours, you should know this. The people we're dealing with here would have no hesitation in making sure you couldn't take a *piss* without someone having to hold it for you. Do you understand?'

The line's gone very quiet so I continue to press home my advantage.

'So, unless you want to be removing lens covers with your teeth for the rest of your life, here's what I'd like you to do. I'm guessing you probably left negative number one and the print you've already made somewhere safe, because you were concerned with what you saw. Am I right?'

'I left it in my locker,' he says, his voice now soft and vulnerable, bolstering my confidence.

'Okay, that's better. So it's still at uni... Great. So tomorrow, you'll go back and get it and you'll go to the dark room when no one else is there and you'll print me a second copy. What's the largest format you can easily print?'

'Ten by eight,' he says.

'Okay, ten by eight is good,' I say, hoping that will be big enough if I have to look for any small clues. 'Then you and I are going to have another little coffee together at six o'clock tomorrow evening, same place as today. Bring the negative and both prints and don't do anything foolish like keeping another copy. Understood?'

'Yeah, whatever,' he says, his indifference far from convincing. I feel sure I've succeeded in freaking him out, and remind myself of Grace's description of him. He's a geek who probably got bullied at school and I'm satisfied he won't be prepared to push his luck with the big boys.

'Thank you Simon. I suppose you would prefer we continue to keep this just between...' The line goes dead before I can finish.

I put the phone down and glance back at the odd photograph. Something keeps drawing me back to the girl's profile but I can't see why. With the light on, the other photos have taken on a more vibrant quality and I try to imagine the mood back on that last evening in December '99. Inevitably, my mind wanders back to my own Millennium Eve celebrations with Sam. I dwell on the scene momentarily and then, without mercy, drown the memory at birth with the remains of the second glass of whisky.

About to stack the photos and put them back into the envelope, I can't resist one final look. That's when I see it, as clear as day. The girl in the unsuspecting shot is also in one of the staged photos. In that one she's looking right into the camera and, like the two friends either side of her, she's got a big smile on her face. The young features are unmistakable. Smiling up at me is Grace.

Totally Blank

I sit here wide-eyed, mind racing. What the hell is going on? My first thought is whether Simon is stupid enough to give me a set of photos of his teenage sister – or whatever relationship she is to him, instead of what was on the camera, as some kind of joke. That seems too bizarre to consider. And although I am starting to feel like I'm being conned yet again, I sense that Simon did exactly what was asked of him. His only deception was to remove one of the shots – and of course to take me for 200 quid. Otherwise, why would he bother holding back one picture if the whole set is fake?

If these really are the photos from the camera, wouldn't he have recognised Grace in them? I'm still convinced the real action revolves around frame one and Simon's seen something on it worth holding onto. I suppose it's possible, knowing he had the real money shot, that he didn't take a lot of notice of the other pictures; a group of kids in a pub.

But something's nagging away at the back of my mind, what he said when he first arrived in the cafe: 'So if you've only just met her, what were you doing with *that* camera?' It threw me at the time. I was feeling under pressure and didn't challenge him on it. Now it makes me think he *did* know it was her. Could he have been trying to protect her, despite the apparent animosity between them? I don't know, maybe I misheard him. Either way, it doesn't make sense and I dismiss the idea of ringing him again and verbally beating him up some more. Not only would I have to come on pretty strong to get him to confess if everything he's given me *is* fake, I'd also risk taking the pressure off him after our last conversation. I resign myself to the thought that everything hinges on how he acts and what he gives me tomorrow. I have no choice other than to let this run its course.

Just then the phone rings. It's Grace and she starts apologising and telling me what Simon told her earlier. The camera was very old, probably ten years or more, and the film had lost its integrity. There wasn't a single frame that could be developed. She says she has the camera and the blank film and can bring them over later.

Her words echo around in my head. I have to bite my

tongue because I really want to challenge her on how Simon knew it was mine and, more to the point, got hold of my name and number.

'Mickey, I know how disappointing this must be. You must be stunned,' she says. She's right but for all the wrong reasons. I don't know what to say.

'Mickey? Are you okay? Should I come over?'

'Uh… yeah, that would be good.'

When she arrives, she gives me a big hug on the doorstep and once we're in the hall she hands back the envelope she'd taken last night. I'm able to hide my continuing sense of consternation behind a mask of disappointment. Grace seems just as upset that there are no photographs to look at. I don't even bother to look inside the package and drop it on the table in the lounge. I'm guessing there's a roll of exposed film in there that Simon returned with the empty camera to complete the con.

'Doesn't get you any closer to finding out what your friend's up to,' she says.

'No. I wish he would get in touch so I can tell him it's all been a waste of time.'

'Yeah, you seem to be stuck in the middle of a farce.'

'You're right there,' I say. The words: 'you and me both' remain unspoken in my head.

Cuckoo's Nest

It's later and we're in bed. I'm feeling slightly uneasy making love to her. It isn't a repeat of yesterday's rampant discovery sex. Don't get me wrong, I'm not complaining; it just doesn't feel right. Afterwards, she's resting her head on my chest and I try to ease my conscience by asking about her family.

'We're not particularly close, as you've probably gathered,' she says.

'Well, I can see you and Simon don't exactly hit it off,' I say, resisting the urge to challenge the nature of their sibling

118

connection. 'What about your parents?'

Grace seems to hesitate as if she's choosing her words carefully.

'I suppose I would have to say they tried to give me a stable home.'

'Not exactly a ringing endorsement.' I can't resist a playful jibe, even though I can hardly brag about having the perfect nuclear family.

'No, it's probably been difficult for them too. I mean I don't suppose I've made it any easier for them.' She's talking in a whisper and I sense it's coming from deep inside. It's the first time she's let me see beyond her tough shell of confidence. I want her to elaborate but don't want to push, so I wait until she fills the silence.

'Simon is their little boy,' she says. 'Always was and always will be. I knew I could never challenge that and I never really wanted to. But there were times I needed more from them than they were able to give. Something I lost a long time ago. I realise now I'm older that they could never have replaced it.'

'What happened?' I ask hesitantly.

'They're not my real parents.'

'Ah, Simon isn't really your brother.' It goes without saying, but voicing it helps to close out the question I'd been desperate to ask.

'It's just easier to say he is. It doesn't stop him being a brat.' She looks at me with a dry smile and I nod back in agreement.

'How old were you?' I ask.

'They adopted me when I was twelve. Not a great age for a girl to try and fit in. I think I was as unprepared to cope with them as they were with me. It was all very nice to begin with... I soon came to realise happy families *is* just a card game.'

'And before that?' I'm starting to feel a bit intrusive, but she seems happy enough to talk.

'Foster homes, social services, Barnardo's. You name it, I did it – the whole Orphan Annie merry-go-round for twelve years. Except it wasn't very merry,' she adds with sigh.

'God,' I say, failing miserably to find the right words. 'It must have been awful.'

'Well, looking back, maybe it was. At the time, I don't know. When you're a kid you just get on with growing up, don't you? When you're little, you think your own life is normal. You haven't got much to compare it with.'

'What's normal anyway?' I say, and then wish I hadn't.

'Well, for me it felt like being part of a big family. Now I realise everyone was at arm's length and there wasn't enough love to go around.' I stroke the soft skin at the top of her arm and she looks up at me, smiling through heavy eyes. 'Maybe I didn't know any different,' she continues and looks away again. 'But deep inside I think I yearned for more affection. In the end, you start settling for any attention as a substitute, I suppose. And it doesn't matter whether it's good or bad... as long as someone notices you. And when you're young you don't understand attention comes in different forms and affection isn't always unconditional.'

I'm not sure if she's trying to tell me she was abused. I remember all the terrible stuff in the news back in the late eighties, happening in care homes. I thought it was all overblown at the time. Now I shudder at the thought that Grace would have been a cute little girl, all curls and dimples, growing up right in the middle of that. Believe me, I want to sympathise, I do want her to talk about it if it helps; I just don't know the right things to say and, more than that, I think I'm afraid of what she might tell me. I realise it's a cop-out but I decide nothing I could say can change the past. All I can do is to hold her closer.

She seems to sense my discomfort and lightens up a little. 'It's not all bad,' she says. 'As you get older, you start to realise you can use it to manipulate situations.'

'You've got me there,' I say, hoping she sees the funny side. She doesn't respond so I venture one last question. 'Have you ever met your real parents?'

'I was told my mum died when I was born.' Her voice starts to crack. 'And my dad couldn't cope...' At that she reaches out of bed and takes my shirt from the chair and drapes it over her shoulders, grabs her clothes and goes into the bathroom. She comes back fully dressed and says she needs to head home as she has work in a few hours.

'Grace? I'm sorry if I upset you,' I say.

'No honey, it's not you. It's me. I wasn't expecting...' She pauses. 'I'm just not ready... yet.' She leans across and kisses me, silencing any further questions.

'I'll ring you tomorrow evening,' I say as she leaves.

It's two in the morning and I'm in shock from her story. I'm also feeling guilty. Primarily because of the photographs of her as a teenager, hidden in the other room. Whichever way you look at it, I'm now deceiving her. And then, when she left, I couldn't even offer to drive her home. Although she had her car here, the least I could have done was to drive her back in it and get a bus home. But, as usual, I'd had too much to drink. I did suggest going with her as her passenger to see her home safely and she just laughed at me. She doesn't seem to share my aversion to drink-driving. Apart from that, I'm starting to feel very protective towards her.

I can't believe she called me honey. God, I *hope* I can be completely honest with her tomorrow.

* * *

Night Vision

Another suburban street, middle class, respectable. Townhouse style. No rooms downstairs. Easy to go unseen.

Watching her leave, he notes the time. No kiss at the doorstep; they've had two hours for that. Front lights had gone off at midnight; main bedroom's along the hall. He knows the layout, windows to the side and rear, but no other lights had come on. Maybe they hadn't made it past the kitchen. Imagining them naked across the slab of granite worktop, he'd breath-fogged the windscreen, remembering the rack of cold Sabatiers on the counter. Heavy, finely balanced, razor sharp.

She gets in the Mazda. Blood-red. Had to be hers. Hairdresser's car. He already wrote down the number. She's so small – so little flesh on the bone. Others would call her pretty, but that's only skin deep. His interest lies deeper than that.

He slides down in the seat, barely controlling the urge to touch himself as she drives past without a glance. His car was here when she arrived, blending in. It's what he does. For a big man, he prides himself on going unnoticed. People only see him when he wants them to. By then it's usually too late.

After a mile of lefts and rights she pulls up outside a featureless cubic block and goes through entrance doors that illuminate a communal hall. He waits until lights through second-storey windows go off in relays from room to room, like a shadow moving across the building. He waits until the entrance hall lantern automatically extinguishes, until the welcome camouflage of darkness returns.

As he reaches to kill the engine, someone walks past – a scrawny youth, with greasy hair, who turns and stares at him through the windscreen. Too late... Usually, instinct would draw him back into the darkness to hide his face. Not this time. Something makes him choose to be seen. Too late... for the boy. He stares back, forcing the lad to turn away and retreat towards the same entrance and be welcomed home by its automated light.

Too late... the kid's features were unmistakeable. Recognisable as the son, but he could have almost been the father... back then. That bent bastard pig. Justice is overdue. For the boss. And for that sweet lass he never knew. A ma who would have loved her wean.

It's a welcome change of plan and he pulls away with a promise to return.

8.

Monday, 21st

Simon didn't show up. The little runt.

I had a feeling he wouldn't fall for my Vinnie Jones routine. I've tried calling his number and Miss Vodafone circa 1999 keeps telling me, with that annoying smugness, his phone may be switched off. Yeah, I know, I agreed to go along with his story that the film was ruined, but he can go to hell. Now I'm desperate to talk to Grace and show her the photos to see if she can shed any light on how they could have turned up years later on a camera in *that* house. I've given up trying to guess what connects five pictures of her and her friends as teenagers with something sinister that surely has to be revealed on the missing shot; something that supposedly had Herb so worried about blackmail.

Talking of the devil, another day has passed without any contact from him. My earlier concern for his wellbeing has been replaced with anger and suspicion. Without any way of knowing what he's up to, once again Herb's got me stumbling around in the dark. Getting hold of that last photo is the only way forward and, in Herb's continuing absence, Grace is the one person I suspect can help make sense of all this. And after last night, I'm keen to come clean with her, if for no other reason than to reassure her she can still trust me. At least that's the plan before I call her this evening.

'Well I'm surprised you've got the nerve.' Her voice stings like salt and lemon without the pleasant hit of tequila; the intimacy of the last few days shattered in a single sentence. She's a million miles away and I'm back to being just another bloke.

'Huh, what's up?'

'Don't play the innocent with me, Mickey,' she says. 'I thought we were getting on well. I thought I could trust you.'

'Grace, you can. I promise you.' My protest is so hollow I can hear an echo. 'What's happened?'

'I genuinely tried to help you and this is how you repay me. I really started to think you were different but you're not. You're like the rest of them.'

'What are you talking about? Grace, you've got me all wrong. I don't know what's going on here.'

'You knew last night and you said nothing. You used me.'

'But Grace...'

'You went behind my back. Took what you wanted and treated me like trash.'

'It's not like that. I wouldn't do anything to hurt you.'

'I really started to open up to you, Mickey. I've never been able to do that before, and all the time... you're as bad as all the others.' She finally stops and leaves an uncomfortable silence, giving me time to think.

'It's Simon isn't it? What's he been saying?'

'You spoke to him yesterday, didn't you?'

'He called me. I wanted to tell you last night but it got too complicated. He stitched me up and then I thought I could bring him back into line. In any case,' I say, matching her tone, 'I'd like to know how he even knew the camera was mine in the first place.'

The line suddenly goes quiet. 'I had to tell him,' she says sheepishly. 'He saw right through me when I said it was mine.'

'And did you give him my number as well?'

'No, he must have got it from my phone,' she says, sounding genuinely upset, before coming back at me. 'But I'd like to know which one of you had the idea to trick me into believing the film was ruined.'

The anger's still in her voice. I'd prefer not to be doing this over the phone, though I imagine it would be pretty scary in person. Our first row and I'm already on the defensive.

'It was his idea.' I sound pathetic.

'And you went along with it.'

'I really didn't have much choice. I was hoping to sort it out with him today so I could talk to you about it tonight. And now he's shafted me again. Honestly Grace, I was going to tell you about the photos.'

'Photos?' Her voice suddenly changes. 'What photos?'

'The ones he gave me.'

'What photos he gave you?'

'There were only five. Didn't he tell you?'

'He didn't mention any others,' she says. Others. The word comes hurtling towards me, but before I can bat it back she continues. 'He gave me two copies of the same print and a single negative cut from the film. Said it was the only one that came out undamaged. He admitted he hadn't known what to do about it yesterday when he told me the film was ruined, but he then decided I might like to deal with it... in the circumstances. In the *circumstances*, I can see what he means.'

'What the hell's that suppose to mean?' My mind starts racing. If she has the first photo from the camera, surely she holds the key to this whole bizarre situation. But what circumstance in Herb's mysterious blackmail caper could possibly be better dealt with by Grace?

'Tell me about the photos you've got first?' she says.

The mood of the whole conversation has changed. The accusations and tearful outbursts have melted away. We're both innocent victims of Simon's childish games and I sense we're back on equal terms.

We both know the other holds a key piece of the puzzle and neither wants to show our hand first. I decide to push my luck and test Grace's change of heart.

'Why don't you come over here and we can look at them all together?'

'I'll see you in The Feathers in an hour,' she says and puts the phone down.

Over Exposed

I'm sitting at the same table as the first time we were in here together. It's been an hour and a half since Grace hung up on me and I'm worried she's not going to turn up. It's becoming a bad habit, hanging around for members of her dysfunctional family. As I hold that thought, a dark cloud of irony hovers over me and asks: *so what does that make your family?* I shake it off and stand up for the fourth time to look across to the other side of the pub, to where I'd first laid eyes on her. But she's not there. Oh well, I'm in no hurry to leave. Back at the bar, the same Aussie girl puts down the pint of Guinness without making eye contact, and announces the price to no one in particular. To make a point, I drop the right money in change onto the bar and turn away. Grace is sitting at our table looking at me.

There's no beaming smile, no warm embrace, no generous kiss. I half-smile, half-frown back at her and put my glass down.

'Tia Maria and Coke?' I ask, hoping her face might soften.

'Thanks,' she says, but the fixed expression remains.

I'm back with her drink and there's an awkward pause. Neither of us wants to start the conversation. I'm not sure why I'm hesitating because I can't wait to see the other photo, although I can sense Grace is unusually nervous. I choose my approach carefully.

'That Simon's a real piece of work,' I say, without looking up from supping on my pint.

'Yeah, a real chip off the old block, that one,' she says and I'm surprised at the ease with which she maligns both her adoptive brother and father in one fell swoop. 'Did you have to give him money?' she adds, as our eyes finally meet.

'Two hundred quid,' I say. 'But that's not what pissed me off. The fact he then held back the only meaningful picture; that's what got me mad.'

'How do you know it's the only meaningful one?'

'Well you've seen it, so you would know!' I snap back. I don't mean to get shitty; I'm just in no mood to continue playing silly games.

'So are you saying the rest are completely irrelevant?' she says.

'Put it this way,' I say. 'I can't see anything there to threaten or be of any interest to Herb.'

'So why are you being so cagey?'

'What if I said I thought you might be amused by them?'

'Amused?'

'Look,' I say, sensing I've briefly got the upper hand, even though she's the one holding the ace, 'I'll put you out of your misery as soon as you hand over the other photo.'

'Okay. I suppose you'll have to see it sooner or later.' Grace reaches into her bag and takes out a large brown envelope and puts it on the table. 'You might want to be discreet,' she adds. 'God knows why he had to print one of them so large.'

'Really?' I say, holding back a smirk as I remember my instructions to Simon. 'Maybe he's not so belligerent after all.' Grace gives me a puzzled look as I take her envelope and place a much smaller one on the table. She makes no attempt to grab it. I have to admire her self-control. I can't wait another second.

Reaching into the large envelope, I start to slide out a ten by eight picture an inch at a time. The photograph that emerges begins with a pair of legs, slender and bare. Immediately, I can tell it isn't a photo of real legs but a photo of a drawing. My eyes follow the direction of the thighs as I pull the whole print out of the envelope to reveal an expertly crafted sketch of a naked, young woman. The label printed beneath answers the obvious question.

EXAMPLE OF A TRUE-LIFE LIKENESS. MODEL IN REPOSE.

The model beams up at me, the face of a cherub with the body of a siren. Looking back at Grace I see the same beguiling eyes, the enigmatic smile. She reaches across with her hand and gently lifts my jaw to close my mouth.

'Oh my God,' I whisper. 'How did this get onto that camera?'

'Don't you think I'd like to know?' she says picking up the other envelope. 'Okay. I've shown you mine; let's have a look at yours.'

As she looks through the five prints, her face contorts. That's followed by a brief moment of recognition.

'I was hoping you would be able to shed some light on them,' I say. 'Do you remember it?'

'Millennium Eve. Sure.' She's smiling broadly and I'm thinking it's because she's remembering good times. She starts to laugh out loud. 'Well, I wouldn't have believed it.' She's shakes her head. All the earlier anxiety has gone. She straightens up in the chair, takes a big gulp of her drink and smiles at me.

'Now *that* explains everything,' she says and continues grinning. I look back at her more bewildered than ever.

Millennium Bug

'It's *mine!*' she says, like that's going to be enough to iron out the creases in my brow.

'Right. I can see that. It's a really good likeness,' I say, picking up the large photo and turning it lengthways, as if studying a centrefold in one of Herb's old magazines. She scowls at me playfully before snatching it away and sliding it face down into the envelope.

'The camera,' she says. 'The *camera's* mine... or at least it was.'

I almost snort the Guinness while nodding to acknowledge at least *that* makes some sense.

'I wanted to take a picture of Mr Johnson's drawing,' she continues. 'For posterity, I suppose.'

'Course you did,' I say, realising how obviously credible that is. She'd enjoyed the whole experience so much it's hardly surprising she would have wanted a secret memento.

'I bought one of those cameras and took it in on the last day of term. Everyone had left early for the Christmas holidays. Taking the photo was the easy bit.' She smiles and shakes her head. 'Of course, it didn't occur to me when I saw you with it on Saturday, that camera gave me the same dilemma all those years ago that it was giving you then.'

'Yeah,' I say. 'At least you knew what was on it,'

'True, but that was my problem. I wanted to make it seem that I didn't.'

'So you took it out on New Year's Eve and hoped it would get filled with dodgy pictures.'

'Well it was the world's biggest party,' she says. 'I was hoping the photos would get more risqué as the night went on, so that when they were developed...'

'Yeah, I get it,' I say. 'By then your child porn wouldn't even warrant a second glance.' She grimaces and looks around to make sure no one heard me.

'I was hoping, by comparison, it might pass as a tasteful piece of art,' she says. 'That was the plan.'

'Sounds like a good one,' I say. The Banker adds silently: *One you could have used yourself if you'd been smart enough to work out the camera wasn't full.*

— Yeah, alright. Give it a rest.

'And it probably would have worked if the camera hadn't gone missing,' she says. 'I never saw it again. For months I was worried sick someone would get it developed and try to hurt me with it, but after a while I forgot all about it.'

'I don't suppose you would have recognised it when I handed it to you.'

'No,' she says. 'They all look the same, don't they? In any case I wouldn't have even remembered what colour it was. And it was the last thing I was expecting. *You*... finding *my* camera... on the kitchen table in *that* awful house.'

The Banker's trying to tell me something, but I put him on mute and thumb back through the other pictures.

'What's that in your hand?' I ask, pointing to the one of her alone.

'I don't know,' she says, leaning in to pick it up.

'It still looks early. I can't believe you would have lit up the sparklers already.'

'Oh,' she says as realisation dawns, casting a warm glow in her eyes. 'I remember. I came back from the loo and they were all huddling over a table. When they turned around they'd lit a candle on a cupcake and started singing Happy Birthday. I was embarrassed and said it wasn't my birthday yet. But they insisted I had to have it then because it would be a huge anticlimax celebrating a birthday the morning after Y2K. It must be the cake I'm holding in the photo before I blew out the candle.'

I smile back at her and nod. While the revelation of her birthday is a welcome distraction, it can't divert my mind from the big question.

'What do you think it all means?'

'I wish I knew,' she says, sighing deeply. 'There was one thing I noticed though.'

'What?'

'Was this the last one on the film?' she says putting the indirect photo of herself back on the table.

'Yeah, it was.' I point to the final exposure on the negatives. 'Why?'

'I'm pretty sure that wasn't taken by one of the group.'

'Yeah, I thought it looked out of place too. Who else do you think could have taken it?'

'I really don't know,' she says, and stares off across the bar for inspiration.

'Well, it was nearly ten years ago. Hard to believe.'

'Yeah, I know. Hang on... yes... I remember. There was this strange man. He was sitting in the corner of the pub on his own when we first got there. Yeah, that's right... He wasn't in the party spirit like everyone else... he just looked pretty drunk already. God, yeah... we thought he was watching us.'

'Do you remember what he looked like?'

'No... not really. Just that he was middle-aged... Oh yeah, he also looked out of place because he was so smartly dressed. I remember, we were mucking about saying he was probably a psycho or a child-molester. God, yeah... We even gave him a nickname. Millennium Pervert, I think it was. Then he left and we didn't see him again.'

'Do you think he could have taken that last picture of you before making off with your camera?'

'Wow, I don't know. I just thought I'd lost it... or someone picked up the wrong one by mistake... or it was just nicked. But... it was no big deal really. Nothing ever came of it, so I haven't really thought about it since.'

'What do you reckon now?'

'Let me see,' she says, studying the photograph again. 'It certainly looks like it was taken from where he'd been sitting.'

We both lean back into our chairs and shake our heads in puzzled synchronicity. There's another question, pulsing like neon in my head, and Grace verbalises it first.

'I wonder what your old friend has to do with the Millennium Pervert.'

'Could Herb even *be* the Mill...?' I start to say, but as much as I've tried to ignore it, the irrational inference festering in my head that the policewoman's comments about Herb somehow associate him with photographs of young people stabs me mid-sentence.

'Well, I suppose anything's possible,' she says. 'Why would *he* be interested in my friends? And didn't he tell you he was being blackmailed because of this camera?'

'First, it looks to me like whoever it was, was only interested in you. It's ironic they didn't realise they got far more of you than they bargained for! Second,' I continue thinking aloud, 'like I said, I can't see anything incriminating here for Herb, regardless of whether he took the camera or not. And even if someone else got hold of it, how would they even know what was on there to threaten him with?'

Grace sits there in silence, looking through her photos, and The Banker reminds me about what she said earlier and prods me to voice the thing that's bugging him the most.

'Whoever took it,' I say, 'doesn't even begin to explain the outrageous coincidence that it's *your* camera I found on *that* table.'

'Well,' she says, apparently missing my point, 'regardless of who took it, I can't understand why they wouldn't bother to develop it.' And she's right; that still doesn't make sense.

'Especially after all these years,' I say. 'To be honest, I'm starting to doubt every word Herb has said.'

'We need to find out what he's up to,' she says, very matter of fact. 'I hope you don't mind. This is now as much my mystery as it is yours.'

'I couldn't agree more.'

'Good. And I've got no appointments tomorrow,' she says, suddenly taking control. 'Here's what I think we should do.'

Cold Comfort

Back at my place, we've set the alarm for five-thirty and decide on an early night. That said, it isn't very early by the time we actually settle down to sleep. What's that they say about it being the best part of breaking up? I'm just glad we seem to be back on an even keel after this afternoon's outburst. But I do feel the need to say something about it.

'I can see how it must have looked when all you had to go on was the photo of the sketch,' I say, absently stroking the soft pad of her palm with my thumb.

'Yeah, I'm sorry. I panicked.' She turns to look at me.

'You thought someone was going to use it against you after all? Herb, I suppose. Or even me.'

'I don't know. Maybe old Mr Johnson had finally got wise to it. Or my old classmates, Paula Harvey and Julie Dixon, had fallen on hard times.' She allows herself a nervous laugh and I reach across and kiss her forehead.

'I can imagine my story of getting the camera from a scary house for an old friend would have sounded pretty flimsy,' I add and she smiles and shakes her head. 'Like maybe I was softening you up for someone else to exploit.'

132

'Oh Mickey, no. I didn't know what to think. But no, not that. I'm not the one being exploited here.' There's sincerity in the way she says it, and yet she abruptly turns away and looks up at the time display projected on the ceiling. 'It's getting late. We should get some sleep.'

Maybe her conscience is clear, because after turning onto her side, she's asleep in no time. As I lay beside her, cushioning the back of her naked body with the front of mine, my mind continues to drift. Thanks to her the photos can be explained, but the fact they involve her is too wild a coincidence. There has to be something she isn't telling me. Her words repeat in my head: *I'm not the one being exploited here.* Sure, it feels like I'm the one being conned by Herb; is that all she means? Right now, I'll settle for the comfort that being in this together feels a whole lot better than being in it alone and I kiss the back of her head and roll over to the cold side of the bed.

As I watch the minutes pass relentlessly in red digits over us, The Banker repeats her other words from earlier. The more I challenge him, the more certain we both are that I didn't tell her I'd found the camera on the kitchen table.

* * *

Killing Time

He hates all this waiting around – unloading in Soho, reloading in China Town. And the bright lights, they don't deceive him. These are grubby streets. West End. East End. No difference. Home from home. Camouflage.

Tonight is strictly business. Even if he wanted to, he couldn't blend in. Not in this thing. White van man. No slapper would get in this, not even in King's Cross.

He's about to head back when he sees the boy. An unlikely coincidence he thinks, and his pulse starts to quicken. Leaving the van, he follows him through dingy backstreets and watches where he goes. When he stops. Who he talks to. He's not surprised when he works it out. Like father like son. Taking backhanders all down the line from the brokers, the late-night traders and the common street hawkers. Many of them the boss's former customers who no longer place orders. Getting better terms elsewhere they say. And using their gains to buy police protection through the agency of this pig-spawn.

Another good reason to settle the score.

9.

Tuesday, 22nd

What a difference the early daylight makes. It can cheer you up and help you see more clearly. It can give new hope and lift your spirits. It can also help make a previously sinister, horrifying place seem so much more benign. Sadly, what it can't do this morning is get us inside Bleak House without breaking a window. Or so I thought.

Today, rather than sneaking around the back lane and coming in over the fence like common burglars, Grace and I have walked right in off the street and down the side of the house. We're at the back door and I'm hoping we can get it open and go straight into the kitchen without having to walk through the dungeon suite. I'm still apprehensive about going in there again, but once Grace had enlightened me about the photographs, it seemed a not entirely unreasonable thing to do. It's not much of a plan; I'm only going along with it because I don't have a better one.

Although I've tried telling her what a mess it was in, I suppose it's easier for her to accept that there's probably a perfectly innocent explanation, but it's much harder for me to rationalise how I felt in there. I'm giving her the benefit of the doubt, because that, along with the bright sunshine streaming in through the grimy windows, is the only way I can contemplate going back inside. And the only way I can dismiss the possibility that I'm about to expose Grace to something really gruesome too.

Assuming we can get inside, she said we'll be looking for clues; anything that might lead us back to Herb. That's a huge assumption, considering the heavy wooden door in front of us. I remember contemplating breaking in this way once before and deciding against it because it would be too noisy. That was until my huge stroke of luck in finding the sash window unlatched at the side of the house. We've already double-checked and discounted that route, given its robust security upgrade. I shake my head in defeat as I realise that whoever allowed me to get in so easily, is now as keen to keep everyone out.

'Let me see.' Grace steps past me to inspect the lock and gives the door a gentle shake with her gloved hand.

'No bolts,' she mutters more to herself. 'And a single lock.'

'Yeah, but it'll take a hefty whack to push it through,' I whisper. 'I expect I could do it, just not without waking the whole street.' I lean my shoulder against the door, trying to gauge its strength, and notice Grace removing something from her pocket. She kneels down at the door handle and I'm about to ask what she's doing when the lock clicks and the door opens inwards.

'Wow! This is a new side to you I wasn't expecting,' I say, following her through the door. 'Don't tell me, your dad's a locksmith.'

'He's not my dad, remember?' I cringe at my own insensitivity, but before I can apologise she adds, 'If you must know, he's a copper!'

'*What?* And you waited until I'd broken into this house for a second time to tell me that?'

'Oh, don't worry about him. We have an understanding. I keep his little secrets and he makes sure I have a comfortable life. We try not to bother each other,' she says without batting an eyelid.

'The old block,' I say.

'Yeah, like father, like son,' she says.

'So, he's not what you might call a pillar of the police community, then?'

'No, not exactly. But he's got his uses. I borrowed these last week and he doesn't seem to have missed them.' She holds up a set of lock picks like it's the most natural thing to have in her pocket.

'And not for the first time, by the look of it.'

'I've had a bit of practice,' she says, dismissing my look of stunned disbelief as if she just told me she sometimes likes to knit.

Déjà Vu

There's rubbish all over the floor: empty fast food cartons, Styrofoam cups and several free local newspapers, the ones full of adverts, still folded in half, unread. Tucked into one of them is a supermarket special offer sheet with glossy photos of baked bean tins and bargain basement garden tools. And scattered randomly among the rubbish is a collection of junk mail envelopes. Grace starts to gather some of them into a pile and puts them on the table.

'I wasn't expecting to start tidying up,' I say with a grin.

'I thought it might be worth flicking through them in case anything's been overlooked,' she says, and I go round and pick up the rest.

'You know last night, Grace?' I say from the other side of the table.

'Yes,' she says without looking up.

'You said about the camera being in here... in the kitchen... when I found it.' I'm tapping the table as I say it and she stops and slowly looks up. Without making eye contact, she shifts her gaze over my left shoulder.

'Yes,' she says. 'You said you saw it from outside. Presumably you meant from that window.'

'Yeah, that's right.' I turn around to look. 'It was that one.'

'Okay. Well I thought you said you saw it through the kitchen window. Didn't you?'

'Maybe. I don't think I said exactly where though.' I look down at the table but she doesn't seem to react.

'So...' she says, looking at me like I'm the one playing games. 'What?'

'It's nothing. I just couldn't remember saying where it was.'

'Maybe I just got the impression it was the kitchen.'

'It doesn't matter,' I say, wishing I hadn't brought it up. 'Forget I asked.'

'Your description was so vivid; it feels almost like I've been here before.' She smirks and returns to her envelopes.

'It must be this place. It keeps messing with my head,' I say and start looking through my handful. 'What are we looking for again?'

'Anything with a name on it would be a start.'

Although we're not planning on spending a lot of time sorting the mail, it's a welcome distraction from opening the inside door and stepping back into the Twilight Zone.

'It's Long isn't it?' Grace asks, sounding perplexed. 'His surname?'

I look across at what she's holding. I've already been through my bundle twice. They're either addressed anonymously to The Homeowner or not marked at all.

'Yes,' I reply hesitantly, wondering when I'd told her Herb's surname, and then feeling guilty for all my sudden doubts. 'Why, what have you found?'

'I think it's only marketing stuff but it's the only one here with a person's name.' She hands me the envelope.

'L. Anglich,' I pronounce aloud as if Grace hadn't been able to. 'It sounds German.'

'Hmm, could be anyone... Previous owner or tenant,' she says dismissively, and I shrug and drop the envelope back onto the floor where we've re-scattered the rest.

I open the doors at the base of the dresser and find it empty except for a large spider that disappears in a panic through a gap in the back quicker than I can close them again. The three narrow shelves above are covered in a thick layer of dust. The top two display a variety of old plates, like they were once part of a proud collection. On the bottom shelf is an assortment of crazed cups. There are circles and other disturbed areas of the surface where the dust has been smudged, suggesting recent activity. At one end is an old transistor radio and I notice the on button and volume knob have a slight shine compared to the other controls.

Careful not to disturb more dust with my gloved fingers, I twist the volume control down a quarter turn and push the button. Classical music briefly lights up the room as I return the volume to its previous level and turn it off again. I'm struck by the contrast that someone who occasionally uses this grimy little room for whatever dubious purpose does so to the gentle strains of concertos and sonatas.

At the other end of the shelf is a framed photograph of a young woman. It looks like it was taken in the seventies judging by the orange circles on the wallpaper behind her. As I reach for it, Grace touches my arm.

'Have you noticed how clean it is?' she says. 'It's the only thing that's been dusted.'

'Or maybe it's only recently been put in here,' I add, picking it up carefully and holding it so we can both look at it.

I would guess the woman is in her twenties. She's attractive with a fresh complexion. Her blonde hair is set into big ringlets and she's wearing a pale blue blouse with puffy shoulders and a ruffled neckline. Her warm smile balances out the gaudy background, and her big blue eyes seem to look through the photo at me.

Grace takes it from me and continues looking at it. I wonder if she's thinking what I am: such a lovely picture doesn't belong in this hideous place. She puts it back onto the shelf and looks away.

'I should probably warn you about this next bit,' I say, changing the mood.

'What about it?'

'Well, the last time I was in there, I thought...' I want to say I heard someone cry out, but I'm not ready to own up to that embarrassment yet.

'House of Horrors, you said.'

'Yeah... and it smelled pretty grim too. I hope your stomach

139

is stronger than mine.'

She braces herself as I pull the door open and we step into the next room. The first thing I notice is there's no bad smell. If anything there's a slightly pleasant odour. I look across to the door that was sealed last time and its bolts are still secured by two combination locks. On the other door, I expect to see the bolts drawn back, but they're also locked with the same heavy duty hardware. I walk towards the second chamber and the bitter-sweet scent of disinfectant seems stronger.

'What do you think these rooms are used for?' Grace is right by my side.

'I don't know. I was able to go inside this one before. It felt like a torture chamber and smelled like something had died in there.'

'Oh God,' she says.

'I didn't tell you before, it seemed too gruesome.' My mind tries to replay the moment I was standing alone in the dark, but here in the daylight I can't recreate the feeling. 'Now it just sounds pathetic.'

'No, Mickey,' she says, gently rubbing the back of my arm. 'It would have been really scary in here on your own at night. I remember the state you were in at The Feathers. Whatever that smell was, it really freaked you out didn't it?'

'Yeah, it wasn't only the stench,' I say, hesitating again, only this time unable to hold it back. 'When I went to close that metal door, it was so heavy that it slammed shut and I think someone heard me.'

'Why? What happened?'

'As I was about to get the hell out of here, I heard something. A woman's scream; crying out in despair. It sounded quite close but muffled like it came from that other room. I thought there was someone locked in there.'

I look back at Grace. She's pulled away from me and has her hand to her mouth and seems to be spluttering. I think she's going to be sick and I grab her arm. And then I see a glint in her eyes and a tear starting to run down her cheek and realise she's

140

actually trying to stifle a laugh. She senses my hurt feelings and turns away, before losing it completely and letting out a loud, high-pitched squeal. A sound that's strangely familiar.

'It wasn't funny, believe me,' I say.

'I'm sorry,' she says. 'Give me a minute and I'll be okay.' At that she rushes back out into the kitchen in fits of laughter.

I leave her to it and slope out into the hallway to nurse my fragile ego. The door to my left is closed. I remember it was the bathroom and I try to open it but it won't budge. The adjacent door, which must be to the front room, is also locked. Turning around I see the small side room where I'd made my exit. It looks the same in there, except the wardrobe doors are closed and the broken mirror is no longer scattered on the floor. I step across the sticky carpet towards the window and look at the nails, driven randomly through its frame and into the sill.

Grace is back behind me and the hand over her mouth is now just to fend off the damp mustiness that lingers in this part of the house.

'What was that all about?' I try to be the adult to her child, to hide my humiliation.

'I'm sorry. I wasn't laughing at you, honestly,' she says, but I'm not convinced. 'It was something else, really. I'll tell you about it later.'

'Yeah, whatever!' I revert back to a sulking teenager.

'Oh, don't be like that. I'll make it up to you, I promise.'

'Okay, you can start by seeing if you can unlock either of those doors.' I point back in the direction of the hallway.

Paper Cuts

We're sitting in a fancy café, a short walk from Bleak House. Grace has a skinny latte with a reduced-fat blueberry muffin on the side. I'm nursing the gravelly dregs of a double espresso. From the window I can see the end of the road with the tube station to one side. The road abruptly turns right at a low wall, above which a robust metal fence marks the perimeter of the over-ground railway line that cuts across, arrogantly claiming right of way. Through a similar fence on the other side of the track, I can see another diverted road, like a mirror image of this one. It's as if someone was meant to build a level crossing but forgot. Pedestrians can cross through the station underpass, whereas cars have to find a convoluted way around. I feel a bit like one of those cars right now.

'Another complete waste of time,' I say, fiddling idly with the empty sugar tube.

'At least we know someone's been in there cleaning things up a bit.'

'What? Like a nice Polish lady doing three hours a week?'

'No,' she says with a smirk, 'but that bathroom was spotless.'

'Yeah, as in clinically.'

'True,' she says. 'But I'm not sure men clean like that.' I'm about to protest, until I remember she's seen the state of my place.

'Maybe not. Either way, there certainly wasn't any sign of the gunge I saw last week,' I say, and keep the thought to myself of what it looked like in the dark.

'What about that front room?' she says, her voice slipping seamlessly into pretentious estate agent mode. 'Apart from its original period features, you'd have to say it had an air of understated decadence and a contemporary minimalist attitude.'

'Thank you Lloyd Grossman,' I chirp back. 'But yeah... one chair, a lamp and a pair of curtains. You certainly couldn't say the place had a lived-in quality.'

'And every room upstairs, completely empty.' She nods sagely. 'Not a carpet between them and all the windows whitewashed.'

'So all we've gained is the recent odour of bleach and a name that's almost certainly a red herring.' I'm feeling despondent again. I suppose I'd hoped we might find something of Herb's there, but there was absolutely no sign of him having been there, of his own accord or otherwise. Having seen those people breeze out of there a couple of days ago is starting to feel like a dream, or perhaps just a brief moment of respite in the middle of a nightmare.

'Yeah, but don't forget about the photograph,' Grace pulls me back with a jolt. I'd completely forgotten.

'You're right; it's got to have been the most significant thing in there. I wish we'd taken a closer look. There might have been something written on the back.'

'Do people even do that anymore?' she says and I shrug.

'Unlikely,' I say. 'Given my recent luck.'

'That must make me your lucky charm!' She reaches into her coat lining and, with a proud grin, hands me a photo frame, wrapped loosely in a glossy supermarket broadsheet.

'Hey! Welcome to my world of grand larceny.' I perk up instantly as if the coffee just kicked in. 'That'll set the cat amongst the pigeons.'

'Do you think?'

'Well, someone's going to be really pissed off about it going missing, that's for sure.' I'm already unclipping the back of the frame. I assume the clips must originally have been too loose because someone's used a folded sheet of newspaper to pad out the gap between the photo and the backing. I let the paper fall onto the table and turn the print over, but my hopes are dashed because the back is blank.

'Oh my God.' I hear Grace's voice and look up. Her face has turned white. She's unfolded the newspaper clipping and is still reading it.

'What is it?' I say. She doesn't seem to hear me and turns the page over. She finishes reading and hands it to me.

It's the front page of the *Epping Forest Evening News* dated Tuesday, 6th December 1983. I read the day's leading story:

FATAL COLLISION: 'A TRAGIC ACCIDENT'

Essex Police have today dismissed earlier speculation that yesterday's high-speed car crash on the Epping Road was the result of drink-driving. One woman died in the head-on collision that happened in the early hours of Monday morning on the A414, east of Epping. The condition of a second woman, believed to have been conscious on arrival at the Princess Alexandra Hospital, Harlow, is reported to have deteriorated overnight. She has since undergone emergency surgery at the Essex Neurosciences Unit at Queens Hospital, Romford where she remains in intensive care. A spokeswoman for the ENU this afternoon described her condition as critical. Police are yet to release the names of the two women, both believed to be in their mid-twenties, and of a third person, a man, who was also involved in the incident. The man escaped with injuries described as serious but not life-threatening and is recovering at Princess Alexandra Hospital.

In a police statement issued today, the traffic officer first on the scene has confirmed the drivers of both cars were women. It remains uncertain whether either driver had been wearing a seat belt, however, preliminary tests have now ruled out alcohol as a factor in the collision, whilst the poor road conditions at the time are considered likely to have played a significant part. The accident happened at a notorious black spot along a remote stretch of the road that runs from Chelmsford to Harlow. The police statement did confirm that the male passenger, whose injuries were less severe, had been wearing a seat belt.

Describing it as a tragic accident, Clive Armstrong, Police Commander of the Epping Forest District, took the opportunity, in keeping with the Department of Transport's national 'Clunk, Click, every trip' campaign message, to stress the importance of wearing seat belts for even the shortest journey.

At the bottom of the article there's a footnote link to an editorial on page 1. I turn the paper over and find it at the bottom of the left column.

Apology – Fatal Accident

Yesterday's editorial referred to allegations purporting to relate to the driver of one of the vehicles involved in the fatal collision in the early hours of Monday morning. It was reported that a man, seen drinking heavily during an after-hours lock-in at The Wheat Sheaf public house near the village of Stapleford Tawney, had driven away at high speed with a female passenger in a white Astra GTE at around 1:30am, shortly before the crash happened. The editorial noted that The Wheat Sheaf is less than four miles from the scene of the collision and that the description of the vehicle matched one of the cars involved. The eye-witness account was believed to have originated from a reliable source.

Following the release of new information, confirming that the drivers of both vehicles were women, Essex Police are treating these accusations as malicious and we are assisting them with their enquiries into this aspect of their investigation. The Epping Forest Evening News accepts that in reporting these claims, it fell short of its usual rigorous standards of journalism and regrets any implied credibility that its editorial may have given to these unfounded allegations. We apologise unreservedly for any distress caused to the victims and their families.

'Wow!' I say, putting the newspaper down. 'I've never heard of Stapleford Tawney, have you?' I look across at Grace who's studying the loose photograph intently. I wait for her to look up. When she does her eyes are glazed.

'What is it?' I ask. 'Does she look familiar?'

'You tell me,' she says, holding the photo alongside her face. I'm drawn more to her expression than the photograph. Her mouth is trembling and her eyes are watery.

'Grace?'

She closes her eyes and tears roll down her face. 'I think it could be my mum,' she says.

Come Again

We manage to find a pub open nearby and I settle Grace into a quiet alcove. She sips at the whisky I've bought her in the hope it will help snap her back into life. She's not said a word since I took the photo from her and replaced it in the frame. She held out her hand and I gave it back. She wrapped it carefully in the advertisement and put it back inside her jacket. She's still holding the newspaper article. I decide it's probably best to wait for her to speak, and so we've sat here for a good ten minutes.

'I've only ever been told,' she finally whispers, 'about a car accident. And that she didn't survive.'

'Didn't you say you were put into care from birth?' I'm trying desperately to understand why she sees such an unlikely connection with the photograph. I'm no expert in psychology. If I was I might wonder if this could be a manifestation of the symptoms of a life with no family and a childhood spent in orphanages and foster homes. Or consider that maybe any tenuous link to a mother she's never met could provoke this kind of reaction. Or be concerned perhaps that she regularly seizes on even the remotest possibility in the hope it might provide clues to her own identity. But like I said, I'm no expert and, although I want to comfort her, at the same time I'd prefer not to say anything to validate what seems to me an irrational conclusion. However, at the same time, I can no longer ignore the screaming voice in my own head, insisting on the resemblance between Grace and the woman in the photo.

'I was told she was six months pregnant,' she says without looking up. 'I was delivered by caesarean while a machine kept her alive.'

'Why would her photo be in that house?' As soon as I say it the thought occurs to me: why wouldn't it? I've already found photos of Grace in there, but she doesn't seem to hear me. She stares into space and carries on talking in a low voice.

'My whole life I've struggled to understand how an unborn baby could have survived that. People talk about miracles, but there were times when I wished I'd died with her, when I thought I didn't deserve to live because she died without ever knowing me.'

'It's okay. This is all a horrible coincidence. Don't let it upset you.' I can tell she's still not listening, but then she looks at me and smiles.

'Somewhere along the way, I started to realise how lucky I was. She died so young, but I'd lived for a reason. To her, my life would have been precious; she'd been alive long enough for me to come into the world. I started to believe I could let her live through me and so I decided to cherish my life and to live it to the full. I at least owed her that.'

I want to ask her what makes her think this is her mother. To say there's no reference in the newspaper to a baby. To point out the date that doesn't even coincide with her birthday. To tell her all the reasons why it's unlikely there's any connection between her and this woman. Instead I move my chair closer and embrace her, and that seems to break the spell.

'Mickey,' she says, looking deep into my eyes. 'There's more I need to tell you.'

'I'm not going anywhere,' I say. 'Take your time, sweetie.'

'I really like you a lot,' she says and I notice one of her eyelids flicker.

'I like you too Grace.' Even in my confusion I want to pinch myself, because I still can't believe a girl like her would make all the running for a bloke like me.

'It wasn't supposed to be like this,' she says. Her eyes are more intense than ever and I stare back into them waiting for her to elaborate, but she seems unsure how to continue.

'It wasn't supposed to be like what?'

'I didn't plan to get so...' she pauses, 'involved. I mean... emotionally.'

'So what did you plan?' I sit back into the seat, picking up on her anxiety, still with no idea what she's getting at.

'Mickey, please don't hate me,' she says. Her head tilts slightly to one side and half a smile settles on her face. I look back bemused and let her continue. 'I'm sorry about my fit of giggles earlier,' she says. I've completely forgotten about it and I'm relieved that's all she's worrying about.

'Grace, if I hated you every time you laughed at me, I don't suppose we'd be getting on so well.'

'Yeah, you're probably right,' she says. 'What I was going to say was the reason I couldn't stop laughing earlier was because it may have been me who spooked you. That night you thought you heard a scream from the dungeon.'

'What?' I say, my narrowing eyes betraying the turmoil in my head.

'I was there.'

'I don't get it. You were where?'

'At the house.'

'What, in that room?' I say in disbelief.

'No, not in the room, I was outside, at that kitchen window.' She grimaces as if bracing herself for my reaction.

'Grace, what are you talking about? What's going on?'

'I followed you. I watched you go inside the house. I saw you come into the kitchen and go straight to the table. You went back through the house and there was a loud bang. It made me jump and I fell into the bushes and screamed. I think that's what you heard.' She's looking down at the table again, but no longer in self-pity. She's hanging her head in shame.

'You followed me? You didn't even know me then...' The thought trails off to the obvious conclusion she must have tracked me back to The Feathers too. I see a rabbit staring mesmerised into oncoming lights.

'I'm sorry,' she says.

'Why Grace? What the hell are you up to? What have you got to do with all this?' Other questions come fast and furious in my head before she's even started on these ones.

'Please don't be angry. I want to tell you everything. I don't want to deceive you anymore. Like I said, I wasn't planning on getting this close. Now I have I don't want to hurt you. Please let me explain.' I've already grabbed my coat from the back of the chair and start getting up.

'No, please don't go. I can explain everything,' she says, reaching across and holding my arm. I stare back coldly into frightened eyes that plead for me to stay.

'I'll get us another drink,' she says. 'Please sit down.' I drop back into the chair as if hypnotised by her touch.

'Mickey, I need to visit the ladies first. Please wait.' Her words are like white noise and she's just a blur as she gets up and walks away.

She's been gone no more than a couple of minutes and I'm still slumped in the chair, jacket in hand, not wanting to stay but unable to move when I feel a tap on the shoulder. I assume it's her checking what I want to drink and I struggle momentarily with the idea that I'm actually not thirsty. Before I can finish the thought and turn around a familiar voice whispers in my ear.

'Hello Mickey, lad. Let's go somewhere we can talk.'

10.

Long Division

I follow Herb from the pub and around the side to where a silver Mercedes is waiting in the car park. We both get in the back and it pulls away sedately without a word to the driver. I'm sitting behind him and can see his massive scalp sprouting short, spiky hair that teases the car's roof lining like a wire brush to a peach. I don't have a clue where we're going and so far I've been unable to say anything intelligible, even though I have a thousand questions.

Moments ago I was stunned by Grace's revelation she'd been following me around before engineering our first and, I had to assume, subsequent encounters. That shock, followed by feelings of relief and then anger at seeing Herb, seem to have counteracted each other and I'm left in a strange, inanimate limbo. I suppose all will be revealed so I say nothing and wait for him to speak. Instead, he gets his phone out and makes a call.

I must be so out of it, my mind doesn't even register surprise when it's a foreign language he starts conversing in. Every now and again he seems to struggle and resorts back to English for a particular word or phrase, but not enough for me to get any sense of who he's talking to and what about. All I can do is stare out of the window. Unable to focus on the landscape flashing past in a blur, I soon lose all sense of direction. Within half an hour we're pulling off a quiet road in the middle of nowhere into a secluded driveway leading through trees and dense shrubs to a rambling country house I couldn't see from the road. When the car eases to a halt outside the gabled stone porch, Herb finishes his call and my frustration boils over.

'Herb! What the f—'

'All in good time, Michael. All in good time.' He cuts me off as he gets out of the car, walks to the porch and unlocks the heavy wooden door, leading me inside to a cavernous panelled hall. To the left, a sweeping oak staircase leads onto a balconied mezzanine. Straight ahead, a corridor extends off towards the rear of the building, reduced to little more than a passageway by the stacks of boxes lining the walls on both sides.

'You'll have to excuse the state of the place,' he says, without any sense of irony, as he opens an ornately moulded door to the right. I follow him into a large square room with a vaulted ceiling, stone fireplace and frescoed walls, decorated tastefully with assorted works of classical art that Grace's Mr Johnson would no doubt have died for. He sits down in a leather smoking chair at one side of the hearth and expects me to take the one opposite. I stay on my feet. When he looks up at me the shadow of a grin flits across his face and he holds out his palms in a conciliatory gesture. That's when I notice his hand no longer shakes.

'Who was that with you?' he says with convincing indifference. It's the last question I'm expecting and I immediately feel protective of the girl who's just admitted screwing me over.

'Don't you think you owe me some *answers* before you start asking the questions,' I snap back.

'Yes. I suppose you deserve that,' he says. 'I haven't been totally straight with you.'

'Well that sure as hell goes without saying.' I raise my voice to bolster my confidence, but in these surroundings Herb is self-assured, and I feel more than a little intimidated.

'It's all right, lad, you're entitled to be angry.' He nods respectfully enough, but he may just as easily be taunting me.

'I thought you were in danger. I was worried about you.'

'That's very touching Mickey,' he says, putting his hand across his heart. 'Really it is. But you know, it doesn't pay to get too emotional in this business.' He looks at me calmly, in control, his eyes brighter, alert, his hair darker, oiled and neatly parted on the side, the lines on his face relaxed. He looks ten years younger.

'Don't patronise me, Herb,' I say. 'I've been all over the place looking for you. I didn't need any of this; it's not what I agreed...'

'You agreed...' he cuts me off, 'because you owed me and because you wanted it. End of story. I may have laid on the hard luck story a bit thick, but at the end of the day if I thought you were doing this out of sympathy, I would have pulled the plug. Your initial reaction was the rational one I'd expected, and I would have left you alone if that had been your final answer. That would have confirmed you were out of the game for good. When you left the door open... I knew you still wanted in.'

He's right and we both know it. It's like he's holding a mirror to my face and the ugly truth burns like acid on my skin.

'Maybe I did,' I say. 'But when are you going to tell me what the hell this is all about?' I struggle to maintain my glare into his eyes, and yet when he locks onto mine I can't pull away, even if I want to.

'And when are *you* going to realise that Grace holds the key to all this?' His words are a quiet, calm punch to my stomach.

'You already know her name,' I concede, groping for fragments of sense.

'Okay, so it *was* her with you back there,' he says with a stinging smile. 'It's been a few years since I've seen her. She was little more than a child. Even then she was beginning to blossom.'

I want to ask why he's so interested in her, to defend her. As confusion and doubt collide violently in my head, realisation begins to dawn: between the two of them I'm caught in a web of lies and deceit. I finally sit down, crushed.

'I did what you wanted,' I say. 'Exactly what you wanted.'

'Credit where it's due, Mickey. You did the job.'

'I did get a buzz,' I find myself saying.

'That's more like it, lad.'

'I've named it Bleak House. That dump you sent me to,' I say, and a wry smile relaxes the muscles in my neck.

'It's a place we use occasionally. You know… for storage.' He says it slowly and deliberately, accenting the last word with a knowing glint, getting the reaction he's looking for, my eyes betraying the shudder rippling up my spine. 'Clearly it's not my usual home comforts,' he adds, proudly looking around the room.

'Smelled like someone… had died in there,' I say, and a frown momentarily furrows his brow. 'I even went back because I thought you might have been locked up in there. Instead, that must have been you who came swanning out the front door as I was leaving. All that, and for what? You were just *testing* me?'

'I needed to know if you still had it in you,' he says, 'or if all that banking had made you soft. I needn't have worried. You passed with flying colours. It was like you'd never been away.'

'So, why the camera?'

'Did you develop the film?' he says.

'Yes.'

'Is that what led you to her?' He's sitting forward in the chair. The question repeats itself in my head. Is that what he'd wanted? Was that his plan all along?

'No, not exactly.'

'We knew Gravesend was an obvious target so we started clearing out.' He pauses and smiles. 'That's when I found that old thing. I was going to throw it away. Don't know why I kept it really… stupid… after all those years…'

I want to ask where he got it from, did he know it was hers, was he the one who took the last photo and then stole it, could he even be the…

'Millennium Pervert.' The words I thought were confined to my head escape my mouth in a whisper.

'What's that?' he says.

'Nothing,' I say. I think I get away with it and decide to keep my own counsel for the time being. I'm feeling so confused about Grace right now, I don't think I even care if he was. Questions that seemed so important an hour ago now go unasked as Herb continues.

'Well, as I was saying, it was pure chance I got chatting to your old dear. She told me your news and I saw an opportunity to help you out.'

'To help *me*?' I say with a nervous laugh. 'By sending me on a wild goose chase?'

'You make enemies in this game...' he says, his face setting like concrete. 'Rivals that will literally steal your business and leave you for dead. It was a matter of time before they'd make their move. But with you on board, we could push back; maybe even recover some lost ground. In time, you could take the lead. One day, we might even be able to take down the whole corrupt empire.' I stare back at him, not knowing whether to be flattered or terrified.

'So why is Grace in the middle of all this?'

'Oh, that was unexpected,' he says. 'I needed to see what you'd do when I had to go to ground, so I had you watched. At first you did all the right things. Then I started getting reports you were sleeping with the enemy.'

'No,' I say. Although I'm shocked to hear he's been watching me, my head is shaking, because I can't believe he's got it so wrong about Grace. 'She thinks she's your daughter.'

'Don't get taken in lad,' he says. 'She's a clever girl, I'll grant her that. Precocious. And cunning. Just like her father.'

'She told me she was adopted,' I say.

'All I'm saying,' he says, hands outstretched with the innocence of Fagin, 'is a bad apple doesn't fall far from the tree. And her old man's the one you should be worried about. He's corrupt and contemptible. He conspired to ruin my life and he *will* pay for it. I'll destroy his family and then I'll destroy him. As for you, you'd do well not to get in the way.'

'I really think you've got it all wrong about her.'

'There you go again,' he says, and just I shake my head as he continues. 'The one thing I've always been concerned about with you, Mickey. You can't stop yourself getting emotionally involved. And here you are again, on the wrong side.'

'What do you mean, again?'

'Oh, I think you know what I mean, lad.' He sneers at me and I have to look away. 'Anyway, it was a big disappointment... at first. And then I remembered where I got that old camera, and maybe it all started making sense. More importantly, it gives you a way back.'

'So, let's just assume I *did* find her,' I say, trying to shift the balance of power by playing along with him. 'What do you want me to do with her?'

'Well,' he pauses, as if thinking aloud. 'As she's joined the game, I'd like you to bring her to me. Not yet. I'll let you know when and where. In the meantime, keep her on a short leash.'

'What do you want her for?' I stare back at him.

'That's not your concern, lad.' He's starting to sound very sinister and I'm struggling to keep up with him, but he just keeps talking. 'How much does she know?'

'I thought it best not to tell her anything until I had some idea of what was going on,' I say, trying hard to maintain eye contact.

'Good, you've done well. I'm glad I bumped into you today.'

'I don't suppose that was down to luck, either.' He smiles and I imagine him in the pub earlier, waiting out of sight for Grace to step away before making his big entrance. It occurs to me for the first time how pissed off she must have been when she got back from the ladies. Truth be told, I can't find much sympathy for her right now. 'So who torched your old house?'

'Oh, I've got a pretty good idea.' He stands up and walks to the drinks table in the centre of the room. With his eyes finally off me I relax back into the chair and the embrace of soft-padded leather emboldens me to tell him something he doesn't already know.

'Someone answered your phone... that night.' He spins on his heels and stares at me, eyes bulging.

'You spoke to him... what did you say?'

'Oh, nothing really,' I say, defensively. 'I thought it was

you... I think I just mentioned the camera and that I had it...'

'You didn't give him your name?'

'Uh... I don't think so... I, uh... really can't remember. I was quite drunk...'

'You need to keep your guard up, lad.' He raises his fists momentarily in a southpaw stance and then lets them drop before adding: 'You'd better let me know if you hear from him again.'

'Who is he, Herb?'

'Oh, don't concern yourself. For the moment that's my problem, not yours.' He looks into thin air like he's weighing up what else to tell me. 'Suffice to say, we were on the same side back at the start. Before... things went bad. Ancient history. Before your time, lad. Should have gone down... instead he sets up on his own and he's been pushing me hard ever since.' His voice drops almost to a whisper: 'That bastard ruined everything. I won't let him do that again.'

'Is he dangerous?'

'No...' he says dismissively enough but turns away so I can't judge his expression. He starts pouring drinks from a crystal decanter. 'No more than an occupational hazard, lad. No harm done. We'd already wound down the operations at the old place.'

'Operations?' I say, trying to sound surprised whilst thinking back to all the stuff I'd seen in his garage.

He comes back with two large blown glasses and hands one to me. The woody aroma of cognac is seductive, but I resist the desire to drink and limit my appreciation to swirling it around.

'You know as well as I do, lad, it used to be a lucrative trade... back in *your* day.' He dismisses my puzzled frown with a smirk and adds, 'It's much harder now. A lot more people involved. It's global these days, what with the Internet. Demand outstrips supply. The stakes have never been higher... And that, lad is what makes it a *nasty* business.'

'So you were lucky,' I say, mesmerised as much by his entrepreneurial zeal as by the whirlpool of liquor in my glass. 'Getting out of there just in time.'

156

'Moved everything. Memories and all.'

'You lived there a long time. And… with your wife before.'

'It's like I said…' I think I hear a crack in his speech until he clears his throat and raises his voice, forcing me to look up at him. 'You can't afford to get emotional. Not in this business. It makes you complacent and that makes you weak.'

'Mum saw you shipping out the evening it burned down.'

'Yes. I know.'

'And at the bank a couple of days before.'

'I didn't mean to be rude, but I did want to keep my distance. I wouldn't want her getting mixed up in something like this, after what she's been through. She deserves better.'

'She's been worried about you too.'

'She's a good woman. I'll miss her.'

'So that's it, you've left Gravesend for good?' He nods back at me. 'I'm sorry,' I say and I mean it.

'Don't worry, those bastards will get what's coming to them soon enough. I'm sorry it meant I had to go to ground for a few days and that left you hanging in the wind.'

'I'm okay,' I say, nodding back with equal sincerity.

'Stroke of luck about the girl, though,' he says. 'It'll be useful to find out what she knows.'

'Really?' The word comes out like a squeak and I try to disguise it by gulping down the brandy, grateful at least for its instant burn.

'Hmm, we'll see,' he says, while I try to stop my pupils dilating too much. 'Anyway, no real harm done, eh?' He gestures around the room. 'I'm still doing okay. What do you think?'

He starts making small talk about the opulence of his second home. It seems this magnificent country pile, a stone's throw from civilisation, has been a regular retreat for a number of years, and has recently become his permanent residence. He offers to show me around, says he's got a games room, even suggests a frame of snooker but I decline. Pool's more my game.

As much as I would love to learn more about his mysterious alter-life, there are only so many surprises I can take

157

in one day, and I'm keen to get out of here. I need time to think and I'm finding it difficult to keep up this act of being at one with Herb when I don't know what his intentions are towards Grace. I find myself fearing the worst, given that he must have watched and photographed her as a fifteen year old, and seems to have used me to find her. To keep the pretence going I have one last question.

'My little challenge may have all been a game to you,' I say. 'To me it was a job and I...' He's seen where I'm heading and cuts me off before I get there.

'Ah yes, your banker's bonus. Let's discuss settling our mutual obligations once you've met the final deliverable, shall we?' There's a menacing grin on his face, and I remember there are always two ways of taking Herb's words.

'I didn't sign up to...' He raises a hand to bat away my protest.

'Don't ruin it now lad, when you're so close.'

'Still being tested, right?' I say, and he nods. I wonder whether he'll pay up in the end. Then again, whether I deliver Grace to him is another matter entirely. At least he doesn't seem to have missed the large wad of cash I took.

'Okay...' I say. 'We'll see. Right now, if it's alright with you, I'd like to be off home.'

'Mac?' Herb calls out and his driver looms into the doorway like a solar eclipse. 'Take young Mickey home, will you. And let him have the phone number here.'

The Giant turns and leaves without a grunt, and I get up to follow him.

'So what happens next, Herb?'

'I'll call you lad... when we're ready.'

During the journey home, with the incongruous strains of Scheherazade wafting from the speakers, I sit in the back seat and ponder the irony that while Grace was following me, Herb's been watching us both. It comes as no real surprise when Mac the Chauffeur doesn't need to ask for my address or directions.

He drops me off and my wits return like I've been snapped out of a trance. I memorise the licence plate as he drives away.

Keeping Mum

Back home, I've just put down my mobile. Grace didn't answer and I'm guessing that's because she's pissed off with me. Right now, I don't know how I feel about her.

Before getting her voicemail, I was going to apologise and tell her about Herb's reappearance. Instead I left a terse message telling her that something came up and I had to dash out of the pub. I need to keep her on the hook, or should that be a short leash? Not least because there are too many missing pieces to this jigsaw puzzle and I need to figure out what to do next before Herb contacts me again.

I've decided that, for the time-being, it's better for her to think she's pissed me off while I try to figure out where my loyalties lie. I guess she'll call me back when she's ready. I hope she does anyway.

I'm thinking about getting some food together for dinner when the landline rings. It can only be Mum.

'Michael,' she says without her usual greeting. 'That policewoman just came back with a detective.' Hairs stand up on the back of my neck.

'What did they want?' I say, breathing heavily.

'They said they were following up on the statement I gave about seeing Herb the other night. They wanted to know if I'd seen a girl or a young woman with shoulder-length blonde hair acting suspiciously near the house when I walked past.'

'What?'

'Yes, and when I said no, they asked if I'd passed the house earlier in the day when I might have noticed her then.'

I slump down onto a kitchen stool and picture Grace snooping around outside Herb's house, having followed me there. This morning the thought would have been absurd. Now anything's possible.

159

'Of course, I *had* to tell them you'd been down that day, didn't I?' she continues, and without giving me the chance to react, adds: 'I said we'd done some shopping and on the way back we stopped off at Gladys Wilmott's before driving past the house. I told them we didn't see anyone hanging around.'

'It's okay Mum, that's true, we didn't.'

'But then they asked for your name, address and phone number. Oh, I hope you don't mind Mickey. They said they might contact you and if I spoke to you first could I ask you to think about it and if you remembered seeing someone to contact them.'

'Don't worry, leave this to me. We've got nothing to hide.'

'Have you got a pen? I'll give you the number. His card says he's Detective Sergeant Melville.'

I don't know why I'm writing this down. It's not like I'm going to be phoning the Old Bill. And if they call me, I'll tell them I didn't see any girl near the house. I'll be telling the truth and that'll be the end of it.

'Oh, there was one other thing,' Mum adds.

'What other thing?'

'The woman said she remembered seeing you at the gate the last time she called in. She said I was very lucky to have a son who would come to see me so often. I knew it was just flannel, especially when she asked if you'd stopped overnight. I told her you hadn't and then she asked if you usually came to see me that often every week. I said no, not every week.'

By now, I'm cringing and starting to convince myself they must have my handwritten note, and before long they'll be more interested in my visits to see Herb than in my caring son routine.

'What did she say to that?'

'Just more nonsense; about me deserving to have such a good son.'

'Was that it?'

'Well, apart from the detective asking as they were leaving how well you know Herb.'

'Huh?' I say a bit too high-pitched as my foot slips from the rung of the stool.

'I told him you knew him as a neighbour but you've been living north of the river for a long time.' I calm down momentarily, until she adds: 'Then he asked if it was possible you might have seen him recently.'

'What did you say?'

'I said I thought he might have been in touch with you, although I didn't think you'd met him. That's right isn't it?'

'And did that shut him up?'

'No, he suddenly seemed more interested that you'd driven down here on Thursday *and* Friday without stopping over. I started to feel a bit threatened. It was like he was suggesting you'd not actually gone back home.'

'Bastard,' I mouthed silently. 'You told him I did though, yeah?'

'I might have got a bit too defensive. I said there was a whole group of friends could vouch for you drinking with them in Hornchurch that night.'

'That's right Mum. You told him!' I say, impressed by her quick wits.

'Yes I did. Coming round here, drinking my tea and making wild inferences about my boy.'

'Then what happened?'

'He started repeating what the woman said; that you must be a good son to drive back down to see me again early the next morning. Then he said all sarcastic like, 'especially with a hangover'. Well, I was livid. I said you came back because you were concerned with what I'd said about Herb the day before and wanted to make sure he was okay.'

'You didn't?'

'I know. It just came out. I was only trying to say you were a good person. Oh, I hope I didn't say the wrong thing Michael.'

'Then what?'

'All of a sudden they needed to leave. I just thought you should know.'

'Thanks Mum,' is all I can manage as I put the phone down.

Park Life

The only food in the fridge is a ready meal and the dessert from Saturday. The chilled spag bol is on its last day; the mascarpone is starting to ferment. I stab the film lid and put the plastic tray of pasta in the microwave. The Harrods cheesecake goes in the bin. What a bloody waste of money.

Quality pasta with a rich, authentic sauce should be accompanied by a good Chianti, but a small bottle of Stella is all this one deserves. I put the piping hot food on a tray with the beer and four slices of bread and butter and take it into the lounge where I turn on the TV. *Crimewatch* is on BBC, showing a reconstruction of a recent aggravated burglary, and I flick over to ITV only to see two coppers chasing a bloke down a dark alley in *The Bill*. I hit the standby button and finish the meal in silence. Cradling the half-empty bottle, I reflect on the fact it's a brew with a reputation. Some people call it wife-beater. But I never laid a finger on her.

With the fork in the sink and the plastic tray and bottle in the recycle bin, I put on my jacket. I need a walk so I can think, make some sense of the last week. I pick up the mobile phone by instinct and then throw it back on the sofa. Right now, there's no one in the world I want to talk to. As I turn the corner at the end of the street, a keen breeze wipes my face. It feels good to breathe it in and I stride on towards the park.

I used to believe problem-solving was a logical and conscious process: you consider all the facts one by one, analysing each element before taking them all together and concluding which one, or which combination, is at fault. You then make adjustments to the erroneous components, re-run the scenario and validate the results. That's how I used to think. Correction, that's how The Banker thinks. Now I just switch off and walk. Somehow the thinking seems to do itself.

I suppose it's since I've had time on my hands, but I find the sub-conscious mind is so much better at sorting things out, left alone to ruminate. Right now, I don't need to run through all the events of the last seven days to scrutinise the facts I know and identify the ones I don't. I don't have to replay the conversations and assess the things that have been said in order to articulate in my head the things that haven't. I don't even find it necessary to separate out what I understand from what I don't. My subconscious mind already knows it all. It doesn't have to systematically sort and file it in an efficient, organised chronology. Its approach is more holistic. Organic. The only input it needs from me is time. So I leave it to do its thing and I just walk.

Harrow Lodge Park is a haven for ducks and dog-walkers, but this late in the day, both have retreated to the safety of whatever they consider home, to avoid their respective predators that lurk in the shadows here at dusk. I stick to the illuminated paths but only to limit my risk of stepping in crap, not because *I'm* afraid of the foxes and the muggers. I head in the general direction of a modest tuft of trees in the far corner, growing around a stagnant pond that seemingly sprung from the ground one day, full of relief and hope, only to find nowhere to run. I know how it must have felt.

The trees bend and sway in the wind and I lose myself in clouds that spread like drops in the water of a blood-stained sky. And as the light fades, I sit on a bench and watch the remnants of colour being reclaimed by the horizon. My subconscious seems to like the darkness. I can sense it shifting a gear as the visual distractions are extinguished. It works better; preferring the low volume hum of the sprawling city at night in its subservience to the sounds of nature. It thrives on the heightened awareness of the damp smell of evening and the cold air on my face. I sit here for an hour, maybe two, maybe longer. I don't know. But strangely, I *do* know when it's okay for my conscious mind to re-take control and I head home, finally knowing whose side I'm on.

When I get there I'm greeted by the chirp of my mobile. It wants to tell me I've missed a call from Grace de M. I can't remember what the M stands for and wonder how a little English orphan girl got such an exotic name. Without dwelling on it, I dial 121 to check if there's a message. This time the voice sounds smug when it tells me there isn't. Perhaps one day they'll programme these robots with a bit more empathy. My disappointment is short-lived because the door bell rings and when I answer it Grace de M is standing on the step. Her uneasy smile reflects back my own conflicted sense of relief and suspicion, and I invite her in with a silent nod.

'I've been worried about you,' she says as I take her coat. She smells fantastic. And she has the black dress on again.

'I thought we could rewind to Saturday night,' she says. 'See if we can run the last few days again... only differently.'

I try to keep a neutral look on my face, although my mind is bouncing off the walls. I had intended to make her suffer, to show her I was mad. I was going to threaten to send her away and to make her beg for my forgiveness. This was going to be my only chance to come out on top, take charge and put her in her place.

I just hadn't reckoned on the black dress.

She knows I'm crumbling and moves towards me. I step back and try to recover my composure but she's already won. I draw deep on my reserves and hold up a hand in a half-hearted rebuttal.

'Grace,' I whisper with a last semblance of willpower. 'If you think you can breeze back in here and start again where we left off on Saturday night, there's one thing you should know...'

Momentarily, the spark has gone from her eyes and her features have dropped. She looks plain, a mere mortal, an extra on life's stage. And for once, for a fleeting second I've got her.

'The cheesecake's dead!'

I keep up the poker face until gradually her eyes light up again and she laughs, resuming her rightful place with the gods. I wink down at her and she launches herself at me and we hold each other in a passionate embrace.

'I'm so sorry,' she says. 'I thought I'd lost you. I can't do this without you.'

'You're not getting rid of me that easily,' I say. 'But you've got a lot of explaining to do.'

'I know. I know. That's why I'm here. Let's go and sit down.' She leads me towards the lounge but I make a quick detour, directing her to the kitchen. We emerge with a bottle of Crianza, a corkscrew and two glasses and she settles onto the sofa.

'Before we start,' I say, 'have you got work tomorrow? It's already getting late and I don't want you driving home after a couple of these, especially as we've been up since dawn.'

'Don't worry about me; I had my beauty sleep earlier. I only have a couple of appointments in the afternoon,' she says. 'So, if that was an invitation to stay the night, I would love to.'

I think I'm the one in desperate need of beauty sleep, but for the moment I'm feeling wide-awake. I only hope the wine doesn't knock me out too soon.

Dedicated Follower

'It was almost a year ago,' she says, staring deep into the crimson well at the bottom of her glass. 'I decided to try and find my real father. I didn't get very far to begin with.'

'I thought they've made it a lot easier these days,' I say, although I don't know why I think that. To be honest I don't know anything about it so I decide to shut up and let her talk.

'Maybe,' she says. 'I don't think my heart was really in it at first. I suppose I was too afraid of what I might find. I wrote all these crazy emails to people I didn't even know, not really expecting any replies. When I kept coming back to the same dead end, it was the easy option just to give up. But then, a few months ago, completely out of the blue, I got a letter from a retired care worker. She said she was at the home I first went to as a baby and someone had sent her a copy of my message. She remembered me and said she recalled there being an address on the original paperwork that had arrived with me from the hospital, which was where my parents were living immediately before I was born. The reason it stuck in her memory, she said, was that she'd been so sad for me that it was the only time she ever broke the rules and sent a personal letter. I was still just a baby and she wanted to see if she could change my father's mind. She said she was sorry but the letter came back marked: return to sender. She also warned me that his surname might be different. It seems they used to let the birth parents change it to make it harder for them to be traced later.'

'Oh, right,' I say, slightly shocked but also glad of the explanation for her unusual name. 'That explains a lot.' Grace flashes me a knowing smile and continues.

'She offered to help me submit a formal request,' she says, 'and shortly afterwards the address was sent to me. It was in Gravesend.'

'My home town,' I say, surprised at the coincidence, but Grace doesn't seem to hear me.

'I thought it would be a red herring,' she says. 'It seemed so unlikely my father would still be living in the same house. But I decided to go there anyway. If nothing else I would get to see where my parents lived when I was conceived.'

The bottle's standing unfinished on the coffee table and Grace picks it up to refill our glasses. Mine's still half full. I'm trying to keep a clear head so I can take in what she's telling me and weigh it up against the conversation I had with Herb earlier.

'I drove down there twice to watch the house but each time it seemed to be deserted. The third time I decided I'd go and knock on the door, but as I approached I saw a big van backed up to the garage and lost my nerve. An hour later it was still there, but as I walked past, a young guy got into the front and drove away.'

'Don't tell me, the garage door closed before you had a chance to see inside?' I say and she nods back unfazed by my clairvoyance.

'I wondered what was going on, so I drove around and parked along the street. I sat there for half an hour, pretending to read the paper, and finally a car pulled up outside and a man, probably in his sixties, and very dapper with it, came out of the house and got into the car and it was driven away. It all happened so fast; all I could do was watch. Anyway I sat there a while longer and when nothing else happened I came home.'

'You know that was Herb, don't you?' I say, and again she doesn't answer.

'Back home, the more I thought about him, the more he looked familiar, but I couldn't place him.' She stops and drinks more of her wine. I notice she's had half the bottle already. I've hardly touched mine. 'I couldn't get him out of my head so I decided to make one last trip. It was early morning a couple of weeks ago. This time I wouldn't hesitate. I was going to park right outside and go straight up and bang the door. As I drove towards the house, I saw another younger man walking up the front path. This time there wasn't a van at the garage door and it looked like this guy had walked there. Before I'd driven past, the front door had opened and the older man had welcomed him inside like they were good friends.'

Now I'm the one grabbing the wine glass and taking a big mouthful. I'm sure Grace realises I've guessed the punch-line but she continues telling it straight.

'I decided to park along the street and wait,' she says. 'About twenty minutes later the younger man came back out of the house and walked right past me. He looked all twisted out of shape, like he'd found a penny and lost a pound. I watched him turn the corner opposite where I was parked and he walked halfway up the side street and got in his car. It was weird he'd parked so far from the house. Mid-morning and the roads were deserted; I remember thinking he could have saved himself the walk.'

I shift uncomfortably in the seat and put my drink back down. Is she dragging this out on purpose to make me squirm?

'I had to make a snap decision to follow him,' she says. 'I needn't have panicked because he only drove a few hundred yards to the next turning and a little way along that road before pulling up and walking to another house. The old woman who opened the door gave him a warm smile and a motherly hug, and he went inside with her.'

I wince at the realisation she's already seen my mum, but she doesn't bat an eyelid. Is there nothing about me she doesn't already know?

'An hour later,' she continues, 'he left the woman's house and drove back the way he came. This time he parked right outside the house and when the front door opened, the old man patted the younger one on the shoulder as he welcomed him back into the house.'

By the time she tells me how she followed me back to the M25, through the tunnel and all the way to Elm Park, she's finally looking sheepish.

'I couldn't believe it,' she says, 'when you pulled up here, a mile from where I live.'

'That was convenient,' I say, no longer with any animosity. I'm starting to get it.

'All I'd planned to do,' she says, her eyes heavy with guilt, 'was see what you did next, just to get some idea of what the old man was up to. I still don't know for sure if he's my father but if it turns out he is, I need to understand what I'm getting myself into.'

'And that ultimately brought you to Bleak House?'

'Yeah,' she whispers and her porcelain cheeks blush. 'That was the biggest stroke of luck; seeing you leave here dressed like a commando that Wednesday night.'

'And then there was The Feathers.'

'Yeah,' she whispers again.

'Nice legs, shame about the shoes!'

'Oh my God. I hoped you hadn't noticed. Those strappy heels cost a fortune.'

'What were you thinking?'

'I'd pulled out all the stops!' she says, defensively before exhaling deeply. 'I'd imagined making my move in a nice restaurant or a wine bar.'

'Instead you got a route march across town.'

'And back again!'

'Well I suppose the rest,' I say, with a sigh, 'is history.'

'I really didn't mean to hurt you, Mickey. I never thought I'd get so close.'

'The middle-aged guy in the raincoat supping whisky on his own in a crowded bar must have been easy prey. And I thought you found me irresistible from the start.'

'I'm sor...' Thankfully she stops herself apologising again. 'I admit it wasn't love at first sight, but once I got to know you...'

It was for me. I don't say it. I don't have to; the schoolboy grin does it for me.

'It was definitely him in the pub on New Year's Eve, 2000,' she says, changing the subject and relaxing back into the seat. 'Can you believe he had that camera all these years?'

'Millennium Pervert,' I say and then wish I hadn't. I can't even begin to tell her what the policewoman insinuated about Herb, photographs and young people.

'I'm just relieved he didn't develop the film,' she says, the smile draining from her face when she adds: 'Especially if he turns out to be my dad.'

'Herb,' I say. 'Your father... I can't get my head around that.'

'Really? Why not?'

'Well, he's so cunning and secretive... manipulative... ruthless and predatory,' I say and her face lowers with each word. 'Come to think of it, maybe it's not such a stretch.'

'Oh, Mickey! I'm sorry!' she says for the umpteenth time, and I smile back at her with the same awkward look on my face.

'So what happens now?'

'What happens with *us*?' she asks and I nod. 'I suppose that depends on you. I'll understand if you hate me. I'm really hoping you don't.'

'I don't hate you, Grace. If anything I feel sorry for you.' I reach across to take her hand and she pulls it back.

'No, don't say that. *Anything* but that,' she says. 'If you *don't* hate me and you *don't* want me to go away and never come back, can I ask you something?'

'Anything,' I say.

'Will you help me find my dad?'

'Well, if it *is* Herb, I can do better than that,' I say. 'He wants me to take you to him.'

'Oh my God! You've heard from him?' Her eyes light up.

I empty the bottle into her glass and tell her what happened after she left me alone in the pub. By the time I've finished telling her about Herb's personal country club and his sinister request to see her, it's Grace's turn to feel hurt and confused.

'It didn't sound like he thought I might be his daughter then,' she says.

'No. He didn't come across as a long-lost father trying to orchestrate a family reunion. Apart from being some bizarre test of my resolve, all of this *does* seem to have been an elaborate plan to find you. What I don't understand is what *other* reason he could have for wanting me to bring you to him.'

'There's only one way we're going to find out,' she says. 'When are we supposed to go?'

'He said he'll call when he's ready.'

Grace goes quiet. I can't blame her for being anxious about meeting Herb, although I am still struggling to understand why she was so cautious in the first place. I get up and put some music on. Back on the sofa I lift my arm and she accepts the offer of a hug as Sinead O'Connor's lyrics seep like graveyard mist out of the speakers. She doesn't move from my embrace until the song comes to its emotional climax and then she reaches up and kisses me.

* * *

Disturbing Sleep

It's his birthday. Uncle Malcolm just slipped into his room. He's not really an uncle. Tonight he's not even drunk. Even at eight, the boy knows the difference. When he's drunk, he soon falls asleep... afterwards. At least the longer he's here; he's not knocking Ma about. Suddenly she's there. Though she hasn't come to save him. Her face is gaunt and lifeless; his last memory of her in Gartloch...

... his sleeping eyes flicker.

Uncle Malcolm is long gone; he died. Father O'Connell's telling him he'll be okay. At the age of ten, he no longer has to beg on the streets. Father O'Connell is kind. He's also gentle. More gentle than Uncle Malcolm. By the time he's thirteen, he knows it isn't right. The policeman seems concerned. At first. Still it goes on for another two years.

Father O'Connell is long gone; he died. Now he tells himself it'll be okay. The priest took his last confessional with a knife to his gut; his cock fed to a stray dog out at Seven Lochs. He's in a garden, looking in through a window. The same copper wants to talk to him. But he's not at home. There's a cat coming out the opening in the door. It purrs and wraps its tail around his leg.

The cat is long gone; it died. He's not fooled by a show of affection any more. He hung it by the tail; the rotary airer still spinning after he'd left. The stench of dead animals is overwhelming...

... his head shakes involuntarily.

His home in Glasgow is long gone; it died. He tells himself he'll get used to the smell as he learns to use the tools of his new trade and to cleave meat from bone. After work, he's in a dark alley not far from London. The lad has a passing resemblance to Father O'Connell. But it's the girlfriend who laughs at him. She's no longer laughing. The boy's blood paints a broad stroke across her face.

She's long gone; she died. He didn't give her the chance to scream. Teeth and fingers need to be scattered in case the pigs at work leave them behind. Pigs... now they're up ahead, with their blue lights flashing. He sees the carnage...

... his flaccid penis awakens.

The woman in the car is long gone; she died. He's at the inquest, watching the grieving husband. And there's a man in a

171

wheelchair with a gash across his head and Meccano around his legs. A younger man wheels him past as they leave and he tries to move aside. He stumbles and kicks the metal frame. The cripple yelps and the kid shouts out: 'Clumsy fucking idiot!' He's used to being yelled at.

The kid is long gone. He died. Guts in a bucket but no blood. Teeth and fingers set aside. The small triangle of steel punctures cold flesh beneath the pale buttock, tracing an arc below the hip bone. Switching hands, he completes the incision in a perfect radius at the crease in the groin and reaches for the hacksaw…

… his ejaculation feels like part of the dream but he wakes mid-way through, moaning loudly.

11.

Wednesday, 23rd

It's mid-afternoon and someone's pummelling on my front door. It sounds like they're trying to knock it through. When I get downstairs and turn the knob the door crashes inwards.

'Police!' is the accompanying announcement, but it's more of a battering ram than a greeting. It isn't the sickly-sweet WPC who's been visiting Mum. Nor is it the slightly pushy Detective Sergeant who accompanied her the last time they popped in for a chat and a cup of tea.

Standing on my doorstep, filling the frame, he says his name is Pinner and that he's a Detective Chief Inspector. I step back to let him in and he launches himself at me.

'What the fuck are you doing with my daughter?' he bellows.

I want to ask him what he's talking about and tell him I don't know his daughter and say who the hell does he think he is, pushing his way into my house and spitting wild accusations at me. But I get the sense he wouldn't be interested in what I had to say, even if I could speak, my protest throttled by the hand gripping my neck and pinning me against my own coat rack.

'You're a fucking pervert,' he roars, heeling me in the chest with his other massive hand, pushing me back against the stairs. 'I'll put you in a fucking wheelchair if I catch you anywhere near her.'

Before I can say a single word, he's left as quickly and noisily as he arrived, ranting as he barges his way back out the house and down the drive, the front door slamming behind him. I sit on the second stair stunned, my throat and chest throbbing.

173

Fair Cop

Several hours later, I'm sitting in the lounge getting meagre comfort from the warmth of an empty glass and even less from the encroaching darkness when the landline rings.

'Hi Mum,' I say half-heartedly, dreading a conversation with her right now. As I've said, I find it hard to lie to her, and this afternoon's dubious brush with the law is still the only thing on my mind.

'This is Detective Sergeant Melville, North Kent CID. Can I talk to Michael Field?'

'That's me,' I splutter.

'It was your mother who gave me your number, sir. Are you waiting for her to call? I can ring back later if you prefer?' He's very civil, in a copper kind of way.

'No. It's just she's the only one who... never mind. What do you want?'

'Your mother told me you may have been in contact with Herbert Long recently.' The hairs on the back of my neck prickle. 'We're keen to trace him in light of the fire at his house last week. We'd also like to ask you some questions about the last time you were in Gravesend and whether you saw anything strange or anyone acting suspiciously near his house.'

'I... er...'

'Mr Field, I would prefer not to do this over the phone so I wonder if I could make arrangements to visit you at home.'

Great that's all I need more fuzz in here giving me grief.

'Whatever. When?'

'How would tomorrow morning suit you, say ten o'clock?' he says.

'Yeah, okay.'

'Can I just check the address I have is correct?' He starts reading it out.

'Oh, it's correct alright,' I say, before he's even finished.

I'm about to hang up when he adds: 'And if it isn't me, it will be my boss, is that okay?'

'You're all the same to me.'

'Right... Well, it's DCI Pinner.' The name spins around in my head.

'Did you say Pinner?'

'That's right sir, Chief Inspector Pinner. Is there a problem?'

'Too right there's a problem,' I yell. 'That bastard's already been here this afternoon throwing his weight around and intimidating me about some girl. I didn't know what the hell he was talking about. Don't you send that psycho back here.'

'Sir, calm down. I don't know what you're talking about. Er... I didn't realise... Look, if you'd prefer to deal with me then that's fine. I'll see you in the morning.' He puts the phone down before I can say another word, and I'm left with the distinct impression it isn't the first time DS Melville has had to pour oil on troubled water in connection with the rogue actions of his boss.

It's later in the evening when Grace calls to ask if I've heard from Herb.

'No, but there's been no shortage of entertainment around here,' I say.

'Why? What's happened?'

'For some reason the police are suddenly very interested in my movements last week. They're investigating the fire and trying to trace Herb. And my old dear's let slip I made several trips down there last week. Apparently, they also want to know about a young woman who might have been acting suspiciously in the area on the day of the fire.' I remember noticing Grace blanch a little the other day when I told her about Herb's house burning down. 'You still there?'

'Yeah, I'm still here,' she says.

'Grace, do you have something to tell me?'

'It wasn't me,' she says. 'The house was fine when I left it.'

'Jesus, Grace! You *were* there? Someone must have seen you. That probably makes you the prime suspect.' When she doesn't respond I realise she's already come to that conclusion. 'Grace? What were you doing there?'

'I was hoping to see what *you* were doing there,' she says, 'with the old man, after your adventures the night before.'

'What, you followed me again?'

'I know,' she says and I can almost see her cringing through the phone.

'You seem to have been more interested in my movements than Herb's.'

'Yes, I know… It's just that I knew you were up to something for him and… well you were a bit easier to keep tabs on that he was. I mean, just living a few streets away.'

'Yeah, okay. But you were wasting your time that day.'

'Not exactly. I kept watching the house for ages, waiting to see if he'd go out.'

'But he wasn't even there,' I say with a certainty that's instantly challenged by her silence. 'Was he?'

'Yes, he was.'

'Not first thing, he wasn't… or when I popped back at lunchtime.'

'It looked to me like he was avoiding you.' Now the line goes quiet on my account.

'Right,' I say with an ironic smirk. 'Nothing should surprise me now.'

'After I saw you on the doorstep getting no answer, I kept watching for ages. I was sure I eventually saw some movement inside and I was trying to decide whether to go and bang on the door. That was when the car pulled up.'

'What car?'

'It was the same one I'd seen the week before. This big wrestler-type got out and went to the door. The old man came out of the house with a suitcase, got in the back of the car and it pulled away.'

'Then what?'

'At first I followed them, but when I realised they were turning onto the motorway, heading north, I didn't fancy a long drive to God-knows-where. So I came back and kept watching the house to make sure it was definitely empty. That's when I decided to take a look inside.'

'So you just broke in,' I say with fake surprise, remembering the ease with which she'd got us into Bleak House.

'Yeah, I went in through the back door,' she says. 'There was an inner door into the garage and I was about to try and unlock it when the doorbell rang. As I watched the front door a piece of paper came through the letter box and then I saw you walk back down the path from the front window. For some reason I picked up your note and put it my pocket.'

'Nice of you to tidy up,' I say. 'It would've ruined the immaculate style of the place.'

'Maybe when you saw it last,' she says. 'By then it was empty. I mean completely bare. No furniture, nothing. It was like he'd moved out.'

'But Mum only saw them loading up in the evening.'

'It must have all been in the garage. I didn't manage to get in because that door was like Fort Knox. Anyway, I didn't see much point in leaving your note on the mat; it didn't look like anyone was coming back to see it... and God knows, no one else would have had a clue what you were on about!'

'That *was* the general idea,' I say.

'Very cloak and dagger,' she says. 'Then I got out of there before anyone else came. I would have sworn I hadn't been seen. I can't believe I'm being suspected of burning it down.'

'Well, the fire didn't start until the early hours of Friday.' I try to console her. 'And in any case, I think I spoke to the person who did burn it down.'

'What?'

'I was trying to get hold of Herb... when I got home from the King's Head. And someone else answered his phone.'

'Oh my God! Why didn't you say before, we could have reported it.'

'I didn't want to tell you. It really freaked me out. Besides, I'm not sure reporting it would be a good idea. Herb made it sound like the people after him are pretty ruthless. I don't think we should do anything hasty until we understand what we're dealing with.'

'But at least we can show I wasn't the last one in there.'

'Sure. All I'm saying is let's keep it up our sleeve until we have to, okay? In any case, you already have an alibi for being back here during the evening. The guys will vouch for both of us if it comes to it.'

'Yeah, I suppose so.'

'Talking of which,' I say. 'Here's a question that's been bugging me: how *did* you know I'd be in the King's Head that night with my mates?'

'Would you believe me if I said *that* time really was a coincidence?'

'Right,' I say, unconvinced. 'Anyway, the cops are coming to see me in the morning.'

'Who's the investigating officer?' she asks, like she might have heard of him. My head starts to spin at the thought.

'He said his name is Melville.'

'Oh!'

'You know him?'

'Yeah... kind of.'

'I don't suppose you're familiar with a Chief Inspector Pinner as well, by any chance?' The line goes quiet again. 'He's already paid me a visit though I didn't get the impression he was on official business.'

'Oh my God! What did *he* want?'

'I think he was just trying to be the protective father figure,' I say. 'It seems he doesn't approve of our... *friendship*.'

'Oh, Mickey, I'm so sorry,' she says exasperated. 'It must have been Simon, that conniving little runt. Don't worry, I'll deal with them. You'll be okay with Melville; he's a good guy. Give me a call tomorrow once he's out of your hair and I'll come over if that's alright.'

'Yeah, fine,' I say with a sigh. 'I'll try not to incriminate you in the meantime.'

Bella Donna

It is a clatty shit hole. He knows it. Deserves better, but he doesn't care; it serves a purpose. And no one ever comes here... ever came here. Just now it's getting like Argyle Street in August. It's as well he cleaned up in time. Especially now he's heard they'll be back again.

He's done as he's been told. Now he's in the scullery, boiling an old whistling kettle on a camp stove. He reaches up to take a mug from the shelf and with the other hand, his large fingers tweak the dial on an aging transistor. The pure tone of a mezzo soprano radiates like sunshine around the room. His smile doesn't reach the surface; it never does. But inside he's floating.

When his eyes re-focus, it's the empty space on the shelf they dilate upon. Where the last time he'd left her. His sweet Jasmine. He lunges at the radio and sends it splintering against the wall, crashes through the door, out into the night air, and howls like a wolf at the moon.

12.

Thursday, 24th

I needn't have worried. Melville doesn't show. He doesn't call to apologise for wasting my time either. Perhaps I should be glad there's something more important keeping him away. I ring Grace in the early afternoon and she agrees I shouldn't bother waiting in any longer. Her voice down the phone seems to bring out the sunshine and we decide to meet in the park for a stroll.

As I walk towards the cafe I wonder if she's spoken to Pinner. I find her outside by the concrete slipway, feeding the ducks out of a bag of bread. She empties the last few crumbs onto the water and takes my hand as we walk off around the lake.

'Simon's an ass,' she says as we approach the wooden bridge. 'It's sad really. We were quite close at first. He was a fragile little boy, physically and emotionally. I think that's why they were so keen to have a second child, to try and bring him out of himself.'

We stop halfway across and watch little coots darting around on the water. Everything about them is black except for their bulbous white beaks that seem to start from the back of their heads.

'Seems hard to believe now,' I say, dismissing the thought of Simon as The Ugly Duckling. 'How come they didn't just have another baby?'

'He was born in Gibraltar while his dad was working there. I think there were complications with the birth and his mum wasn't able to have any more kids.'

'What's she like?'

'Who, *Gillian*? She was really nice.'

'Was?' I say, dreading the inference.

'She's gone back to Gibraltar but we still keep in touch.'

'Doesn't sound like the perfect environment for an adoption,' I say as we continue to walk.

'It was okay back then. I was the one with the problems when I first met them. By twelve I'd already been in trouble with the police a few times. I knew the father was a copper so I was a bit apprehensive. At first, little get-togethers were orchestrated in parks and zoos. There'd be three or four of us from the kids' home and a couple of families looking to adopt. Course, they didn't tell us that.'

'They didn't want to build up any hopes?'

'I suppose the idea was to see how everyone got along without putting pressure on any of us. I was the eldest. And starting to realise adoption was becoming unlikely.'

'I suppose most people want babies.'

'Yeah, the little ones never seemed to hang around for long,' she says pensively. 'Except for me; I must have used up all my luck getting born in the first place. Course, by then, after all the problems, a lot of the homes had been closed down and they were trying really hard to get the older kids back into families.'

'So the Pinners took a shine to you.'

'No one was more surprised than me. I suppose Simon must have only been six and I remember there was a boy of a similar age in the group, probably younger. I'm sure everyone was expecting the two boys to bond. But for some reason, right from the start, Simon latched onto me. I was flattered. Like I said before; unconditional affection was a bit of a novelty. And he was quite sweet back then...' She stops momentarily as we reach a simple log bench at the top of the hill. We sit down and look back at the view across the park.

'I started looking forward to the meetings,' she continues. 'I suspect the people around me could see it was having a positive effect, so they encouraged me to think about spending some time with the family. I got on really well with Gillian. She was a lovely mum before things went sour with Terry.'

'Terry is Simon's dad, right?'

'Yeah, Detective Chief Inspector Terence Pinner to you,' she says and I cringe at the thought of his spit on my face. 'Back then even he seemed like a nice guy. Although I got the impression he would have preferred another boy; one who was a bit more outgoing and adventurous. But he probably noticed that Simon's confidence grew when he was around me so Terry made all the right noises and welcomed me into the family.'

'Sounds like it was just a formality in the end.'

'I suppose so,' she says. 'Terry generally gets what he wants. I stayed there for a weekend, which went really well, and before I knew it I'd moved in with them permanently.'

I know nothing about it but I assume when kids get adopted there's a legal process that results in them taking on the adoptive family surname. It seems insensitive to ask about hers; I figure one day she'll tell me. There's a lot about her I still want to know.

'So you became the big sister?' I say.

'Yeah, it really was like that at first. I suppose he did look up to me. That made me feel wanted; he was someone I could protect.'

'So where did it all start going awry?'

'He grew up!' she says, shaking her head. 'It's ironic. I suppose I helped to give him the confidence to become the son Terry always wanted him to be. As he went through his teens his father started to mould him in his image. I feel a bit responsible for that.'

'No. You just helped him reach his potential. You couldn't have known he would turn out bad' I say, putting my arm around her waist. 'From where I'm sitting, he seems to have helped you move in the opposite direction.'

'Thank you,' she says before looking away embarrassed. 'That's probably why I still bother having anything to do with him.'

'That and the fact you have to live under the same roof.'

'I don't *have* to stay there,' she says. 'If I wanted out badly enough, I'd only have to ask his dad.'

'Really?'

'Sure. Terry just wants me to be happy,' she says with a wry smile.

'So you keep saying. You must have some hold over him. Don't tell me he turned into a monster and now you're old enough to ruin him.'

'That's one way to describe it,' she says. She must see the look on my face because she quickly adds: 'No, not like that. He's never laid a finger on me.'

'I'm relieved to hear it,' I say, rubbing my neck where I can still feel his grip on my throat.

'You know, I actually think he's afraid of me,' she says.

'We are still talking about the big bloke who pushed into my house yesterday and threatened me with physical violence, yeah?'

'I'm sorry. He won't do that again, I promise.'

'How can you be so sure?'

'Well...' she says, 'it all goes back to five or six years ago, when Gillian's drink problem started and she and Terry began fighting a lot. Simon and I would try to keep out of the way but I felt really sorry for her because she had a lot to put up with. She didn't fit into the circles Terry mixed with, and I think she would have preferred to have stayed in Gibraltar. She hated the weather here. And as we later found out, it wasn't just the sunshine she was missing. She's back there living with a Spanish guy she knew before.'

'Happy families,' I say.

'Yeah, right,' she says with an ironic laugh. 'Before that, when her drinking got really bad, Terry made her go into rehab. And it was while she was away on one of her special holidays, as he used to call them, this guy turned up at the house.'

She proceeds to tell me about the night in July, 2004 when a stranger knocked at the door...

Hard Case

Terry had invited him in and they were chatting away in the lounge. Simon was out and Grace was upstairs. After trying to listen to the muffled voices through the floor and being unable to hear what they were saying, she got fed up and went downstairs for a drink. Terry heard her and came out of the room, closing the door behind him. He was acting strangely and asked her why she wasn't going out. It was even more out of character when he produced a £20 note from his wallet and told her to go and have some fun.

Grace went to a friend's house for an hour or so and returned home, thinking the man would have gone. But he was still there. No one heard her come in and she listened at the door for a while. The two men had been drinking heavily and were talking loudly.

'... deserved it.' The visitor's voice reverberated like a double bass. 'He's better off out of it.'

'Maybe so,' Terry said. 'But how is any of this my problem?'

'Because, Terry, my old son,' the guy bellowed, 'I'm making it your fucking problem!'

'Keep it down, will you. This is my home don't forget. My boy's upstairs asleep.'

'All I'm saying is we go back a long way.' His voice had dropped to barely audible, allowing Grace to hear something being unclipped. 'I pay you to make problems like these go away. Just like you have before.'

'I don't know if I can this time.'

'Of course you can, Tel. And the reason why is sitting right here. And there's plenty more where that came from.' There was a long silence.

'This is the last time, Ray.' It was Terry who finally spoke, and while Grace only just made out what he'd said, it made her skin crawl.

'He's a good lad, that Simon,' the man called Ray said. 'You wouldn't want anything to happen to him.'

'Okay, okay. Leave my son out of it, alright.'

'And then there's the girl, yeah...'

When her hand came up to cover her open mouth, she accidentally brushed against the door handle and it clicked. She stood there rigid, trying to decide whether to walk in and pretend she'd just got in, or to scurry up to her room. The man seemed to keep talking and she thought he said: 'Could all be very different for her, you know.'

She stayed long enough to hear one of them walk across the room and as she shot upstairs, she barely recognised Terry's voice.

'Alright, I get the message,' he said, defeated. 'Let me see the fucking money, then.'

She went to bed and couldn't sleep until she heard the visitor leave and Terry go to his room. After a fitful night, she woke up early with a headache and went downstairs to take a painkiller. The door to the lounge was open and she could see a briefcase on the floor. She went in and tried to open it but it was locked.

Back in her room she lay awake staring at the ceiling until she heard Simon getting ready for school. The front door slammed behind him just after eight o'clock. Normally, Terry would have been up and out first and she would have been the last to leave the house. That day she had showered and dressed for work before he even surfaced. When she saw the state of him coming down the stairs, she no longer felt quite so awful, but her stomach still wasn't up to having breakfast and she settled for a peppermint tea.

'That was a heavy night,' she said. 'Do you want a coffee?'

'Thanks, you're an angel.' He lurched into the lounge rubbing his temples.

'That man last night,' she said as she brought the drinks in and put them on the table. Terry had been slumped in an armchair with his head back against the cushion. He sat forward and looked at her through heavy eyelids.

'What about him?'

'Is he a colleague, like Jim Melville?' She was used to Jim coming round before Gillian's problems got too bad.

'No, he's just a contact.'

'What's in there?' she said, nodding across the room.

'Huh?' His features tightened into a grimace as his head jerked around to follow her gaze. 'Oh, God! That... It's only paperwork. Police stuff. You know, files and statements. Nothing to worry your pretty little head about.' He was suddenly animated and jumped out of the chair, picked up the case in one hand, grabbed his coffee in the other and went upstairs and didn't reappear before she left for work.

A couple of days went by and he seemed to be avoiding her. He was out late into the evening and had left the house before she got up the following morning. The visitor's threatening words kept repeating in her head and there were lots of questions she wanted to ask. The next night, after she'd gone to bed, she heard him come in and put the TV on, she went back downstairs.

'Thought you'd gone up,' he said as she came in and sat down.

'I couldn't sleep. What's this?'

'Spaghetti Western,' he said, and she watched for a while as Clint Eastwood stood opposite four men, poised to draw his gun.

'Why are they called that?'

'They were made by Italians.'

'Nothing to do with the tomato sauce everywhere?'

'Hilarious,' he said without looking up from the screen and a thunderous blaze of gunfire rattled the speaker. He twitched in his chair with each blast and she found herself wondering if his inner gunslinger was pulling the trigger or taking the bullets. Then there was silence and The Man With No Name was the only one standing.

'Are they all dead?' she asked.

'Just keep watching.' On the screen Clint Eastwood walked past an old man with a beard and said, *My mistake; four coffins.* 'There you go. All dead.'

'Talking of dead men,' she said. 'Who was the one you were talking about the other night?' That's when Terry went ballistic.

'I won't tell you again... keep your fucking nose out of my official business!' he yelled, throwing the remote control across the room. She was stunned; he'd never sworn at her before. She ran upstairs and locked herself in her room.

Later that week, she sneaked into his bedroom when he was at work, and managed to unlock his wardrobe with a paper clip. The briefcase was on the top shelf and she carefully lifted it down. Both sides were locked with their numbers each set at 999. She thought that was corny until she realised that when she rotated the barrels one way the three individual rollers kept turning but when she flicked them the other way, they all stopped at 9. He'd just spun them all as far as they'd go. She gave up and put it back.

A couple of weeks went by and she noticed how he was using more cash, even for big things that he'd usually have put on a card. He never used to have any cash on him. Gillian would call him The Queen whenever they were out and she'd end up paying for things. All of a sudden he was throwing it around like it was going out of fashion. One morning, he had to leave in a hurry to go to a crime scene and as she walked past his room she saw the briefcase lying on the bed. She noticed that the right-hand combination had changed. It now showed 490 and when she pulled the slider with her thumb, the catch sprang open on its hinge. The other number was still 999. She smiled to herself, lifted the case onto its back feet and changed the three nines to 010. April Fool, she thought as the second catch flipped open. It was Simon's date of birth.

She opened the case while it was still upright and the contents started to fall out. She tried to shut the lid quickly but it was too late. One had already escaped onto the bed and several others had shifted, preventing the case from closing. She lifted the lid again, this time more carefully, and her eyes opened wider. Apart from the bundle on the bed and the ones that had moved, neatly bound blocks of £50 notes filled three-quarters of the case. She had no idea how much and didn't get a chance to count them when she heard the front door open. She only just managed to rearrange the contents, lock the case and get out of the room before Terry came back upstairs cursing. He brushed past her, went into his room and she heard the wardrobe door being locked.

She was sure she'd left the case exactly as she'd found it, but it seemed too much of a coincidence when he surprised her that evening. He asked her to come with him and wouldn't say why. She was nervous and kept asking where he was taking her. He just rambled away as he drove.

'You need to understand things aren't always perfect,' he said. 'You have to take your opportunities when they come along. And when things fall in your lap, who's to say you don't deserve them?'

'Are you talking about bribes?' she asked.

'What harm's the odd back-hander if it takes money out of the pockets of criminals?' She didn't answer and he added, 'If I don't take what comes my way there are plenty more out there who will.'

Then he pulled in at a filling station. She thought he just wanted to get some petrol for wherever they were going, but when he parked up and told her to follow him, she started to get concerned. Her anxiety was short-lived when she saw on one side of the forecourt a second hand car lot with a row of little sporty two-seaters, all shiny and nearly-new. He told her to take her pick.

Dirty Cash

'Bloody hell!' I say. 'What did you do?'

'I said, "I like the red one!"'

I suspect my face has taken on the appearance of a dead guppy, yet she continues unabashed.

'He took me back a week later to collect it and paid in cash,' she says, picking idly at the long grass growing under the bench.

'He told me not to mention it to Gillian when she came home. And the briefcase disappeared.'

'Aren't there a load of formalities,' I say, 'for large cash transactions like that? You know, to stop money laundering? We were always having it drummed into us at work.'

'Of course...' she says with a cheeky grin, 'the girl from Compliance.' I shake my head and blush. 'But no,' she continues, 'I think the salesman knew him. At least he didn't *seem* to ask any awkward questions.'

'And what about you? Did *you* ask any more awkward questions?'

'Well I suppose I should have.' She inhales deeply through clenched teeth. 'But a few days later, I found £1,000 in my current account. It definitely wasn't mine. I was only earning trainee money while I was still going to college. I thought the bank had messed up so I kept my mouth shut.'

'Like you do,' I say.

'Well, the following month there was another thousand. That time I did check with the bank and they said it was a new standing order from the account of T Pinner. When I asked him about it, he said he'd decided a young woman like me should have an allowance. He said he wanted to make sure I always looked nice and he knew good taste didn't come cheap. It's gone up every year since. It's now over £3,000 a month.' She stands up and looks across the lake towards the distant tower blocks, before adding: 'Last year he gave me an advance so I could buy the salon.'

'You own the...?'

She starts walking back towards the woods.

'Simon only told Terry you'd taken lewd photographs of me as a kid,' she says changing the subject as I catch up with her. 'He told him you were probably some creep from my past coming back to blackmail me.'

'I don't suppose it looked good from his perspective,' I say, giving him the benefit of the doubt.

'I suppose not,' she says, before changing her mind. 'No,

he's just a trouble-maker. He's always trying to get one over on me with his old man. And I'm pretty sure Terry's motives for coming to see you were more to do with self-preservation than defending me. Now you know why.'

'And is Simon aware of your arrangement with his... Sugar Daddy?'

'I'm not sure,' she says, her brow knitted in a brief show of indignation. 'I've suspected for a while he's been brought into the family business. That's why I took him for a drink in The King's Head last week; to try and find out what he's up to.'

'And you seriously thought a free pint would buy his confession?'

'I don't know, sometimes it feels like the only way to get his attention for more than ten seconds,' she says. 'But no, as you probably saw, it didn't work. He got defensive and stormed off.'

'And I thought you sent him away so you could spend the evening with me,' I quip.

'I told you, that wasn't planned.'

'I believe you. Even *you* couldn't get a student to leave a free drink on the table against his will.'

'He was a bit shocked at how much I knew about his father,' she says. 'He'll probably be buying me the drinks in future.'

'That explains how easy it was for you to get him to develop the film so quickly.'

'I suppose. He certainly seems keen to stay on my good side.'

'And to defend your honour,' I add. 'Did you speak to Pinner as well?'

'No, but you don't have to worry about Terry. I told Simon to sort it out. You won't be getting any more off-duty visits.'

'Strange that his henchman hasn't been in touch on more official business,' I say.

'Yeah, hopefully that's good news,' she says.

'So,' I say. 'This is a really bad habit of yours; breaking into people's houses.'

'And you can talk!' She gives me a playful push and I trip on a branch and exaggerate my fall into the bracken. She starts laughing and I'm about to grab her when my phone rings. This time there's no doubt it's Herb because I've added the number he gave me to my contacts.

'It's him!' I say as I take the call and the laughter drops from her face.

'Mickey, I'm glad I've caught you, lad. Do you know where the girl is?' He comes straight to the point leaving me no time to think.

'Her *name* is Grace,' I say holding a finger to my lips. 'And yes... I'm sure I can track her down,'

'Here's what I want you to do,' he continues. 'Tonight at nine o'clock, I'd like you to bring her to me.'

'Your place in the sticks?' I say. 'Only, I'd need directions.'

'No Mickey not here; somewhere you're more familiar with than here. One of my less ostentatious properties that you've visited more than once. You know the one.'

'Herb, why do you need her to go there?' I say. 'It's not the nicest place to meet.'

'I have my reasons,' he says and a shiver runs up my spine.

'What do you want with her exactly?'

'Mickey! Just complete your part of the arrangement. Bring the girl at nine, and we'll be even.'

13.

Point Blank

It's eight-fifty and we're parked under a large tree a hundred yards from Bleak House. We've been sitting here for ten minutes, after first driving past and seeing no sign of life. Once more, the place is dark and forbidding and I'm finding it very strange to be here for the first time at the invitation of the owner, not needing to snoop around in the shadows or worry about getting caught, yet I feel more anxious than ever.

Grace is the first to see the car pull up outside and we both watch as Herb gets out of the passenger seat and walks towards the house. The large figure of another man expands like foam from the driver's door and I recognise him from the other day. Big Mac. He's about six-four and wears a dark suit, no tie. He looks like a rugby player and it strikes me he's probably not just Mac the Chauffeur. He scans up and down the street and seems to look straight at us. I'm no longer sure we're so well-concealed, parked tightly in the shadows between two other cars. Regardless, he turns away and follows Herb into the house.

We've spent the early evening establishing some ground rules. Given that Herb's intentions towards Grace are not paternal, we've agreed to stick together no matter what; we'll let Herb do all the talking and under no circumstances will either of us go into the torture chamber. The other thing we decided was that I would go in alone first and try to assume some level of control.

The front door opens before I have a chance to knock and Mac the Butler leads me into the front room. With the heavy curtains drawn and the lamp on, the place seems unexpectedly cosy. Herb sits in the armchair and two bars of an old electric fire are starting to take the chill out of the musty air. He doesn't get up as I enter the room, but a frown creases his forehead. Before he has a chance to speak, I seize the initiative.

'Very homely, Herb,' I say, looking around the room, trying to remain cool.

'It has its uses.'

'Not your usual style though.'

'It tidies up nicely, don't you think?' He looks across at Mac, whose expressionless stare remains fixed on me. 'We're used to... tidying up mess.' He unsettles me without even trying and already I'm on the back foot.

'Let's get to the point, shall we?' I say.

'Well that all depends, lad. I take it you didn't come alone?'

'Look, I just want to know what's going to happen first.' I try to keep my voice strong and even. 'What do you want with her?'

'That's between me and the girl. You don't need to get involved.'

'Look, she agreed to come because she wants to talk to you about her father,' I say and his eyes narrow.

'I'm not frightened of *him*.' he says.

'That's not what I mean,' I say, but he's not listening.

'I thought we had an agreement, Mickey. For you and me, this is strictly business. All you have to do is deliver the girl and walk away. The sooner we can get past this, the sooner we can start talking about the future.'

I realise he's trying to deflect me with a far from subtle reminder of the offer he made back at his country house. Words that have repeated in my head since: '*With you on board, we could push back, maybe even recover some lost ground. In time, you could take the lead. One day, we might even be able to take down the whole corrupt empire.*'

'Not until you tell me what you want with her?' I push back, surprising even myself with the strength of my conviction. My pulse is racing and adrenaline is making me light-headed;

outwardly I'm just managing to keep my composure.

'You're breaking the first rule lad. You're getting too involved. Just tell me where she is.' As he says it, I notice that Mac the Butler has morphed into a gorilla, shifting his weight in a territorial posture. I instinctively step back before Herb holds up a hand and the ape gets back into his cage.

'I'm not always this forgiving to people who play games with me, lad.' His voice lowers and he shakes his head while his eyes remain locked on mine. 'We go a long way back and I value your loyalty agreeing to help me out after all this time. So I really don't want to have to do this the hard way. But that's your choice.'

'But I didn't say I...' My feeble protest tries to surface, but I'm almost grateful when he plunges it back underwater.

'We don't seem to be getting anywhere with this.' He raises his voice and the window frames vibrate. 'Like we said before, you'll be well-rewarded, Mickey... when you bring her to me. So, where is she?'

The room suddenly feels colder and the hairs on my neck bristle as I try to compete with his stare. Seconds of deafening silence seem endless until the door crashes open and we all jump. It's Grace, standing at the threshold, with a gun pointing at Mac. That wasn't one of our ground rules.

'Mickey, what's he talking about?' she shouts and her eyes dart around the room as if she's trying to watch everyone at the same time. 'What reward do you get for bringing me here?'

'Grace, it's not like that,' I say, but instantly freeze when she spins and points the gun at me.

'I thought you were on my side!' she shrieks, stepping into the room towards me.

'Put the gun down.' Herb intervenes, his voice now gently calming. 'No one needs to get hurt tonight.' He's holding out his hand towards her and as she looks back at him, the intensity in her eyes seems to ease and her grip on the gun loosens. It's like she's been mesmerised.

In that split second, Mac makes his move and lunges at her.

194

They both have hands on the gun and it's being waved wildly around the room. I duck for cover and then hear a loud click, looking up in time to see Mac holding the weapon, and Grace sitting on the floor dejected.

'Huh,' he snorts before letting the pistol fall to the floor and the silent impact sends a piece of plastic bouncing across the room.

'That was very foolish,' Herb says. 'If you're going to carry, you should be ready, willing and able to use it. Toy guns are for children.'

Grace gets to her feet and looks at me with a face full of contempt. I shake my head to protest my innocence but she looks away.

'So, now I'm here old man,' she says to Herb, 'what is it you want from me?'

'Have a seat.' He gestures to the only other chair in the room; a wooden one I recognise from the kitchen. 'Let's try to be civilised.'

She remains standing but he ignores her defiance and turns back to me. 'Mickey, your job is done. Mac will see you out. And, don't worry... we'll sort out the money.'

'I'm not going anywhere.' I look across at Grace and she's still glaring at me. 'We came here together and we're leaving together.'

'That's very sweet.' Herb mocks me. 'But remember, a moment ago? She was pointing a gun at your head. This is just between me and her now.'

'I'm not leaving her alone,' I insist. It's a futile gesture because this time when Mac makes a move Herb doesn't intervene and I'm manhandled out of the door, all the way to the pavement.

'Go,' he says pointing to where my car is parked.

'I'm waiting here,' I say. 'I'm going to be taking her home.'

He shakes his fat head and I make a lunge to get past him. He almost dislocates my shoulder pulling me back and wraps his huge arms around my chest so I can't move.

'Walk!' he growls. *While you still can* is implicit in the way he sends me hurtling towards the lamppost. I manage to avoid it and remain on my feet and slowly walk backwards in the direction of the car, while he stands on the pavement watching. I try to come up with a new plan but he's still there when I start the car.

'Tosser!' I yell as I drive past and he swats it like a fly and returns it to me deftly on the tip of his stubby middle finger.

Around the corner I stop the car and dial the number I stored earlier. A mobile rings five times and I start to worry it was only for daytime use. Then I hear a familiar voice.

'Melville,' it says.

'It's Michael Field. We spoke on the phone yesterday.'

'Ah yes, Mr Field,' he says, sounding a bit off-guard. 'Sorry about this morning. Something came up and I couldn't...'

'Yeah, don't worry,' I say, only the dire circumstance forcing me to let him off the hook mid-cringe. 'It's not about that. Well... I suppose it *is* related.'

'What is?' he says.

'I know where Herbert Long is.'

'You've seen him?'

'Yes. I'm not far from a house he owns in South Woodford. I had to leave but I'm concerned about a friend who's still there with him.'

'Concerned about what?'

'Look,' I say, wishing I'd thought this through. 'We haven't got time for a long explanation. He's gone to a lot of trouble to get her and it looks like there's been some weird stuff going on in that place.'

'Her?' he says, his tone more urgent. 'Who is she? And what kind of weird stuff?'

'I can't explain it over the phone. I'm just really worried about Grace.'

'Grace?'

'Her name's Grace de Manton,' I reply, surprising myself with the instant recall. 'She said she knows you.'

'de Manton?'

'Yeah. She's m...my... girl... she's a friend.' I stutter with frustration at having to explain myself to him and then remember how our previous conversation ended. 'She's the reason your guv'nor paid me that personal visit yesterday.'

'Oh, *that* Grace. Right... where exactly is this house?'

Near Miss

Melville's suddenly very concerned and says I should have dialled 999. He can't attend because it isn't his patch and it would take too long anyway, but he promises to get his Met colleagues on the scene urgently. I drive around the block, park at the far end of Bleak Avenue and shadow-hop back towards the house. The first thing I see is Mac the Bouncer standing at the front door, which forces me to go round the back and over the fence.

Everything's dark and quiet at the rear, so I venture around the side and give the back door handle an optimistic twist. Grace's simple philosophy of breaking and entering without the breaking part makes me smile as the door opens and, thanks to her, I make a dignified entrance into the kitchen. Already I can hear voices and I prickle. They're no longer in the front room. They're much closer. That's another of our ground rules compromised.

The inner door is ajar and I stand behind it for cover should anyone come through. At first the talking is very quiet and I only pick out the occasional word. Herb says something like: not worth living. Grace's tone is too subdued for me to catch her response. Herb's getting louder. His voice echoes around the concrete walls, but the outburst is muffled by the time it arrives at my ears and I can only make out the occasional phrase.

'... the bastard...' he says with crystal clarity, before his voice falls away again to a mumble. '... in it together...' The ebb and flow continues, each sentence ending like a wave crashing onto rocks.

'... long time for this day ...had the chance ...paid the price ...that bastard Pinner's turn.'

These final, chilling words are followed by a loud bang that reverberates around the house, shaking me into action, and I look around the kitchen hoping to arm myself. I burst into the room brandishing a fire poker.

But the room is empty. The second thing I notice is that the heavy metal door on the right is open and the dialogue is continuing from inside the chamber. That spiteful little room has tricked me again, ruining my heroic entrance. At least my embarrassment is spared as I dart unnoticed into the corner and stand with my back to the cinderblock wall, just a few feet from the open door. Opposite me, the other cell remains stubbornly locked.

'...covered it up!' Herb's still yelling. 'Might as well have put a gun to her head and pulled the trigger. And all I ever wanted was the truth. But he denied me that. Now it's time for justice.'

'But this isn't the way,' Grace says.

I move closer to peer into the room. All I can see is Herb's hand resting on the bench and a lump hammer within his reach. I tighten my grip on the poker.

'I want him to suffer. I want him to know how it feels.' Herb continues to rant and picks up the hammer and slams it down on the bench. I've heard enough and I'm about to burst in when I hear Mac shouting from the front.

'Filth!' he yells, accompanied by the sound of police sirens approaching.

Relieved I don't have to challenge Herb to a medieval duel, I move back into the kitchen and manage to pull the door behind me before Knuckles makes it in from the hall. I don't think he's seen me but I don't wait to find out. I'm out the back door and over the bottom fence even faster than the last time I had to leave in a hurry.

By the time I emerge from the alleyway onto the street, the blue lights have stopped flashing on the police car parked along the road. I find a vantage point behind the neighbour's front hedge, where I have a good view of the front door, and it must be ten minutes before Herb opens it and steps aside to let a policewoman out. Another cop emerges behind her but there's no sign of anyone else. I crouch there, completely bemused as the three of them conclude what appears to have been a polite conversation.

'No harm done,' Herb says.

'Well, I'm sorry to have disturbed you sir.' The woman puts her notebook away, replaces her cap and, with a nod of her head, turns to the other copper and they walk down the path towards the front gate.

'What a waste of time,' she says as the front door closes. 'They must think we haven't got enough to do.'

'Bloody provincial CID. Who is this Melvin anyway?' the man-cop adds as they get into the car.

When it pulls away I want to jump up and down and wave my hands about to stop them. Instead I squat there in stunned disbelief; so much for calling the cavalry. My thoughts return to Grace and I imagine her hidden in the house, restrained and silenced so the Old Bill couldn't see her. Not only could they not see her, they didn't even seem the slightest bit suspicious that someone could have been locked up in one of those grisly cells.

I sneak up the side path and around to the small kitchen window at the back when the sound of a snapping twig sends me scurrying for cover. I turn to see Mac emerging from the far corner of the garden. He stares straight towards me but then looks away, panning the wilderness for movement. I hold my breath, waiting for the moment he sees me and charges. Luckily, he doesn't. He just clambers noisily through the dense wilderness across the bottom of the garden and peers over the fence. Presumably seeing nothing, he turns and comes back towards the house, by which time I've been able to bury myself deeper into the bushes. He looks back in my direction again. By now I'm well-hidden. He gives up and goes indoors.

I hear the key turning in the lock and find the courage to reach back up to the window. The inner door is open and I get a quick glimpse of Mac talking to Herb in the hallway before it crashes inwards, rebounding with a bang off the dresser and closing back on itself, leaving me with a freeze-frame of Herb, his fists clenched and his face set with rage. I'm guessing Mac saw me when the police arrived; they're pissed off with me for raising the alarm and want to make me pay for it. The door remains closed and it looks like they've given up trying to find me, so I decide to go back around the front and squat in the dark recess at the side of the bay.

No sooner am I in position, the light inside goes out and, seconds later, the front door opens and the two men come out of the house. Herb secures the door while Mac walks to the car and unlocks it. I think about Grace left inside and can't decide whether to confront them or wait until they've gone, in the hope I can get back in and rescue her. I make a hesitant move towards the car but they drive away before I'm anywhere near them.

The house is dark and silent again and I walk down the side path to the back door and reach for the handle. I already know this time it won't yield. I feel nauseous with the thought of Grace locked in. I call her name but there's no reply. I tell her I'm not leaving until I can get her out. Without a plan I sit on the doorstep with my head in my hands and wallow in my own helplessness. It feels like I'm sitting here for ages before Melville jumps back into my head. This time I'll insist he comes. Only problem is, when I reach for the phone on my belt, the case is empty. I try to stay calm and persuade myself I left it in the car. The Banker's not convinced; he knows I didn't.

'Don't worry Grace, I'll come back for you,' I call through the airbricks and head back to the car.

Told you so, says the know-all in my head when the phone isn't on or under the driver's seat. I leave the door open and rush round to the other side and start rummaging around on the floor, desperate to avoid having to retrace my steps back and forth around this bloody house tonight.

'Are you looking for this?' It's Grace's voice that hits me like a bullet in the back of the head. When I look up she's standing on the pavement, one hand on her hip and the other holding up my phone.

'Thank God,' I say. 'I was worried sick.'

'Well, you should be more careful,' she says. 'It was lit up like a Christmas tree at the bottom of the fence.'

'I meant thank God *you're* okay.'

'Quick, come here,' she says as headlights pan around a side turning along the road.

When I get to her she plants a big kiss on my lips and wraps her arms around me. I'm not complaining, but it is a bit unexpected. She must be pleased to see me. As the car slowly drives past I try to watch, but Grace pulls my head around so I can't see it and carries on kissing me and caressing my head with her fingers, keeping her own face hidden in the process. The car rolls on beyond the next tree before pulling up outside Bleak House. Grace finally releases me.

'Quick,' she says with a gesture. I get back in my car like it all makes perfect sense. 'Start the engine and drive away casually.'

'Who is he?' I say, even though that one is ridiculously low on my list of burning questions.

'Don't look at him,' she says as we ease past the house.

'Don't look at who?' I say struggling to keep my eyes fixed straight ahead.

'That's Jim Melville.'

Hanging Out

Ten thirty and we're sitting in the dark in a deserted car park a couple of miles east of Redbridge. Apart from agreeing it would be best to avoid going back to either of our places for a while and deciding to just park up and calm down, we haven't spoken since driving away from Bleak House.

'Talk to me about the gun,' I say, slicing through the silence.

'It wasn't a real one,' she says and looks away.

'It sure as hell looked real when I was staring down the

barrel.' I glare at the back of her head.

'Okay,' she says, turning to face me to deliver her stinging counterpunch. 'So talk to me about the money.'

'I didn't know the job had anything to do with you, remember?'

'Yeah, but it seems to have changed somewhere along the line, doesn't it?' she says, and without giving me a chance to speak, starts impersonating Herb. '*Like we agreed, Mickey, my boy, you'll be well rewarded when you bring her...* What the hell did he mean by that exactly?'

'That's not what he said,' I say, splitting hairs. 'As far as I'm concerned he was only paying me to get the camera. But maybe he's twigged about the other package.'

'What other package?'

'It was lying there. As far as I knew it belonged to whoever was blackmailing him. I figured I was doing him a favour.'

'And you took it?' she says, jabbing at my conscience like a prize-fighter, probing for a weakness. 'To help good old Herb?'

'The truth is; I don't know why I took it. It was just there.' I'm on the ropes, floundering. 'I've tried telling myself it looked like the first package and I wanted to be sure I got the right one... I know that's bollocks. It was obvious. I knew I already had the camera. I just couldn't resist. It was there for the taking. Low hanging fruit they call it in the City.'

'Yeah, but they're not taking other people's money.'

'That's a matter of opinion,' I say trying to tease out a smile but she's intent on keeping me dangling.

'You could have given it back,' she says. 'As soon as you knew it was his, you *should* have given it back.'

'I'm sorry,' I snarl, pummelling the steering wheel with the heel of my hand, 'but I didn't have a spare twenty grand in my wallet when he decided to reappear as the lord of the frigging manor.'

'Twenty thousand? Jesus, Mickey. Now you owe him.'

'Yeah,' I say. 'Don't I know it?'

'And a man like that isn't going to let you forget it.'

'Yeah, I know that too.'

'What do you mean?'

'That's the only reason I got involved in all of this. Because I already owed him.' She finally turns and looks straight at me, wide-eyed.

'What for?'

'It was a long time ago – a lifetime,' I say. But it no longer seems so distant, so incongruous. 'It doesn't matter now. Forget it.'

I count to ten, waiting for the knockout blow. Thankfully it doesn't come. I'm saved by the bell.

'It was lucky the police showed up when they did,' she says.

I'm so relieved by the let-off, I can feel my collar slip from the hook and my feet return to the ground. Relieved I don't have to tell her about my fledgling career as a burglar at the tender age of seventeen. How my very first job went horribly wrong. And that it was Herb who cleared up the mess. I've often reflected on how he effectively gave me a second chance that night, allowing me to choose another path, so I could go on to live a perfect life. The cynic in my head stifles a laugh, but the irony isn't lost on him either. If those were Herb's intentions back then, his motives have changed. He seems to be trying to lure me back in. Why else would he set out to test me?

'I called Melville,' I say, glad for the opportunity to be smug. 'He seemed really worried for you; said he'd send in the local plod. Fat lot of good *they* turned out to be.'

'Thank you,' she says. 'I'm not sure what would have happened if they hadn't arrived when they did.'

'I suppose so,' I say. 'You know, while I was waiting for them I sneaked back into the house. Thanks for leaving the back door unlocked, by the way.' At last I get a smile as I continue recounting my heroics. 'I couldn't hear much but I did see Herb banging the bench with that hammer. Did he try to hurt you?'

'No,' she whispers. 'He doesn't realise.'

'Doesn't realise what?'

'He just thinks I'm Terry Pinner's daughter.' She looks

straight ahead into the darkness.

'Sounds like Pinner owes him something too.'

'Yes,' she turns to face me again, her expression now subdued. 'But it doesn't sound like something that can be repaid.'

'So what does he want with you?'

'Revenge?' she says and a cold chill runs up my spine.

'You'd better tell me everything,' I say, and she starts from the point I was frog-marched out of the house...

Relatively Speaking

Herb had told Mac to stay at the front door and asked Grace to follow him to the storeroom.

'No way,' she said, staying seated. 'I know what goes on in there.'

He laughed dismissively and replied 'Of course. You've been here before.'

'We came back because of the camera.'

'Ah,' he said. 'He *has* told you about it. He said he hadn't. Never mind, I don't suppose it really matters now you're here.'

'It was you in the pub ten years ago,' she said.

'Yes it was me.'

'You stole my camera.'

'Yes. I should have got the film developed years ago, either that or thrown it away. I didn't think there was likely to be anything on there of much use. Six frames, one I took, the other five just party shots of you and your school friends. Nothing there to get back at him with.'

Grace tried to ignore the additional irony that had he developed the film there was certainly something he could have used against *her*. Instead she simply echoed him.

'Get back at him?'

'Your old man, the bastard that helped ruin my life.'

'Terry?'

'Terry Pinner.' He spat out the words like venom. 'Even his own daughter can't bring herself to call him Dad.'

'He's not...' she started to protest, but the intensity of his glare and her confusion at his next words cut her short.

'Why don't I introduce you to *my* family... what's left of it,' he said and started to get up.

She reached inside her coat and took out a package. 'Is this your wife?' she said, holding up the framed photograph she'd removed from its gaudy wrapper. Now it was his turn to be shocked.

'Where did you get that?'

'It is her, isn't it?'

'I thought I lost that, weeks ago. Where was it?'

'Here, two days ago.'

'Hmm, bring it with you,' he said. 'There's someone else you should see.'

A wide metal shelf spanned the entire length of the store room, suspended on brackets against the bare wall, doubling as a workbench, with two chairs tucked neatly beneath. He pulled them out and offered her a seat. Apart from a variety of wooden crates, stacked in order of size on the bench, the room was empty. He held out his hand and she gave him the package, watching as he carefully placed the photograph on the work surface and then discarded the glossy paper in a crumpled ball onto the floor. Reaching into one of the boxes, he produced two items. Both made Grace's pulse quicken.

First he put a lump hammer onto the table without ceremony, like it was a mug of tea. The second item was another photo frame, smaller and virtually identical to the other. He kept it in his hands and looked at the picture.

'I once had a daughter,' he said before standing the frame alongside the other one. 'This is all I have left.'

Grace turned hesitantly to look closer at the second photograph. A newborn baby, swaddled in hospital-issue pink, her tiny fingers clinging loosely to thin air, eyes closed, contentment spoiled only by the transparent tube looping from her little nose, blissfully unaware of her harrowing birth and uncertain future.

As tears welled up in her eyes, she couldn't find the words to say to him; to claim the image as her own. For one thing, she couldn't be certain it was her, but also she could tell Herb was in no mood to have his memories violated. She had to accept this wasn't the time or the place.

The room was spinning and she was finding it hard to focus. Although Herb was speaking, his words didn't register. She had a vague awareness he was talking about someone. Someone else – another man.

'...he killed my wife,' he said.

The last words broke the spell, and she was able to take her eyes off the photograph. Trying to refocus, she realised he'd mentioned a name, but she hadn't heard it. She wanted him to say it again but he didn't. All she could gather was the other man was a rival. She tried to concentrate.

'I lost everything,' he said, putting both photographs into the box. 'After that it was almost not worth living.'

'What's it got to do with Terry?' she said.

'Pinner, the bastard. They were in it together from the start.' His voice rose to a crescendo on every other phrase as if this was a mantra he'd repeated in his head many times.

As he continued, he took the hammer and bounced the cold metal on the palm of his hand. 'I've waited a long time for this. I should have finished it before when I had the chance. The other one has already paid the price. Now it's that bastard Pinner's turn.'

Grace jumped when he slammed the hammer down, narrowly missing his own thumb. The noise obscured his shout but she thought he said, 'It was rigged!'

'He killed her,' he yelled as the metal bench hummed like a tuning fork. 'And your old man covered it up. Might as well have put a gun to her head and pulled the trigger.'

He ignored her attempts to reason with him and continued ranting about wanting revenge. Although she couldn't explain why, when he pounded the bench a second time, she knew he wasn't going to use it on her.

'And then,' she says to me, 'I managed to slip out when the police arrived.'

'Well that makes me marginally less pissed off with their incompetence in being so easily conned,' I say. 'Surely, they had to be suspicious of an old guy and a thug shacking up together in an empty dump like that. Even if they'd held hands, the state of the soft furnishings would have given them away.'

'No,' she says with a chuckle. 'The big guy was hiding in the garden the whole time. He was literally on the other side of the fence from me. I could hear him huffing and puffing after he'd run out of the house. I thought he was after me but he just went to ground and let me get away.'

'I still think they gave up a bit lightly. They couldn't have been in there long enough to even search the house, let alone have a look around the back.'

'Maybe,' she says. 'Then again, without a warrant they'd have had to suspect a crime was being committed.'

'Right,' I say. 'I forgot you lived with the Old Bill. But... I really got the impression that Melville bloke believed me. Wouldn't that have given them sufficient cause?'

'He probably only has so much influence up here.'

'Hmm... you're probably right. The locals didn't seem to have a lot of respect for him as they left. So what did you do then?'

'I stayed the other side of the fence until everything had gone quiet.' She looks down at her feet. 'I had to see what you would do next. I realised everyone else had gone when I saw you talking to me through the wall and sitting on the step with your head in your hands. That's when I decided to follow you back to the car.'

'Are we okay?' I say, reaching across and taking her hand in mine. She squeezes it gently and smiles.

'Herb obviously has some grudge against Terry,' she says. 'Thinks he's somehow caught up with some other Mr Big and the crash that killed his wife.'

'You said yourself, Pinner's no angel.'

'I know. But all those years ago?'

'Dish best served cold,' I say and she returns my frown with a nod. 'So, again he planned to kidnap you. Then what?'

'And why now?' We sit in silence, both trying to find a logical thread to unpick.

'Let's say,' I say, tracing a timeline with my finger on the fogged-up windscreen, 'Herb only became aware of you about ten years ago, before gate-crashing your Millennium Party. If he'd known Pinner all along, wouldn't he have known he already had a son long before you joined the family?'

'Not necessarily. Remember, Simon was born in Gibraltar. Terry and Gillian hadn't long got back before they started thinking about adoption. So it's possible, by the time he discovered that Terry was back, I was already part of the family with no reason for Herb to think I hadn't been there all along.'

'Maybe,' I say. 'But even if he did know about Simon, he might have been more interested in you because of the loss of his own daughter.'

'That's probably true. He said the other man had already suffered, whatever that means. I got the impression he believes in an eye for an eye. Yet, there was something about him that made me doubt he could carry it through.'

'So, Pinner returns to Herb's manor and starts his meteoric rise through the ranks. After a year or two he's back on Herb's radar. Herb does some digging and finds that the copper has a teenage daughter. He tracks her down to a pub on New Year's Eve and watches her. Then decides to take a little memento with him and snatches one last shot before he leaves. Make sense so far?'

'Okay,' she says, watching me embellish my screen graphics with little stick-people and stick-children. 'But if he wanted to kidnap me why didn't he do it then? Instead, he goes home and throws the camera in a drawer and leaves it there for ten years, waiting for some mug to show up!'

'Hey, that's not nice.'

'Harsh but fair,' she says, callously wiping out the little camera I've drawn on the glass.

'You're probably right.'

'He said he didn't think there was anything on the camera to get back at Terry with,' she says, shaking her head.

'Lucky for you he didn't develop it,' I say and she returns my smirk with a nervous laugh.

'But it's strange he kept it all that time and did nothing with it. It doesn't make sense.'

'Yeah.' I nod. 'He said he was going to throw it away, but maybe Pinner's pissed him off again.'

'Anything's possible with him.' She nods back. 'Or maybe he's come across some new information.'

'Surely if he's got new evidence about his wife's death, he could pursue it through official channels.' As soon as I say it I realise my naivety.

'Pinner *is* the official channel and even if he wasn't, men like Herb don't settle their differences in court.' She was right. Especially after twenty-five years of simmering, they don't.

'How did he seem?' I ask. 'When you were alone with him?' It felt like a daft question, but from what I'd heard of their conversation in the dungeon, I couldn't really gauge Herb's state of mind, especially as he's a man who seems to value emotional detachment.

'That's something I've been thinking about,' she says, staring back out into darkness. 'Although he acted like he wanted to frighten me, and don't get me wrong, I was upset and stressed with the situation, I didn't feel intimidated by him. What he was saying was all between him and Terry. It was like he wanted me to understand, to see his side. He was looking for my sympathy. He wasn't aiming his anger at me. He spoke to me like he knew me. He came across as very lonely. In spite of what he was saying about Terry, it felt as if he wanted me to like him. Or at least respect him.'

A tear forms on her long eyelashes. She blinks and it drops

onto her cheek. I want to wipe it away, but at the same time I want to watch it rolling slowly down the contour of her beautiful face.

'You know, it's funny,' she says with a sad smile. 'When I saw the opportunity to run and get out of there, I hesitated. For a fleeting moment, I really wanted to stay and talk to him.'

I nod as if I understand, and give her a few moments of silence. 'Remind me why we ran from Melville?' I say. 'I thought you said he was one of the good guys.'

'He is. But, did you seriously want to explain all of this to him tonight?'

'Fair point. I'm not even sure I could,' I say, peering out the side window and starting to consider our next move. 'He's going to catch up with me sooner or later and want to know why I wasted police time and ruined his evening with the wife and kids.'

'Don't worry,' she says. 'He's not married.'

'How well *do* you know him?'

'He came to Terry and Gillian's a few times back when things were still normal,' she says. 'Before their divorce. I've only seen him a couple of times since.'

By now the windows are weeping and the word *divorce* ricochets around the car. It's not one I want to dwell on at the moment but I do want to move the conversation away from nice bloke Jim Melville.

'Why am I not surprised that Pinner couldn't keep a happy family together?' I say.

'Remember it takes two to tango,' she says. Great. Now I'm thinking about Sam and what part I might have played in causing her disaffection. I'm struck by the ease with which I've taken sides with Gillian without even knowing her, based on what little I *do* know of her husband. Luckily, on this occasion, Grace hasn't read my mind.

'The penny only dropped for him,' she's saying, 'when Gillian went back to Gibraltar last year and moved in with that Spaniard. Then it looked like she was the marriage-breaker all along.'

'So did you move out when they split?' I ask, moving the conversation away from the complexities of relationship breakdowns as much for reasons of self-doubt as out of a genuine desire to know more about her life.

'Yes,' she says. 'Part of their settlement included buying the flat for me and Simon to share. Once they bought it I was keen to move in straight away. Simon wasn't eighteen and had to stay with his mum, so I had the luxury of a place to myself for a couple of years. He only moved in when he started at university.'

'Lucky girl!'

'It's not so bad. I probably only see him once or twice a week unless he wants something. I suppose one day we'll sell it and split the money.'

'You didn't fancy following Gillian to a warmer climate then?'

'She wasn't exactly good company at the time. When she was drinking, her moods were like a pendulum. If you timed it right she would be your best friend. A minute later she could be screaming at you.'

'No wonder Melville stopped calling round,' I say.

'It's a shame. He's a really nice guy.' Her voice tails off.

'The feeling must be mutual. He certainly seemed to drop everything to come and rescue you tonight.' I suddenly feel uncomfortably jealous and straighten myself up by pulling on the steering wheel. 'He's a bit old for you though isn't he?'

'We're just friends.' She looks back at me with a wry smile.

'Right,' I say, unconvinced. 'Well if you're such good friends, wouldn't it be best for us to go and see him tomorrow and try to smooth things over?'

'I don't know,' she says. 'Let me sleep on it and see how I feel in the morning.'

* * *

211

Clean Sweep

The front door opens with a click. He steps inside and closes it silently behind him. Even though the little space behind the door is in virtual darkness, he knows the stairs straight ahead are steep and narrow. His arm brushes against coats hanging from a rail on the wall to the side. He pats them down carefully with his gloved hands and frowns when he finds something bulky in an inside pocket. As he carries it upstairs, he doesn't believe it can be either of the things he came for, even though it feels like it could be one of them. There's no way it would have been left lying around. In the neon light of the landing his suspicion is confirmed, and he takes the item into the front room and puts it on the coffee table.

Slowly he goes from room to room. Meticulously, every cupboard is searched, every concealed space exposed and every hiding place revealed, so everything is left exactly as it was. Every rug and loose floorboard, every shelf and wonky picture frame, every tin of food and frozen pizza, every bath towel and wardrobe top, every pair of socks and box of condoms, every darts trophy and LP rack. All seemingly untouched.

After one final search of the front room, he takes the first item from the coffee table and slides it into his other coat pocket. He came hoping to retrieve two things after all. And while it's not one of them, it might still be useful. He slips out as easily and unnoticed as when he arrived.

14.

Friday, 25th

We stayed in a motel last night. It didn't seem like a good idea to go home. We'd no doubt managed to piss off just about everyone in a single evening and Grace was paranoid that any one of them would be able to follow us back to either of our places. I tried to reassure her that the only reason I seemed to be of any use to Herb was because he couldn't track her down in the first place. But that convinced neither of us. For a while I'd been harbouring a nagging doubt that getting me to find her wasn't his real motive anyway. The more I'd thought about it, the more convoluted that theory had become. It was just so unlikely he would have planted her camera with her undeveloped photographs on it in a run-down old house as a viable means of getting someone like me to find her.

I was coming to the conclusion that Grace's sudden appearance on the scene had been a complete, if not unwelcome coincidence. Besides, I didn't doubt for a second Herb had the capability to discover both of our addresses, passport numbers and shoe sizes without leaving the comfort of his rural retreat.

I didn't like the look on the receptionist's face when we gave false names. Grace had joked about calling ourselves Mr and Mrs Smith. I said I wasn't ready for another sham marriage so we gave single names.

Buck Shot

Once we're off the M25 this morning, Grace calls Melville from my phone.

'Hello, I was hoping to speak to Jim,' she says. 'Oh, but I thought this was his direct... I see. When will he be back? Okay... No, there's no message. I'll call again later.'

'Out on the beat?' I say. 'Or out the back polishing his truncheon?'

'Neither,' she says, disdainfully shaking her head. 'Not due back until late afternoon.'

'I suppose we could go and see Pinner.'

'Not one of your better ideas,' she says and turns away to look out the window. We're through Dartford and I'm about to ask if the trip is really worth continuing. Then she turns around and catches me stone cold.

'Last night, when you said you owed Herb...' I steal a sideways glance and wish I hadn't because I can see the question in her eyes before she's even asked. 'What did you mean?'

'Oh, nothing really,' I say. But feeling her glaring at me with the unseen eyes of a priest behind the confessional screen, I'm forced to offer at least some words of contrition. 'Look... we go way back... ancient history. There's stuff... Grace, I will tell you but can we talk about it later?'

'Hmm... another one of your *long* stories, I suppose,' she says; I'm sure, no pun intended. I'm off the hook again as the road widens into two lanes and I'm grateful to pull out of the traffic, speeding off like the one that got away.

'Anyway,' I say, reasserting myself against the raised engine noise, 'as we've now got hours to kill and you won't introduce me to your family, I suppose I could show you mine.' I'm half joking and expect a similar rebuff.

'Why not,' she says. 'That would be lovely.'

'Okay...' I say. 'But not a word about recent events, agreed?'

'Oh!' she says, piling on the sarcasm. 'I really wanted to tell your nice, conventional parents all about my perfect family background.'

'Did I tell you my mum lives alone?' I say.

'No, but I did get that impression. Didn't you also say you had a brother?'

'Yeah. John.' I hesitate, unsure how far to go with this. I've just realised there's a big risk taking Grace to meet Mum so soon. And I don't mean the one involving embarrassing baby photos or the awkward references to Sam having been such a nice girl. It doesn't even worry me that Mum probably still has our wedding photo on the wall. The real risk is that Grace will ask her in all innocence about my dad and my brother. I can either spill the beans now or take a chance it doesn't come up.

'What does he do?' Grace asks, making the decision for me.

'At this moment,' I say, 'he's probably peeling spuds.'

'Oh, he's a chef.'

'Some days,' I reply. 'And other days he gets to be a listener.'

'What's a listener?'

'It's when someone's on suicide watch and he sits with them to help them through it.'

'Oh, he works with offenders. Sounds like an interesting job,' she says.

'Yeah, that's one way to put it. It depends what privileges he's earned.'

'Oh God,' she says. 'He *is* a prisoner.'

'Yeah.'

'Mickey, your mum and dad must have been devastated.'

'Mum was,' I reply, building up to the big punchline.

'Is your dad... no longer alive?'

'Oh, he's alive alright.'

'But he isn't still with your mum?'

'No, they're divorced.'

'I'm sorry, that must have been terrible,' she says. 'Was there someone else involved?'

'No, he didn't stray like that, but the deceit was probably worse.' Grace says something and puts her hand on my arm. I don't really hear her and just kept talking. 'For over a year she thought he was still working the nightshift. We all did. He'd been laid off and couldn't bring himself to tell her. Seems he just retrained as a housebreaker. I think she could have got over the lies and the sense of foolishness, even the shame of it. She probably would have stood by him.'

'But she didn't?'

'No,' I say as we take the slip road off the A2 and head towards Wombwell Park. 'By the time she knew about it, he'd moved up to bank robbery and had roped her eldest son in with him.'

'Oh God,' she says again. 'Are they both inside?'

'They were. Forty years between them. Dad's been out on licence for five but he stays away. John's still got at least five to do.' I look out the side window and try to compose myself.

'Jesus,' she says, blaspheming a third time. 'What did he do, kill someone?' I almost swerve into the central reservation.

'The security guard... at their first bank job,' I say, exhaling slowly through trembling lips. I really want to leave it at that, spare her the grim details, but her silence eggs me on and I take another deep breath. 'He pulled Dad's mask off, just as they were leaving. John was already outside. He could have got away. Dad came out and told him and they panicked. John went back in and shot the man in the face.'

Grace is now silent as I take the right turn into Hamilton East.

'He was only twenty,' I say, as we pull up outside the glowing hearth of my family home. 'Now he's a lifer. Minimum twenty-five years. No guarantee of parole. And Mum's disowned him.'

I look across at Grace. Her face is ashen and she has a hand over her mouth.

Mamma Mia!

The pristine white tablecloth is adorned with best china. Plates, cups and saucers I didn't even know Mum had. Within minutes of us accepting her invitation to stay for lunch, fresh sandwiches, a bowl of tossed salad and another one full of crisps have appeared as if they've been waiting in the wings. They're followed by a delicate cake stand, half a dozen fondant fancies, arranged colourfully around its tiered edges, and an elegant teapot wafting aromatic steam from its spout. Mum's face is beaming like the proverbial Cheshire cat and she seems to float in and out of the room with every new delivery of food. Each time, she looks at us sitting together and smiles, and each time Grace smiles back.

They've already had an awkward hug on the doorstep. I wish I could have given Grace more time to get her head around my family history before she stepped over the threshold, but she seemed to put it out of her mind once I'd made the introductions.

I can understand this is a bit strange for them both. Mum's so used to fawning over Sam on our infrequent visits together, and I know she's still really upset that Sam would cheat on me. I think she felt more deceived than I did because she'd only ever seen the outward appearance of a happy marriage and thought Sam was the perfect daughter-in-law. God knows, my mother needed some family bliss to be proud of back then.

'Mum, come and sit down and stop fussing,' I call after her as she heads back to the kitchen. She returns with a big tin of assorted Belgian chocolate biscuits that were almost certainly tucked away somewhere out of reach for Christmas.

'It's so nice to meet you,' she says to Grace for the second time when she finally sits down at the table.

'I've been looking forward to meeting you, Mrs Field. Mickey's a lucky man to have such a lovely mum.'

'Mums are supposed to be lovely, that's our job,' she says and beams even brighter as she looks across at me before turning back to Grace. 'And... how's *your* mum?'

'I was adopted,' Grace says surprisingly confidently and gives Mum a very upbeat version of her life story. At the end of it you'd be forgiven for thinking Terry Pinner is the people's champion and Simon is angelically following in his father's footsteps. I look across at her and try to hide a knowing grin. She smiles back at me and reaches across to gently squeeze my hand.

'So tell me, how did you two meet?' Mum says, offering

Grace another sandwich.

'Oh, you know,' Grace says. 'The usual things, a furtive look across a crowded bar, a clever opening line, the offer of a drink.'

'Michael always was good at chatting up girls before... well, when he was younger.'

'I bet he was.' Grace winks at me. 'Then we got chatting and soon realised we had a lot in common. We were both looking for the same thing. I suppose you could say we just clicked.'

I almost choke on a crisp at Grace's camera pun, but she continues to describe the second time we met and takes great delight in telling Mum how I conned my mates out of their money. I start to protest my innocence and realise there's no good way of telling that particular story.

Pretty soon the two of them are nattering away as if they've known each other for years and I sense that Grace is grateful for the chance to relax in the warmth of a mother's love. There's just a danger we're getting a bit too comfortable. It's not until we're onto our second cup of tea, having made a serious dent in the Christmas biscuits, when Mum snaps us both back to reality.

'Michael, have you heard from Herb yet?'

'Yes,' I say.

'Oh, you have. Is he okay?'

'He's fine, Mum. He sends his regards.'

'Where's he staying?' She looks at Grace. 'He's an old neighbour of ours whose house burned down last week. We've been worried about him, haven't we Michael?'

Grace smiles and nods.

'He's been with family, Mum. He's fine. There's no need to worry anymore.' She looks at me with relief in her eyes and turns back to Grace.

'Poor old chap. Some say he's a bit of a rogue,' she says, and before I can stop her she adds: 'Even the police said they were worried he might be involved with handling photographs of children.' Grace's eyes widen and she shoots me a questioning look.

'Mum!' I say with a withering glare. 'All they asked was whether he'd ever offered you any photographs?' Out of the corner of my eye I can see Grace's jaw drop, but Mum doesn't let that deter her.

'And...' she says, indignantly, 'they made it sound like there was a young girl in his house that day. How do you explain that?' Grace is about to say something but I cut her off.

'Mum. He's old school. He's not like that.' She sees me looking furtively at Grace.

'Well, I hope you're right,' she says, lowering her voice. 'He's always been very pleasant to me.'

'There you go then,' I say.

'But he did start...'

'Mum, I've seen him and he's okay. He's staying in a nice, big house out in the country and someone's there looking after him.' I give her a pained expression and look sideways towards Grace.

'Oh, don't mind me dear,' she says to Grace, seeming to take the hint. 'I have to say it like it is. Honesty's the best policy. Nobody likes being lied to, do they?'

'No, Mrs Field, you're right.'

'But he was acting strange before he disappeared.' She makes a point of finishing the sentence I'd interrupted, before adding. 'And the police *did* say there'd been a girl in there.'

'Well I expect...' Grace says, before I cut her off again.

'Mum!' I say, 'Can we change the subject, please?'

'Mrs Field?' Grace says, looking daggers at me. I hold my breath.

'Yes dear? And please call me Annie.'

'Mickey told me you haven't been well. Are your legs feeling better?'

Wiggle Room

We've decided I'll go in alone to see DS Melville while Grace waits in a coffee shop. After my pathetic attempt to take control of her reunion with Herb last night, I'm amazed she even suggested it. But here I am, counting ceiling tiles for what must be twenty minutes, before the meeting room door finally opens.

'Sorry to keep you, Mr Field. Has anyone offered you a coffee yet?' I'm surprised at his courtesy, given the nature of our last conversation.

'No, I'm fine. We've not long had lunch with Mum.' I cringe at the unnecessary detail and keep talking to disguise my embarrassment. 'Look, about last night. There was a bit of a misunderstanding. I honestly thought Grace was in danger and I couldn't think who else to call.'

'I take it she's safe and well?' he says, taking the seat opposite me, across the table, before leaning forward on his elbows; so much for an informal chat.

'Yeah, she's fine; just a bit shaken up,' I say and ease back in the chair.

'I gather she wasn't in the house when the Met arrived.'

'No. She managed to get away when they heard the sirens. Just as well... for what good that lot did.'

'Hmm, I gather Long was happy for them to have a look around and, apart from the place being a bit run down, they didn't see anything there to give them cause for concern,' he says, ignoring the irony in my laugh and the shake of my head. 'By the time I arrived everything was deserted.'

'Right,' I say. 'But I thought you said you couldn't come.'

'Yes, well I just wanted to be sure. Anyway, I was hoping to talk to *her*.'

'She's okay, really,' I say. 'She asked me to come and explain everything. She's feeling a bit upset and confused at the moment. She thought you'd understand.'

'Yes, that's all very well,' he says leaning further forward, 'but I do have some questions I'd like to ask her.' I shrug my shoulders and he adds, 'Well... as you're here perhaps we could run through the things I wanted to talk to you about?'

'Sure,' I say, slightly less anxious about discussing that than trying to articulate the nature of yesterday's rendezvous at Bleak

House. He seems to have let me off lightly on that one, but my sense of relief is short-lived.

'So, what do you know about the arson at the property belonging to Herbert Long... the one in Gravesend?' He looks straight into my eyes. I blink and look away to give myself time to construct a reply, conscious of having reminded Grace earlier that I wouldn't be mentioning the stranger who answered Herb's phone.

'Well... ' I say, trying to stay calm and laidback, in spite of beginning to feel like the chair's infested. 'I drove past the house last Friday morning on the way to see my mum and saw the fire damage.'

Melville leaves the silence unfilled and I fall into his trap and start rambling. 'I didn't know it was arson, although I noticed it was all sealed off like a crime scene, so I suppose I wondered if there were suspicious circumstances. That's really all I know.'

'So you just happened to drive down to see your mother that morning?'

'Yeah. She'd worried me a bit the day before. She seemed anxious about something.'

'And it was her you were concerned about?'

'Well, yeah. Just something she'd said. I knew she was worried and I wanted to make sure she was okay.'

'Something she'd said about Herbert Long?'

'Maybe,' I say, pushing myself up on the arms of the chair. 'But like I said, I was concerned about her. After what she's...' I manage to stop mid-sentence.

'Been through.' He finishes it anyway, nodding sagely. 'Yes, I can understand that.'

'Good,' I say. Although I'm now sitting upright, he's still towering over me. And the room suddenly feels much smaller.

'So presumably you came from the Dartford Crossing?'

'Yeah,' I say with a shrug. 'And down the A2.'

'What, towards the golf course?'

'That's right.' I try to disguise the frown that's pinching my forehead as I stare back at him.

'Bit of an indirect route isn't it... to get to your mother's house?' Now I'm hoping the slits of my eyes at least conceal the cogs and wheels that have gone into overdrive in my head.

'Yeah, well... we used to live in Sussex Road, didn't we?' I say, relieved my wits haven't completely deserted me. 'Sometimes I like to go past the old house. Big deal. What's your point?'

'Have you discussed the fire with Miss Pinner?' His change of tack throws me. It's also the first time anyone's called her that.

'With Grace?' I say and he nods. 'Uh, well, she's aware of it if that's what you mean. What's it got to do with her?'

'When's the last time *you* were in the house sir?' His questions are darting all over the place.

'I've only been in there once recently; a couple of weeks ago.' I'm getting agitated. This is starting to feel far too formal for my liking.

'You didn't visit Mr Long's house last Thursday afternoon?'

'I drove past with my mum on the way back from shopping. But no, I didn't go in.'

'Apart from your mother, was there anyone else with you?'
'No.'

'Did you see anyone else near the house? A young woman, perhaps? Someone you might have recognised?'

'No. Like who?'

'Why did you visit Mr Long two weeks ago?' By now, I've had enough.

'Look... *Sergeant*. I don't want to be rude, but I did *volunteer* to come and answer a few questions. Before I say anything else, I want to know where this is going. And if I'm a suspect, perhaps you'd better read me my rights.'

'That won't be necessary sir. Just one last thing, how long have you known Miss... er, Grace?'

'Hang on a minute. Sounds like you have your own personal reasons for wanting to know about me and Grace, or am I still helping with official enquiries?'

'I'm simply trying to establish any possible connection between Miss Pinner and Mr Long and so far you're the only common denominator.'

'Am I really?' I say. 'Well maybe you'd better ask her about that.'

'Well, precisely. Like I said I was hoping to speak to her today. Can I make a suggestion?'

'Go for it.'

'I'm sure we'd both prefer to keep this discussion on a casual footing. Would that be a reasonable assumption?'

'Go on.'

'You implied earlier that Miss Pinner was with you at lunchtime, at your mum's?' he says and I squirm inwardly. 'I suppose she's waiting somewhere nearby. If I could accompany you to see her, it would be far better than me having to formally invite her into the station. Do you understand where I'm coming from?'

'Ah, I get it. He doesn't know about this particular line of enquiry does he?' I say and Melville glares back at me. 'You've gone off-piste haven't you? You want a little chat with the guvnor's daughter behind his back. Would *that* be a reasonable assumption?'

'Mr Field,' he says, straightening up in his chair. 'Let's just say it would be much easier for all of us if we could keep this unofficial.'

'That's ironic,' I smirk.

'Look, don't push your luck, Field.' He stands up and leans across the table, his eyes bulging. 'Make no mistake, I have reasonable grounds to detain you here and now in connection with the criminal destruction of property. But there are other matters I would prefer to discuss in due course without such constraints and I would appreciate your cooperation on that basis. Do I make myself clear?'

'Yeah, yeah, yeah. All I was going to say was that Grace told me you were the good cop.' His eyes give away a suppressed smile and then he exhales dramatically.

'And all I'm asking of you is the chance to prove it.'

'Okay. I'm going to trust her judgement on this. Let me ring her first.'

'I'll see you at the front desk,' he says and leaves me alone in the room.

Mug Full

We barely speak during the ten-minute walk to the café and when we get there Grace is sitting in a quiet corner. A huge beaker with the frothy remains of a skinny latte is on the table in front of her and the *Daily Mail* is folded open at the financial pages. She stands and smiles awkwardly as Melville holds out a hand. She squeezes it gently and seems to lean in for a kiss, but he stays upright and she sits back down again.

'How are things, Jim?' she says like they're old mates.

'Oh, you know, cops and robbers. Too many of them and not enough of us.'

I flinch and look over to the counter. 'I think I'm ready for that coffee now,' I say. 'Do you want another one Grace?'

'No, I'm okay,' she says and Melville shakes his head – like I was including him – and sits down opposite her. I join a seemingly permanent queue and, when I eventually get back to the table and put down the ceramic bucket in which a thimble of espresso has been drowned without trace in a gurgling sea of foam, the subdued conversation stops a bit too abruptly for my liking.

'The sergeant said he wanted to ask you some questions Grace,' I say, louder than necessary. Melville bristles and looks around, but we've got the rear half of the cafe to ourselves.

'Let's keep this low key, shall we?' he shoots back at me and I put my hands up in fake surrender.

'What is it Jim?' As she says it the tension seems to slide from his shoulders and I realise what a calming effect she has on him.

'I've come across an anomaly I'm struggling to understand

relating to a house fire we're investigating. I realise this is unorthodox but as it's you I'll get straight to the point.'

'Okay,' she says.

'What were you doing in Herbert Long's house on the day it was torched?'

She looks across at me stunned. I stare back helplessly. This isn't a scenario we'd rehearsed and all I can do is wait to hear what she comes up with.

'Oh, God, what did I leave behind?' she says.

'You know I can't discuss the details of forensics found at a crime scene. However, there are reasonable grounds...' He starts all officiously, sitting up straight in the chair, fiddling with his notebook before pausing to look up at her. Then he sighs and slouches forward, putting his hands on the table. For a moment I think he's going to touch her fingers but he stops short. When he continues to speak, his tone is more relaxed. 'All I can say is there are suspicions you were in that house, in all likelihood, on the day that it was later set on fire. I need you to help me understand when you were there and what you were doing. I'm hoping I can eliminate it as a factor in the arson. That way we can leave the conversation here and, in good conscience, I can dismiss the evidence as inconsequential. So, would you mind telling me why you were there?'

'This doesn't sound like you, Jim, keeping all this unofficial,' she says. In the circumstances, I can't understand why she's goading him, especially when she adds: 'It's all a bit cavalier, isn't it?'

'I suppose you might say I've had a good mentor,' he says. 'Maybe it was inevitable for some of his... methods to start rubbing off.'

'I take it Terry isn't aware we're having this conversation?' She looks deep into his eyes.

'No. He's already told me to drop it.'

'I suppose I should be grateful for that. Thank you for giving me an opportunity to explain.'

'Take your time.'

'Did you know I was adopted by Terry and Gillian?' she says, as if she's expecting to surprise him.

'I've suspected it for a while but I've only just found out for sure,' he says, leaving Grace looking shocked. 'I always thought you seemed a bit out of place with them, if you don't mind me saying.'

'Did he tell you?' she says.

'He didn't have to.' He sighs again and seems to choose his words carefully. 'Although at this stage it's all circumstantial, I've come across the juvenile offender records of an eleven year old girl with a string of misdemeanours. She was in care at the time. Her surname was James.

'Oh,' she says, looking down at the table.

'I requested clearance to trace her through social services and that was when the boss told me to back off.'

'I bet he did,' she says.

'It wasn't the first time he'd told me to overlook details I thought might be significant. But this time it seemed to be personal.'

By now I'm feeling confused and left out.

'So let me get this straight,' I say, breaking the tension, and at the same time increasing my own anxiety about the direction this is heading. 'There's recently been a little girl in Herb's house?' Melville stays silent and Grace stares into her empty cup, like neither of them has heard me.

'Could someone please tell me what this is all about?' I say, raising my voice again to get their attention and then lowering it back to a whisper. 'It's just I keep hearing that Herb is somehow connected with children and photographs, and excuse me if I'm starting to get a little bit paranoid.' Melville gives me a perplexed look but it's Grace who answers.

'It's me,' she says. 'I was that little girl.'

I'm guessing that's supposed to make everything clear.

'You're twenty five,' I say. 'And that's not your surname.'

Melville shifts in his chair and I look at him, but he shrugs and we both turn back to Grace.

'Okay,' she says. 'I grew up as Grace James.'

'What about de Manton?'

'It's...' She takes a deep breath and briefly closes her eyes. 'It's silly I know... it's just a name I use sometimes.' As she says it I feel a chasm open up between us.

'Grace?' My mind starts bouncing around the room.

'Can we get back to the point?' Melville's saying. 'Why were you in Long's house that day, Grace?'

'It's all very simple really. I've been trying to trace my real parents.'

I can hear her words and I let her continue uninterrupted, but my head's preoccupied with a conversation I realise will have to wait until we're alone.

She's telling him how she found the house where her real parents had lived and how she became intrigued with Herb and the strange comings and goings. She leaves out all references to me before admitting that when she came back to find the house deserted, she couldn't resist having a look inside.

He asks her to tell him exactly what she did and where she went in the house, and when she starts by saying she got in through the back door, his eyebrows raise, I'm guessing because he won't have found any signs of forced entry. She doesn't tell him she used regulation lock picks to open it, but she does say that once inside, she was shocked to find the house completely empty. When she thought she heard a noise coming from the front garden, she hid behind the front door and left the way she'd come in, going home none the wiser about the man who lived there.

'I don't need to tell you I could charge you with breaking and entering,' he says.

'I know,' she sighs.

'Not to mention how this looks, given the subsequent criminal damage to the premises,' he continues, and she nods back at him nervously. He seems to hold her gaze intentionally. 'But I'm not going to. And that's not just because DCI Pinner told me to drop it.'

'Thank you,' she says, and something in the way their eyes meet tells me he trusts her. Not because of her connection with his boss but for some other reason in spite of it. After a moment he looks across at me.

'I'm not finished with you yet Mr Field. That will have to wait. I need to get back to the station, but you'll be hearing from me once I've made some further enquiries.' Then he turns back to Grace. 'I'm glad to hear you didn't need my assistance in the end yesterday evening. Is there anything you want to tell me about your meeting?'

'No Jim, not at the moment. There are still a few things I need to work through first. But thanks for caring.'

'Well, you know where I am.' He gets up and walks towards the door without another word. All I can do is glare at her.

Return Address

Grace is asleep in my bed. It's all getting a bit too much for her. We got back earlier this evening, after I convinced her to stay at my place while we sort all this out. By the time I'd made her a cup of green tea, she'd already crashed on the sofa. I carried her through to the bedroom and covered her over. It's seven-thirty and I'm sitting alone in the half-light, listening to Sade's sultry tones caressing the dusk, thinking through what Grace said earlier, about her imaginary name. In the car coming home, she told me that James was the only surname she'd ever known before being adopted...

'I've no idea how I got it,' she said. 'And when I was old enough to ask, no one seemed to know where it came from. For some reason, it never felt right, so I invented a name of my own.'

After her adoption, she became Grace Pinner, but she never really liked that either because it sounded so bland. At school, kids being what they are, they turned it into Grey Spinster, which to the average insecure teenage girl must have been the ultimate in mental cruelty. I told her I prefer de Manton. It suits her. It's bold and provocative.

'That wasn't the intention,' she said. 'I was only ten when I dreamt it up.'

I asked her what it meant but she wouldn't tell me.

'Just something silly,' she said. 'An escape from the reality back then, I suppose. An alter ego to live out my dreams.' She sighed before adding, 'You should be flattered. I hadn't used it for years until I met you.'

I've written it on a scrap of paper in big capital letters and I've been studying it for clues. Finally, I see it. It's so simple and yet so elegant. I walk to the darkened window and hold the paper at an angle and the reflection confirms it. I think about the little girl with no name, turning her lost identity into such an enigmatic new persona.

Deep in thought I start to draw the curtains. That's when I see the car parked across the road. It's a silver Mercedes, and getting out of the driver's door is Mac the Chauffeur. When he starts walking towards the house, I pull away from the window and weigh up my next move. I rush through to the bedroom and before I can decide whether to wake Grace, the doorbell rings. The sound is followed by a muffled thud. Together they're enough to rouse her and she looks at me through bleary eyes as I signal for her to be quiet.

'Who is it?' she whispers.

'It's Herb's heavy,' I say. 'Don't worry I'll get rid of him. Just stay here.'

I go back into the front room and, sticking close to the wall, look down towards the path. I'm relieved to see him walking back to the gate and out onto the street. He gets in the car and drives away. I'm guessing that with no lights on he figured the place was deserted. When I go back to the hall, Grace is peering around the bedroom door with a questioning frown.

'Don't worry, he's gone,' I say. 'Must have thought we were out.'

'Really?' she says.

'Yeah I know. Feels like he gave up a bit too easily if he was looking for...' I look down the stairs to the front door and see a large envelope on the mat.

'Okay. So maybe he was just the messenger,' I say and she follows me halfway down.

'Don't touch it,' she says looking over my shoulder. 'What if it's a...' I stop in my tracks two stairs from the bottom. The heavy brown packet is wound tightly with rubber bands and otherwise unmarked.

'No, that wouldn't be his style,' I say, reaching down slowly to pick it up. Whilst the feel of it in my hand is worryingly familiar, I carry it back upstairs like it's a bottle of nitroglycerine and put it carefully on the coffee table.

'What do you think it is,' she says, but I don't answer. Instead, I cross the room and open the hi-fi cabinet. I touch a button on the turntable and the needle rises, silencing Sade's assurances that my love is king. I wait for the arm to finish its robotic return and slide the stack shelf forward before reaching behind it into the back of the cabinet.

'What are you doing?' I hear Grace say as I pull out the jumble of leads nestling in the gap between the record rack and the back panel of the unit. I continue feeling the unseen corners of the compartment with increased desperation.

'It's gone!' I yell. 'Someone's been in here.' I spin around and see Grace holding the parcel and picking nervously at the elastic with her fingernails.

'Wait,' I say as I head out into the hall and back down the stairs to the coat rack. Last night I left the decoy bundle in my jacket pocket, but it's a futile search as I pull the lining inside out. I know as soon as I grab it that the envelope is no longer in the pocket. I run back upstairs and into the lounge just as Grace is removing the last rubber band and ripping open the sealed envelope and a pile of neatly stacked yellow paper fans out across the table.

'What the...'

'Fuck!' I say, finishing her sentence. Scrawled across the top sheet, written in large red letters:

DON'T SCREW WITH ME, FIELD
YOU OWE ME £200

It's been an hour since our special delivery. We've calmed down and started to rationalise what just happened. I've told Grace about my fake package of yellow banknotes. I wasn't able to give her a particularly good reason for making it in the first place. The best I could come up with was because I'd originally thought the money belonged to some thug who was blackmailing Herb. So I figured if I got into a tight squeeze with someone desperate to get it back, I might be able to buy myself some time with a decoy. She's not convinced, but it doesn't matter now.

'Not only did they get in here; they were able to find both bundles and get out without leaving a trace,' I say, as much to myself as to Grace.

'And then to send one back... just to make a point,' she says continuing my train of thought. 'Maybe it's Herb's way of saying you didn't deliver on your side of the deal.'

'Like I said before...' I say, through gritted teeth, 'when it came to you there was no deal.'

'That's not how he sees it,' she fires back, disarming me with simple logic.

'Yeah... you may be right. It also tells us a lot about what he's capable of.'

'Why would you still owe him £200?'

'Yeah right,' I smirk. 'Make that Simon owes him... his fee, remember? For developing the film.'

'Oh, I see. But surely you're now even as far as Herb's concerned.'

'Maybe... perhaps he's trying to tell me I'm out of the game.'

'Either way, I can't leave it there. I still think he's my father. He doesn't realise it yet and although he's angry now, I can't give up on him until he looks me in the eye and refuses to accept me as his daughter.' She looks right into mine and adds: 'I've got to see him again.'

I get my phone and call the number of his country house. It just rings and rings.

15.

Saturday, 26th

I fell asleep on the couch last night. Grace was tired and went back to bed. I finished off the last three inches of a bottle of Jack Daniels that had sat in the cupboard untouched since Sam left. Hard to believe I know, but Bourbon's not my thing. She would drink it with Coke but I've never been one for mixers.

I'm woken by blinding sunlight. I hadn't bothered closing the curtains in case there were any more mysterious visitors, but all had been quiet until the early hours. At least that's the last time I remember getting up to look out the window. There's a gnawing pain just behind my eyes and I block out the light with my hands. On the coffee table there's a message written on a yellow sheet of paper, tucked beneath the empty bottle:

BACK AT FIVE – G x

The smile that crosses my face at the thought of the decoy bundle's reincarnation as a notepad is tinged with guilt that I didn't at least see her before she left. I knew she had to work today and I wanted to make sure she was up to it. I told her last night I would take her to the salon this morning but she said no. I was still going to anyway. I'm reminded how many times I used to promise to do things for Sam, only to get too worse for wear and then let her down. She said I had a problem. When she cheated on me I was able to reassure myself *she* was the problem. Now, I'm not so sure.

I snap out of my self-pity and go into the kitchen, looking for something to eat. There's no bacon in the fridge and only one egg. Grace has left low fat bagels and a carton of cranberry on the breakfast bar. I decide to give the bagel a try and pass on the juice. The wrapper suggests I might like it with low fat crème fraiche and blueberries. I just toast it and spread it thick with butter. It goes down well with black coffee and I toast another one.

After a quick shave, I grab the mobile. It's got a missed call and I hope it's Grace. It's not. I smirk at my own joke when the phone says Lucky Jim called an hour ago. I was being ironic when I added him to my contacts list, but after yesterday's cosy little tête-à-tête, maybe I should have put him in as Clever Dick.

I call Grace first and get her voicemail. I feel strangely nervous about calling Melville back before speaking to her. She seems to be able to bring out a softer side in him than the one I had to deal with at the station. I tell myself to stop being a prat and ring him back. I needn't have worried because I get his voicemail too. I leave my name and number and head back into the bathroom.

Stark Choice

I've just got out of the shower when I hear the phone ringing. I'd rather not proliferate the game of ping-pong with Melville so I dash to the kitchen naked and pick it up. That's when my heart jumps into my throat, because it says the caller is *Bleak House*.

It's the name I added against the number that made me jump the time it called me that night I was skulking around outside, worried that Herb might have been incarcerated there.

I press the green button and lift the phone without speaking.

'Mickey Field?' Slow and deliberate, the deep voice is disturbingly familiar.

'Who's asking?'

'We've spoken before,' he says.

That much I already know.

'Uh... how do you know my name?' I say slowly, trying to

control my breathing.

'You introduced yourself... remember?'

'When?' I say and he leaves me in limbo struggling to make the connection until I hear a click and then another vaguely familiar voice that's instantly enlightening and equally alarming.

"Sorry I woke you, Herb. It's so good to talk to you." A recording of my own pathetic drunkenness slurs back at me down the line. "Thought you were in trouble..."

'Does that help?' the other voice adds in startling contrast.

'You're the bastard who burned the house down,' I yell. 'What do you want from me?'

'So many questions... and so much anger, Mickey. You don't mind if I call you Mickey?'

'You can call me Monty-bleeding-Python if you want, but I still want to know who the hell you are and what you want.'

'For the moment,' he says calmly, 'I'd prefer it if you didn't know my name. Before that happens, I'd need to be sure what side of the line you're on.'

'What's that suppose to mean? What line?'

'Things have become... complicated.' I dwell briefly on the irony of my own words, this time from the mouth of a stranger, when he continues, 'There's your alliance with Long, on the one hand... that reminds me, was he pleased with the camera?'

'What's it to you?' I say, suddenly feeling very exposed, here in my kitchen, without so much as a tea towel for cover.

'Oh, just curious. It's good to know he's resurfaced.'

'I didn't say...' But of course I had. Undeterred, I stay on the offensive. 'So, what's so complicated about that? I've known him most of my life.'

'Yeah, I'll grant you that. But you'd have to admit there's been something of a reunion of late. The complication is that, on the other hand, you're spending all this time with Miss Pinner.'

'What about Grace?'

'I think she's taken quite a shine to you, Mickey. That was very unexpected. I suppose you know who her father is.'

'That copper, you mean...'

235

'Chief Inspector, no less. I'd expect you to show a little more respect for the boys in blue, considering your... dubious background.'

'Yeah? What else do you know about me then?'

'Oh, I'm pretty well-connected. Let me see... first there's your father. I think they call him The Sheriff... in certain circles... on account of the way he shafted your brother. Poor Little John. Need I go on?'

'Yeah, okay. You've made your point. What do you want?'

'Well that all depends... like I said... what side of the line you're on.'

'I don't get it. And even if I did, what's it to you anyway?'

'This can get to be a very messy business, my friend. Oh, and there's the rub; are you my friend, Mickey? That's all I need to hear.'

'That's a stupid question... I don't even know who you are.'

'Oh no, it's a very important question. You see, you appear to have a foot in both camps. So I need to find out if you're my friend. Because... well, if not, there's really only one alternative.'

'How about you tell me who the hell you are and why it matters to you what company I keep and then maybe I can...'

'It's very simple. Really it is. They are like two sides of the same coin, young Grace... and Long. I'll give you a little time to figure it all out. And when you do, I'd rather you got back to me to confirm I can count on you, than having to discover from someone else that I can't. Believe me, by then it'll be too late.'

'You don't frighten me, you bastard...'

'Look Mickey, how can I put this? If you find Herbert Long in any way menacing, I can protect you from him; that's a promise. And if you think he's capable of making your life really difficult, at a stroke, I can make things very simple for you. But... if you think you can stand against me and that I couldn't change your life in a way that is... profoundly uncomfortable, then I urge you to reconsider.'

'So you want me to drop Herb... or else, what exactly?'

'Well, we tend to settle our differences... how should I say?

Indirectly. You see I have no interest in hurting you. Like you said, we hardly know each other... okay, perhaps that's only half true. Sometimes people need a bit of encouragement, and I find the best way is to make sure that those they love the most... stay safe and sound.'

'You leave Grace alone!'

'Oh, that's funny. I could almost say the same to you. You're probably fed up with hearing that. No, I won't intervene on that score. At least as long as it makes her happy. And just to reassure you, I have no intention of harming a single hair on her head. No, I was thinking of someone much closer to home. Perhaps... Mrs Field might be surprised if one of my associates were to pay her a visit.'

'Leave my wife out of this, you bastard.'

'Yes, of course... there's *that* Mrs Field too. And I would have put money on you thinking of family first... poor old dear, all on her own down there in Gravesend. Maybe blood isn't thicker than water after all. I've never understood what that meant, have you? Probably best not to dwell on it. I'm sure you'd rather not find out. Anyway, it's useful to know you still care about her too... Samantha, isn't it? Or maybe you call her Sam...'

I open my mouth to speak, but my vocal chords have turned to sawdust and nothing audible comes out.

'I know you're still there. If not for the deafening silence I might have thought you'd left me hanging. No, I expect you're just wondering how I know so much – well-connected, like I said. *And* you're probably worrying what else I might have on you. So you should be... Anyway, give it some thought Mickey. You've got my number; don't be a stranger.' The line goes dead long before I lower the phone from my ear.

Scenting Danger

When Melville calls back an hour later I'm still feeling very exposed, though at least now fully clothed. He says he wants to meet up again and wonders if I'd mind him coming to my house.

He says it's nothing to worry unduly about and it relates to some other lines of enquiry. He sounds very courteous and, I might even go so far as to say, quite friendly, but the word *unduly* stands out like it's written in capitals. He says he'll be here at three this afternoon.

He arrives unfashionably on the dot. He's sitting in the lounge while I make some tea.

'You've got a nice place,' he says when I come in with the tray.

'Thanks.'

'I'm glad Grace has found someone she feels she can trust.'

'Yeah.' I'm not sure what else to say to that.

'She *can* trust you, can't she Mr Field?'

'Call me Mickey,' I say, and try to nod reassuringly.

'She's not had it easy, you know.'

'No. I suppose not.'

'I've known her a while.'

'So she said.' I shift uncomfortably on the sofa, irritably pulling the cushion from behind my back and shoving it out of the way.

'I suppose... I've been like an older brother.'

'That's good to know,' I say, relieved but hoping not to sound it.

'It's just... I couldn't stand by and see her getting hurt.'

'You don't need to worry about that.'

'Good,' he says. 'I'm glad we understand each other.' He sips his tea and then throws me by asking if he can use the bathroom.

'Uh, yeah,' I say, almost getting up before sitting back and nodding enthusiastically, as if needing to confirm it's a perfectly natural thing for him to ask. 'Across the hall, door on the left.'

He seems to be in there a long time and I'm left sitting in my own lounge, anxiously twiddling my thumbs, like I'm waiting for the plumber to come in and tell me how much it'll cost to fix a dripping ballcock.

A smile creases my face when I hear the loo flush and

remember all of Grace's smalls hanging up to dry over the bath. Maybe it's all to do with male hormones and animal instincts, but the thought of him fighting his way through her knickers and bras in the intimate sanctuary of my lair gives me renewed confidence.

'So, is that all you came to see me for?' I say as he comes into the room. He looks back down the hall and turns to me, puzzled. 'No, I didn't mean... I meant... to see that I was treating her well?'

'Look, I'll come to the point, Mr Field,' he says, returning to his seat. 'I'm very concerned for her safety.'

'Well you really don't need to be,' I say. 'And if you don't mind me saying, this is all a bit beyond the call of duty, isn't it? Coming here to check the place out, with your not-so-subtle threats and accusing me of putting her in danger.'

'No, you don't understand,' he says, holding up a calming hand. 'It's not *you* I'm concerned about.'

'Who then?' I lean forward and massage the creases in my forehead.

'Terry Pinner's a very powerful man,' he says, and reaches across to take a fly biscuit from the plate I'd brought in on the tray. I hate them; the packet's been in the cupboard for months.

'Sure. I've already had the pleasure, remember? So I know he's a thug.' I wait for him to jump to defend his boss but he doesn't.

'It's not just him.' He says it with an intensity that makes my head jolt.

'I'm not sure what you're saying... Grace seems to be able to keep Pinner off her back.'

He nods like he knows what I mean. 'All the same, he's a very powerful man.'

'Like I said...'

'But there's always someone more powerful, Mr Field.' He's choosing his words carefully, and keeps looking down as if he doesn't really want to be telling me this.

'What, like up the chain of command?'

'No... not necessarily,' he says.

'So... where?'

'You should be more concerned about people outside the force than within it.' I wait for him to elaborate. Instead, he puts a hand across his mouth as if to prevent anything else coming out.

'Come on! You're going to have to give us more than that, surely? It's not much of a warning if you can't be specific.'

'Just look out for her, will you?' he says. 'And you. You should be on your guard too.'

'Is it Herb Long we need to be wary of?' All my wolverine bravado of two minutes ago has evaporated. Now I'm a lamb and he's the shepherd.

'Long's a toerag, make no mistake,' he says, finishing his tea. 'But even he's not quite the monster some would have you believe. Even though he might swim with the sharks, he's as much a target in all this... though I'd hesitate to call him a victim.'

'What do you mean *in all this*?'

'Look Mr Field, this is an ongoing investigation. You'll understand I can't comment further.' He's fiddling with his phone and then starts to get up like he's ready to leave, but I have to get him to trust me enough to keep him talking.

'Mum told you he'd contacted me,' I say as he stands up. I stay seated. 'It was a couple of weeks ago.'

'Yes, she did. But I got the impression yesterday you didn't want to talk about it.'

'I know, but what you just said... He told me he was being blackmailed.' As I say it he sits back down. 'We met to discuss a proposition. It was a job he wanted me to do. Break into a house and recover a camera. I agreed to do it.'

'Are you sure you want to tell me about it?' he says, fumbling for his notebook. 'There's only so far I can go with this, off the record.'

'Bear with me,' I say. 'I didn't break any laws. It turned out the place was his and it was all a prank. Anyway, I did the job and suddenly the joke's on Herb because Grace had been following me in an attempt to get closer to him, thinking he might be her real father, like she said yesterday. Then, would you believe, she recognises the camera and it's her photographs that are on it. It was all a big mystery until she finally got to meet him.'

'It didn't sound like that went very well.'

'No. As far as Herb's concerned she's Pinner's daughter and he saw an opportunity to use me to bring her to him.'

'What for?'

'Well, not for tea and biscuits,' I say and offer him the plate.

Melville sits forward, declines another stale garibaldi and thinks for a while.

I say I'll make another cup of tea, and when I come back in with the tray he's on the phone, so I leave him to it and use the toilet myself. I know that's how a dog shows dominance, by urinating where another one's already been, but really I just want to put Grace's things away in case he needs to go in there again before he leaves.

'Mr Field,' he calls and this time when I go in the lounge he's standing up again. 'I'm sorry, I need to head back.'

Just as I think I've failed to get any more information from him, he hands me a scrap of yellow paper he's taken from my pile.

'You didn't get this from me,' he says, and without waiting for me to read it, heads out of the room. 'I'll see myself out.'

I unfold the paper.

RAYMOND RIGGS

Who the hell is Raymond Riggs? As I look up, a ribbon of bird shit splats across the front window and I grimace.

Red Rag

Grace doesn't get back until almost half six. I was getting worried and had already left two messages. She lets herself in with the key I gave her. We agreed she shouldn't go back to her flat for the time being, and I've told her to make herself at home.

She puts her head around the doorway and beams. I smile back with relief and want to give her a hug, but all I can do is nod as she holds up a bunch of fresh flowers. I put my hand over the phone and tell her where she'll find a vase in the kitchen.

'Okay, thanks. Monday at ten forty-five,' I say and hang up.

'I was starting to worry about you, babe,' I call out, and her face reappears at the door.

'I'm fine,' she answers with a nervous grin. 'I tried calling when I was on my way but you must have been on the phone.' I look down at the mobile that's now telling me I had a missed call ten minutes ago.

'Where've you been?' I ask.

'How was your day?' she says, at the same time.

Then like some corny scene from a sitcom, we say together, 'It's been an interesting afternoon.' We both laugh and she walks over and gives me a hug.

'Let's get something to eat once I've freshened up,' she says. 'Then we can compare notes.'

'Good idea. How do you fancy Spanish?'

'*Olé!*' she sings, holding imaginary castanets over her head while stamping her feet.

'You really are amazing,' I say and shake out an invisible cape.

'*Gracias!*' she sings, launching herself at me with fingers pointing out from her head.

'And, very horny,' I add as we land in a heap on the sofa.

'Horny and hungry.'

'Sounds like a film I once saw,' I say. 'Maybe if we shower together we can save some time.' The twinkle in her eyes ignores my hopelessly-flawed logic and I carry her to the bathroom.

An hour or two later we're in a local tapas bar, tucking into Serrano ham and tortilla. I know the manager, and he's given us a quiet table in a cosy alcove. It's not too busy for a Saturday night and I suspect we're both glad the food's arriving quickly. If we were hungry before the shower, now we're famished.

'Tell me about your day first,' I say as the next round of dishes arrives.

'Well, my last client cancelled, so I was finished just after three,' she says, reaching for the chorizo. 'I was going to surprise you, but I wasn't sure what you were doing and I didn't want to come back to an empty house. So I treated myself to a coffee and a cupcake.'

'Very civilised,' I say.

'Yeah, until it reminded me of yesterday and I remembered what Jim Melville had said.'

'Which bit?' I say. I'm still getting my head around Little Grace James, the young offender. At least I was seventeen when my brief period of juvenile delinquency kicked in.

'That Terry had told him not to follow up on the evidence... about me being in Herb's house.'

'I just assumed he would be trying to protect you.'

'Hmm, unlikely. Like I said before, he's usually focused on protecting himself first. Anyway, I got to wondering how much he actually knew about my past. Was it possible he'd been aware all along... you know... if I *am* Herbert Long's abandoned daughter? But then, I couldn't be sure if he even knew him?'

'I'm pretty sure he does,' I say.

'Well, I had a sudden urge to find out,' she says. 'He's not easy to get hold of but I only had to leave one message and he rang me back within five minutes. He agreed to meet if I could drive down there, something about having an important meeting tonight. So I got in the car and was in his office by four-thirty.'

She proceeds to tell me how she has always found it better to act dumb with him. It plays to his sense of superiority. He's also wary of her because she knows so much about him...

She planned to tell him the truth; that she'd been trying to trace her real parents, and to ask what he knew about them. To her surprise, she didn't have to. Before she even sat down he went

243

on the offensive.

'What the fuck were you doing in that house last week?' His voice was intense and she knew this wasn't the concerned parent routine. He was on edge.

'How well do you know my real father?' she countered, expecting a big reaction. But there was nothing. He stayed calm and composed.

'We've been through this Grace. There's nothing to know. The records were lost, you've always known that. In any case, what's that got to do with this?'

It was enough to confirm he really didn't suspect Herb might be her father. But something in the way he'd said *that house* told her there was more to this than he was letting on, so she quickly changed tack.

'I was in there because I saw the man who followed me and stole my camera. That New Year's Eve, remember?' He shrugged and shook his head. 'I followed him to the house and watched him. When I knew he'd left I sneaked in the back to see if I could find it.'

'I remember you saying something about an old guy in a pub years ago,' he said, the frown beginning to lift from his brow. 'Are you saying it was that sick fuck that was watching you?'

'I'm pretty sure it was him.'

'Jesus!' He yelled, the capillaries in his cheeks glowing red. 'I should have put him away years ago, when I had the chance.'

'So you do know him?'

'Of course I do, but why...'

'Why do you think he followed me and took my camera when I was fifteen?'

'That fucking pervert probably likes watching little girls and taking their photos.'

'What makes you say that?'

'As far as I'm concerned,' he said with a smirk, 'it doesn't matter whether he's a child-molester or not. He's a nasty piece of shit that needs to be flushed away.'

'Either he is or he isn't.'

244

'What does it matter? He's a criminal, that's for certain. Sometimes we just have to get them on whatever we can.'

'There was a photo of a young woman in his house,' she said. 'Made me think he must be married.'

'He was,' Pinner said, suddenly less animated.

'But it looked like he lived there alone.'

'She died in a car crash, years ago,' he said.

His mood had changed and when she asked if they'd had any kids he flinched and took a long time to answer.

'She was pregnant at the time,' he said.

'Did you know her?'

'No,' he said, 'not really.'

'What does that mean?' she said and he glared back at her.

'If you must hear the gory details,' he said, 'I was one of the last people to see her conscious.'

The blood must have drained from Grace's head because she started spinning. She could hear him telling her he'd been a traffic cop back then, and had been the first on the scene. But her mind was in free-fall. He asked if she was alright and offered her a glass of water.

'You did ask for it,' he said.

'What did she look like?' she said, barely holding herself together.

'They say she was an attractive woman,' he said, 'but I don't suppose I saw her at her best. God knows how Long ended up with her.'

'How did she die?'

'I really don't know. She was lucid when I spoke to her, but her legs...' He didn't finish the sentence.

'Did she say anything?'

'I remember she was concerned for the baby. *Don't worry about me, save my baby*, she was screaming as they lifted her out.' He looked across at Grace and their eyes met. 'What does it matter anyway? What makes you so interested in her death?'

She held his gaze for what seemed like forever.

'Because I think I'm her daughter.'

Just Desserts

There's a load of food left and I'm hoping she hasn't completely lost her appetite when she sets down the knife and fork and pushes her half-empty plate forward. I call for another bottle, although I'm not sure my news is going to help her digestion.

'Sounds like we've both been idling away our afternoon in the company of North Kent CID.' My clumsy attempt to lift the mood has the opposite effect, and Grace looks up in a panic. 'Don't worry. It was just a social visit from your old mate, Jim Melville.'

'Really?' she says. 'I know he said he hadn't finished with you but I didn't expect him to get back quite so soon. What did he want this time?'

'You know it's weird. The more I think about it, the stranger it seems. He called and asked if he could come to my house. When he got there it was like he was your big brother, checking me out.' I look up from eating and Grace is smiling. She starts picking at her food again. 'He didn't want to talk about Herb or the arson. It was like he'd driven all that way to make sure I was good enough for you.'

'He's very sweet. Just not my type,' she says unprompted and I let her continue. 'He asked me out after I moved into the flat; must be three years ago. I had to turn him down. He's too serious. I told him he was too old for me. That's funny... I'm pretty sure he's younger than you!' She smirks and I send it back to her with extra sarcasm.

'Well he certainly still carries a torch for you,' I say.

'So was that it? He wanted to make sure you were being nice to me?'

'That's what I thought, and so I offered him a cup of tea. It was all very cordial at first. Then he told me he was worried about you. I thought he meant because you were with me and I started getting a bit narked by his pathetic jealousy.'

'I don't think *he's* the jealous type,' she says.

I ignore the implication and tell her how the conversation

went and how he then got all cagey before handing me the cryptic note.

'What was it?' she asks. The sparkle has returned to her eyes and I notice that her plate is now empty. I hand her the piece of paper.

'Who's Raymond Riggs?' she says.

'Good question. I got seven million hits on Google.'

'Great.'

'I think I narrowed it down,' I say, and her eyes widen again. 'Well, I had nothing better to do than worry about you coming home late.'

'Riggs,' she says and repeats it back to herself.

'What is it?'

'I don't know,' she says, gazing up at the ceiling. 'It has a familiar ring to it. It might come to me in a moment. Tell me what you found out.'

'Well, it's amazing how popular the name is and there's a lot of rubbish on the web,' I say. 'But there were several newspaper articles that looked quite promising. They all referred to a Ray Riggs of the same age, born in London in 1960. In the earlier articles he's described as a promising young footballer in his late teens. That seems to have fizzled out because later on he's a bookmaker. And by the end of the nineties he's a successful, if slightly controversial, businessman.'

'Not exactly the sort of man you'd lose any sleep over,' she says, picking up the dessert menu. 'Why would Jim give us such a useless warning?'

'Yeah, but,' I say, 'there was one less-than-glowing reference.'

'What?' she says. I can tell she's lost any enthusiasm for my hunt-the-needle in the haystack of the Internet. She carries on studying the desserts, but I seriously doubt she's going to be tempted to indulge after this.

'Five years ago he was in the dock when the jury failed to reach a verdict and the case was dropped.' I still haven't got her full attention. She seems to be torn between the pears in sherry and the flan. Then she lowers the menu and looks up at me.

'Riggs,' she says again, this time with conviction. 'Yes, that must have been it. When Herb was banging that hammer on the bench, remember? At the time I thought he was saying: it was rigged. What if he was saying it was Riggs? It was Riggs who killed her.'

I stop momentarily to take in what she's said. It warrants further thought but I don't want it to ruin my big finale.

'Well, apparently,' I forge ahead in the most judicial tone I can muster, 'when the trial uncovered irregularities in his business dealings, the judge directed the jury to stay focused on the matter at hand and a lot of the circumstantial evidence was thrown out. It seems that weakened the prosecution's case and in the end, the jury wasn't sufficiently convinced Riggs was responsible... directly or indirectly... for the death of his business partner.' I look at Grace and finally get the reaction I was expecting as she closes the menu.

'Murder?' she says.

'Yeah, and it gets better. The newspaper report highlighted what it described as the turning point in the trial. The senior detective involved in the case had been called as a key witness and his testimony served to validate the defendant's alibi.' I pause to watch the realisation rise on her face like an Arctic dawn. 'I bet you can't guess who that detective inspector might have been?'

'Terry Pinner,' she whispers and the menu falls from her hands.

* * *

Cold Calling

It's a recorded voice that answers. She says there's no one home. He hears the beep and puts the phone on the table. The sound of his breathing is all they'll hear. He'll phone again later and keep trying until someone picks up. Then he'll hang up and he'll do it again tomorrow night. And the next night, until he's certain when someone's there and when they're not. And whether it's him or whether it's her.

16.

Sunday, 27th

We slept in late and chilled in front of the TV this morning. Then I drove Grace to her flat so she could grab some things. We waited for a while to make sure Simon wasn't there.

'Aren't you going to come in?' she said.

'I'd better keep watch,' I replied. Really I just didn't want to see where she lived her independent life. I suppose I was getting used to the idea she's with me now.

Back home, we cooked a roast dinner that we ate late in the afternoon. We took turns trying to call Herb, without reply. Apart from that, it was a Lionel Richie kind of Sunday. That was until Grace persuaded me to drive out to see if we could find Herb's house in the country.

We set out under the cover of early evening darkness, and soon find the pub where Herb first reappeared. I show her where the Mercedes was parked and we drive away in the general direction it took. Apart from remembering that when I was in the car with Herb we hadn't gone on either of the nearby motorways, I felt sure we'd travelled beyond the perimeter of the London Orbital. Even so, the A roads and place names we see don't ring any bells. There are several junctions where I can't be sure which way to go, and before long we're on a narrow and totally unfamiliar country road. By now all I *do* know is that some miles back we went under and beyond the M25, and with no junctions joining it along this stretch, we're heading out into rural Essex with no idea where we're going.

'We're lost,' I finally admit.

250

'Never mind,' she says. 'It was a long shot anyway.'

We keep going for no other reason than the road isn't wide enough to turn around.

'Let's enjoy the ride,' I say. 'We're bound to come to a main road, sooner or later.'

It turns out to be later, because we drive along endless hedgerows until an orange haze lights up the horizon and we get a vague sense we're heading back towards civilisation. The light rises and falls as we drive up and over the rolling countryside, shifting playfully from one side of the car to the other as we meander through the labyrinth of fields. Just when we think it's on another road and we've missed the turning, we see it straight up ahead. But it's not the light of a junction with clues to our journey home. As we come closer, a solitary building, lit up on all sides by amber floodlights, comes into view. The little country pub is welcoming and I pull into the car park, suggesting we avail ourselves of some rural hospitality.

'Hopefully someone will be able to help with directions,' Grace adds.

The homely crackle of an open fire greets us inside, and the only patron sitting at the bar turns in surprise as the heavy door rattles back into place behind us.

'Evening,' he says and continues reading his paper. I return the greeting and walk towards the bar, looking around for the landlord. Grace takes a seat near the hearth that dominates the far wall.

'Out back,' the man says, gesturing to a low, narrow door behind the bar, just as the landlord squeezes his huge bulk through the opening and solicits my custom by raising his bushy eyebrows. A shake of his beetroot head informs me that, perhaps unsurprisingly, Tia Maria isn't in his repertoire so I order Grace a whisky. I could murder a Guinness but settle for Coke. I hand him a tenner and he returns the change without even a grunt.

'Where are we?' I ask and immediately feel stupid – not least because he ignores me and lumbers back through the doorway. I give him the benefit of the doubt but decide not to repeat myself.

'You're about a half mile from the village.' It's the other customer that answers. 'Just keep going and you'll see the sign.'

'Thanks,' I say and raise the tumbler.

'Cheers,' he says, reciprocating with a virtually empty pint glass. 'Whereabouts you headed?'

'Oh, we were out for an evening drive, you know. Got a bit lost to tell the truth and then we found this place and thought we'd come in for a crafty one. Hoping to find our way onto a motorway back towards London.'

'You won't easily get onto the M25 from here,' he says, confirming what I already know.

'How close are we to the M11?'

'Not far, but you'd have to go up towards Harlow and pick it up at junction seven. I suppose it might even be quicker for you this time of day.'

'Well, we're in no hurry either way.'

'Okay. Go through the village,' he says, pointing in the direction we'd been heading. 'Straight ahead, you can't miss it. At the first junction, go right, right again at the next, then left and left again. That'll bring you to the main road. You'll see directions there; turn left and you'll be heading towards the motorway.'

'Thank you, that's very kind,' I say and he raises his dirty glass to me again. I turn away and take the drinks to where Grace is glowing in the firelight.

'Our humble host sends his profuse apologies for being clean out of cocktails,' I say. 'So I got you scotch instead.'

'I'd rather have had the Coke,' she says. 'You're a bad influence on me.'

'It's the one you like,' I say with a grin. 'I even asked for extra peat.'

She shakes her head with a tired smile.

'I'm sorry. I'll get you a Coke.' I start to get up and she puts her hand on my arm.

'Don't worry. It looked like more trouble than it's worth.'

'Yeah, but if you really don't want it...'

'I'll tell you what,' she says. 'How about if I drive home and you have the whisky?'

'Okay. If you're sure.' She nods and I swap the glasses before she can change her mind. 'Sorry, it's not Diet.'

The guy at the bar doesn't move from his perch and the landlord remains out of sight. The blazing fire seems to be the only thing grateful for our presence.

'I've been thinking about this Raymond Riggs,' Grace says and a cold draught bristles my neck as if the pub's warmth has suddenly been sucked up the chimney.

'Yeah, so have I,' I say. 'I've been wondering if he's got a really deep voice.'

'Why do you say that?' she says with a nervous laugh.

'You said you thought Herb might have been saying *Riggs* when he got all upset with you about his wife,' I say and she nods. 'Well, could that make Riggs the guy who's after him now?'

'Yeah, it's possible,' she says with a shrug.

'And that in turn might make him the deep voice that answered Herb's phone.'

'Oh God, yeah,' she says.

'And it gets worse. Whoever it is, he rang me yesterday while you were at work.' She puts down her glass, almost missing the table. 'He seemed to know a lot about me. He knew about the two of us, my mum, John, everything.'

'What did he want?' she says, and I notice her rosy glow start to fade.

'It was more of an ultimatum. He told me to choose... between you and Herb.'

'What? Why?'

'I don't know. He said something about you two being different sides of the same coin. It didn't make sense, except he clearly wants me to abandon Herb.'

'Therefore... putting me on the other side.'

'Apparently. And with the threat of violence if I make the wrong decision.'

'Jesus! No wonder Jim was so keen to warn us.'

'Yeah... what a bloody mess.'

'And,' she says, 'that kind of confirms my theory.'

'Oh yeah, sorry, I interrupted. What were you going to say?'

'I think it does... Oh my God!'

'What?'

'Well, if Terry gave him an alibi, like you said...'

'Right,' I say, lowering my voice, 'for murder.'

'And his name's Raymond...'

'Yeah...'

'So... he's *Ray*.' She says it quietly, conspiratorially, like it's supposed to mean something to me.

'Okay, short for Raymond. Go on.'

'You said the trial was five years ago, right?'

'Yeah... 2004. I think it was July. What about it?'

'That's the year after that horrible man came to the house.' She reaches for my hand and squeezes it tightly.

'Oh God,' I say, finally understanding what she's getting at. 'You said his name was Ray.'

'Yes,' she whispers.

'Didn't you say they were talking about someone being better off out of it?'

'And Terry took the money to make the problem go away...'

'Just like he had before.' I finish her train of thought. 'But how does that put you on his side?'

My brain gets there with the question hardly out of my mouth. It's still a shock when she says: 'My allowance... That's where all the money's been coming from.'

'Shit!' I mouth back.

I finish the scotch and down the rest of the Coke that Grace slides across the table as she gets up to leave. We walk towards the door and the man turns around and watches us.

'One last thing,' he says as we reach the door. 'Remember I mentioned that main road to Harlow? Well, it can be a bit hairy at times if you take my meaning. Especially at night. Folks around here call it The Mad Mile. So take it steady.' I thank him again, and this time his empty glass stays on the counter.

Overtaking Time

As we walk out into the sharp evening air, my eyes are drawn up to the illuminated sign that creaks on rusty hinges. It's framed at the top of a high wooden pillar, set into the ground on the opposite side of the road. Beneath a traditional painting of a bushel of straw is the pub's name: The Wheat Sheaf.

I shrug to myself. There must be hundreds of pubs with that name out in the sticks. Grace hasn't noticed it, so I dismiss it as a coincidence as we walk to the car. I get out the keys and am about to get in on the driver's side.

'Aren't I supposed to be driving?' she says.

'Oh yeah. Are you still feeling up to it?'

'Definitely.' She gets in and starts adjusting the seat.

'Remember it's a bit different to yours. It'll probably seem huge after driving that little soft top.'

'I'll be fine,' she says and turns the key. She pulls away smoothly and then slams on the brake just as we get out onto the road.

'What is it?' I screech as the seat belt throws me back against the headrest.

'Sorry,' she says. 'Must try to remember it's automatic.'

'Okay... if you want me to drive. I've only had the one.'

'No, I'll be okay,' she says, and tucks her left foot back out of the way. She quickly gets the hang of it and pretty soon we're approaching more buildings and looking out for the first turning.

'Where are we exactly?' she asks as a junction appears up ahead.

'He didn't say,' I answer. 'I think we must have missed the welcome sign already. Maybe there'll be one on the other side as we leave.'

'Just don't blink,' she says. I'm relieved that her mood has lifted since we left the pub, and when she asks me where I think the village might be twinned with, I join in with the joke.

'Timbuktu?'

'Maybe,' she says. 'I was thinking Outer Mongolia.'

She pulls up at the crossing and we look at the direction signs opposite. The left turning has village names we've never heard of and points in the direction of the A414. I look at Grace, but she doesn't seem to have made the connection and pulls away, this time thankfully without trying to change gears manually. A few hundred yards up on the opposite verge we can see the back of the village welcome sign.

'Quick, look behind,' she says. 'What's it twinned with?'

I look back just in time to see it doesn't say a twin. All it says are the words of the village name and a shiver goes up the back of my neck.

'What was it?' she says. 'I bet it was somewhere in Belgium? Somewhere no one's ever heard of.'

'I couldn't read it. It's too dark.'

'Never mind, let's see what the next one is.'

Her driving gets more confident with each twist and turn. At the tiny hamlet of Toot Hill, she feels the need to honk the horn, and then takes the turning at Greensted Green without even braking. I try to smile – I want her to have fun – but it's probably more of a nervous grin.

'The Mad Mile!' She smirks and puts her foot down as we turn left onto the A414, Epping Road. I can't believe she hasn't seen the significance; I distinctly remember that was the road identified in the newspaper article we found with the photograph of Herb's wife. The road where her fatal crash happened. And The Wheat Sheaf was the pub where an eye-witness claimed one of the cars had set out from minutes before with a drunk driver at the wheel. I stare straight ahead as Grace continues her one-sided banter.

'There's probably some European directive,' she's saying, 'that means we now have to call it The Crazy Kilometre!'

I know she's waiting for me to join in and I do think about giving her the politically correct lobby's alternative. But I'm feeling increasingly uneasy and my proposed suggestion of The Mentally Impaired Carriageway probably wouldn't be funny anyway.

'Just concentrate on the road ahead,' I say. She takes my point and starts to steer gingerly around the bends. Ahead we can see taillights and pretty soon we're right up behind them.

'A tractor at this time of night!' she says. 'Hopefully, he'll pull in.' But he doesn't and we crawl along behind it.

I can sense she's getting impatient as the road starts to wind around into a broader section. The tractor illuminates cats eyes that trail straight ahead and up into the darkness. Initially Grace hangs back and allows a gap to open up but then, just before we start to climb, she makes her decision and hits the accelerator.

As she starts to pull out, two things happen simultaneously. First, glaring headlights crown the top of the hill. And second, the tractor indicates right and moves across to block our path. As the lights ahead sweep down the hill towards us, Grace eases off the gas. But as she does, the driver of the tractor realises we were overtaking. He slows down and pulls back into the left, leaving her only one option. Now she's committed and floors the pedal again. The engine roars its objection. Its response is slow but sure. We begin to pull alongside the tractor. The oncoming vehicle speeds towards us, with gravity on its side. We're accelerating too. The gearbox kicks down. Headlights flash manically. Blinding as we speed towards them. A catastrophic impact seems inevitable. Lights flash larger and brighter. Time slows. Silence. I look to my left. The tractor's no longer beside me. Then to my right. Grace is already turning the wheel. Pulling back, hard left. I'm drawn towards her, against the momentum of the car. Black hedgerows beckon. The choice is stark. Into the light or into the dark. We twist back. I'm pushed hard against the door. Tyres screech and slide. Then bite firm and we straighten with a jolt. The blurred outline of the approaching car whistles past as the sound of a receding horn fades away behind us.

'Wow!' she says, sinking back into the seat. 'This thing's not got the oomph I'm used to.' I just nod and exhale deeply.

Now I'm definitely not going to tell her the village we went through was Stapleford Tawney.

17.

Monday, 28th

There are three things I hate about visiting my brother in Wandsworth. The first one is getting here – three tubes and a bus. The second is the waiting. The third is the smell – a cloying combination of boiled vegetables, cold sweat and barely-suppressed testosterone that perspires through the cinderblock pores of the Visit Room. But worse still is how it makes me feel, seeing him the way he's become. I usually have to have a few pints on the way home to help me get over it. But today's going to be different. Today I've driven here. I'm on a mission.

I go to see him two or three times a year, even though the visiting orders still arrive in the post every couple of months. They're issued at John's request, which is the only reason I still go at all. I assume Mum's still getting them too.

Being a convicted murderer puts him pretty high up the pecking order in prison but even so, John's virtually had to grow up, from being a naïve teenager to a hardened criminal, in an environment of constant threats and intimidation. I find it increasingly difficult to recognise the person I grew up with; the older brother I once looked up to. He's become resentful of my life because his was buggered, as he puts it, so long ago. I've started to believe we're poles apart. In recent visits we've found less and less to talk about. All he ever wants to know is whether Mum's okay. Usually, once I've given him her news, he'll go back into his shell. If I ask him how it's going, he'll get angry with me. And if I try to tell him what I've been up to, he'll shut down. My monologue soon dries up and I just sit there, waiting for him to call the guard to take him back. We rarely take up more than a fraction of the hour. Then I'll watch him walk away and thank my lucky stars.

You have to book a visit at least twenty-four hours in advance. I tend to leave it to the last minute to make sure he still wants to see me; it wouldn't be the first time he's changed his mind, making me turn around to go back home. Hence the call I was making when Grace got back on Saturday evening. When you arrive, half an hour before your allotted time, you have to present the VO and a driving licence or passport. I've still got the old green paper licence, but they want something with a photo on it so I have to take my passport. Thanks to John – or should that be Dad – I never get the same buzz most people do when they dig it out of the drawer every summer. Without taking off your shoes, you walk through the metal detectors before being frisked. You're not allowed to wear hoodies or scarves, or take through any bags or personal possessions. You used to be able to hand in cash to be added to a prisoner's account, but now all you can do is take in loose change to spend on them in the cafeteria.

There are lockers in the Visitors' Centre where you can leave your stuff and, once through the double airlock doors, you get to stand in a room while the most un-spaniel-like Cocker has a good old sniff around. I always thought they were after drugs, but I made the mistake of taking in my mobile once and the dog went ape. So did I, when they accused me of trying to smuggle it in. They only let me off because it was in my coat pocket and not a body cavity. That was the last time I saw John show any sign of empathy. It was no more than a shake of his head as he said it could have been worse; if I was on the inside and they suspected me of concealing something like that, the screws would have subjected me to a technique they like to call spooning. It sounded like a real pain in the arse. From there it's into the waiting room, or Chavs-R-Us as I like to call it.

Today, I'm sitting in the corner chair and feeling very conspicuous. First, because I'm not wearing a velour tracksuit in a choice of pastel shades, and second because I'm not a woman.

You might even say, thirdly I'm over the age of twenty-five – and mentally over the age of twelve, but that would just be nasty. It's not their fault. Unless they knew what their man was like before they got too drawn in, of course. They say you can choose your friends, and I'm sure that applies as much to husbands and boyfriends. Family you're stuck with.

Another half an hour goes by and I'm starting to get hungry. I don't know why they bother giving a set time; they always make you wait longer. The entertainment value of trying to imagine the bad luck stories that each of these women represents is wearing thin. Fortunately, my name is read out in the next batch, and I'm the first to reach the door and head up the queue. It's like I'm at the departure gate and want to be the first onto the plane. Usually, I'd be one of those that stay seated, thinking that unless you're at the front, you'll just get held back by the fat ones in the middle. Today I want to get my full timeslot and, before long, I'm walking into the Visit Room and anxiously looking from table to table.

I needn't have rushed because when I eventually see John, he's sitting at a table in the far corner away from everyone else, and so I'm one of the last to sit down anyway. Most of the prisoners are in their own gear, jeans and T-shirts, but the green mesh bibs they all have to wear make them look like some unruly Sunday league team, meeting in the pub before going off to kick seven bells out of their opponents in the name of amateur football. Under John's team vest I can see he's still got on a prison-issue blue boiler suit. The wide yellow sash down the front tells me he's been playing up again. Twenty years in and he's still rarely off the Category A blacklist.

I used to offer to shake his hand but he stopped taking it.

'Hi,' I say and he barely nods as I sit down. 'How have you been?' It's a stupid question, considering the cut above his right eye and the heavy dressing on the side of his neck.

'Fuckin' marvellous,' he says, rubbing the back of his head with his left hand. My eyes are drawn to the diagonal scars down the inside of his forearm; some of them look new. I don't understand why but I know he does it to himself. He once told me it relieved the boredom. I think that was just his way of saying it gives him a few minutes relief from the stress and gets him some attention. He sees the look on my face and quickly drops his arm to the table. 'How's the old dear?'

'She's fine. I've seen quite a lot of her lately.' I want to get his attention quickly so he's more likely to open up, but my first attempt falls flat.

'Well, lucky you,' is all he says.

'She asked after you and sends her love,' I lie.

'Piss off. Tell her I can still read and I'm guessing she can still write.'

'There's nothing to stop you writing first,' I say and he just glares at me. This hasn't started well. 'Look, the reason I've been down there a lot is to see Herb Long. Remember him?' I'm hoping that might pique his curiosity.

'He's still alive? I heard Riggs had taken him out.'

'Riggs? What have you heard?' I must sound a bit too eager. I'm the little squirt again, in awe of my big brother, hoping he might let me in on something only the big boys know.

'Ah, you don't want to hear about all that shit. The stuff that goes on in here. Half of what you hear is bollocks anyway. What you don't know can't hurt you. Best to keep it that way. Especially for a big pussy like you.' He didn't used to be so spiteful. I hate him for it but I have to try again.

'Herb did say there was a gang of thugs looking to blackmail him. And they had some shit on him that could bring him down.' I've told him something he hasn't already heard and I swear if he was a dog his ears would have pricked up.

'What kind of shit?'

'Photographs.'

'Really. What did he want you to do?'

'Get them back.'

'So... did you?'

'Yeah.'

He does something I haven't seen in twenty years. He

smiles. Suddenly, my older brother is back, sitting in front of me and looking at me like he used to. I smile back and he moves in closer.

'Problem is,' I go on, 'I need to find out about Riggs. I think he might be onto me.'

'Whoa... go easy bro,' he says and the hairs on the back of my neck twitch. I'm not sure if it's because he called me bro or because a warning from him is one to be worried about.

'What can you tell me?'

'He's good. Shit never sticks to him. It all looks legit but a lot of it's fake. Top end stuff. Not your crappy Rolex knock-offs. Premium brands and high fashion, all mixed up with kosher businesses. No one's ever been able to pin anything on him.'

'So what makes him so dangerous?'

'To start with he's a twisted bastard. A fuckin' psycho from what I've heard.'

I've always been able to reassure myself that John's reaction in the bank was some kind of pre-emptive, self-defence. It's a stretch I know; justification for shooting a complete stranger in the face point-blank with a sawn-off 12 bore. But it's the only way I can still think of him as my brother. From what he's saying, though, in the hierarchy of criminals, Riggs is off the scale.

'Others always take the fall for him,' he continues. 'There's plenty in here would like to see him gone.'

'All because of some counterfeit goods and dodgy dresses?'

'Think about it, numbnuts. It's big money. Creates big risks. Once you've got an empire like that, you'd do anything to protect it. Surround yourself with thugs and pay them well. Create enough daylight between the top man and the operations and it's almost impossible to trace it back. That's Riggs, if you listen to any of the jabber in here.'

'So, what's the connection with Herb?' I ask.

'God, you're so fuckin' naïve; sometimes I can't believe we're related. Of course there's no love lost between those two. Join the dots.'

'Really?'

'For Christ's sake, Mickey! Riggs was in a massive car crash, years ago. Still walks with a limp. Remember Long's wife died in a crash? Like I said, join the dots, Sherlock.' I'm thinking he's listened to too much jabber and is starting to believe his own bullshit.

'Bit of a stretch isn't it?'

'Take it or leave it. Deadly enemies or not, one thing's for sure, they're both in the same game. That makes them rivals whichever way you look at it. And Long's way out of his depth.'

'The bloke that rang me said I need to choose which side I'm on.'

'Huh! Good luck with that!'

'Jesus.' I look away and my mind starts to wander. 'How do you even get to be like that?'

'Money,' he says. 'He's got fuck-all else.'

'No family?'

'The business *is* his family.' He pushes his chair back and raises his hand to indicate he's ready to go back to whatever hell exists behind the grey door. The guard behind him takes a step forward, but then John changes the signal to a single index finger, prompting the man to retreat like an attentive waiter. My big brother leans back in even closer. I can smell his rancid breath and I try not to pull away as he finally adds: 'Especially now his old woman's disappeared.'

'Really?'

'Rumour is she went out one morning a few weeks ago and still hasn't come back.'

'What, just up and left?'

'Hit, more likely. They're still waiting for a body to turn up.'

'God, that's enough to screw anyone up.'

'Yeah!' He smirks. 'Lightning striking twice.'

'What?'

'Well that's what made Riggs the vicious bastard he is.' He glares at me like I should know what he's talking about.

'Lightning?'

263

'Well it's not the first time, is it?' He's losing patience with me and I can only look back long-faced, like a banker without a bonus. 'It happened to his kid brother too.'

'Did it?' My eyes widen.

'Christ, where have you been?'

'So, were they... close?' It's a stupid question and he punishes me for it.

'What, like us?' He leans back and sneers at me through yellow teeth. 'More like junior Krays, those two.'

'And he just disappeared?'

'Urban fuckin' myth among those in here that knew him. The lad was only eighteen.'

'When was that?'

'Long time ago. Late eighties. Around the time I was nicked,' he says, and a muscle in my neck twitches.

'So... what happened?'

'Riggs was just a rookie back then,' he says. 'Thought some of his gear had been blagged. And he finds out about this other gaff. Nowhere near his own manor, and for some reason he decides that's where it is. Sends his little bro in after it. Big mistake.'

'Why?' I mouth but no sound comes out.

He turns to the prison guard and they exchange nods and he scrapes back his chair. As he gets up he leans in like he's going to kiss my cheek and as his stubble scuffs my face I feel a spot of his saliva tweak the soft folds of my ear. But it's his words, cruelly mimicking my whisper, that make my skin crawl.

'The boy... was never seen again.'

As he walks away, part of me feels like following him through the grey door. Instead I sit here and let the walls close in around me.

Criminal Fraternity

I'm sitting in mid-afternoon traffic, driving back from Wandsworth, but my head is somewhere else. The events of late-

January 1988 flash through my mind and I realise how hard I've tried for most of my life to suppress them. There's something strangely therapeutic about letting the memories play out. And there's a new angle I'm being forced to consider...

It was almost one in the morning and I was hiding behind an old shed in the back garden of a house a mile from home. Dad was at work and John was out drinking with his mates. He seemed to be going out at night a lot, often getting home in the early hours. I'd told Mum not to wait up. At seventeen it was unusual for me to go out so late, and so I'd had to lie to her. I'd never done that before. She was settled in front of the telly for the night and, as luck would have it, an old school friend had phoned for a chat. That provided the cover I needed. I told her I was going to see a mate who just broke up with his girlfriend. I said he was in a pub getting drunk and needed someone to talk to, so I'd offered to pick him up and get him home. I couldn't believe she fell for it.

I left the car parked on the road and walked the last few hundred yards. I'd been told the best place to break in was the side window. The instructions were clear. The path was dark and narrow and the window was old and rotting. All I had to do was break the small pane at the top. With several layers of duct tape over the glass, a sharp blow with my elbow shattered it with a muffled crunch. Standing on the window ledge, I reached in and stretched down to easily lift the handle on the lower window. I tried several times to keep the handle disengaged while I pushed with the same arm against the glass to try and open it outwards. The swollen frame was held firmly in place on rusty hinges and I couldn't get enough leverage to force it open. I tried pulling on the frame from the outside, but with nothing to grasp I couldn't shift it. I didn't have any hardware with me to jemmy the frame as I'd been told it was always best to go light and nimble. So I had to resort to Plan B.

It bothered me that I had to deviate so soon, but if I was going to complete the task and earn his respect, I at least needed to get inside. It was such a big piece of glass to try and break with my elbow and it was going to be a lot noisier. I unrolled more tape, lots more, and found a large stone in the back garden. I managed to make the first crack without much more than a dull thud. The hardest part would be stopping large pieces of glass falling outwards and smashing noisily on the ground.

I pushed against it with my shoulder. It flexed, though not enough to break quietly. I had to hit it again, and that time it splintered. Only a few fragments fell inwards. The rotting wood did me the favour of gripping all the outer pieces and I was able to take out two or three large shards and place them carefully against the wall behind me. I wanted them out of the way for when I made my getaway. More pieces came free until the last one was hanging like a giant fang. I didn't notice it was cracked, and as I wiggled it to release it from the wooden groove it snapped and I was left with a small fragment while the large corner piece fell out and shattered on the concrete path. I ran back to the shed and watched from the darkness.

Ten minutes felt like an hour, but when I was sure no one was coming to look I went back and climbed in through the opening.

Inside, the place was surprisingly tidy given the run down facade and, although the layout was unfamiliar, I was able to move easily from room to room. With a torch in one hand and a large holdall in the other, I started compiling a mental inventory of the contents of the endless shelves lining the walls. It was more like a warehouse than a dwelling and I was amazed by the array of goods stacked floor to ceiling. My old school holdall was going to be totally inadequate. That problem was soon addressed in the front room where I found large bags and suitcases in all shapes and sizes. It was quality stuff; Louis Vuitton, Gucci, Mulberry. Now the problem was going to be staying focused and not overdoing it.

I grabbed two of the large bags and headed to the next room. Devoid of shelves, and any other fixtures, this one was filled with rows of clothes rails and each one was loaded with polythene-wrapped dresses and outfits. It was like being backstage at a fashion show. I didn't quite know where to start and I began wishing I hadn't left the car so far away. That's when I heard it.

The crunch of glass underfoot sent a bolt of terror through me. I dived between the rows and stayed silent. I had to hold my breath to stop my lungs from giving me away, even though my heartbeat could probably be heard in the next street. I stayed there motionless, forcing my breath to escape in long whispers, and having to stop myself from then gulping it back in. Seconds crept by and all the time I could hear muted footsteps in the hall and, one by one, in each of the downstairs rooms, until finally, torchlight beamed around the room, turning the covered garments into translucent ghosts. Without searching for long, the light receded and the sound of footsteps became exaggerated by the creaking of stairs. Floorboards took up the load overhead.

I decided to make my move and got up from behind the rack and went to the door. I could see the room ahead of me down the hall where I came in. I'd have to cross the foot of the stairs to get to it. I hesitated and lost valuable time. I knew I had to leave then but something wasn't right. I'd left my bag along with the other two behind the rails. Another instruction rang in my head: *whatever you do, don't leave anything behind*. I had to go back. I still had time. The footsteps upstairs had moved to the front of the house. I went back into the room and grabbed my holdall but its handle got caught on the bottom frame of the end rail. It started to glide on wheels across the rough wooden floor behind me. Before I realised what was happening it struck an uneven floorboard and, as I looked back and tried to unhook the bag, I saw the rail falling towards me.

In slow motion, the garments began sliding along the pole, adding to its momentum. Although I caught the metal bar cleanly, its shifting load was uncontrollable and the heavy wooden hangers started clattering to the floor. For a fleeting second I held on to prevent more items from falling, but it was too late. I had to get out. I let the rail go and it crashed thunderously to the ground.

In no time I was out in the hall and running towards my exit. I should have kept moving, but at the foot of the stairs I couldn't stop myself looking up. Staring back at me with eyes like headlamps was a lad of about my own age. He was standing on the half landing and for a second he looked about as terrified as I felt. Before I could move, his face seemed to narrow and his mouth set into a grimace and, with a deafening shriek, he launched himself down the stairs towards me.

I didn't see the knife until it flashed past my face. I held his arm but he was stronger than me. Then he lost his balance and I wrestled him to the ground. He brought his hand around to try and stab me below the ribs. I managed to grab his arm again. I was on top with the weight advantage. He kept yanking his arm, trying to free it from my grasp. I was preoccupied with the knife. I didn't even notice his knee rise up until it connected with my groin. The scream of shock and agony died in my chest. The air had already left my lungs. I rolled to the side, doubled-up on the floor. Excruciating pain radiated from my nuts into the pit of my stomach. He wasted no time and swung the blade at my head. I pulled away and kicked his supporting leg from under him. He was sent sprawling back to the ground. I was finally able to take a breath. Air rushed into my chest and adrenalin coursed through my veins. The nausea in my throat subsided.

Again I grabbed for the arm with the weapon. This time I got a firmer grip around his wrist. With my other hand I pushed his face into the bare floorboards. He struggled to slide his head from under the heel of my palm that was pinning him down. There must have been a splinter pointing out from the edge of a plank. And he yelped like a whipped dog when it pierced his cheek. He turned his head towards me. I saw the thick end of the sliver of wood jutting out below his eye. He stopped struggling momentarily. I relaxed my grip too. He snatched his hand away from me. Again thrusting the knife towards my face.

As he did, I turned my head to the side. I grabbed his sleeve at the elbow as his arm arced towards me. Not enough to stop the speed of his lunge, but enough to change its course. The blade connected with something soft. I braced myself for the impact to reach my brain and explode my senses.

Nothing. The body beneath me continued to writhe wildly. But something was different. Its energy was no longer directed at me; its struggle was against another force. It jerked and convulsed but no longer fought. The fight had also left me and I pulled away, not understanding my repulsion as something sprayed across the room like the spout of a fountain, pulsing to the sound of music. The bitter taste on my lips made me gag as I got to my knees and looked down through stinging eyes. There was a warm, sticky fluid, as black as oil in the darkness, soaking into my shirt and dripping from my face. The movement of his body slowed to a rhythmic judder and a shiny, viscous pool spread outwards and around his head. At its centre, glistening like rubies, the hilt of the knife hung loose from an opening in the side of his neck. About a third of the blade remained in the wound. It flashed red with a receding pulse. The seeping blood finally slowed. Then it stopped.

Bile burned my throat as I emptied my stomach onto the floor. *Don't leave anything behind.* But I just ran.

Mea Culpa

The image of me covered in a stranger's blood, running from the house headlong into Herb, is the last memory I have of that night. I assume he must have calmed me down, cleaned me up and sent me home. But I can't picture any of that; where he took me, what he said, how he seemed. All I know is it got sorted and no one ever spoke of it. Not even Dad. I did it for him, and he didn't even ask how it had gone.

I waited anxiously for a knock at the door, for the police to come and take me away; a recurring nightmare even now. When they did come, a few days later, it was Dad and John who left in handcuffs. I suppose in time I was able to rationalise what had happened, to distance myself from it. That and the tidal wave of their subsequent convictions, swept me away from that life.

As I arrive home and pull into the driveway, I think about John's last words before returning to his cell block. Is it conceivable, by some hideous twist of fate, that it was Riggs' brother I fought with and killed that night? The possibility hovers like a scavenging bird looking for a place to perch. The longer it circles there, the less of a coincidence it seems, until finally it finds a place to settle in my head. Another thought joins it as I'm forced to consider the idea that for the last twenty years, while I've been anxiously waiting for the law to catch up with me, Herb Long has been protecting me from his greatest enemy.

Grace gets back from work late again. This time she's just been busy. The woman who cancelled on Saturday was desperate and offered to pay extra to be spray-tanned after hours. I've made dinner and we're sitting at the table. I didn't tell her I was going to see John; I plan to tell her about it tonight.

'I can't believe your wife left you,' she says after tasting the lasagne verdi I've spent the last hour preparing. 'You're such a great cook.'

'Technically, I kicked her out, remember?' I say, ignoring the compliment.

'Yes, but for good reason. You know what I mean.' She's trying to be sympathetic, and I'm not really in the mood.

'To be honest I rarely did much in the kitchen the last few years.' The undercurrent of self-loathing that's been niggling away all afternoon starts to rise, and I'm failing to suppress it.

'Mickey, you're a lovely guy. She didn't deserve you. She must have been mad to start mucking around behind your back.' It's a subject that's been largely taboo between us and I realise she's only being supportive. The problem is she's caught me on the wrong day.

'Look, if you must know I was a lousy husband.' I slam down my fork, spattering the tablecloth with sauce. 'I didn't do anything for her, I didn't take her out, I never bought her flowers, I drank too much and I let her down once too often.'

'Mickey!' she says offering me a comforting arm. 'What's

brought this on?'

I regain some composure, pick up the fork and start moving the pasta around on my plate. I'm not sure how to continue.

'I saw a ghost today.' I say, finally looking up at her. She waits for me to continue. 'A young lad who died twenty years ago.'

She looks back, even more confused, wanting to understand. In the end I can't bring myself to tell her what I was going to say.

'I went to see John in prison,' I say, opting instead to describe the metaphorical spectre of his wasted youth. She falls for it and suddenly shifts her sympathy towards him. Somehow that makes me feel better and I continue eating.

I tell her what I found out about Riggs, about his dodgy business empire and his long-running rivalry with Herb. I mention the coincidence of his car crash years ago, but I leave out the bit about his carelessness when it comes to losing his nearest and dearest.

'We have to find Herb again,' she says as we load the dishwasher. 'If this guy Riggs *was* behind the fire at his house, Herb's in real danger.'

'If you choose to swim with sharks you probably learn not to get too attached to your limbs.' I immediately regret the insensitive analogy. After all, he probably is her dad, even if he doesn't know it yet. 'I'm sorry. I wouldn't want him getting hurt, even if he *has* been acting like a prat.'

'We have to find out what he's really up to.'

'You're right,' I say. 'If he's in trouble I'd still want to help him.'

'We just need to make him realise we're on his side.' As she says it I realise she's already made the emotional crossing. From wanting to check him out from a distance, she's now prepared to protect him, in spite of the way he treated her when they eventually met. Similarly, my sense of loyalty towards Herb, which, don't get me wrong, has been severely tested, has also strengthened, the more I reflect on what he did for me... and has carried on doing ever since.

Though he's becoming increasingly subdued, The Banker tries to remind me what that means for both of us in light of the deep voice with the ultimatum, that we're now convinced was Riggs. I dismiss him without a second thought. It's time to stand up and be counted.

'I'll keep trying,' I say. 'I get the impression he doesn't want to be contacted.' She sighs as I phone his number again. No one answers.

* * *

Work Shop

The tip of the screwdriver slips from the groove in the locking nut, gouging a furrow across the large, stubby knuckles of his other hand that grips the Stanley knife. He curses and throws the offending tool across the floor, making no attempt to wipe the blood or rub away the pain. Instead, he thumbs the button on the knife to test the sliding blade, before putting it back in the metal tray. Alongside a pair of bolt-cutters that have also been cleaned and oiled, a cleaver shines up at him with a newly-sharpened edge. He lifts the lump hammer and balances its weight in his hand. It feels good, and he lets the square head drop into his palm.

'Huh!' he snorts, picking up the large carrier bag with its supermarket logo, as if to appreciate its eco-friendliness. Multiple uses it might have had, but when he drops in the hammer, adding to its contents of a billiard ball and a length of nylon cord, the real irony is lost on him. It's not a bag for life.

Leaving the tray on the bench, he goes out and closes the heavy door behind him.

18.

Tuesday, 29th

I find it written in black ink on yellow paper, propped up on my bedside table; I've no idea how long it's been there:

DIDN'T WANT TO WAKE YOU – YOU LOOKED SO SWEET! HAD TO POP HOME FOR SOMETHING I FORGOT. NOTHING TO WORRY ABOUT (WOMEN'S STUFF) HOPEFULLY BACK BEFORE YOU'VE EVEN MISSED ME. G x

Red digits on the ceiling say 03:34. We were in bed by eleven, and I'm guessing asleep in minutes. My brain's gone from comatose to microprocessor in seconds – four seconds to be precise. Having originally woken me, my straining bladder has to endure a fruitlessly-thorough inspection of the entire house, garden and street. But when I finally get to the bathroom, and in full flow, I start checking behind the shower curtain - as if we're just kids playing hide and seek - it registers its disapproval in yellow spatter on the white ceramic rim.

Moments later, her mobile rings. I can hear it in both ears – one through my phone, the other much louder... much closer. I find it lighting up the living room. I'm tempted to take it with me, especially when mine's so low on power, but I decide to leave it there in case she gets back before me. By now I've got jeans on over my Calvin Klein bedtime boxers and the coordinating T-shirt is also moonlighting as daywear. Shoes without socks are so uncomfortable, but I don't stop to think about blisters, and I'm out the door with my coat and keys within minutes of lowering the toilet seat.

Miss Take

I count twenty cars on the move between my house and the road before her turning. None of them is a little red soft-top. I'm so preoccupied looking for hers and eliminating every other colour, make and model, that it's not until I've driven halfway down her road that I see the silver Mercedes parked outside her flat. My whole body goes rigid.

I drive past and take some comfort that at least her MX-5 isn't in its reserved bay. There's no sign of activity at the front and inside all the lights are off. I park the car further up, get out and instinctively stay close to the front hedge of the neighbouring house. Approaching her flat, I can see the communal entrance door is propped open with a fire extinguisher, even though the inner light is off. I noticed last time how it acted like a car's courtesy lamp, coming on automatically when the door opens and turning itself off after a short delay once it closes. That thought gives me a sense of dread as I tiptoe across the residents' parking area, exposed in the full glare of streetlights, and handicapped by my inappropriate choice of footwear. The first pair that came to hand was my ex-work shoes. It was all part of the image back then; Blakey's in your heels to announce your arrival across the marbled floors of rival banking halls. Not so impressive when you're in stealth mode, and excruciating without socks.

Slipping quietly through the glass doors into the lobby, I edge my way along the inner wall and back into a shadowy recess, when something clinks gently against the skirting board; an object I must have kicked along the carpet. I bend down and brush the floor gently with my hand until I feel something round, brittle and not completely cold: a light bulb. I suppose I should be glad I didn't break it, yet I get no sense of relief when I look up and see the lantern pendant hanging empty from the ceiling.

Ignoring the service lift behind me, I head across the hall and open the fire door to the stairwell, desperate to maintain the strangely-reassuring stillness. But I'm not even halfway up the first flight when the mechanical din of wheels and pulleys shatters the brittle silence.

Staying close to the wall, I feel my way back down the linoleum steps and peer through the narrow meshed glass of the door, back into the lobby. Above the lift door, the down arrow is lit and, alongside it, the number one illuminates briefly. The lift's descent must have started on the second floor. Grace's flat.

I keep watching, momentarily ignoring my sense of dread, hoping the door will open and she will step out, female essentials in hand, looking lovely, flustered only by the lateness of her departure to get back before I wake up and find her note. Then I'll push open the door and surprise her.

But it's not her. At first it looks like the tiny lift is crowded, and for a split second I think it's just a couple of other residents having crammed in, their intimate embrace reluctantly untangling only when the doors fully open. The figure at the front, a man I'm guessing, is wedged in with his back to the door. He seems to be hunched forward over another figure whose shape I can barely make out. Like a contortionist emerging from an impossible aperture, a giant of a man unfurls backwards out of the lift. By contrast, the object behind him slumps forward and the man has to reach in to support it. This time, when he straightens up, he turns, and I instantly recognise Mac's huge bulk. When he manhandles what appears to be a loosely-rolled carpet out of the lift and carries it like a sack of potatoes to the main door, my brain starts to pixelate.

Before I've regained my wits, he's outside, halfway across the parking bays, and by the time I reach the outer door he's opening the boot of the Mercedes.

'Hey!' I shout as aggressively as I can muster. He's got one hand on the bundled rug, propped against the side of the car, and as he turns to look at me, he loses his grip and it slides away from him and hits the ground with an audible thud.

'You!' is all he grunts, as he bends down to gather up the loose folds and proceeds to re-wrap his quarry.

'Leave it there!' I scream and he ignores me as I take another time-lapsed step towards him. I still can't make out any shape, but as he lifts the roll back upright, a bare leg slips out up to the calf. The small limp foot, its toenails dark, like purple varnish, drags into the kerb where it wedges momentarily against the tyre, the ankle stretching and twisting horribly before recoiling as he tugs hard on the dead weight to lift it over the rim of the boot. That fleeting glimpse is all I get, but it's enough to reinforce my worst fears that it must be Grace.

I grab for the phone, about to hit the nine, when realisation hits me like a bullet. The battery's dead.

'Shit!' I yell and throw the phone at him. It bounces off like a Lilliputian missile. He doesn't even feel it. 'Leave her alone, you sick bastard.' I run at him as he's closing the boot. He turns and swats my approach, sending me spinning under my own momentum onto the tarmac. My shoulder screams out with the impact. I'm back on my feet, but he's made it to the car door. I aim a kick towards him as he twists to drop into the seat. It misses the un-missable target. I manage to keep my foot up and the heel of my shoe redirects towards his trailing right hand. His knuckles crunch against the door's edge. Metal studs grind gratefully against fragile bones and soft flesh. He bellows an unintelligible roar and reels in the damaged paw. His other hand reaches across to close the door. Before I can regain my balance, the engine fires up, and as he drives away the last thing I hear is an absurd accompaniment of baroque harpsichord.

The music fades in his wake and I'm left standing in the middle of the road, frozen in confusion at what just happened and uncertain what to do next. Instinct takes over and without further conscious thought I'm in my car and chasing. He's already taken the first turn off Grace's road and by the time I do the same, I see the Merc pull away at the next junction. When I get there, sod's law, several cars are coming and I'm trying to inch out and look ahead at the same time. I think there's a big enough gap and pull forward, when a souped-up little hatchback with ridiculous wheel arches flashes vindictively and swerves around me. I get right up behind Mighty Mouse and he slams on his brakes and forces me to a virtual stop, long enough to see his cupped fist gesturing in a vertical motion over his shoulder before he speeds off again.

Looking ahead, I think I can still see the Merc, and I accelerate hard, but Boy Racer has other ideas. You'd think he'd be up for The Fast and The Furious. But no, he's only interested in holding me back; he's Driving Miss Daisy and we're going the long way. After several attempts to pull around him fail, I catch a glimpse ahead and realise there's no longer a silver car in front. I've lost it. I pull into the kerb and the tosser in front speeds away with a victorious blare of his horn. I don't have time for road rage tonight so I spin the car around. I need to get back to Grace's flat and hope I can get inside so I can use the phone.

This time I drive straight into her parking bay. I race up the stairs to the second floor and find the door wide open. I've not been inside before, but it's obvious there's furniture out of place in the sitting room. There's a lamp on its side and a bare expanse of polished wooden floor where I'm guessing a rug used to be. Everything else looks normal and I quickly check the other rooms. The only sign of recent activity is in the kitchen where there's a used dinner plate, knife and fork in the sink and a half empty glass of water on the drainer.

I find the phone back in the lounge and I'm about to pick up the receiver when I notice a blue 4 flashing on the base unit. I press the play button and hear a woman's voice. She's leaving a message for Simon, and I decide it must be his mother. She asks him to call her back. The next message is confusing because it starts off silent with just a vague background noise like someone's there but not talking. Then there's Simon's voice saying, 'Hello, who's there?' The line goes dead and the message ends. I'm guessing he picked up the phone after the answer machine had kicked in. The third message has the same kind of background noise like heavy breathing. Eventually, Simon picks up and says, 'Whoever this is, just piss off and leave me alone.' This is starting to feel like telephone voyeurism and it isn't helping me save Grace so I lift the receiver and dial 999.

'Police,' I say, and as I wait to be connected the answer machine serves up another silent message, only this time the call is cut off presumably by someone – Simon – picking up the phone and slamming it back down.

'What's the nature of the emergency, sir?'

'Uh... abduction!'

False Dawn

It's a quarter to seven and the cops have finally let me go. You'd have thought I'd been the nutter with the giant roll-up by the hard time they've just given me. They could see by the furniture out of place that there must have been an "altercation", as they liked to describe it. Apart from that, there was nothing to say a huge thug had just drugged, if not killed, a young woman and driven off with her in the boot of his car. Nothing, that is, except me. And, call me insecure around the Old Bill, I got the distinct impression they didn't quite believe me. Not even when I gave them the number plate of the Merc that I'd added to the piece of paper I've been carrying around with me. They only let me go after I eventually persuaded them to get Melville on the phone to vouch for me. And they weren't prepared to get him out of bed until six-thirty. I was never so grateful to an officer of the law.

That said, right now I'm pushing my luck, testing the alertness of early morning commuters and provoking the speed camera outside the pub where Herb had reappeared. Remembering the route we'd taken on Sunday when we got hopelessly lost in the dark, I try a few alternative turnings at the main junctions. Several times I have to turn around and go back and try again. The problem is, on the way there, in the back of Herb's car, I was so disoriented, I didn't really take a lot of notice of the scenery. When I was chauffeured home, I was able to get a better sense of where we were and the things around us, but of

278

course, it always looks different going back the other way. Even so, helped by the first traces of daylight, every now and then I spot a familiar landmark.

Driving along an open road with nothing but trees and hedges to guide me, I'm about to resign myself to being lost yet again. There's no traffic so I reverse into an opening in the hedgerow so that I can drive back the other way. As I pull forward, I spot a black letter box, attached to what was probably once a gatepost. I pull the car onto the grass verge a few yards down the road and get out and walk back to the opening.

Approaching the mailbox, I notice the gold lettering that stands in bold contrast to the black painted casing:

L. ANGLICH

I sigh loudly, partly in relief, but mainly trepidation. It's the name we'd found on the junk mail at Bleak House. Once I'd discovered all I needed to know about Raymond Riggs online the other day, I'd typed 'langlich' into Google. That's when I discovered it's German for rectangle – or long-ish. And that's when I realised Grace's predilection for inventing cryptic names might well be hereditary.

I decide to leave the car where it is and walk. As I approach the turn in the long driveway that brings the house into view, I get off the noisy gravel and use the shrubbery for cover. The first thing I see to the left is the front of the Mercedes, deserted in a narrow lane off the main driveway. My heart pounds faster when I realise it's been backed up to a side entrance.

Everything seems still and quiet and, at risk of being seen from the front bay, I quickly cross the drive to take cover at the side of the house. I figure the window I'm crouched beneath looks into the room where I had my discussion with Herb.

Slowly I raise my head until I can just see through the glass. There's a light on and it takes a split second to get my bearings, until I realise I'm staring straight at Herb, who's sitting in the same fireside chair. I duck quickly, fairly certain he hasn't seen me, and move to one side of the window so I can stand up, while taking some cover from one of the heavy drapes hanging inside. Now I can use one eye to watch Herb and I can see he's talking. He's looking and gesturing across the hearth to the other chair with its back to me; the one I'd sat in before. Occasionally a hand appears from behind it though I can't make out who it might be. Man or woman, friend or foe. Probably friend, as the conversation seems to be cordial and there's a teapot and best china on a small, ornate table between the chairs.

With no other cars on the drive, if it's a visitor they either walked in like I did or, heaven forbid, arrived in the Mercedes. One thing's for sure though, it isn't Mac. I can't see Herb sharing a civilised morning repast with the hired muscle. And the guest is far too energetic to be him. In any case that possibility is disproved when the door opens and The Monster himself walks into the room.

At that point, the person in the second chair stands up, still hidden from my view by the high back of the leather seat. The way that only the top of a head appears suggests the person must be very short, and I'm trying to dispel the thought that it could be a child. I really can't tell. Herb seems to deal with Mac who leaves the room. He then gestures to the other person to sit down. I can hear their raised voices but I can't make out what's being said. And rather than dropping down out of view, the top of the head stays visible above the chair and becomes more animated. I'm willing whoever it is to step out from behind the chair and turn towards me, but right then instinct drops me to my knees as I hear the door opening at the front of the house. Footsteps crunch across the path as I edge towards the corner. Before I can peer around, a long blade flashes in front of my face.

'Field,' Mac says, stepping out in front of me. 'Inside... now!'

Red Sauce

I'm struggling to admire my surroundings. If circumstances were different, I'd be darting from row to row, in awe, like a kid in a sweet shop; pulling out bottles and blowing dust from their labels, attempting to pronounce the grand French chateaux and appellations. Instead, I can only squat and gaze at the racks of vintage wine that stand like regiments in Herb's cavernous cellar. From its scale and order, and the layer of grime that's been allowed to settle like a noble shroud, this has to be a collection amassed over many years. I turn my head as far as it will go but I can't see the door. It's too far behind me. That and the fact there's a nylon cord biting into my neck...

I had to accept it was no contest when Mac the Knife steered me into the house. It wasn't going to be the most dignified entrance to the breakfast party, but I figured at least I'd be able to challenge Herb on what the hell was going on and find out what's happened to Grace. But once inside the panelled hall, I was frog-marched straight ahead, halfway down the corridor that was no longer narrowed by piles of boxes, and into a little room where a bank of CCTV monitors lined the walls. On one screen I saw the front of my own car out on the road and on another, a rear view of the Mercedes with its boot open.

'What have you done with her?' I yelled, but that just prompted Mac to remind me he still had a weapon by piercing my T-shirt with its cold steel tip, and introducing it to the soft flesh behind my left kidney. That propelled me through another doorway, and once we'd descended a steep drop into the cellar, he proceeded to impress me with his mastery of bondage.

Don't get me wrong. There was nothing sensual about the way he tied my feet together with a length of cord. Nor was I aroused when he forced me to the floor with my knees up to my chin while he took up the slack and wound it several times around my waist. Once he'd finished securing my hands behind my back and tying off the loose end around my neck, I really couldn't see the appeal. Thankfully, he didn't then hoist me into a compromising position. I don't know if he enjoyed it, but he didn't say a word, and left me with nothing but the cold stone wall for a backrest. I didn't say anything either. On account of the billiard ball behind my teeth and the length of duct tape he stretched tightly from one ear to the other.

I'm left squatting here, helpless and desperate to know what he's done with Grace. Is she here? Is she still alive? It's been several hours now since I saw him drag someone from her flat. I keep telling myself that her car hadn't been there. But the sight of a small, delicate foot twisting grotesquely at the ankle keeps flashing before my eyes to convince me it was her. Who else could it have been? She said that was where she was going. And Herb has been after her for years. I should have done more to protect her. Instead I've led her right into the hands of a man that I called my friend, and that she had hoped to call her father. And now, I can't even help her.

The only thing I can do is concentrate on drawing deep breaths through my nose and try to fix my eyes on something calming. Usually, in the only remotely comparable situation I can think of, I would have to settle for the pattern in the lens of the dentist's overhead light. Today it's a darker glass I'm focusing on; a Louis Latour Montrachet Grand Cru. I think the label says 1998.

Realisation starts to dawn that I could be down here for hours. Worse still, Mac the Dominatrix might return to knock me about a bit, just for kicks. I need to find a way out to look for Grace, but twisting my head past the next row of bottles only causes the noose to tighten further. And before I'm forced by reflex to turn back to ease the pressure, I catch a fleeting glimpse of something hideously familiar that causes the air in my lungs to escape the only way it can, exploding in a torrent of snot from my nose.

When I regain my breath, I try to vocalise her name in my throat. It dies unheard in the mucous that's clogging my airways. I take deep breaths to clear my nose, and try humming it loudly, but it's useless. I need to get a better look to find out if she's even there. I try again to stretch my neck and force my eyes to the right. Even then, all I can see is no more than the hint of the edge of the rug behind the metal frame.

Overcome by a total sense of helplessness, I feel the muscles in my legs start to spasm and I slump back against the wall, resigned to staring straight ahead for what feels like hours. But maybe only minutes later the door opens behind me, and I recognise the sound of Mac's lumbering footfalls.

I think about trying to look around but my neck's had enough of this tourniquet. It's not just the way the rope tightens when I move my head that makes it protest; it's the fact it doesn't then loosen off as much when I turn back. While that may be true, the real reason I don't look around is because I don't want to see him coming. There's nothing I can do, no matter what he has in mind. All those instinctive fight or flight chemicals flushing through my body have nowhere to go, and I'm locked in a pre-mortis rigor. Let's just get this over with. I close my eyes and wait for the inevitable.

Instead of approaching me, he rushes past, and when I open my eyes he's crossing my field of vision at a speed that defies his bulk, huffing and puffing as he goes.

'Fockin dae-light,' he mutters and I realise he's not come for me.

Perversely, I now *want* him to acknowledge me, to show that he can hear the bizarre noises I'm trying to project, to at least meet my pinpoint stare so I can see into his soul. But he passes without a glance, and I don't even get any relief that his obvious agitation isn't directed at me. My neck's refusal to move means he disappears momentarily until, in a replay of the earlier scene, he staggers backwards, dragging the rolled-up rug from out of the recess. Again he struggles to control the dead weight, and I see streaks of red in stark contrast to the pile's neutral tones. And when a limb slips free, this time it's a pallid arm that hits the cold concrete. But now, when he fails to prevent the bundle from unravelling, it does so completely and all I can be sure of, as it rolls out of my sight, is that the body is completely naked.

I close my eyes, imagining the slim thighs and delicate

calves ending in small feet, one of them twisted at an impossible angle, and my head spins. I hear him hastily re-rolling it and hoisting it onto his shoulder with a grunt. As he heads back to the door, I watch him turn in my vague direction, but even now he denies me the validation of looking me in the eye.

'Ye took ma money,' he says, seemingly to the wall above my head. 'And ye came back... and took ma property. No one touches ma stuff.' The words are the most I've heard him say, and in an accent as uncompromising as the Clyde.

If I had the strength and the means to do more than mumble unintelligibly, I'd ask him what the hell he's talking about. Okay, the money, I get that. It's pretty obvious it wasn't Herb's or he'd have said something by now. But what would Mac the Bruce be doing with a photograph of Herb's wife? I doubt the question is even discernible in my eyes, but he still won't look at them anyway.

'Coming back for you,' he says. It's a promise that offers me no hope, and once again he gets away. And this time there's quite literally nothing I can do about it.

Present Arms

There are crashes and bangs as Mac climbs the stairs, and I feel every knock as if it's my own body being bashed against the rail and bumped into the doorframe. When the door slams I close my eyes and give into the wave of grief. I don't have the luxury to sob; even so, when I blink and the first tear runs down my face, a steady stream soon follows.

When my head begins to clear, a new sound registers in my brain, and I sense someone else in the room.

'Mickey?' he says and I realise it's Herb, slowly coming towards me. I raise my head and his movements become more urgent and he reaches me and immediately starts to peel back the tape from my mouth. He cups his other hand under my chin, encouraging me to spit out the ball and I make no attempt to hold back the glob of saliva that also plops into his palm.

'What has he done?' he says, and I see the genuine horror in his eyes. He reaches around behind me and starts picking at the knot behind my neck.

'Over there!' I shout. All that comes out is a rasping whisper. 'Go and see... over there.'

'Let me get this undone,' he says, but I twist away from him and he comes back to face me. 'What is it, Mickey?'

'Over there.' He turns in the direction of my eyes.

'What is it, lad?'

'Grace,' I screech and the effort scorches my throat. 'I think it was Grace.'

'No,' he says, as he walks away. 'It can't be.'

'Did you tell him to take her?' I shout, at last finding some volume.

'Oh God,' he says, looking into the recess before tracing the dark stain across the floor with his eyes. He reaches down to touch it and lifts his finger to his nose. Before he can confirm what I already know, a different voice that's as deep as it is familiar shouts from the direction of the door.

'Stay where you are!' The words precede the clomping of a cumbersome descent, and the irony that I couldn't move if I wanted to is lost in the moment when the voice adds: 'I've got a gun.'

My view remains limited and nothing seems to change for several seconds. I'm guessing Herb is doing as he's told out of shot. I wait like the captive audience at a West End show for someone new to take the stage. But it's not a confident entrance when a middle-aged man with a limp and a boxy brown suit shuffles into my peripheral vision.

'What do we have here?' the stranger says, pointing a pistol with his right hand and reaching up with his left as if to scratch his forehead.

'Riggs!' Herb exclaims, and I have to push back against the wall to stop from rolling onto my side.

'And you must be Mickey Field,' the gunman says, now standing square in front of me like he's reached some invisible mark on the floor. He looks at me with a fixed smile, but keeps the gun pointed stage left. This time when he strokes the skin above his eye, I notice the gristly white scar that divides his brow like a tectonic ridge. 'I thought you were on his side. What *have* you done to piss him off? ' I haven't a clue how to answer that and I'm glad when Herb draws his attention away from me.

'What are you doing here, Riggs?'

'A little bird told me there'd be some action here this morning. And I've been wondering where you sloped off to after our recent little barbecue in Gravesend.'

'You bastard. You'll pay for that.'

'No, Long.' Riggs' voice booms around the cellar. 'I've paid all I'm going to pay for your pathetic vendettas. I'm still convinced you killed my brother when he was just a boy.'

'That wasn't me,' Herb says. 'I didn't kill him.' I still can't see Herb but I'm half-expecting Riggs to look daggers back at me. I'm glad when he doesn't.

'And what have you done with my wife?'

'I've never met your wife,' Herb spits back at him. 'You never were much good at keeping hold of your women.'

'Fuck you!' Riggs yells. 'With your pathetic ransom note.'

'I don't know what you're talking about. But from what I've heard, she was better off without you, you sadistic bastard.'

'Hear that?' Riggs says, turning back to me. 'There you are, trussed up in his cellar like a gimp in a fetish bar... and *I'm* the sadist.'

'He didn't...' I say, but Riggs cuts across me.

'So what's that then?' he says to Herb, pointing to the floor with the gun.

'I don't know.'

'Is that blood?' Riggs stoops precariously to touch it. 'Is that... her blood?'

'I don't know,' Herb says louder and Riggs points the gun back at him.

'If you've killed her...'

'Like you would give a shit.'

'Fair deuce,' he says, nodding as if in civilised agreement. 'She's good for nothing. Couldn't give me a son. Even a daughter would have been something. Does fuck all and spends my money. So, yeah... I'm not losing any sleep. But if it was *you* who took her... *you* who killed her...' he says with an evil grin. 'Then I'd care.'

'What, like you killed mine...'

'It's Grace's blood!' I shout, and they both turn to look at me. 'I was there... at her flat, when Mac took...'

'Yeah, nice try, Field.' Riggs scowls back at me. 'Thought you'd be in on it somehow.'

'Do I look like I'm in on *anything*?' I protest, but he dismisses me with an ironic shrug.

'What have you done with her, Long?' he yells.

'Not me. I just came down here and found Mickey like this. It's all Mac's doing. Listen to the lad.'

'That Jock... is *your* pit bull, Long. Don't play the innocent.'

'He's right though,' I plead. 'I saw it all happen. Then the bastard tied me up and took her away. You should be going after him. She might still be alive.'

'She might, might she?' he says, but remains focused on Herb. 'The body... where would he have taken it?'

'I've no idea,' Herb says.

'You can't give up on her,' I splutter. 'It wasn't just a body.'

'Don't expect him to care about Grace,' Herb says. 'He's the one who killed her mother.'

'That was an accident,' Riggs counters. 'You're the one intent on wiping out an entire family.'

'Don't talk to me about family,' Herb says. 'You took mine... before all this even started.'

'You still had something left,' Riggs says, again rubbing at the scar on his forehead. 'But you threw her away like rubbish. I've taken more of an interest in her life than you ever did, you selfish piece of shit.'

'What, by buying her loyalty?' I say, surprising myself with the strength of conviction given my precarious position.

'What do you know about it, Field?' Riggs turns and points the gun at me; I flinch.

'Enough to know you've got Terry Pinner over a barrel.'

'Just enough to keep young Grace in a lifestyle to which I'm sure she's become accustomed.' He sneers at me and adds: 'A bit out of your league, I would have thought. What are you? A failed banker.'

'Pinner's been in your pocket for years.' Herb joins in. 'Protecting you.'

'Wasn't he there the night of the crash?' I add and Riggs' face visibly twitches. He tries to conceal it by rubbing his forehead and just stares at me. 'Funny how you got out alive and everyone else died.'

'Not everyone,' he says. 'Don't forget the child... I never have. Even if *he* didn't care.'

'You bastard,' Herb says, though this time with less rancour.

'If it wasn't for me, she wouldn't have even got through her teens,' Riggs says.

'If it wasn't for you...' Herb counters. 'She'd still have a mother.'

'You're missing the point, both of you,' I shout. 'If you care for her, why aren't you trying to find her? You do know she's your daughter Herb.'

'Yeah, right!' It's Riggs who scoffs while Herb seems to be nodding. 'We'll see about that.'

'What's that supposed to mean?' Herb says and Riggs grins back at him.

'What is she to you, Riggs?' I say, and as he looks at me, I notice Herb edging forward and I try to keep up the distraction. 'You seem intent on protecting her. But you know what? She doesn't have a good word to say about...'

Before I can finish he swings the gun down at my head and, although it's only a glancing blow, it's enough to send me reeling onto my side. The noose around my neck tightens mercilessly as I try to hold my head off the floor to stop it closing my windpipe completely.

In the same moment, Herb takes his chance and throws the billiard ball. It narrowly misses Riggs and ricochets off the wall into the nearest rack of wine with explosive force. Riggs is thrown off balance and Herb makes a grab for the gun. Herb is deceptively strong, with the element of surprise and a good few inches advantage. Riggs' movements are laboured under the assault and he struggles to stand his ground. The gammy leg appears to be more than just a minor disability and gives him a pronounced weakness on one side. Herb soon overpowers him and I hear the gun clatter across the floor.

While it's good to see Herb overpowering Riggs, it's bad I have to watch it all happen sideways. While they're fighting each other, I'm wrestling with gravity, trying to prevent my head resting on the floor. I'm hoping Herb can help me sit up, but the thought is interrupted by distant voices. Muffled shouting reverberates though the open door and heavy footfalls stomp across the timber ceiling. I daren't move, although I can see Herb heading back towards the stairs and Riggs getting back to his feet. I try to call out, but the door slams somewhere behind me and then there's silence... except for the rhythmic dripping that draws my eye to a pool of red liquid, laced with shards of glass.

With an arm wedged beneath me, my shoulder grinds into the concrete. The tendons down the side of my neck strain against the weight of my head. I can't let it drop. The cord has pulled so tight around my throat. Breathing is now the only priority. I draw the filthy air into my lungs in a thin, painful whistle. I'm struggling to clear my lungs as the dirt clogs my throat. Movement only constricts the noose more. The fight to free myself has the opposite effect. I'm feeling light-headed. Panic setting in. One last gasp... every sinew... desperate... for movement... some loosening... My head jerks... up and down... seeking the slightest opening. Violent spasms... I can't control... squeeze it tighter. My lungs... at bursting point. Conflict in my head... deafening...

Then it stops... Everything stops.

Domestic Bliss

As a little kid, I loved to lie in bed, warm and snug on a Saturday morning, and hear Mum vacuuming somewhere in the house. Something about the low resonating ebb and flow would send goose bumps down my back as I curled up tight beneath the covers. There must have been something comfortingly womb-like about that feeling. I always knew, sooner or later it would stop, and when it did I would lay there, hoping she was just moving to the next room. Then it would start again. I never wanted it to end but it always did. Eventually. I don't know if it's the old cylinder cleaners that made such a wonderful hum or if it's something you grow out of because I haven't had that feeling since. Not until now.

The voice is so gentle it makes me want to sleep forever. It rises and falls, interrupts and then soothes. The words seem urgent, panicked, but I want to ignore them and just drift away on their glorious sounds. I know it's her voice, although I can't remember her name or what she looks like. That doesn't matter because I'm not sure who I am either, or what I am. I just know she's lovely and I want her to keep talking so she stays with me forever. If she stops I'll be on my own. And I couldn't bear to be alone. I'm willing her to speak, hoping again that the pause is temporary, as if she's just finished one room and is about to start on the next as she vacuums an endless house. I'm holding my breath waiting. Will she start again or will I hear the dreaded click of the power switch and the plug being pulled from the socket? Come on, surely it can't take that long to decide whether to start again or stop for good. I can't hold on much longer...

Something makes me decide to inhale. It's a deeper breath than I was expecting. And someone's turned up the volume to full blast. It's not the comforting sound I was waiting for. I think my head's going to explode. There's also a light in my face and I screw up my eyes to blot it out. I want to go back to the darkness where the sound caressed me, where I could be alone with it.

Instead, something reconnects. Somehow, I know who I am again. And that it's Grace's voice I can hear. And when I open my eyes it's her face I see. I start to rationalise and my first semi-lucid thought is that there must be a heaven after all, and we're both here together. If that's the case, why does she look so worried? Then she smiles and I'm instantly certain of one thing. We're both still very much alive.

I'm aware of someone else behind me and my arms are being freed. They feel numb, although the wonderful sensation of pins and needles reassures me that blood is starting to flow. I want to look around to see who is helping but I can't move my head. And anyway, I don't want to look away from Grace.

'Thought we'd lost you there for a minute.' It's not a voice I recognise. I'm grateful anyway that he's unravelling rope from around my waist, and moving to my ankles to loosen the slipknot.

'You're okay, Grace,' I croak as recollection floods back into my head.

'Don't worry about me Mickey. Let's get you up,' she says. My legs are very shaky and I almost fall before they both support me and lead me over towards the exit. The quick movement sends a jolt of pain into my head, but it's my neck that suddenly cries out for attention. I rub my hand carefully around my throat. It doesn't feel like mine. I don't remember pulling on a turtle-neck over my T-shirt earlier. There's an indentation where the cord dug in and my skin burns in protest at the touch. I wince and Grace gives me a reassuring smile as she helps the stranger lower me onto the bottom stair.

'He'll be okay now,' she says, nodding to the man who seems reluctant to leave us, until he dutifully heads off up the stairs.

'How did you get here?' I manage to say. Although it's painful, my voice is starting to sound less like a Dalek. 'I went to your flat. Your note... You said...'

'Sorry Mickey, I had to...' she says, looking hesitantly up to the man who is now standing at the top of the stairs in the doorway. She joins me on the bottom step with our backs to him.

'Why?'

'I had to talk to him...' She lowers her voice. 'He *is* my father.'

'Huh?'

'He thought I'd come to trick him... that I was just Terry Pinner's daughter... and working for Riggs. I finally got through to him, persuaded him I was here to warn him. He told me about the camera on Millennium Eve... that he'd wanted to snatch me. Teach Terry a lesson. He was too drunk. He couldn't do it.' She pauses for a moment. 'He started talking about my mum. Her name was Jasmine. He said he can see her in my smile...'

I put my arms around her and hold her gently. My shoulders are still getting used to bending that way. She realises my discomfort and lets me go.

'How did you get here?' I say.

'They're going to raid the place later this morning... the police. Terry told me yesterday and I got him to give me the details – I had to warn Herb. He also told me you were in serious danger from Riggs. That's why I didn't want to tell you I was coming here this morning. I thought if I could keep you away, I could make everyone see sense. Make things right. The last thing I wanted was for you to get hurt.' She turns and looks up the stairs.

'Are you okay?' I say.

'Yes. I'm fine. The good news is: I've found my dad.'

'Yeah, well... he could have told me... earlier.'

'Told you what?'

'Well... that you were alright. That you were here all along.'

'I'm fine Mickey, really I am.'

'You are sure about him, yeah? About Herb?'

'Yeah... I think so. Why?'

'I thought you were dead.'

'Dead?' She lets out a nervous laugh.

'Over there.'

'Where?' I lean forward to point to the trail of blood. Before my arm will obey the instruction from my brain, we're interrupted by the man at the top of the stairs, shouting down at us.

'You ready to come up here yet?'

'Yeah, I think my legs are coming back,' I say and turn back to Grace and whisper: 'Is he a cop?'

'No,' she says. 'He's with Riggs.'

'Oh! How many are there?'

'He's one of two... plus Riggs.'

'If *they're* in control, where does that leave us?' I say. She just shrugs. 'And what about Mac? Have you seen him?'

'No. Why?'

'There was a body, over there. He came back for it.' Her eyes widen and her mouth falls open. I squeeze her hand and realise I have to tell her the rest. 'I thought it was you... it looked like the toenails were painted. But now I think it must have been...'

'Right then, you two... up here now.' The guy upstairs cuts me off again. We both look up and he flaps opens his jacket to reveal something shiny holstered beneath his arm.

I take the stairs slowly, one at a time, and pretend to slip so that Grace comes closer, just long enough for me to say it without being seen.

'Have they got Herb?'

'Yes,' she breathes into my ear. 'That's the bad news.'

19.

Body Blow

Herb is sitting in his favourite chair by the fireplace. Thug Number Two is standing behind him, resting the heel of a gun in one of the deep leather dimples of the high back, and Riggs is seated opposite. With his head bowed, Herb reminds me of a woodlouse under attack; two spiders waiting patiently for their prey to unroll. As we enter the room, Riggs gets up and walks towards us.

'Any news on the Jock?' he says, turning to Thug Number One, and the man following us in shakes his head.

'Has he said anything?' Number One nods towards Herb, whose hunched shoulders remain motionless, and gets the same wordless response.

'Maybe you can talk some sense into him,' Riggs says to us, 'before I completely lose it.' I hold Grace's hand and lead her to the seat Riggs has vacated, and drag another one noisily across the parquet floor and put it alongside. Riggs takes up a position behind me, and Number One retreats to his customary place in the doorway. With the stage set, I'm not quite sure what's supposed to happen next. I needn't have worried because Riggs continues giving direction.

'Tell me what you've done with her?' he yells and Herb lifts his head to reveal a red lump the size of a duck's egg under his left eye.

'Oh, God!' Grace brings a hand up to cover her mouth, but Herb seems unfazed by the injury.

'Like I said, I've never seen your wife,' he says slowly and defiantly. 'And I don't know where she is.'

Before I can react, from behind, Riggs brings his right arm around my purl-knit collar and presses the cold tip of his gun barrel into my temple. Whoever said one pain can cancel out another was having me on because the agony from these two places is singularly and cumulatively excruciating. I don't move. I *can't* move. I literally stop breathing. As if to compensate, Grace visibly jumps in her chair and gasps.

'Leave him out of it!' she screams. Riggs has got me in a firm grip and there's nothing I can do but stare straight ahead at Herb.

'That doesn't change anything,' Herb says, remaining calm and composed. 'I can't tell you something I don't know.'

'What about now?' Riggs says, tightening his arm around my throat, whilst moving the gun to the side and pointing it straight at Grace. This time, Herb is the one to flinch. 'I'll ask you again, where is she?'

'I... don't know,' Herb says, failing to conceal the panic in his voice.

'Are you sure?' Riggs says. Now he's the one calm and assured. In control. 'You really have nothing more to say.'

'I don't know about your wife...' Herb splutters and Riggs' finger bends against the trigger. 'But I do know what happened to the lad.'

'What lad?'

'Your brother,' Herb says, and the air leaves my lungs like a burst balloon.

'Go on.' Riggs continues, holding the gun steady.

'Tell him Mickey,' As Herb says it, Riggs reunites the end of the barrel with its imprint on the side of my head. Only now it threatens to remove the circle of skin like a hole punched in leather.

'Uh... oh, Jesus... yeah. He had a knife. I had to fight him off...' I gasp.

'You killed him...' Riggs says and I can't tell if it's a question and decide not to answer. 'What happened to him?'

'It was an accident...'

'What did you do with him?'

'We fought... the knife... he would have killed me...'

'Then what?'

'I... ran away.'

'You killed my brother,' he says slowly. 'And then... you ran away.'

'I was just a kid.'

'*He* was just a kid!' he roars, twisting the gun. The pain is unbearable and blood starts to trickle down the side of my face. 'What happened to him... afterwards?'

'I don't...'

'Mac tidied it up,' Herb says, rescuing me, much as he did before.

'I knew you must have been involved, Long,' Riggs bellows.

'I didn't want to be involved,' Herb says, glaring at Riggs. '*You* involved me, when you decided to send your kid brother into *my* lock-up, to nick *my* stuff.' Like a bullet through my brain, realisation dawns after all this time; that's exactly what Dad had sent me to do too – to break into Herb's lock-up and steal his stuff. And yet, Herb still helped me, cleaned up my mess, covered my tracks and let me go.

'So what did you do with him?' Riggs shoots back.

'Mac... dealt with it. I don't know what happened to the...'

'I want to know where the boy's resting.'

'Then you'll need to ask Mac... I never have.'

'That doesn't cut it, Long. He's one of yours... the same as this punk.' Riggs releases his grip around my neck and pushes my head away with the pistol. I don't get the sense I'm off the hook. Grace leans towards me and I'm glad for her concern. I turn to her, in need of reassurance from her eyes. But they'll no longer meet mine; instead they dart back and forth and there's a look of panic as if she's drowning.

'Take him back downstairs,' Riggs says to the man who hasn't long ago untied me, and my brain goes into overdrive as I scramble for my life.

'Like he said...' I blurt out. 'It's Mac you should be after.'

They all stop and stare at me and, although this isn't how I would have wanted Grace to find out, I have to make the biggest impact while I've got their attention. 'All that blood down there... There *was* a body. I saw him taken from her flat.'

'Saw who taken from the flat?' she says.

'Like I've been saying, Grace... I thought it was you, but then... of course, I was the only bloody fool who didn't know you were here all along. So it can only have been... Simon.' I look around the room at the others and repeat the name for maximum effect. 'Simon Pinner. Mac took him. He might still be alive. You have to get after him.'

It seems to have worked and Riggs is on the move in no time. He takes out his phone and leaves the room. Number One disappears with him and Number Two steps out from behind Herb's chair, walks over to the window and turns back to face us. He keeps his gun trained in our general direction but seems otherwise disinterested.

'Simon... is he dead?' Grace whispers.

'I didn't get a proper look,' I say. 'I thought the toenails were... but they must have just been blue. It didn't look good.'

When I look at her she's staring into space. Her face is white.

'What is this Mac anyway, a psycho?' I say. Herb shakes his head.

'No...' he says, unconvincingly. 'He... gets a bit enthusiastic, that's all... takes his job too seriously.'

'Not just the driving, then?'

'His job is to protect me and my interests.'

'So he goes after your enemies?'

'Sometimes you have to take the initiative...' he says with a shrug before his body language changes and he sighs. 'He's always been very loyal... but just lately... I've had to turn a blind eye.'

'Because he's started enjoying it too much?'

'I don't think... I can control him anymore. That's why I wanted to bring someone else on board.'

'Well, thanks for that,' I say. 'He almost killed me too.'

'I'm sorry lad. That was never my intention.'

'Maybe he was after Grace last night,' I say and look across at her. At first she doesn't react. 'Otherwise, why Simon?'

'Why does anybody kill anyone?' she finally says with grit in her voice. Now she's looking at me and I'm the one trying to avoid eye contact. 'You killed Riggs' brother.' It's a statement, loud enough for everyone to hear, but there's a question mark disguised in her tone.

'I didn't mean to...' My words are empty; spoken aloud, but not for her benefit. She locks onto my gaze, crying out for me to elaborate. It's Herb who fills the silence.

'People die all the time, Grace. You'd be surprised how many just disappear.' She's still looking at me like she hasn't heard him.

'I didn't mean to kill him, Grace.' I say it quietly and search her eyes for some flicker of understanding. All I get is my own reflection. 'It was an accident.'

'An accident?' she says, her words cold and sharp like a blade. 'How can you kill someone and just get away with it?'

'I don't know... You heard him... He made it go away.' I look from her to Herb as if he has all the answers.

'My hands are clean,' he says, and as if to prove it he holds them out like Pontius Pilate, before adding: 'Don't ask, don't tell.'

'So it never bothered you before... what Mac gets up to?' she says.

'I'm not his keeper.'

'Did you know he had Simon down there?' she says. 'All the time we were up here talking?'

'No,' he pleads, shaking his head. 'I didn't know where he was when I called him. When you said about the police coming, I wanted him back here to make sure there wasn't anything in the house for them to find. I didn't see him come in and he soon loaded up the van and left. When he got back that's when he came in and said there's an intruder. That must have been you, Mickey.'

'And then he had his own tidying up to do,' I say. 'You have to admit Herb, he might have kept it from you, but it looks like he's been doing all this in your name. Riggs' wife... Now Pinner's son.'

'And Riggs' brother,' she adds and I cringe.

'Grace... I didn't...' I say but she doesn't even look at me.

'Some advice,' he says leaning towards her in his chair. 'A lesson Mickey learned a long time ago. It helps if you don't ask too many questions.'

Grace looks from him to me and shakes her head.

'Yeah, very paternal,' I say. 'Fatherly guidance on turning a blind eye to the sick elephant in the room.'

'You want to talk about father figures?' he asks. 'Your old man was a bloody fool, Mickey. Probably still is. I offered him the chance to become my partner after Riggs... But, no, he thought he could do it better his own way; just taking stuff that didn't belong to him. Not only did he turn me down but he then turned against me.'

'It was your lock-up,' I say, exhaling deeply. 'I never knew.'

'Exactly,' he says. 'Because you didn't *need* to.'

'So I was burgling you...' I look across to Grace. She's still shaking her head, but I figure she already knows the worst, she may as well hear the rest. 'And you let me go?'

'You'd done me a favour, remember, sticking it to that kid.' Grace draws in a sharp breath and he continues in a whisper. 'Once the body was gone and the place was cleaned up, no one would have ever suspected. Only your old man knew you'd been there that night, and he wasn't talking.'

'Does he know... my dad?'

'What, that both his sons are killers?' Grace says, in a disembodied voice. She slumps back in the chair when Herb holds up a conciliatory hand. Number Two seems to have become distracted, watching something out of the front window, and Herb starts stretching to look over the top of my chair. I wonder if he's thinking about our chances of making a move while we're not being watched. Instead he settles back and continues talking.

'I told him to keep you out of it,' he says. 'When he went down and took young John with him, I figured you needed a chance to decide which way you'd go. The boy's death was burden enough. I was glad you turned away from the life *he* had planned for you. If I'm honest, lad, I was slightly envious that you made a success up there in the real world.'

'Some success,' I say. 'In the end it was just a house of cards.'

'Don't knock it, Mickey. I would have had your life if things had been different. Jas would have had me running the Post Office by now. And she would have been a successful designer.' He looks across at Grace, but she's lost all interest in her family history. 'After she died, I had to clear out her things, and that's when I found how easy it was to integrate good quality fakes with the real thing. She had things she didn't even know were counterfeit. When I started trying to sell them on, I found a willing market. It's grown from there. I've always told myself it all came from her... Though I doubt she would have approved.'

'So where does that leave *us*?' I say to no one in particular. Grace's doesn't react. She's a million miles away.

'Back then I wanted to give you the chance to decide,' Herb says. 'And here we are now, full circle. I'm giving you that chance again.'

'Yeah right,' Grace says, bringing us both down to earth. 'That assumes we all get out of here alive.'

Rough Justice

Number Two's preoccupation with something outside shifts to the door, as raised voices can be heard in the hall. They get louder and louder until the door crashes inwards and, before any of us can move, the uncompromising energy of Detective Chief Inspector Terence Pinner shatters the peace with the discriminating subtlety of a drone strike. He's hurling abuse at Herb before he even sees where he's sitting and, after reaching the middle of the room where he acknowledges Grace with a momentary pause, he turns and starts raining blows down on the old man's head.

'Where's my son, you sick fucking pervert?' is the gist of his enquiry.

Grace jumps out of her chair and grabs her adoptive father by the arm and starts pulling him. He's in such a rage that he throws his arm outwards and catches her full in the face with the back of his hand, sending her flying across the room. I jump to her side and Riggs is not far behind me, seemingly as concerned for her well-being as I am.

Pinner finally stops his assault on Herb and turns to see Grace on the floor.

'Grace! Grace!' he says, 'I'm sorry.'

In response, Herb starts competing with me in who can yell at Pinner the loudest and the melee is only brought to a head by the loud discharge of Riggs' gun. A large, decorative chunk of cornice drops in a snowstorm of powder onto the head of Number One, whose only mistake was to follow too closely in the unpredictable wake of his boss.

'Steady on, Ray,' Pinner says, lowering his hands from his ears. 'If you're going to shoot anyone, make sure it's him.'

'Let's stay focused, Tel,' says Riggs. 'He's already said he doesn't know.'

'And you believe him. I've always had him down as a nonce. This just about confirms it.'

'He's not a pervert!' Grace screams, pushing through to stand between Pinner and Herb. 'He's my father.'

'Yeah, whatever. Whether he is or he isn't, I'll bring him down one way or another. That's why I wanted to raid the place. I'm sure we'll find more than enough here to put him away.'

Herb's too busy nursing several more bruises on his face to contest his innocent on either charge. I've seen no evidence of dodgy designer goods stashed around the place, although I'm sure there's plenty of scope here for the odd store room or two. But it's pretty clear now all the insinuations about Herb's predilections for minors is no more than an elaborate smear campaign put about by Pinner to hasten his incarceration.

'Talking of raiding the place,' Grace says, 'where's the rest of the hit-squad you said you had lined up for this morning?'

'It's been pulled,' he says despondently. 'God knows why. Someone up the line got cold feet. Anyway, it's just a matter of time.'

'Ah,' she says, turning to Riggs, 'that'll be why your old mucker's still here with his boys. No doubt got the nod earlier.' Pinner lowers his eyes and Riggs laughs out loud.

'The reason I'm here,' Riggs says, smiling back at her, 'is to look out for you.'

'What, by pointing a gun at her head?' I say, causing them all to turn to face me as if they'd forgotten I was still here. Pinner bristles and looks at Riggs.

'No harm intended,' Riggs says, disarming him with an assured grin. 'Just testing the strength of this new family tie we're all hearing so much about.'

'Did you know about this?' Pinner says, still looking at Riggs. 'This... family connection.' A strange grimace breaks across Riggs' face as he looks around the room from Pinner to me, to Herb and finally stopping at Grace.

'I've known all along...' he says. 'That is... that she's Jasmine's child.'

'You what?' Pinner's the first to react.

'Oh, I've always taken a keen interest in her. Since that... fateful night.'

'That'll be what a guilty conscience does to you.' Herb says.

'It was a terrible accident,' Riggs says, his fingers tracing the scar on his forehead.

'Just like your brother,' I say. He bats that away with the shake of his head.

'No, this was a tragedy,' he says looking down at his leg. 'And one I've been reminded of every day since.'

'Don't try to dress it up any other way Riggs,' Herb says. 'You killed her and it's pure luck you didn't kill the baby too.'

'I didn't kill her, Long. And the child lived,' he says. 'And you... didn't want her. So in time I found someone who did.'

'After twelve years?' I say, and look across at Grace who seems stunned into silence.

'As long as it took,' Riggs says, before turning to Pinner. 'And when you told me about your difficulties trying for another child, I decided you'd make the perfect surrogates.'

'But how?'

'Oh, come on Terry. You know how these things work; a discreet word here, a small donation there. And the authorities back then, being so keen to find those poor little orphans new homes after all that trouble. What better than into the family bosom of an upstanding officer of the law?'

'And all because you killed her mother,' I say. Riggs glares at me and I decide a more conciliatory approach is my best option. 'Even if it was... like your brother... an accident.'

'I didn't kill her. I wasn't even driving... Terry, tell them. Tell them I was the passenger.' He looks at Pinner, who still seems to be getting his head around the revelation about Grace.

'Of course,' Grace says looking at the DCI. 'You were there. First on the scene. You saw her still alive.'

'And you helped him cover it up,' Herb says, struggling to get out of the chair before being manhandled by Number Two.

'He... wa... wa...' Pinner's words seem to stick in his throat. 'He was... the pass...'

'There you go,' Riggs says. 'I wasn't driving. He's the only living witness and he vouched for me then... and he'll vouch for me now. Thank you Terry.'

'Someone else was there,' Herb says, and Riggs spins around and aims the gun at him. 'Go ahead and shoot me, Riggs. It doesn't matter anymore.'

'You're bluffing Long,' he says.

'There was a witness!' It's Grace who breaks the tension and they all look at her like she's mad.

'*In utero* doesn't count, my dear.' Riggs dismisses her.

'In the newspaper!' she counters, scornfully.

'What newspaper?' Pinner says.

'It was an old cutting. Someone reported a man driving from the pub with a woman as the passenger.' She points at Riggs. 'That was you.'

'That was never corroborated,' Pinner says. 'That so-called witness never came forward.'

'Because he didn't trust any of your lot,' Herb says.

'Ah, now it's all coming out,' Riggs says. 'What do you know? You weren't even there.'

'No. But I know someone who was.'

'Bullshit,' says Riggs.

'It's true. There *was* a witness. Someone *did* see you that night...' Herb glares at Riggs and then points to Pinner. 'And you, conspiring to cover it up.'

'Who?' Grace says. 'Who was there?'

'It was Mac. He saw it all.'

Riggs lets out a deep laugh. 'So after all these years... your witness is that Jock sociopath you keep in a cage in that shit-hole in South Woodford. The animal that you now say took Simon and, you'd probably have me believe, killed my wife too. Good luck getting *him* in the witness box.'

'Oh, don't you worry.' Herb smirks. 'I think he's got his own idea of justice.'

'Ray,' Pinner says, visibly agitated by the reference to Simon. 'I've heard enough. I'm calling this in. We need to find that freak. You and your boys should probably get out of here.'

'What about him?' Riggs aims his gun at Herb.

'He's not going anywhere,' Pinner says, getting out his phone. 'Just go.'

'That's right Riggs,' Herb says. 'Run along now, so your man on the inside can cover for you once again.'

'You're pathetic, Long!' Riggs yells. 'You were always jealous of me. Accept it, you've always been a loser. And I've always come out on top.'

'And to think we were once partners,' Herb shouts back.

'We were more than that, Long. At least I thought so.'

'What, best friends... you and me? That's not what best friends do, Riggs.'

'She was with me first. You wouldn't have even known her if it wasn't for me.'

'It was me she chose... me she married,' Herb says, wrestling with Number Two.

'You may have had the piece of paper, Long, but that's all it really was.' Riggs sneers.

Herb becomes so animated that Number Two has to lunge forward over the back of the chair to pin him down by the shoulders, restricting him to threatening Riggs with just his eyes.

'Ray!' Pinner yells. 'Enough...' Riggs nods to Number Two, who dutifully releases his grip on Herb and heads towards the door. Riggs turns to follow him before Grace stops him dead in his tracks.

'So, are you saying... you were having an affair... with my mother?' she says.

'Like I said...' Riggs returns her stare with equal intensity. 'It was a tragedy.' With that he limps out of the room.

Softly, Softly

When the cops arrive, only minutes later, it's pretty obvious DCI Pinner can't quite believe their speed of response. He isn't alone in that. And like the rest of us, I bet that's not the first thing that crosses his mind. His explosive entrance earlier is reduced to a damp sparkler in comparison to the storming of Herb's country house.

'Armed police... Nobody move!' The shrill command is the first thing we hear. The second is the door bouncing off the wall. By the time six armed response cops in full SWAT gear have swarmed into the room and lit up our chests with little red dots, all four of us have frozen.

'Arms... behind your heads! Drop... to your knees!' We all comply, except Pinner, who starts reaching into his jacket.

'Do it... Now!' The deafening scream is accompanied

305

instantly by the synchronised migration of two red dots from Pinner's chest to his forehead.

'I'm DC...'

'Shut it!' Screaming Balaclava inches forward as two others enter the room, and through the door I can see several more helmeted, bullet-proofed shadows streaming through the hallway. Once we've all surrendered, four men circle around behind us and lower our hands one at a time and zip-lock them behind our backs. The other four keep their weapons trained on our hearts.

'Names!' Screaming Balaclava looks at us one by one.

'Herbert Long.'

'DCI...' he says, loud and indignant. 'Pinner.'

'Grace... Long.' Screaming Balaclava locks onto her eyes like the sun through a lens until she spits out: 'Pinner. Grace Pinner.'

'Michael Field.'

'Anyone else... in the house?' To my surprise the question is aimed at me.

'Raymond Riggs... and two men...' My voice comes out unintentionally loud and staccato. 'Left a few minutes ago.... And Big Ma—... *his* Scottish driver... got away earlier... took someone with him... may have been dead.'

'Anyone else?' He's turns now to Herb, who shakes his head, at which point another balaclava with the same monotone voice appears at the doorway.

'All clear!' he yells.

'All clear!' Screaming Balaclava shouts back for no apparent reason.

'Need SOCOs in the cellar!'

'Why? What's down there?'

'Lot of blood!' With that the man in the doorway steps away and Screaming Balaclava lowers his voice into the radio clipped to his flak jacket.

'OIC!' he says, no less assertively.

'OIC receiving.' The scratchy response is barely audible.

'You're authorised to enter!'

306

'Roger that.'

'Need SOCOs in the cellar!'

'On their way.'

'Need you in here... for IDs!'

'Understood.'

'Theatre's all yours!'

'Coming in.'

Screaming Balaclava reels in his chest. His job is done and four of his men follow him from the room. The ones who've searched the house are also filing out past the door. They move out silently and the hallway seems to sigh, but none of the tension has left this room. We're left in the capable hands of the four ninjas with semi-automatic guns pointed at us. And they're still very much on the job. That is until the Officer in Charge breezes in.

'Morning Grace,' says Detective Sergeant James Melville.

'What the fuck!' Pinner shouts.

'Sir.' Melville's reply is respectful but cool as he dismisses his boss with a raised index finger and turns to the Men in Black. 'This... is Grace Pinner... and Michael Field. They can be released.' The red dots drop like broken buttons from our clothes as the guns are lowered. One balaclava leaves the room and the other rushes to cut the cable ties from Grace's wrists and then mine before also heading out the door. I watch them leave and catch sight of men in white paper suits and hoods entering through the hall.

'Sergeant?' Pinner yells 'What's going on?'

'This man,' Melville says, turning to his left, 'is Herbert Long. He is a person of interest in the case but not a suspect at this time. He can also be released.'

'But sir...' the marksman shouts, keeping his gun trained on Herb's chest. 'The blood... in the cellar?'

'We're already onto that. And I know it wasn't him. Let him go.' The red dot falls from Herb's shirt and his hands are freed before the penultimate sharpshooter leaves the room.

Herb rubs his wrists and sits back in his chair. Grace and I are still standing and I move closer to her. I brush her hand with mine in a way that could be construed as accidental but I'm glad when she doesn't pull it away. She sits down and I test her further by perching on the arm of her chair.

Now there's only one red dot left and it's on DCI Pinner's forehead.

'Mel-ville!' Pinner raises his voice again. 'My boy's out there. Get me out of these fucking PlastiCuffs.'

Melville waits until Pinner stops cursing him.

'Have you finished, sir?' he says, and Pinner just glares back at him. 'Okay, I'll take it from here,' he says turning to the one remaining shadow, who now seems strangely out of place. 'You can let AC know they can come in.'

'Sir!' the man shouts and leaves the room.

'What the fuck...?' Pinner spits, but runs out of venom before ending the sentence, 'Are AC doing here, Sergeant?' Melville holds up a hand like he's halting traffic, but his boss, who's still kneeling on the floor, has visibly given up the fight.

A grey-haired officer in pristine uniform enters the room, carrying a braided cap, followed by a woman and a man both younger and in plain clothes, all of whom we later discover work in Anti-Corruption. Melville steps back deferentially as if waiting for the senior rank to take over.

'It was all your good work, Sergeant,' the brass says. 'Please... go ahead.'

'Sir.' Melville nods respectfully before turning back to Pinner. 'Terence Pinner... I'm arresting you on suspicion of corruption and conspiracy to pervert the course of justice. You do not have to say anything, but it may harm your defence...'

By the time Melville gets to the end, Pinner is slumped back on his haunches and the two younger investigators, who have crossed the room, take an arm each and lift him to his feet. He looks plaintively back at Grace as he's led away. When I turn around she's looking down and shaking her head.

'Sir?' Melville says. 'Do you mind if I take a moment...'

'Have as long as you need, Sergeant. Excellent work. Carry

on.' After a very civic nod in our general direction, AC/DC replaces his cap and turns with a flourish, slicing the air as he leaves, with the creases in his trousers.

20.

Untold Suffering

'What about Riggs?' I say as Melville sits down in the chair I vacated.

'We're onto him,' he says. 'Do we need a paramedic out here?' He looks from me to Grace and then to Herb, and I realise we've all got various lumps and bruises, but we all shake our heads.

'And Simon...' Grace says. 'What about Simon?'

'Since your call earlier,' he says, nodding at me, 'we've been looking for the car.'

'He was here... Mac. He can't have gone far. But I don't think Simon...'

'We'll get him,' he says, more to Grace than me.

'What was all that about with Terry?' she says, and Melville smiles back at her kindly.

'It started when I saw your birth certificate,' he says. 'It was in the name of Jasmine Long... after your mother. It names your father as Herbert Long, a junior manager in the Post Office. Date of birth says the first of January '84. Probably the only fact you ever knew.'

'I suppose that's something,' she says. 'But how did you come across it?'

'It all started when we were investigating the fire...' Melville says, looking across at Herb. 'We found a blonde hair and a small fingerprint inside the front door.'

'Oh, yeah,' she says, smiling furtively at the look of bewilderment spreading across Herb's face.

'At first Pinner said it was just further evidence confirming his belief that Long... was in the habit of having kids in the house. A proposition he'd asserted many times. That you,' he stares into Herb's eyes like he's looking into his soul, 'are a paedophile.'

'That dirty bastard!' Herb mutters, a look of disgust distorting his features.

'What, on the strength of a hair and a small fingerprint?' I say in disbelief.

'Exactly,' Melville says, raising his voice and prompting Herb to straighten up, 'But I now know that was a malicious lie he'd been putting around to incriminate you for years. And once again, here he was trying to use it to dismiss evidence and divert attention away from the arson investigation.'

'Because he knew who did it,' Herb says and Melville nods back at him.

'So how did you know it was my hair?' Grace says.

'I didn't,' Melville replies. 'Not at first. We couldn't get a match on the fingerprint either.'

'But you suspected me anyway,' Grace says.

'What, you tricked her?' I butt in. 'Last week in the café... into incriminating herself?'

'Hold on a minute,' he says. 'Let me explain. At first Pinner didn't want us wasting time on these pieces of evidence because we couldn't be sure how long they'd been there. Even when we found a small shoeprint in the mud by the back door he wasn't interested. Then, all of a sudden, he completely changed his tune and it was as though they were the most important leads we had. I couldn't understand it. He'd made up his mind they belonged to the arsonist even though there were other aspects of the fire that just didn't fit.'

'Like what?' I say.

'Well, it bore all the hallmarks of a professional job, done in the dead of night. This was no act of teenage vandalism. I told the guv'nor there was no way a serious arsonist would use a back door for access and then hang around behind the front door, leaving fingerprint and DNA evidence, when that part of the house had any chance of not being destroyed in a subsequent fire. Whoever started that fire would have entered and left the building as close to the point of origin as possible.'

'What did he say?' Grace asks.

'He said, what we had was as close to a smoking gun as we were going to get, and to stop wasting time on fanciful theories and deal with the evidence in front of us.'

'Again, to lead you away from Riggs,' Herb says and gets the same acknowledgement from Melville.

'So, at his insistence and based on the tenuous correlation of the size of the fingerprint and the shoe impression, we went back and narrowed the fingerprint down to a number of possible juvenile records on the system. None was conclusive. But that's where Mr Field came in.'

'I did?'

'Remember, you called me to report a disturbance involving someone called Grace de Manton? When I realised you were talking about Miss Pinner I had an idea. I didn't understand what was going on with you three that night; especially when that house was dark and deserted by the time I arrived. But it gave me a hunch and I went back and expanded the search to include de Manton. Something very interesting came back under that name. But when I met with you on Friday,' he turns to look at Grace, 'I have to admit I still only had a reasonable suspicion you'd been in Long's house on the day of the fire.'

'Grace?' Herb says. 'What were you even doing in there?'

'I don't know...' she says. 'I just wanted to find out more about you. I'm sorry, I shouldn't have broken in.'

'But it wasn't the first time you'd been caught housebreaking, was it?' Melville asks and Grace responds with a silent nod while her cheeks flush loudly. 'At the age of eleven, you got yourself arrested. The record said you initially gave a false name. Fortunately for me, the name was added to the database as an alias. That record, together with the fingerprint, the blonde hair and the size-three shoeprint, that couldn't have been there before the rain earlier that day, provided a reasonable probability that it had been you... in the house just before the fire. But before I decided to confront you, I showed the results to the boss. As you might imagine that was a challenging conversation.'

'That's when he told you to drop it,' I say, remembering the previous conversation.

'Yes. At first he was in denial; to the point where he almost cracked my head open on his office wall. Then he started acting strangely. He said he'd known all along you'd committed some minor offences before they adopted you, but he said that was all in the past. He told me to bury any proof that you'd ever been in Long's house. When we then met in the afternoon and your admission matched with the evidence *and* once I'd heard your explanation, I started to realise there was more to this than Terry Pinner just trying to protect you. It didn't add up and I got the impression there was someone else he was covering for. You came to see him on Saturday afternoon, didn't you Grace?'

'Yes.'

'I don't know what you said to him but when you left he was in a foul mood – even for him. When he headed out for a meeting no one else seemed to know anything about, I decided to follow him. That's when I saw him with Riggs.'

'I've known it all along,' Herb says. 'Those two have been in league.'

'In the meantime,' Melville says, 'something had made me go back and look further into that little girl's history. But I had to go over his head to get authority to see her records at social services. It didn't quite work out the way I'd planned because my request was referred back to him, along with the information I was asking for. He summoned me into his office early on Sunday morning, and it was a very different conversation. He threw the file across his desk and when I opened it, on the top was a copy of the birth record of the little girl previously known as Grace James, more recently Grace Pinner and, it seems, occasionally Grace de Manton.' He looks into her eyes. 'Like I said, the birth certificate confirmed the baby was originally named Jasmine Long.'

313

'What did he say?' I ask.

'That it didn't change anything. He wanted me to stop wasting time following up on what he called coincidence and innuendo. He said he was closing down the arson investigation, given that the owner hadn't been traced, and he wanted me to take over a new case right away. Instead, I spent the day looking back through some old files relating to Riggs where Pinner had also been involved, and a pattern started to emerge. I got in touch with the Assistant Chief Constable and he brought in Anti-Corruption. From one of the files we picked up a reference to Riggs being injured in a bad accident years ago. When that led us to the car crash that killed Mrs Long I knew we were onto something.'

'*He* killed her,' Herb says through gritted teeth. 'I always said he killed her. No one would believe me.'

'When I went to see Terry,' Grace says, 'he admitted he was first on the scene.'

'Yes, that's what I discovered,' Melville says, 'in his initial assessment report. It said the drivers of both vehicles – a red saloon and a white hatchback – were women. The one driving the white car was pronounced dead at the scene and she had a male passenger. The male was identified as Raymond Riggs and it said, although he was conscious, his legs were badly crushed. Apart from that, he suffered injuries to his neck and a deep laceration to his face. Pinner's report stated that he dragged Riggs clear of the wreckage as a precaution because he was concerned with the risk of fire and a possible explosion. It was less detailed about the injuries to the woman travelling with Riggs, but as I read through the file I saw that the post-mortem showed massive trauma to her upper body, including fatal injuries to the head and spine.'

'Jesus!' says Herb.

'In contrast...' Melville hesitates then continues in a subdued voice, 'Mrs Long's injuries, at least as determined on arrival at A&E, were remarkably similar to those sustained by Riggs – predominantly to the legs, some restraint bruising across the chest and what was described as minor impact bruising to the head. She was also conscious, but there's no reference to her being moved from the vehicle before the paramedics arrived.'

I can see Grace's eyelids brimming and she blinks, releasing the suppressed grief in a torrent down her face. I turn to comfort her and at the same time Herb leans forward and touches her hand.

'I'm sorry,' Melville says,' I don't want to make this any worse than it already is.'

'Go on,' she says. 'I need to know.'

'Subsequent documents confirm the leg injuries in each case were sustained from the displacement of the engines through the foot wells of each vehicle and this led me to become suspicious. Pinner's report states the collision was head-on and the photographs show the point of impact being off-centre, on the driver's side. It says that Riggs' girlfriend had misjudged the bend and the steep incline ahead. That she had lost control and crossed the carriageway. And then didn't make it back into the left lane before hitting the oncoming vehicle.'

'Oh my god,' I say with a shudder, getting a flashback to our drive home from the country on Sunday.

'I had to believe,' Melville continues, 'that both drivers should have had the same leg injuries. There was the added confusion surrounding the use of seat-belts. The report said only Riggs was buckled up, but made clear that while his passenger was ejected through the windscreen, Mrs Long remained seated in her car. One photograph showed the front of the car Riggs was in and the windscreen was shattered across its entire width, not just on the drivers' side. I started to become convinced Riggs had been driving. He survived because he was wearing a seat belt and because, by pure chance, his head injuries were only superficial. I believe Mrs Long was also wearing her seat belt, but her injuries proved to be more serious than originally thought.'
He looks down as he says it and Grace looks into Herb's eyes.

'They missed it,' Herb says. 'She was only concerned for you... She told them to stop fussing over her and to check the baby. They said it was fine and they moved her to the obstetrics ward for observation. Because of that they missed the skull fracture. She'd been bleeding in her brain and the blood clot put her into a coma. They rushed her to neurology but it was too late.' Grace looks back at him, too traumatised to speak.

'I found a gap in the evidence inventory,' Melville continues, almost in a whisper. 'There was no witness statement and only a vague reference to a case of mistaken identity involving a suspected male drunk driver leaving a nearby pub on the night of the crash.'

'That's because there wasn't one,' Herb says and Melville frowns at him. 'He made it all up... Mac. He's your eye-witness. But he didn't see them leaving any pub.'

'What *did* he see?' Grace says.

'He came across the crash scene by pure chance. He saw Pinner drag Riggs from the driving seat and tamper with the evidence to make it look like the passenger had been at the wheel.'

'Why didn't he come forward?' Melville says.

'Believe me, I tried to get him to. He said he called the newspaper because he didn't know how else to make things right. And then he didn't think anyone would believe him if he went back and changed his story. Over the years I've come to suspect there was more to it than that. I know he has a phobia of the police; doesn't trust anyone in authority. But if I'm honest, I think he probably had something of his own to hide that night. I've never asked.'

'How did you get to know him Herb?' I ask.

'He came up to me in the pub after the inquest and told me what he'd seen. He was sleeping in his car at the time so I gave him somewhere to stay and he's been loyal to me ever since.'

'Witness statement or not,' Melville cuts in like he's keen to finish up and leave, 'it was an anomaly that gave me reason enough to be concerned. With Pinner's name all over the file, I couldn't help wondering if he was as quick to remove inconvenient evidence back then as he is today. That's when I found it, buried deep in the file. The blood test results from the hospital. It showed Riggs four times over the drink-drive limit.'

'There,' Herb says. 'I always knew.'

Leaving Alone

Melville left after an uncomfortably long hug from Grace and a word of warning to Herb not to get too relaxed, on the basis that they'd no doubt be having further conversations in due course. All the balaclavas have now gone and Pinner's been driven off in an unmarked car by the corruption cops. The white paper suits are still doing their thing in the cellar and there's blue and white tape being unrolled everywhere – in the hall and outside. It seems unlikely Herb will be allowed to stay here while they continue to investigate. Finally there's just the three of us in the room.

'I didn't get to see you,' Herb says to Grace, 'when you were born. They wanted me to. I suppose they thought it might change my mind. I just couldn't. It'd all been too much. They'd already kept her... your mother alive for almost a month. They wanted the pregnancy to reach twenty-six weeks to give you the best chance. I had to sit and watch her breathing through a tube with no hope of her ever waking up. I'm sorry. At the end of that, I had nothing left to give you.' He looks across to Grace with heavy eyes and she moves over and puts an arm around him. I finally see him looking at her like a father should look at his daughter.

'The hospital gave me that photograph of the baby... of you,' he says. 'But it stayed in the envelope for years.'

'When did you put it in the frame?'

'After I sobered up on New Year's Day. Ten years ago.'

'What were you hoping to achieve that night?'

'All I knew then was that you were Pinner's daughter. I didn't really have it in me to hurt you, but I suppose I thought if I could grab you... shake you up a bit, that would be enough to send him a message.'

'So, what stopped you?'

'It was the perfect opportunity; you'd gone to the toilet alone. But I hesitated long enough to see one of your friends produce a cake with a candle on it and I heard her say something about not waiting for the next day to celebrate your birthday. It felt like just a hideous coincidence, but it was enough to cut me off at the knees. I'd lost my nerve, and with your friends distracted, I just took the camera. When you came back, they gave you the cake and I took a photograph and went home. In the long hours of that night I opened the envelope and saw the picture of the baby for the first time. I knew it would have been her birthday too.'

'It was my sixteenth,' she says.

'What changed your mind last week?' I say, but he doesn't seem to hear and continues looking at Grace.

'When I sobered up, I felt ashamed of what I'd been planning to do – to kidnap a girl with the same birthday... So I threw the camera into a drawer. I didn't give you another thought until I was told Mickey had found you...'

'She found *me*, Herb,' I say. He acknowledges me with a sigh and turns back to Grace.

'Anyway, last week things were different. You were grown up. And you were getting close to my friend here. That made you a threat. That's why,' he says, now looking at me, 'I had to adapt my plan and use you to bring her to me. I wasn't about to offer you a cut if you then had divided loyalties, lad. Not if you were then consorting with the same girl, all grown up; the daughter of one of my two worst enemies.'

'And you honestly never considered... ' I say, thrusting my finger at him, 'it might have been the truth? That just maybe... she really was *your* daughter?'

'What do *you* think lad? My wife gets killed and Pinner covers it up. The thought that I gave up my daughter and she ended up adopted by him was preposterous. Knowing it was true now is... killing me.'

They stay sitting together and now I'm the outsider.

'At least he'll get to pay for it,' I say. 'Prison won't be much fun for a corrupt copper.'

'Huh! Prison! I've always believed in punishment to fit the crime,' he says. 'Prison's too good for him.'

'So what now?' I say, more to Grace than Herb, but he's the one to answer.

'There are going to be repercussions,' Herb says. 'I'm going to have to lie low for a while. But once they catch up with Riggs, the game will get easier. You can still help me keep it all together. The two of you would make a great team.'

'The two of *you*,' Grace sneers and we both turn to look at her, 'are *already* a great team.' She gets up and leaves the room without another word.

I tell Herb I'll be in touch and rush out after her, nodding to the copper outside to let Melville know we're heading home.

I catch up with her as she reaches her car that's been parked around the back.

She turns to face me and says, 'You killed a man.'

'It was self-defence. I was young. Stupid. Just doing a job…'

'Breaking into a house because someone told you to,' she says cutting me to the quick. 'Sound familiar?'

'He would have killed me.'

'Well, that we'll never know.'

'Do you honestly think I haven't thought about that? Just once or twice…' I say, before lowering my voice. 'A thousand times since?'

'Yeah, well,' she whispers, getting into the car. 'I thought we were being honest when we told each other the most outrageous things we'd ever done. You certainly win the prize now.'

'I was hoping I wouldn't have to tell you.'

'What else are you hoping you won't have to tell me, Mickey?' She shuts the door and lowers the window.

'There is nothing else.'

'I need time to think,' she says, starting the engine.

'What are you going to do… about Herb?'

'I really don't know.'

'He is your dad.'

319

'Right now I don't know how to feel about that. I don't know how to feel about any of this.'

'Is there anything I can do?'

'I'll call you, when I'm ready. But for now, just let me go... please.' Before driving away she asks the one question I can't answer. 'I need to decide, Mickey. Will that be you in thirty years?'

Dead Ahead

Back in my car and a mile down the road, I can see the little red soft-top up ahead. At the next junction, rather than turning left, she drives straight on like she's forgotten the way. Of course, I'm going to have to follow her before she gets completely lost. So much for letting her go. She takes the next left. Easy mistake. I'm sure any moment she'll pull over and do a U-turn. No, she goes straight ahead. There's a sign for the motorway coming up. That's it; we'll get on at the next junction. She'll be alright now; at the roundabout, first exit...

Okay, she would have been alright. Instead she goes straight across. We're now heading south-west rather than south-east, and I'm starting to lose my bearings. On we go until I start seeing familiar names of London suburbs ahead. This has to be the longest route home she could have chosen. And then I get it. The next list of destinations includes South Woodford. We're heading back to Bleak House.

She nips in and out of the busy traffic and I lose her before we even get close. I curse the fact my phone is dead and hers is back at my place. When I eventually turn into Bleak Avenue, a Chelsea Tractor attempting a three-point turn blocks my progress. The driver's taking forever to manoeuvre the beast between all the cars that line the street. I think about leaving the engine running and getting to the house on foot.

Before I can decide, I see Mac's lumbering bulk emerge through the gap between the houses up ahead to my right. He runs along the pavement back towards the house and disappears out of view behind the four-by-four that's still trying to turn in the road to get past me. The next thing I see is Grace hurtling out of the same alley, and I blast my horn. She turns long enough to see me.

'Quick, he's getting away!' she yells. 'Get after him.'

The car in front is now starting to ease towards me, and the woman is gingerly guiding her front wing, millimetres from my bumper. I can't wait any longer and her mouth drops when I suddenly wheel-spin away, taking a layer of paint with me from the side of her pride and joy. With a clear road ahead, I'm doing twenty when I pass Grace, running along the pavement. Ahead, I can see the red Mazda parked outside the house, and further up on the left is a silver saloon. By the time I see Mac between the trees and put my foot to the floor, I'm pushing forty. I know, once he's in the Merc, that this old estate will be no contest, so my aim is to get ahead of it before him to stop him pulling out. The gearbox shifts up as I continue to accelerate, and I curse the fact it's an automatic. But the needle's approaching fifty as a wing-mirror goes pinging off from one of the cars on the left. I'm close enough to the Mercedes now to ease off, but just then Mac appears between parked cars ten yards ahead, and looks back towards me. He only has to cross the road and he'll be in the car. I can't let him get away again. I can see the whites of his eyes when he steps into the road. I'm now doing fifty-three and he still thinks he can make it. For me, it's a split second decision. Brake. Or don't brake.

Sitting on the pavement some time later, with Grace holding me tight, I can't remember which one I took. Does it matter? His head shattered the windscreen before his body was thrown halfway down the road. They're still trying to remove one of his legs from under the engine.

They found Simon in one of the chambers. Men with faces as white as their paper suits are bringing him out now. In body bags, one at a time.

EPILOGUE

Late October

It's over a month since I've seen or spoken to Grace. And I'm now getting to the point where I only think about her four times a day. I've avoided the temptation to contact her. It's hard, knowing what she must be going through, wanting to offer some comfort, desperately hoping we can reconnect, even just to keep in touch, if only to be friends. But at the same time I have to respect her wish not to call; to accept she will call me if and when she's ready, and accept that may mean she never does.

Sam has split up with Dean. Apparently, he wasn't looking for that level of commitment and now she's crashing on a girlfriend's sofa. She's decided to rent a place nearer town and we've talked about formalising our separation. It makes sense and I've started tidying up the place, knowing that I'll have to put it on the market.

All of Grace's things are back in her suitcase because I can't bear to see them lying around anymore. When I went through my stuff, I ended up with a box full of confidential paperwork that needed to be destroyed; old bank statements and the like. I'm now in the garden where I've set up an old, cracked concrete planter as a make-shift incinerator. As most of the stuff is already blazing away, my mind starts to wander...

I suppose I could have taken up Herb's offer. We spoke on the phone a few days after and he said he'd also heard from Grace. She told him she's glad they finally met but that's as far as she wants to take it. He said there was a lot I could still do for him. He wanted me to take up the reins on the distribution side, while he concentrated on the offshore suppliers. That was the last I heard from him. After the police found a horde of his dodgy merchandise in the locked chamber, I suspect he went abroad. The fallout when they caught up with Riggs in Thailand sent shockwaves through even the legitimate side of the luxury brands market. Although there may now be fewer sharks in the shallow end, the water is becoming too transparent for a business model like that to survive. And there's a new predator out there with bigger teeth, called Her Majesty's Revenue & Customs. This time I'm glad I turned him down.

During the forensic search of Bleak House, the contents of the second chamber turned out to be the least of my concerns. The recently-promoted Detective Inspector James Melville was interviewed on the BBC's South East News the week after they dug up the concrete floor. I was eating liver and onions at Mum's when it came on.

'The most disturbing aspect of the grim discovery in Woodford,' he said, 'was the fact that the young man's severed head was found inside a Gravesend High School holdall.' As the owner of the house, Herb is now an international fugitive. And as the owner of the holdall, I'm struggling to sleep at night.

In my dreams I hear a woman screaming and now I *know* it's coming from inside the dungeon. I want to help her but each time I'm chased from the house by a pale young lad who waves something shiny at me through the kitchen window. It glistens like rubies in the night as I try to unsnag my bag from the barbed ledge of an overgrown fence, eventually letting it go and surrendering to a dark, endless drop...

I can't help smiling when I see the stack of yellow paper I've thrown absent-mindedly into the box of rubbish. I fan them out and add them to the fire. There's something cathartic about watching my fake money burn.

Next is a box of business cards with my name and former office embossed on them. I kneel and feed them into the fire a few at a time, mesmerised by the flames as they lick around the edges, slowly bending the corners before turning a vibrant green as the heavy ink burns.

'Hello lad,' a voice whispers in my ear.

Although it instantly makes my pulse race, it's too soft to be threatening, and I spin around to see Grace beaming at me.

'Bit early for Bonfire Night,' she says, all bright and breezy. She's wearing everyday blue jeans and a black puffy jacket. She looks great, but there's something different; she seems somehow... unpolished.

'Wow!' I say, getting to my feet. 'It's great to see you.' For weeks I've thought about what these first few seconds might be like, remembering some of the hesitant greetings we've shared before and reflecting on the fact that at first she was just acting, intentionally flattering me, with ulterior motives. I'm no longer sure what to expect from her, and so I promised The Banker I'd keep my guard up. Her smile is warm and genuine and as I get up I want to take her in my arms and kiss her, but I manage to resist. Instead of offering an embrace, she takes my hands in hers and squeezes them gently.

'So how have you been?' I say, leading her across to the patio.

'Okay,' she says, but her eyes aren't convincing.

'Good. Me too.' I lift a couple of plastic chairs off the stack and we sit down in the autumn sunshine. 'At least I was, once the CPS decided not to prosecute for the... you know.'

'Yeah, good riddance to that creep,' she says. 'Jim told me they've started reviewing missing persons' cold cases going back thirty years. Sounds like you did them a favour.'

'Doesn't feel good though.'

'No. I know. I've been feeling terrible too,' she says, and her mouth quivers. She takes a deep breath. 'About taking Terry's money all these years and keeping my mouth shut. All along, he's been getting it from the man who killed my mother. I feel just as guilty.'

'But Grace, you didn't know that.'

'That doesn't change anything,' she says shaking her head.

324

'I've had to get rid of everything he ever paid for. The police came and took a lot of stuff and most of what they left, including half my wardrobe, I took to the charity shop.'

'Not the black dress!' I wink at her, but she suppresses even a guilty smile.

'No. I'm saying I paid for that from my own money,' she says and then adds with an ironic laugh, 'Who am I kidding? Everything I have and all the money I get derives from him.'

'Grace, no. You mustn't think that way. What about all the work you've done, your training, running a business, employing people...? You've put a hell of a lot into it; don't underestimate how much of it is rightfully yours.' She's nodding her head and I think I can see a glimmer of light in the depths of her eyes and I try to reel it in. 'And that's before you even consider all those sad lily-white people you've sent out with a happy bronze smile on their faces!'

'I suppose you're right,' she says, and when the sparkle breaks through it's a whopper. 'Thank you Mickey, I've missed you.'

'I missed you too,' I say and squeeze her hand.

'I'm still waiting to hear what's going to happen about the flat,' she says with a sigh. 'It'll probably have to be sold.'

'That sounds familiar.'

'Why, what's happened?'

'Well, I can't afford to keep the house and settle up with Sam, now we've decided to formalise the separation.'

'I'm sorry,' she says.

'I spoke to her on the phone. It was all very confusing. I didn't know what to think. She seemed sad and distant, but there was something else. She was a different person to the one I knew. But then, I've probably changed too.'

'Did you tell her about us?'

'No, it didn't feel right. Besides, I didn't know what to say... You know, about us.' She looks back at me and nods. 'Anyway, after I put the phone down, I realised there was no going back. I rang her the next day and told her I wanted a divorce. We agreed to keep it clean and simple – irreconcilable differences, no other parties, everything split down the middle. We're meeting next week to go through it all and get the house on the market.'

'I'm sure it'll be for the best,' she says.

'You *will* get half the money from your flat, right?'

'At the moment I don't know if I'll be entitled to any of it.'

'Really? What about your car?'

'That's already gone. They're calling it all the… proceeds of crime,' she says. 'Next thing is what they're going to decide about the salon.'

'No! Surely they have to leave you with something,' I say and Grace sits forward, shaking her head. 'That's your livelihood. They can't take that away from you. I won't let them.'

'We'll have to wait and see.' She relaxes back into her chair.

'What about Melville? I'll talk to him; he wouldn't let you lose out like that.'

'I already spoke to Jim and he's going to see what he can do,' she says. 'But I can't keep expecting special treatment.'

'I understand how you feel, Grace, but like I said, you've worked so hard. It would be crazy if they couldn't see that.'

'I know. But it was all a sham from the start. I've had to go right back to the beginning and find out who I really am. If I have to start again, at least this time I'll be doing it my own way.'

'Looks like we've ended up in the same boat.'

'Nice to have you on board,' she says, breaking out in a smile before getting up and leading me back across the garden by the hand. 'I've got something else to keep your bonfire going.'

'Really,' I say. 'What is it?'

She reaches into her pocket and produces an envelope that she hands to me. 'Look at the postmark,' she says as I'm about to open it.

The envelope is franked across the corner of a brightly-coloured stamp depicting a tiger, and I can barely make out the words Hong Kong. It's dated a week ago. Inside is the photograph of her mum that we first saw in Bleak House and a letter that she encourages me to read out loud.

326

Jasmine,

Perhaps it was too much to wish you would want to take the path I offered you. I hope you will understand it is all I have to give. Your mother wouldn't have approved of the life I have led or the opportunity I have given to you. It will remain yours to take should you ever change your mind. Believe that I once was, and would still be, a better person with her at my side, but I think she was busy all those years watching over you. I know she would be so proud of you. How you came to be known as Grace must have had something to do with her. You have her eyes and her strength. I wish I could come to know you better because I am sure I would find her spirit alive within you. I will need to stay away for a while and maybe it's better for you that I do. If you never want to hear from me again, I will understand.

Mickey is a good man, if in some ways much like me before I met your mother – too eager to bend with the breeze, too easily led. That remains his greatest strength and weakness in equal measure. Like she was briefly to me, you can be the wind that blows him towards a better course if you choose. If you leave him adrift, he will no doubt be drawn back in my direction. Either way, I would be content. And if he makes you happy, I would be happy too. His efforts went unrewarded and that is not my way, but if you decide to stay with him I would consider my debt repaid.

Remember, this all started from your mother's things. Perhaps it might be better to think of him as a gift from her.

H

I look up and her face has a serene look of strength and pride. Gone are the sadness and the tears at the references to her mother. When I hand it back to her, she keeps the photo and drops the letter onto the fire.

As the blue paper scorches to brown and the flames engulf it, she takes a large brown envelope from inside her jacket and tells me to burn that too while she goes indoors to make us coffee.

I empty the envelope, letting it fall into the flames and look at each photograph before adding them. For one last time, the glow near the bottom of one of the pictures lights up the face of the young girl out celebrating on the eve of her birthday and of a new millennium. I'm loath to burn the larger print of the portrait labelled: "Example of a True-Life Likeness – Model in Repose". It goes on the fire anyway. But only after I've looked furtively towards the house and slipped the smaller version into my coat pocket.

The remaining items from my box go on last. They cling together but catch quickly and curl in the heat, twisting and objecting, as if wanting to free themselves from the flames. They represent a side of me I've had to confront a lot recently. I decided to reject them in the hope I can finally shed the demons I've allowed to tempt me all my life. Yes, the girl from Compliance was right to be suspicious all those months ago. Taking them was a stupid act of impulse and perhaps should have been a warning of what was to follow. They were the last in the book and I thought when the new one was started no one would miss them. Of course I should have realised, Rick's attention to detail was the *reason* he was the boss. According to Jake, no sooner had he spotted the gap, he'd stopped the missing ones anyway. I threw away my job for absolutely nothing. I watch as the three cheques blacken and disintegrate, their grey smoke drifting up in spirals.

As the flames subside, I stoke the smouldering remains with a stick and blow gently into the glowing embers, bringing them briefly back to life until all that's left in the bottom of the tub is ash that I render into grey powder with the heel of my boot.

When I get upstairs, Grace is sitting in the lounge. She hands me a mug and I join her on the sofa.

'So what now?' I ask.

'Okay, Mickey. No more games. No more mysteries.' She sits upright, the tone of her voice having changed. 'I want you to know I've missed you, and I like you a lot. I think I want you. But I need to understand who you really are.'

'What you see is what you get, Grace,' I say, holding out my hands.

'Is it?' she says, and her blue eyes won't let me look away. 'There was a lot said back at my father's house that caught me off-guard. Most of it I found hard to believe, like you had things in your past that didn't fit with the man I thought I'd seen in you.'

'There is nothing else. That's everything there is to know, the good and the bad. I wish I could, but I can't change the worst of it.'

'We've all done things we're not proud of, Mickey. God knows I have. I don't want to dwell on them. I want to look to the future and I'd like you to be a part of it... if you want to. I just can't afford to make the same mistakes again. I need to know I can trust you.'

'It's funny,' I say, after her eyes release me from their spell. 'I've been thinking a lot about the future too. You're right. You have to settle up with the past and then leave it behind so you can move on. And there's something I've come to realise.'

'What's that?'

'The only good decisions I've ever made have been after really bad things happened. Sure, I thought I'd made it up there in the real world as someone recently put it. But it was all an illusion because I didn't stay focused on what really mattered. When it all fell down, I blamed everyone else. In the end it was all down to me.'

'Now you're the one being too hard on yourself,' she says and rubs my arm.

'Maybe. What I'm trying to say is I may not always get it right in future, but now I think I understand what's important. Whatever happens, going forward I want the decisions we make to be shared. I want us to always be honest with each other. No secrets, no hidden agendas... Grace, I would love to be in your future and I want you to trust me.'

'So why didn't you call me?' At first I think she's joking and I smirk innocently, but the frown remains on her face and I shift awkwardly in my seat.

'You told me not to.' I say and she just nods back at me. 'I would have done, if you hadn't said.'

'Michael Field.' Now she's shaking her head in playful exasperation. 'Do you *always* have to do exactly what you're told?'

'But...' I continue my pointless protest, 'I was thinking about you all the time, I was desperate to know how you felt about me and if there was anything I could do or say that would help. I didn't want to make things worse. Believe me I wanted to be there for you, but your words kept repeating in my head. You said you didn't want me to contact you.'

'You're right, I'm sorry. I shouldn't have said it,' she says, and then adds: 'And you shouldn't have believed me. Always doing what other people tell you keeps getting you into trouble.'

'Fair comment,' I say. I've never really thought about it but she's absolutely right.

'Why is that?'

'I don't know. Laziness? It's usually the easy option. I tend to go with the flow.'

'The problem with letting other people determine what you do is that you're still responsible for it. The path of least resistance can have just as awful consequences.'

'You're right. It's about time I started making my own decisions.' Her face lights up with her beautiful smile when I add, 'The first one is this: I'm never going to let you down.'

'I love you Mickey.'

'I love you too, Jasmine,' I reply with a wink.

She smiles and leans across the table before stopping momentarily.

'I'm sticking with Grace,' she says.

'Amazing,' remains unsaid on my lips, silenced by her passionate kiss.

THE END